CROCODILE
TEARS

Alan Carter was born in Sunderland, UK. He immigrated to Australia in 1991 and now lives in splendid semi-rural semi-isolation south of Hobart, Tasmania. In his spare time he follows the black line up and down the local swimming pool or drags on his wetsuit and braves the icy waters of the D'Entrecasteaux Channel. He is the author of six previous novels: the Fremantle-set DS Cato Kwong series *Prime Cut* (winner of the Ned Kelly Award for Best First Fiction), *Getting Warmer*, *Bad Seed* and *Heaven Sent*. His New Zealand-set *Marlborough Man*, featuring Sergeant Nick Chester, won the Ngaio Marsh Award for Best Novel and the sequel *Doom Creek* is out now.

ALAN CARTER

CROCODILE TEARS

 FREMANTLE PRESS

'Some worked out satisfactory substitutes for the discarded life, and some ran amok.'

Charlotte Jay, *Beat Not the Bones*

PROLOGUE

6th September, 1999. 11.52 a.m.

There had been little sleep in the night: babies crying, people coughing and snoring, everybody sweltering. There must have been two thousand of them, all slowly suffocating. Everybody terrified and waiting to die. Around dawn they had heard the motorbikes and the trucks draw up outside. The shouted threats, the goading, the cruel jokes and laughter. Surely they wouldn't violate a church? The house of God? Surely nothing. She knew now – nowhere was safe.

Wasn't this how it had always been? How it always would be? You lift your head for a brief defiant moment to sniff freedom and somebody is waiting with a machete to chop it off. Freedom? She had never known such a thing, nor had her parents, or grandparents. She glanced down at her daughter. Nor would she. The shouts and threats growing from outside and the heat building inside. She became aware that people were staring at her.

'What?'

'You,' said an old man, a neighbour from down the lane. 'They're shouting for you. They want you.'

She listened. Yes. No mistake. Hand her over and you will all be safe.

'Don't worry.' It was the Father. 'We will not do it.'

'Why not?' A voice from the crowd. 'They only make trouble for us. Why should we die for them?'

'Fool.'

She lifted her chin proudly. 'I will go. Who will look after my child?'

'Mama! No!'

'Nobody,' said the Father. 'No need. You will stay here with us. Together we are strong.'

'Who is the fool now?' the voice from the crowd retorted.

'Those men outside, they are hoodlums, gangsters.' The priest tried to calm their fears. 'The army will not let them do anything to us.'

'They belong to the army, idiot.'

Again her name was called. A man reading from a list, the megaphone distorted with feedback. Four people. Hand them over. Save yourselves.

Seconds ticked by. Minutes. The shouts and threats died down. Footsteps receding. Engines rumbling. Vehicles moving. Maybe they were going? They dared not violate this house of God after all. The Father was right – miracles do happen. Have faith.

No. Those men had not gone. Windows smashing, gunshots, explosions. Gas. They were being tear-gassed. The children screaming and crying. People trampling each other to get to the door. She grabbed her daughter and hugged her close, eyes streaming from the gas and from her own real tears. She knew what awaited them outside but there was no choice. You have to head for the light. For freedom, whatever the cost.

Angeles City, Philippines – September, 2013

'What mob are you?'

It was a large gun. Like something from a cartoon, or a Clint Eastwood movie. A Magnum .357, the Harley-Davidson of pistols. The barrel was digging into the corner of his left eye. Driscoll had suspected when he walked over the club threshold ten minutes ago that this wasn't going to end well. The dance floor was filled with bored, writhing, scrawny girls barely out of high school. Their sparkly G-strings looked sad and cheap and some of them still hadn't learned how to apply their makeup properly. The place reeked of cigarettes, watered-down beer, and stale perspiration. The sweat oozed from the sunburned middle-aged gubbas, mainly Australian if their T-shirts and Southern Cross tatts were anything to go by, lining the cubicles around the walls. Their greedy, predatory faces and overhanging guts multiplied in the mirrors. Girls sat on laps, feeling hands go where they shouldn't, maybe wondering how, or when, or if ever this might end.

A few pesos in the paw, some reassuring Tagalog in the ear of the bouncer, and Driscoll had muscled his way up the stairs and along the corridor to the back where the thumping crap music no longer bounced off your ribs. There he'd found Dean stretching a polo shirt to breaking point across wide gym shoulders, hunched over a laptop that seemed way too small for him. Driscoll knew Dean was Noongar and the only Noongars he'd met were real tough bastards but funny as hell. Growing up in a schizoid town like Perth would do that to you. Dean was probably well-suited to running a girly club in the fleshpots of Angeles – one big sprawling Sodom clinging to the fence line of the old US air base at Clark. He was Perth through and through – focused on dollars, on winning. Nothing else mattered.

'Gunditjmara. Warrnambool,' Driscoll said.

'Fierce?'

'When pushed.'

Dean grinned at the man holding the gun. 'Be careful, Mikey. This man Driscoll is "Fighting Gunditjmara". Fierce mob. Complete fucking cannibal. Eats Lebs for breakfast. Got that?'

'No problem, boss.' Mikey was feeling cocky. He would be, he was holding the cannon. Driscoll had pulled his file too before he flew in: Michael Aboud from Punchbowl, NSW – running from a gang feud that had killed four of his erstwhile comrades back in June over a period of less than a fortnight. They were fighting among themselves. The Brothers-in-Arms were a mixture of third-generation Lebanese and second-generation Afghan Tajiks. A wrong word, a tiff over a shared girlfriend, a spilled drink: whatever it was, it had split the gang down ethnic lines and they'd been doing drive-bys on each other ever since. Mikey had been next on the list so he'd taken the first plane out – an AirAsia flight to KL and on to Clark. Now he was Dean's property.

'Coconut though, eh?' Dean, back on the subject of Driscoll. 'Errand boy for the wadjela. Tracker ...' he glanced at the fake ID card in Driscoll's confiscated wallet. 'Tracker John? That you?'

'This is the deal,' said Driscoll. The gun in his eye was beginning to give him a headache and he was sick of holding his hands in the air. It was hot and sticky in that office and he was craving one of Dean's watered-down San Miguels. 'You withdraw your blackmail demands on Charlton's wife and employers, give me any dodgy pics and other materials you have, and erase him from your system.'

'And?' said Dean, faintly amused.

'You get to stay in business.'

'You reckon you've more clout than the local police chief and district army commander? I pay them good money to leave me alone.'

'It won't be enough this time. Play the game, mate. Hand over the stuff on Charlton and we go our separate ways.'

Patrick Charlton was the embassy's IT specialist. He was known to pop down from Manila to Angeles every other weekend to satisfy his nasty carnal urges on girls his daughter's age. The embassy had opted to turn the other cheek. Geeks of his calibre were hard to come by; most had been snapped up by the miners or internet monoliths with much deeper pockets. Seventy-two hours ago, Charlton had been found in the club's VIP room crouched over a thirteen-year-old who'd been unable to extricate herself from beneath his bulk. His face was blue and his heart had exploded from a dodgy batch of street Viagra, recently imported from North Korea. Pictures and extortion demands had turned up in his wife and line manager's emails the next day. It wasn't hard to trace them back to Dean. The pictures were bad enough but what galvanised the embassy was the bigger threat of Charlton's missing thumb drive and the classified documents and codes therein.

Enter Rory Driscoll. 'The cops and army are back in our pockets, Dean. Don't get greedy or stupid.' He realised, as soon as he said it, that he probably shouldn't have. Greedy, okay. Stupid, not.

Dean was on him with fists the size of Christmas hams and a mean look in his eye. Mikey stood back to enjoy the show, the Magnum hanging loosely at his side; he obviously had a great deal of confidence in his employer. He probably wasn't expecting the wrench and snap that broke his boss's neck a few seconds later. And Mikey definitely wasn't ready for the top of Driscoll's head driving into his nose. But he did seem to want to hold on to his big gun and, with a strength that surprised, was gradually twisting it around towards Driscoll's armpit.

'Michael, you need to stop this, right now. Really, mate.' The barrel scraped Rory's shirt, their fingers fought for the trigger. 'Khalas!'

Mikey's eyes registered surprise at the Arabic command to desist. Driscoll swung Mikey's arm away and the gun went off with a deafening roar. A framed photograph of John Worsfold and Ben Cousins hugging in a sea of blue and yellow exploded into a large hole in the wall. Driscoll was a Hawthorn man himself. He managed to bury his elbow in Mikey's eye then got a grip on the poor bloke's nose with his teeth. It must have hurt because Mikey finally dropped the gun. Driscoll punched him a few times to encourage him to stay down.

He found the thumb drive in Dean's pocket and took the laptop with him; Dean wouldn't be needing it anymore.

Mikey was in a foetal position under the desk, blood all over his face. 'What the fuck are you?'

'Fighting Gunditjmara.' Driscoll bent down and dabbed Mikey's face with a tissue, offered him some bottled water. 'Best to keep your head down for a while, mate. Maybe find another country? Keep your nose clean and we won't tell the Tajiks where to find you.'

Driscoll's phone went. It was his boss, Aunty, sole proprietor of Hope Springs Strategic Consultants and old chum of everybody who mattered in government. 'Rory, my boy. Job done?' A symphony was playing in the background. She liked Mahler. Pretentious old fairy.

'Yep, sorted.'

'Casualties?'

He looked over at Michael, snivelling and bleeding under the desk. He'd recover. At Dean, the floppy doll. 'Just the one.'

'Do I detect a lighter touch these days?'

He wasn't sure if it was a compliment or a reprimand. He could hear sirens approaching and raised voices down the hall. They'd probably reported the gunshot.

'Anything urgent, Aunty? Only I need to be making tracks.'

'We've had a request from Canberra. What's your thoughts on Operation Sovereign Borders?'

He'd been expecting this, had even done some preliminary training for it. The new government was filled with men with a cold gleam in their eyes and scores to settle. They'd been mandated to 'Stop the Boats' and no doubt had all sorts of crazy schemes bouncing around their bitter little brains. Driscoll was right up their street.

'Well?' said Aunty.

He thought about Patrick Charlton and his craving for very young girls, about the sweaty predatory gubbas lining the booths downstairs, about Michael Aboud and his taste for big guns. About poor Dean and his ideas above his station. 'Operation Sovereign Borders, Aunty? It's about two hundred and thirty years too late.'

PART ONE

1

Fremantle, Western Australia
Wednesday 18th April

Cato Kwong would have killed for a sandwich and said so. He'd been going all day and somehow never managed to grab a bite. It had finally caught up with him, that growly, low blood sugar feeling when civilisation goes out the window and we are returned to our primal state of foraging mammal.

'Anything in the fridge?'

'You serious?'

Cato shrugged. 'Depends what's on offer.'

Deb Hassan opened the door and peeked inside, rummaging with rubber-gloved hands. 'Milk,' she sniffed the carton, 'still fresh. Cheese, bacon, some tomatoes going soft, carrots, marge – heart tick, two stubbies of wife-beater, half-a-dozen eggs, marmalade. Oh,' a pause. 'And this.' She stepped back with a see-through plastic tub, the kind they give you your olives in at the supermarket.

Cato looked closer. 'The missing ear.'

'Still hungry?'

In spite of the bloody specimen in the tub and the abattoir in the next room, the answer was still yes. His phone went: caller ID Pavlou, his boss. 'Howdy.'

'What's the latest from the crime scene?'

'The victim is a sixty-three-year-old white male, Douglas Peters, lives alone according to the neighbours. Stabbed multiple times and body mutilated.'

'Mutilated?'

'They chopped an ear off, the left one. And put it in a plastic tub in the fridge.'

'Nice. Any thoughts?'

Cato limped over to the doorway; his leg was playing up today. An old bullet wound will do that. Once again he surveyed the lounge room: the spray of blood around the walls and on the rug; the body still in situ, being photographed and videoed. Family snaps on a shelf: weddings, graduations, birthdays. All splashed with crimson. 'Bit early, but I'd say at this stage we're dealing with a nutcase.'

'Forced entry? Burglary? Meth head?'

'Doesn't appear to be forced entry. Still looking at what might be missing. The body was found by a Jim's Mowing contractor who'd called round to do his regular clean-up. Wondered why the back door was open when the bloke was usually out on lawnmower day to escape the noise. Saw the blood trail.'

'What time was this?'

'Around one.'

'Hmmm.' The sound of a door opening and traffic noise. Pavlou must be stepping outside for a ciggie break. 'Media?'

'Gathering beyond the cordon. Usual suspects.' He looked out the window: a no-longer ordinary sunny Wednesday afternoon in outer suburban Fremantle. 'Couple of choppers up there too, and drones.'

A sigh and some rustling at the other end. 'When do you expect to be out of there?'

'Half an hour, an hour maybe. Leave everything to the techs. Doors are being knocked, everything more or less in hand for now.'

'Fair enough. Had any more of those funny turns of yours, Philip?' She rarely used his nickname. A racially-charged epithet could come back to bite you on your career trajectory.

'No,' Cato lied. 'All good.'

***

The room was full and DI Sandra Pavlou held the stage, petite and wiry with swimmer's shoulders. Late afternoon sun slanted through the windows. Cato had grabbed a drive-through burger on the way back and it sat heavily in his gut. Sharon had pinched his hips playfully last night, said something about middle-aged spread. She'd been up at sparrow fart on a morning run while he sleepily attended to two-year-old Typhoon Ella who'd recently discovered the word 'no'.

'What do we know about him so far? Chris?'

Chris Thornton was in charge of collating the blizzard of information into a useful narrative. He was made for this job. He'd finally been prised away from Fremantle into Major Crime; he should have come over earlier but he was recently married and had been loath to do the commute from the southern suburbs into the city. Cato knew the feeling. Thornton adjusted his new specs, swiped his iPad and stood up. Compact, boyish, uncomfortable in a grown-up Major Crime suit.

'Douglas Peters, sixty-three. Widower. One adult offspring, a daughter – she lives in Melbourne. Peters was in the Job.'

'Tell me more.'

'Retired seven, nearly eight, years ago. Last position was as a sergeant up in Derby.'

'Anything jump out on his service record? Notable enemies he might have made?'

'Not so far. We're still digging.'

'Anything else?'

'We've got the boffins going through his computer, telecom and financials. According to the phone records he'd spoken to somebody late last night so it appears he was still alive at around ten p.m. We're following up on those people he was in touch with. Nothing stands out on the finances yet, although there are statements for an offshore family trust account that might be interesting. We're also looking at his career before and after being a cop.'

A quizzical lifting of the chin from Pavlou but there was nothing more forthcoming. She twisted her head. 'Duncan?'

The forensics honcho uncoiled his lanky frame from behind a desk. 'Blood all over the place. Peters was pretty much hacked to death. Machete most likely. It might have been personal or maybe just somebody who was really enjoying themselves. No sign of the murder weapon. There'll have been blood all over whoever did it. And there's a trail going out the backyard over a fence into Milky Way, the laneway running along the back. Looks like there was a car waiting, but too hard and dry to get any useful tyre impressions.'

Thornton butted in. 'We've got somebody chasing down CCTV and traffic cameras.'

Pavlou nodded. Back to Duncan Goldflam. 'Any other traces?'

'Bloody sock prints around the house. Size tens. Some fibres on the Colorbond fence. No fingerprints. Some other stuff: plant life, seeds, all going under the microscope.'

'When do you think you'll have a full report?'

'Hopefully a useful prelim by end of tomorrow. Full-ish monty by the end of the week.'

Cato was feeling hot and light-headed. Looking around the room he recognised very few faces: Duncan Goldflam folding back into his seat, Chris Thornton absorbed in his iPad, and Deb Hassan scribbling a note to herself. She had come over to Major Crime shortly after him, putting in the long hours to assuage Pavlou's doubts and repay Cato's support. Hassan caught Cato's eye, nodding towards the front of the room.

'Philip?' DI Pavlou leaned forward. 'You with us?'

He'd done it again. Zoned out. 'Boss?'

'Post-mortem. Tomorrow morning. You okay for that?'

'Sure.'

The meeting broke up and Pavlou brushed past him. 'My office, please.'

***

'What's going on, Philip?'

They were sitting in Pavlou's glass-enclosed lair. Door closed. Cato had his back to the world and he couldn't see the curious glances over the partitions. Just Pavlou, her geranium and a photo of the family somewhere near the Parthenon. He knew he couldn't keep saying 'nothing' and 'I'm fine'. Nor could he say 'I'm just tapering off some heavy-duty anxiety medication. Bear with me for a while.' She'd stand him down and if he didn't have the job to occupy him what the hell was he supposed to do? 'Just overtired, I think. Ella's a handful at the moment. Not sleeping.'

'Commiserations, mate, but half the people on the squad have little kids. Been there myself, once or twice.' She softened. 'Had a health check recently? You seem … a bit peaky.'

'Yep, last week.'

'And?' Pavlou visibly restrained herself. She had no right to ask for specifics. 'Everything okay?'

'Far as we know.' Cato fingered the foil of pills in his pocket.

'How's Sharon. She well?'

All these questions, dancing around the subject. 'Great.'

'Back in the Job I see. Saw her on the news at that airport meth bust last week.'

'Yeah, loving it.'

'You two good now after that ... time?'

'Good as gold.'

She was running out of solicitousness. 'This is a nasty one, Philip. And the victim was in the Job. One of ours. We need all hands on deck. Full focus.'

'Absolutely.'

'You need to buck up and sort out whatever it is that's going on. If you won't tell me what it is, I can't help you. The ball's in your court.'

'No worries.'

'My door's always open.'

'Thanks.'

Cato went straight to the toilets and doused his face with cold water. He popped a pill from the foil and necked it. He'd be right as rain in fifteen.

***

Thornton was hovering when Cato returned.

'Everything okay, Sarge?'

'Bonzer. What have you got for me?' The clock on the wall nudged six. He needed to be home, the nanny had to go by six thirty and Sharon was on evenings at the airport. He wondered if he could summon the reserves of energy he would need for a fractious Ella. This was no life for any of them. So why had he accepted Pavlou's offer to join her squad? Why hadn't he walked away like he said he would? He still didn't know – or maybe he did but wasn't prepared to admit it.

'Sarge?'

He'd lost it again. Wandered off into his thoughts, had to be dragged back. 'Sorry. You were saying?'

'Peters. A first-run potted biography. He's certainly been around.'

'Highlights?'

'Joined nineteen eighty-one, first posting Kalgoorlie. No distinctions, no scandals. Three years on, he moves to Newman. Ditto. Every three to four years he moves to another regional posting: Busselton, Southern Cross, Geraldton, Meekatharra, Derby, et cetera. All points north, south, east and west.'

'Except the city?'

'Yep, country boy through and through.'

'And nothing remarkable in his career? No big busts or scandals which might make him some enemies?'

A shake of the head. 'A plodder, on paper anyway. Looks like any promotions that came his way were by virtue of length of service rather than dashing leadership acumen.'

A pause. Cato sensed a 'but'. He voiced it.

Thornton slid the iPad on to the desk. Cato had started wearing glasses; he'd been getting these headaches, cryptic crossie clues turning blurry. Tragic. Thornton used his fingers to helpfully enlarge the font. 'Meekatharra, two thousand five. An Aboriginal woman died in custody, not on his watch, he'd gone off duty that afternoon. There weren't any specifically suspicious circumstances. She had an undiagnosed pre-existing medical condition. Neglectful maybe, but no malice intended. Nobody officially sanctioned.'

It was remarkable how many of those tragic statistics from country lockups would be interpreted as neglectful but not malicious. Nothing personal. Add them all up, and they do begin to seem malicious after a while. 'So if he wasn't directly involved, what's the "but" about?'

'He transferred shortly after. Earlier than his usual pattern – he'd only been in that job about eighteen months.'

'Maybe an opportunity arose, an offer he couldn't refuse? Plum posting?'

Thornton nodded. 'Derby? The plum is in the eye of the beholder I suppose. But he certainly liked it there. Good fishing, I hear. He stayed until he retired late in two thousand eleven.'

'Six years. Longest stint anywhere. And he would have been …'

'Fifty-six when he retired.'

'Went longer than most. Anything after that?'

'Two years with private security – a company called CPS. We're trying to get the details. They're a cagey, bureaucratic mob.'

'And then he finally decided to come and live in the big smoke after all these years.'

'Beaconsfield.' Thornton retrieved his iPad. 'Smoky as.'

Cato was ready to go home. 'Thanks Chris. Let me know how you go with CPS.'

***

Cato woke about two a.m. just as Sharon slipped into the bedroom.

'How was work?' he murmured sleepily as she spooned into him.

'Slow. There's a couple of mugs due in from KL tomorrow night who'll be getting the cough and squat treatment. Vietnamese. Poor bastards are payback for an arrest in Sydney last week – tit-for-tat turf war. They're dobbing each other in every second day. I'm losing track.' She yawned. 'You still awake?'

'Yep.'

'Your day?'

'Somebody got chopped up in Beacy. Old bloke, used to be in the Job.'

'Lovely. Did Ella go down okay tonight?'

'Fine. Julie had her fed and bedded before I got home. Apparently she ran out of steam at the playground down South Beach and was nodding off before she even got to the yoghurt and banana.'

'Hasn't stirred since?'

'A murmur around ten but she went off again quickly.'

Her hand crept across his stomach; lightly brushed the old knife scar there. 'How about you? Are you sleepy?'

He turned to face her. 'Not anymore.' Enjoying the smell and the touch, the pressing intensity. Her breath warm and greedy. She straddled him.

His phone went. On silent, but throbbing and dancing on the bedside table.

'Leave it.' Sharon drew him in. Held him tight. He focused on the moment.

Light flashing on a left message.

After a while a soft sob escaped her. Cato too was spent.

The phone again. The double beep of a text this time. Sharon rolled away. 'Want to get that?'

'No.'

'They're determined.' Sharon fluffed her pillow and pulled the covers up. 'Put them out of their misery or turn it off.'

He checked: unknown number on the missed call, a hiss and background pacing noises on the voicemail. Accidental butt call? Twice? The text.

I know who did Peters

Nothing to lose. He texted back. **Who?**

And waited.

No reply.

After five minutes he snuggled in to Sharon and fell asleep.

2

Thursday 19th April

The next day there was a breakthrough. A neighbour over the back from Peters had reported that on the morning of the murder, around eight, she had been putting out her wheelie bin for collection when a car nearly cleaned her up. A Toyota ute: white, no trade markings but dried mud splashes on the wheel arches.

'Rego?'

'She didn't catch it,' said Thornton, scanning the entry. 'Too fast to get a glimpse of the driver, beyond generic male with dark clothing.'

'Ethnicity?' asked Cato. 'Big, small, skinny, fat, old, young?'

'No mention.'

'Get it followed up, jog her memory. And chase the vehicle, CCTV, traffic cameras, neighbours, witnesses, bus drivers, regular delivery people on or near that route at that time.'

'Boss.' His expression conjured images of grandmothers and eggs.

'The mud splashes should help.' Cato showed Thornton his phone and the overnight text. 'Can you run a trace on that number?'

'Sure.' Thornton noted the details. 'If they know who did Peters why don't they just get to the point?'

'A tease. Just what we need.'

Thornton nodded. 'Had some thoughts about Peters too.'

'Yep?'

'Stuff that might not be on the official record. Former colleagues, that kind of thing.'

'Got somebody in mind?'

This time Thornton showed him a text on his own phone.

I might be a useless old duffer but I'm not dead yet. Get him to call me.

Cato recognised the caller ID. 'Hutchens?' His old boss at Fremantle.

A grin. 'He wants you to buy him lunch. OBH at North Cott. Today. One-ish?'

'Since when did you become his appointments secretary?'

'Not his, Sarge, yours. Always and forever.'

'Tell him I'll see him there, maybe he can wear a carnation so I recognise him.'

'I've reserved a table by the window. Nice day. Should be a perfect view over to Rotto. Very romantic.'

***

Ex-DI Mick Hutchens was looking well. Tanned, fit even. Shorts, T-shirt, canvas boat shoes. A bicycle helmet?

'Rode here.' He nodded towards a mountain bike chained to a rail outside. 'Had a swim over at the beach before you arrived. Lovely.'

'You ordered yet?' said Cato, sliding out a chair. Thornton had been right, it was a perfect day: Indian Ocean as flat as a pancake and blue as a sad song. Rottnest Island shimmering on the horizon.

'Just a drink, so far.' Hutchens lifted the middy to his lips. 'Sook strength.'

They scanned the lunchtime menu and Cato went to the bar to order their food and get a lime and soda for himself. 'Driving and on duty,' he said on his return.

'Never said a word, mate.' Hutchens leaned in. 'Still limping, I see. How is it?'

It was over a year since Cato had taken a bullet in the leg and he'd felt it every day since. 'Some days are diamonds, some are stones.'

'Sharon and the bub?'

'Sharon's back in the Job and loving it. We're ships in the night these days. Ella's two, big time. How's Marjorie?'

'She's taken up French and says everything with an accent and a pout. Keeps things spicy, I suppose. She wants us to go there in July so she can immerse.' He enclosed the last word in finger quotes and over-pronounced the second syllable. Their food arrived, burger and chips for

Hutchens and pasta for Cato. 'Enough about me, I hear you've got Dougie Peters on a slab?'

'Yep. Know him?'

'Worked with him in Kal in the early days, then again in Meeka.'

'Meekatharra? That would have been around two thousand five, six?'

'Guess so.'

'Weren't you in Albany by then?'

'Transitioning. I investigated the death in custody.'

'And?'

'Jacobs, I think her name was. Connie Jacobs?' A confirmation nod from Cato. 'Pre-existing cardiac condition; something to do with how the electrical currents move through to keep the thing pumping. Hers had packed up. Word is she should have had a pacemaker but the waiting list was too long. One of those things, eh?'

'What had she been arrested for?'

'Non-payment of fines and an altercation at the pub, the Commercial.'

'Where did Peters fit in?'

'He was custody sergeant at the time of her arrest but went off duty within a couple of hours. She died on somebody else's watch.'

'End of story?'

'Pretty much.'

'Except he took an early ticket of leave and transferred up to Derby where he stayed until his retirement, disrupting a pattern he'd set for the previous thirty years or so.'

Hutchens grinned through a mouthful of chips. 'Still not slow on the uptake.'

'The official record suggests the career opportunity arose and there was nothing suspicious about the timing. I'm guessing you think different?'

'We had a farewell meal in the Commercial, Dougie and me. They do a good parmie. I'd written my preliminary report and assured him he had nothing to worry about.'

Cato wound some fettucine around his fork. 'Why did he need reassuring?'

'Exactly.'

'Guilty conscience, or just your average middle-aged worry wart? He'd followed all the correct procedures and protocols I take it?'

'Yep.'

'But?'

'But he seemed to think people in town would hold him responsible anyway. There was no official sanction, just an air of disapproval, disappointment. It stung him I guess.'

'Duty of care?'

'That kind of thing. She'd been well regarded in the community. Very active.'

'Which people? Anyone in particular he feared?'

Hutchens moved his chair to let someone squeeze past. 'Family, I suppose. Payback, maybe?'

'But it wasn't his fault, was it? And you usually need to belong to the tribe to come under tribal payback law.'

'S'pose so.'

'The altercation in the pub, the arrest.' Cato dabbed some sauce off his lips with a napkin. 'What was that about?'

'There'd been some argument with a whitefella. She'd slapped him. He'd pushed her over. The hotel manager called the cops and they decided she was the one who should be arrested.'

Funny that. 'Who was the whitefella? What was the argument about?'

'A mining contractor or something. Bit of racial abuse. She took offence.'

'As you would,' said Cato.

'Barman reckoned they'd both had a skinful.'

'The whitefella she argued with, remember his name?'

'You'll have to check your files. My memory's not that good.' Hutchens pushed his plate away. 'You keeping okay?'

'Yeah.' Cato finished off his pasta. Saw Hutchens still sizing him up. 'Why?'

A sniff. Whatever he was thinking he'd decided to keep it to himself. 'I forgot to ask. How's Jake?'

'Coming along. He didn't make it through to the end of year twelve. He's doing a uni bridging course through TAFE, living full-time with his mum these days.'

'Fully recovered?'

'On the outside, yeah. He gets these anxiety attacks.'

Hutchens shook his head. 'Must be tough.'

'At times,' Cato admitted. 'We're focusing on the positives.'

'Give him my best when you see him.'

'Will do.' Cato told him about the mystery text in the middle of the night. 'Any thoughts?'

'Wasn't me.'

'Joe Public doesn't know it's me on the case. I haven't been in the news or anything.'

'Somebody else in the Job wants to tip you off?'

'Possibly. Why the cloak and dagger?'

'It's what we thrive on. Keeps the juices flowing.' Hutchens drained his middy. 'Speaking of which, enjoying the cut and thrust of Northbridge? The big city?'

'An office is an office. Sometimes I get to take the train, enjoy the view, read a book.'

'Books. That reminds me, I've got a deadline.' Since retiring, Hutchens had signed up for a Masters in Criminology at Edith Cowan. A great source of merriment to some.

'Thesis on track?'

Hutchens nodded. '"The Postcolonial Detective: Memoirs of a Renaissance Man".' He unhooked his bike helmet from the back of his chair. 'Dougie Peters was a thirty-year man. You don't go that long without making a few enemies. I should know.'

'Watch this space.' Cato jangled his car keys. 'Good to see you. You're looking well.'

'Cheers. And you know what? I don't miss the game as much as I thought I would.' A wave. 'Look after yourself, okay?'

***

'We've had a sighting of the muddy ute.'

'Where?' The daydream dissolved. Nudged by Hutchens' enquiry, Cato had been thinking about his son, Jake – guilt and sadness the main ingredients. Both were the last things Jake needed from his father these days. Or ever.

'Heading south on Carrington, a few minutes after the bin-lady sighting.' Thornton checked an incoming on his mobile. Ignored it. 'Swung a left on Winterfold. Witness described it as "reckless driving", nothing out of the ordinary for that area, he reckoned.'

'Witness?'

'An old bloke coming out of Red Rooster with his chook.'

'Red Rooster? Early morning?'

'That's when he does his walk. Puts it in the microwave when he's ready. Adaptable, these oldies, eh? Resilient.'

'How'd you find him?'

'He found us. Follows us on Twitter and Facebook. Saw the appeal.'

Praise be for tech-savvy pensioners with time on their hands and bees in their bonnets. 'And?'

'He said he got a look at the driver. Described him as Aboriginal, only he put it less politely.'

'Any detail?'

'Driver looked about fortyish, not a young bloke anyway. Dark T-shirt with some words and pictures. Floored it down Winterfold and disappeared into the distance. We're following the trail. How'd the chat go with Mr Hutchens?'

'Good. That Meeka incident, the death in custody. Can you track down the close family, see if any of them have moved to Perth, got any records for violence? And find out the name of the guy Connie Jacobs slapped in the pub before she got arrested.'

'Do my best. Why?'

'Diligence. The barman and hotel manager too, please.'

Thornton looked sceptical. 'Sure, no problem.'

'Anything on that private security mob yet?'

'CPS? Their public affairs people said they'd get back to us as soon as possible.'

'Tell them we want some answers before close of business today or I'll get a warrant to go and search their files myself.'

Thornton grinned. 'Nice one.'

***

CPS was Cormann Protective Services, a division of the Cormann Logistics Group CLG, and they had offices on the twenty-third floor of a St Georges Terrace skyscraper in central Perth overlooking the Swan River. Cormann, the founder, was long dead and the company was now fronted by his son-in-law, Graham Winter, but effectively owned and run by faceless venture capitalists in Sydney. They'd deigned to provide a half hour late afternoon for Cato and Deb Hassan to meet with their public affairs guru. Winter made the introductions himself before handing them over.

'This is Jacinta. She's from New Zealand but we won't hold that against her.'

Jacinta smiled and nudged him pantomime style. 'He's a card, isn't he? And a top-class underarm bowler.'

They jousted like comic medieval knights a moment or two more before Winter made his excuses. 'You'll be in fine hands with Jacinta.' When he'd receded, Cato had the impression of him never really being there in the first place – the consummate grey man. He could have been the prime minister.

They had adjourned to a comfy room with armchairs, a low table, flowers, tea and biscuits. The river sparkled in the late afternoon sun, as did Jacinta. 'I'll never get tired of looking at that view. Ever.' She turned back and pressed the coffee plunger into place. 'I'm from Invercargill, bottom of South Island. Sun shines about three days a year. How do you like your tea?'

'White and none,' said Cato, all friendly.

'Straight, no extras,' said Hassan.

'Help yourself to biscuits.' Jacinta pushed the plate Deb's way. 'Afternoon slump, eh?' She curled a rogue lock of blonde hair behind her ear and turned back to Cato. 'Have I seen you in the news, on TV or something? You seem familiar.'

'Perth's like that.' He lifted his chin at the folder on the table in front of her. 'Douglas Peters?'

'Yes.' She picked the file up and riffled it. 'Bit flimsy I'm afraid. He wasn't with us for that long. Between you and me, and not wishing to speak ill of the dead, he didn't make that much of an impact.'

'What did he do?' said Hassan.

'Sorry?'

'His job. What did he do?'

'Client Interface Specialist – Senior Grade Three, North West Point Processing Centre.'

'Meaning?'

'Guard. Christmas Island.' She gave a wry smile. 'Bulldust, isn't it? We don't use that kind of poncy language anymore.'

Cato failed to hide his double take. 'Sorry, I didn't expect such … candour.'

'No point beating around the bush is there?'

Cato was beginning to warm to Jacinta. 'What did the job involve?'

She shrugged. 'Keep a record of comings and goings. Supervise the guard rosters, log staff and inmates – sorry, "clients" – in and out. The younger guys took care of any difficult stuff.'

Like a custody sergeant at a small town lockup, guessed Cato. 'Was there any "difficult stuff" during his tenure?'

Jacinta snorted. 'You kidding? There's difficult stuff every day. Somebody self-harming, acting up, sewing their lips shut. Who wouldn't, stuck in a place like that?'

'Forgive me but you don't seem like your usual spin doctor,' said Cato. 'This level of frankness. It's …'

'Counterintuitive, I know.' She nodded. 'That's why they hired me. Little blonde Kiwi from World's End, looks and sounds like a kid, doesn't know when to shut up. Brilliant, eh?' A sip of tea. 'Blind them with so much truth they don't know what to believe.' Cup back in the saucer. 'Oops, there I go again.'

Hassan leant over, stretching her hand out for the file. 'Can I …'

'Yeah, nah, sorry.' Jacinta clutched it to her breast.

'But I thought?'

'Rules. I can say whatever I like, particularly if it relates to stuff already on the public record. But I can't give you any paperwork.' She offered up a rueful smile. 'Crazy isn't it, but there you go.'

The warmth was wearing off. 'You realise this is a murder investigation?' said Cato.

'Sure. It's a very serious business.'

'And I can seek a warrant for those records.'

'Have you read the relevant border control laws lately?' said Jacinta, smiling again. 'Good luck with that, eh.'

***

DI Pavlou left Cato to run the end-of-day Peters team briefing. She was juggling four other killings on top of this one: a domestic stabbing up in the Hills – empty nesters who could no longer hold it together now the youngest was off on her gap year; a king hit in the Northbridge nightclub district; a toddler shaken to death in the Wheatbelt; and some bloke down in Bunbury bludgeoned to a pulp. She needed to go over to HQ and talk resources with the brass and the beancounters.

'Any word on that mud-spattered ute?' she'd said as she fired off a message on her phone.

'Nothing conclusive yet but Chris Thornton tells me he's making progress.'

'I hear you had lunch with Mick Hutchens today.'

Thornton telling tales? Did Cato need to look over his shoulder now? 'Hutchens knew Peters. He investigated a death in custody he was linked with.'

'Any merit?'

'Might be.'

'How's the old bugger doing?'

'Well. Enjoying retirement, it seems. Not missing the Job.'

'Yeah? So why's he getting in your ear?'

Cato had shrugged. 'Helping out a mate.'

'Nice.' And off she'd gone.

Cato cleared his throat. 'So tell me about this progress on the muddy white ute, Chris.' Heads turned in the meeting room, except those that were studying their phones, or spots on the ceiling, or colleagues' anatomies.

'We've picked him up again, combination of traffic cameras and eyewitnesses, total of five sightings taking him to the Thornlie area. Got a fix on the plates now too and turns out they're stolen, don't match the vehicle in question. After Thornlie, there's no more sightings.'

'That's it?' said Cato, knowing Thornton hadn't finished.

'You also asked me to check on rellies and associates of the Meeka death in custody.'

'Connie Jacobs.'

'Yep, her brother Lenny lives in Thornlie as of six months ago. His mobile number is on the list of calls received by Doug Peters the previous night, plus he owns a ute of the same make and colour.'

'But not the same rego, I'm guessing. Or you'd be saying so.'

'Could have swapped the plates. And he has convictions for violence.'

'What kind?'

'Fights mainly. In pubs. But it shows he has a temper.'

'Is somebody bringing him in?'

'He's not been to work since the day of the murder. Nobody has seen or heard from him.'

'Make him a priority. Family, associates, haunts, the lot.' Cato tried to tamp down his excitement. 'Anything else? Anybody?'

Cato broke the meeting up with a directive that Jacobs be found. Thornton sidled up. 'That other mobile number you asked me to follow up?' Cato nodded. 'Prepaid. Lost or stolen a month ago.'

No surprises. Cato wiped a foggy spot on his specs. He was tired, finding it hard to concentrate.

'Meekatharra.'

'What?' He realised Thornton was still speaking. Another zone out?

'The phone was lost or stolen in Meekatharra. An amateur gold prospector. Thought he'd lost it out bush somewhere when we asked him. He'd never bothered reporting it, just replaced it.'

The mystery text – **I know who did Peters**

'Is that where the message was sent from? Meeka?'

A shake of the head. 'According to the techies it was sent from a location in the CBD. Probably within about a two hundred metre radius of where we are now.'

Hutchens' speculation: an insider who knew Cato was running the case and probably had access to his mobile number. An insider who seemed to know what happened to Douglas Peters and why. Somebody in this building? In this room?

But why so coy?

And another link back to Meekatharra. 'The staff at the Commercial Hotel, the mining subcontractor Connie Jacobs argued with. Any word on them?'

'Nothing. The contractor in the police report was from South Africa. He went back there about four years ago. The hotel staff? High turnover, lots of casuals. Shoot-throughs.'

Cato chewed his lower lip. 'Okay, they'll wait. Let's find Lenny Jacobs.' He observed his colleagues filing out of the room. Wondered who among them might be playing games with him.

3

Friday 20th April

Rory Driscoll throttled back when he saw them, allowed the boat to drift a while in the stiffening breeze. The water was the colour of gunmetal and a bank of black-grey storm clouds boiled on the horizon; the rain would be here by the afternoon. At the jetty, a silver four-wheel drive and four people lined up side by side, hunched against the wind. One lifted her arm, giving him a wave. No, not a wave, an impatient get-a-move-on. Aunty. It had to be.

As he drew closer he was able to take the measure of Aunty's companions: a middle-aged bloke – glasses and miserable, a suburban lawyer used to getting his arse kicked. Next to him, a woman in her late twenties or early thirties, sharp features, no nonsense allowed. The third seemed vaguely familiar, maybe ten years older and ten centimetres shorter than Driscoll but holding his shape well. Wary, alert. Last, of course, Aunty, with a twin-set and pearls under her Driza-Bone jacket.

Theirs was a strange relationship. He sometimes wondered if he should be seeing a counsellor about it. An old-school purveyor of the dark arts of spookery, Aunty had been a talent-spotter, catching his eye at a guest lecture at ANU one autumn afternoon maybe twenty years ago. She'd noted his proficiency with languages, his isolation from the flint-eyed youths around him, his physique and his black eye. Been fighting, she'd observed. None of your business, he'd replied. You need taking in hand, she'd concluded. And he'd let her. Maybe she was the mum he'd always wanted his mum to be. Decisive and encouraging.

'Rory, my love.' She blew out a wreath of blue smoke. 'Keeping well?'

Driscoll chucked the rope to Mr Vaguely Familiar who caught it and started tying up. 'Good, Aunty. What brings you all the way out to the wild west of Victoria?'

'Dire straits, as always.' She waved a hand in front of her face and grimaced. 'Fish?'

'Boxes of the stuff. Help yourself.' He killed the engine, checked all was well and stepped on to the jetty. Paid attention to Fit-and-Fifty first, holding out a hand. 'We met?'

'Don't recall.' A firm grip. 'Mason. Willie Mason.'

Sharp features and no-nonsense next. 'Mira Soares.'

'Hi,' said Driscoll.

Aunty took charge of the last one. 'This is Brian.'

'Hi, Brian.' The handshake was brief and damp, like he'd never touched an Aborigine before. 'Why the long face?'

'D'you have to be so direct, Rory?' Aunty turned on her chunky boot heels and lifted one of her chins at the cluster of buildings up the road. 'Anywhere up there we can get a coffee?'

Rory checked his watch. Just gone ten. 'The bakery should be open if Janelle didn't have a skinful last night.'

They all looked tired, Aunty included. Over coffee it emerged why.

'You drove all the way from Canberra?' Driscoll took a bite from his egg and bacon toastie. 'That's like …'

'We did it over two days,' said Mason. 'A few detours here and there. Nice, if you don't have too many stops and share the driving.'

'Another day and you could shoot through to Adelaide.' Driscoll finished chewing. 'Or beyond. Just keep going.'

Aunty could read him. Of course she could. 'I know you've moved on, Rory, but this is big. I wouldn't be asking if it wasn't.'

Mira Soares was absorbed by the fern pattern on her coffee froth. Brian No-name met Driscoll's gaze for the first time. Pleading. Only Willie Mason seemed cool about all this. Professional detachment, years of experience. Whatever it was they needed of him, Rory wondered why they couldn't just give the job to Mason instead; he seemed capable enough.

'Tell me.'

The bakery was empty, them aside. Out of holiday season, kids at school, farmers farming, fisherfolk fishing, bogans sleeping off whatever they did last night. Nobody listening in, not even the proprietor who was out back grabbing a ciggie. Aunty looked like she wanted to do the same. 'Two weeks from now there's going to be a committee from The Hague –'

'The Hague?' interrupted Driscoll.

'It's in Holland. But this committee is having its meeting in Darwin.'

'Darwin?'

'Northern Territory. Fuck, Rory, your geography's gone downhill since you went into hibernation. They're having a meeting about East Timor.'

'Timor-Leste,' said Mira Soares. 'That is the name now.'

'Right,' said Aunty. 'This committee is going to be hearing from Mira, Brian, and from Willie here.'

'What about?'

'No need for detail right now. But somebody doesn't want them to talk to the committee.'

'Who?'

'Good question. Whoever, they are they're not messing about.' Aunty explained herself: the existence of a hit list, threats already made, houses torched, pets butchered, trollings on social media, midnight phone calls, the usual.

'You're taking it seriously?'

'Wouldn't be here otherwise, Rory.'

'What's it got to do with me?'

Aunty grabbed her ciggie packet and lighter, nodded for him to join her outside. 'You're on the death list too, dear.'

***

'Where do they all fit in?' Rory stood upwind from Aunty so her smoke wouldn't bother him. The storm clouds had crept closer. Rain by lunchtime now, he predicted.

'Brian's a solicitor. Not a high-powered one. He tends to do wills and conveyancing. Bit of divorce work, family court matters.'

'How'd he find himself on a hit list?'

'A client of his lodged some secrets with him. Left a time bomb ticking away in the poor bastard's life.' A slow suck on the coffin nail. 'Ms Soares is a journalist, blogger, podcaster – you name it, she does it. Came here as a kid just after the independence referendum in ninety-nine. Freelances for an investigative news website and dug herself into some trouble.'

'Willie Mason?'

'Worked at the embassy in Jakarta and then, after Timorese statehood, the one in Dili.'

'Must be why he seems so familiar.'

'Know him?'

Either I've met him or I just know the type.' Driscoll's gaze passed over Aunty's head, through the cafe window. Mason chatting amiably with Mira Soares, at ease. Soares less so but, if the body language was anything to go by, responding to his flirtatious manner. And poor Brian staring into space, lost in his fears.

Aunty pulled her Driza-Bone closer and folded her arms against the wind. 'You were there in the mid-noughties, wee slip of a lad. I was still working out what to do with you.'

She'd found a place for him within the shadowlands of the intelligence community, testing his abilities, seeing what his potential was. 'I don't recall doing anything warranting a death sentence.'

'Maybe you know or saw something but you don't realise it?'

'Maybe.' Driscoll studied her. She should be retired by now, collecting her pension, drawing on her super. Doing a Rhine cruise. 'What's all this to you?'

'Do you see me being put out to pasture? Seriously?' She handed him a business card. 'Hope Springs Crisis Management Consultant.'

'You used to be Hope Springs Strategic Consultant. Why the change?'

'Everything's reactive these days, isn't it? Nobody seems to want to think ahead and consider consequences. I blame the internet.'

'Same logo anyway,' said Driscoll, slipping the card into his pocket.

'I mostly deal with footballers caught sending dick pics to teenage girls. Old bishops, actors and comedians whose pasts have caught up with them. My job to muddy the prosecution waters. What was it about supposed funny men and the nineteen seventies?'

'Bit sordid if you don't mind my saying so, Aunty.'

She pouted. 'Pays well, though.'

Driscoll nodded through the window. 'They don't seem to fit that picture.'

'I keep my hand in. The old-school network chucks me the odd morsel. Mason came looking for me. And you.'

'Why?'

'He wants you to keep them alive until The Hague committee meets.'

'Why me?'

'He reckons you're the key. If you survive, they all will.'

***

While doors were being knocked and leads followed in the hunt for Lenny Jacobs, Cato sat in on the autopsy for Doug Peters. It had been postponed from yesterday because of staff shortages and a backlog; a colleague had called in sick, the pathologist explained.

'I might well be Wonder Woman but I can't be two places at the same time.' Professor McKenzie finished off the 'Y' incision on Peters' torso and glanced Cato's way. 'Poor bugger took a fair hiding, eh?' She lifted her chin towards the specimen on a nearby counter. 'And what's with the ear?'

Cato shrugged his shoulders. 'Don't know yet whether it's meaningful or just somebody's idea of a joke.'

'Ha-bloody-ha.' She put her scalpel down and reached for something else sharp. 'How are you finding the new job?'

'Pretty much same as the old one, although now I don't have to fight so hard for the interesting cases.'

'Interesting? Interesting is an interesting concept, isn't it?' She peeled back a sheet of skin. 'I heard you were ready to walk away from all this interesting stuff. What changed your mind?'

Cato winced at the squelching and tearing noises. 'Sucker for punishment?'

'Join the club. I don't know why I do it either. Used to think I was a force for good, letting the dead speak, that kind of thing. Sometimes still think it. Other times? Pushing shit up a hill might best describe it.'

McKenzie was far more loquacious today and Cato wasn't sure he liked it. He preferred the dour terse Scot with the occasional wisecrack dropped in, like a boiled lolly tossed to some street urchins. He said as much.

She nodded. 'Did a job late yesterday on an eighteen month old brought in from Narrogin. She'd been shaken to death by her dad. Snapped neck, bruises all over, sores. She's not the first I've done and won't be the last.' Her breath sucked at the mask. 'Some days you look into their eyes, see those last moments through them, and wonder what the fuck it's all about.'

McKenzie returned to the task, observing aloud Peters' injuries and general state of internal and external health while Cato made notes along the way. No real surprises. The victim had been hacked, with a machete most likely, and most parts of his body had sustained terrible injuries. The severing of the ear seemed almost superfluous.

'Coup de grâce?' wondered Cato aloud.

'God knows. That's your department.'

'Time frame?'

'I'd say he died somewhere between the middle of the night and early the next morning. Might be able to tighten that up after a few more tests.' McKenzie stepped away from the gurney. 'He was in the Job, wasn't he?' Cato affirmed so. She nodded. 'I remember him.'

'What?'

'I did the autopsy on the death in custody from Meekatharra. He sat in on it. Devastated he was.'

'You remember him from, what, thirteen years ago?'

'Like I said earlier, some stay with you, others don't. This one I remembered more because of him than her. She was routine. Dodgy ticker. End of story.'

'So what was special about him?'

'He was shattered, took it all personally. I told him at the end, he couldn't have known, it wasn't his fault. But he just kept insisting it was. "I'll pay for this one day," he said.' She moved over to the taps and started stripping off the scrubs. 'Not wrong there, was he?'

***

It took them until the end of the afternoon to locate Lenny Jacobs. He'd looked up drowsily from his middy in the Thornlie Tavern to find he was surrounded by TRG ninjas. For all his stocky, pugilistic demeanour, he came quietly and now sat opposite Cato and Deb Hassan with a lawyer from the Aboriginal Legal Service at his side. Questions had been raised about the heavy-handed approach.

'No heavy hand was lifted against him,' Cato had pointed out. 'But he was hard to find and there was some urgency. We're investigating a murder here. Time is of the essence and we'd appreciate your client's cooperation.'

'So he's not under arrest?' The Aboriginal Legal Service lawyer, Bob, was a tall, skinny man with the air of a resting academic. He just wanted to clarify. 'And free to leave at any time?'

'Sure,' said Cato. 'As things presently stand.'

'What's this all about?' Jacobs said, for what must have been the tenth time. 'Who's this dead bloke you're on about, and what's that got to do with me?'

Really? They'd get to the phone call later. As an opening gambit they'd asked him to account for his whereabouts on the day of the murder of Douglas Peters and in the time since.

'How about you just answer the question,' said Cato. 'Please.'

A nose scratch. 'Been crook.'

'Map it out for us,' said Hassan. 'Start at the beginning.'

Jacobs worked as a contract delivery driver in the burgeoning gig economy. He even had his own ABN, which was a source of some pride. 'First in the family to have a self-employed business number,' he said. 'Just need to get my first million in the bank now.' On the day of the murder he'd collected and delivered parcels in the southern suburbs, weaving back and forth along Leach Highway and South Street.

'We should be able to confirm that through Uber Rush records.' Bob turned to his client. 'Shouldn't we?'

'Yeah, that's right.'

Hassan took down some details and zapped them through to Chris Thornton for follow up. 'And you don't mind if we crosscheck with your satnav?'

'Nah, but it's busted anyway.'

'Since when?' asked Cato.

Since the day before the murder, funny that. A different tack – did Jacobs know Douglas Peters?

'The dead bloke? No, why would I?'

'He was the officer in charge of the station in Meekatharra when your sister died.'

'Connie? No shit. Really?'

'But back in the day you knew him well enough, didn't you?' Hassan prodded the papers in her file. 'Barely a month went by without you spending a night in the cells: drunk, fighting, domestics. You name it.'

'Turned over a new leaf since then. Sorted myself out.'

'Good to hear,' said Cato. And it seemed true enough. No convictions or arrests for over four years. 'But you'd have got to know Mr Peters, Sergeant Peters as he was then, well enough during that time. Even arrested you himself once or twice.'

'This was at least thirteen years ago, right?' said Bob the lawyer. 'And my client was often drunk or otherwise indisposed at the time. It's drawing rather a long bow to say he knew Mr Peters well, isn't it?'

'I didn't say "well", I said "well enough".'

Jacobs interrupted. 'Peters, yeah, I remember him now you mention it. Good bloke. Stopped those other cunts in the station from giving me a flogging, once.' A shake of the head. 'So he's the one that's dead? Fuck. Shame.'

'You gave him a hard time after your sister's death,' said Hassan, studying the file again. 'Fronting a couple of demos outside the lockup. Broke his windows at home. Weren't so sure he was a good bloke then, were you?'

'I was upset. My sister had just died. In his custody.'

'But you're saying now that you think he was a good bloke. You want us to believe you don't still hold that grudge?'

'Time's a great healer.'

'Why did you phone Doug Peters the night before he died?'

'Did I?'

'According to the records, yeah.' Cato slid a printout over to the lawyer, pointed out the highlighted number.

'Must have been a butt call,' said Jacobs. 'I had him on my contacts from all those years ago. Forgot to delete him I expect.'

Implausible but not impossible. 'How come you haven't been to work, been seen by anyone the last couple of days?' Hassan looked up from her file. 'Been lying low?'

'Like I said, crook. Bit of gastro.'

'But not at home all that time according to the neighbours. Where were you?'

'Friends.'

'Names?'

'Can't remember. Only just met them. Nice people though.'

A few more questions and they had enough for a first account interview. Enough to begin tripping him up and unravelling his story. 'Do you mind if we take DNA samples?' said Cato. 'To help exclude you from our enquiries?'

'What if I refuse?'

'We'll arrest you and take some anyway,' said Hassan.

Jacobs leaned back in his chair, cupped his hands behind his head. 'Same old story, eh?'

***

The Uber Rush records showed that Jacobs' deliveries were all carried out promptly on the day of the murder. Many of the pickup and delivery addresses provided eyewitnesses who recognised Jacobs as being the delivery driver – some knew him from previous jobs. In particular a witnessed collection in Myaree and a drop-off out near the airport had him elsewhere when the neighbouring bin-bag lady said she was nearly bowled over by a muddy white ute. So Jacobs was free to go until and unless they could find more on him or match his prints or DNA sample to the crime scene. But he would be tailed by a surveillance team in the meantime.

'Think he's our man?' asked Hassan as they logged off for the day.

'Think so. Hope so,' said Cato. 'It would be a nice quick result.'

'But he has alibis.'

'For the timing of the speeding ute. Not necessarily for the murder.'

'So who's in the ute?'

'Don't know, not him it seems. Maybe it's coincidental, somebody in a hurry for their own good reasons and nothing to do with the murder.'

She frowned.

'It happens,' said Cato. 'You know it does.'

Thornton would continue building the background picture on Jacobs. Forensics would comb Jacobs' ute and Thornlie unit as secondary crime scenes, and the labs would take a look at his DNA. He'd have to couch surf until his home was freed up again.

Jacobs was philosophical. 'Used to it, brother. Make sure you tidy my place up when you've finished.'

Hassan was tasked with her outside enquiries team to fill in the gaps on where Jacobs was in the days before the murder, before and between deliveries on the day in question, and on his sickie days off since with the mysterious unnamed friends.

'He's shitting us on that, but why?' Hassan squinted into the glare of the sunset. 'Still, he doesn't seem like the mad machete-man type to me.'

'I'd like a dollar for every time I've heard that,' said Cato.

***

Sharon was on a split shift so they got to spend the evening together. Ella had taken a while to go down; snotty and irritable, harbouring a virus from day care and possibly a new tooth coming through. Cato could already taste the greasy, acidic germs of yet another bug in his throat. Sharon, braced for a restless night, had fortified herself with half a block of chocolate and a peppermint tea.

'Tired?' enquired Cato, lifting her legs to his lap and massaging her feet.

'Been tireder.'

'So you don't fancy making a little brother or sister for Ella?'

'You offering?'

'Always and forever.'

She yawned. 'Not tonight, maybe tomorrow. I think the Drug Mule Wars might be dying down. Might even be able to take a long weekend soon.'

'Work's going well?'

'It's good to be back in the fray.' She laid a hand on his. 'How about you?'

'Yep, all good.'

'Really?'

'You don't think so?'

She tilted her head. 'Sometimes you seem like the old you. Other times, I don't know. You seem flattened out. No edges, no highs, no lows. Not present.'

That'll be the drugs, thought Cato. 'Probably just tired.'

'Yeah, probably.' She tapped his hand. 'That part's good now.'

'What?'

'The arch of my foot. You've been rubbing it for a while.' She smiled. 'You can move on if you like.'

'Sorry. Right.'

'Are we okay, Phil? Anything going on?'

'Everything's good. Really good.' Why couldn't he tell her about his reliance on the antidepressants? His fear of falling off a cliff. Why, over a year after the avenging angel Jai Stevenson had ripped into his life, couldn't he put those pills aside and get back to normal? He was trying, he really was. Tapering the tablets under medical supervision from a daily to a weekly slow-release dose. And a secret mini-stockpile of the dailies for emergencies. Result? The odd migraine, lapse of concentration. Nothing he couldn't hide or handle. Sharon had stuck by him. Jake was recovering. He too was recovering. Everything was back on track, wasn't it? No, Sharon already had enough on her plate with the new job. He couldn't add to that.

'I'd better get ready for work.' Sharon lifted her feet from his lap, grabbed their cups to take to the kitchen. 'The twelve thirty from Kuala Lumpur awaits.'

4

Monday 23rd – Tuesday 24th April

'Jacobs' prints and DNA are in the murder house.'

Duncan Goldflam's lanky frame filled the doorway. Cato closed his laptop. 'Magic. Whereabouts? How?'

'Partial palm and some fingers on a wall and doorway and around a coffee mug. DNA on the rim of the mug.'

'He had a cuppa while he was chopping up Peters?'

'Thirsty work I suppose.' Goldflam checked his notes. 'And we've got some matching fibres from the crime scene with clothes we've found at his home. Recently washed.'

'Sweet.'

A surveillance team had Jacobs under watch at a house a couple of streets away from his unit. Cato told them to bring him in. Over the weekend more had been added to Thornton's backgrounder on Jacobs. A fellow inmate at Hakea when Jacobs had been on remand for yet another assault charge recalled him saying, quote: 'He was going to do that cunt Peters.'

As recently as sixteen months ago.

'I thought he'd finished with all that bad behaviour four years ago?' Cato had wondered aloud. 'Changed his ways.'

'Moderated maybe,' said Thornton. 'He was acquitted of the charge, mainly based on confused and conflicting accounts. A melee on Australia Day in Meeka. Cops reckoned he was in the thick of it. He reckoned the cops just rounded up the usual suspects. He won in court.'

'How reliable is the prison snitch?'

Thornton had grinned. 'Blue chip, boss. Aren't they all?'

'How'd you find him?'

'He found us. Heard we had his old cellmate in the frame. Offered his services.'

'That's some grapevine. I don't like the sound of this.'

Thornton had shrugged. 'Keep it in reserve?'

'Bottom of the pile. Anything else?'

'Mobile records. Jacobs attempted to phone Peters' landline twice the evening before the murder. Two short calls, the length of an answering machine message. But, as we know, he didn't bother talking after the beep.'

'He reckoned it was an accidental buttcall.'

'Twice?'

'Not impossible.' Cato stifled a yawn. The fitful night's sleep leaving its mark. 'So he paid him a visit in person the next morning instead?'

'That's one scenario.'

'Phone records, forensics placing him at the scene, past history and motive' Cato scratched his chin. 'It's becoming a pretty compelling scenario.'

'People have been locked up for less. Especially here in the State of Excitement.'

'That's good enough for me.'

***

Things moved swiftly from there. After a further interview, during which Jacobs still denied any wrongdoing but failed to provide anything new to strengthen his case, Pavlou saw enough in what they had to charge him at least with manslaughter. By the end of the day a magistrate remanded Jacobs into custody and the investigation shifted gears. They no longer had a killer at large but now they needed to make sure they had sufficient evidence for a strong prosecution brief and hopefully an upgrade to a murder charge.

Pavlou was beaming. 'Good work, Philip.'

'Thanks, boss. Team effort, as always.'

'Fancy a trip to Bunbury?'

One of the other recent murders: a bludgeoning if he remembered rightly. 'There's still a case to build here with Jacobs.'

'That'll trundle along in the safe hands of Hassan and Thornton with oversight from me.'

'Short notice on the home front: Sharon's on nights and Ella's coming down with a bug.'

A thin smile. 'Fair enough. See what you can arrange and let me know when suits.'

Code, he knew, for Not. Good. Enough. 'Is Bunbury urgent?'

'Murders tend to be.' Pavlou checked an incoming on her mobile and frowned. 'A few people off sick, shortage of experienced hands.'

Julie the nanny was sometimes prepared to sleepover. 'Bunbury D's not able to run with it?'

'If I thought that, I wouldn't be asking you, would I?'

'Complicated?'

'There's a certain flamboyance that bears further scrutiny.'

'Flamboyance?'

'Post-mortem. After caving the skull in with a claw hammer, the eyes were gouged out with a dessert spoon.'

'Definitely a dessert spoon?'

'Left on display, in a bowl, with the eyes.'

'Ah, right.' Cato scrolled through his phone for the nanny's number. 'I'll see what I can do.'

***

Driscoll was driving with Willie Mason riding shotgun – tasked to keep him awake. Mira was asleep in the back. Brian slumped beside her, nodding fitfully against a rain-spattered window.

'You must have been shipping in as I was shipping out.'

'Hmmm?' Driscoll's attention was on the headlit road out front, the steady rain, and any suicidal roos lurking in the gloom.

'Timor.'

'Must've.' It was around three a.m. They'd been going for about four hours along the Great Ocean Road after spending the weekend in his Warrnambool shack catching up on sleep and showers. Sometimes they veered inland for a while to keep people guessing. Aunty had donated the four-wheel drive, taken a Cessna out of the Portland airstrip, paid in cash with no ID and no questions asked – a mate of Driscoll who owed a favour. The satnav had been disabled way back in Canberra. Likewise, all phones confiscated, batteries and SIMs out.

'Miss it?'

'What?' said Driscoll.

'Playing away from home. The discarded life. The Great Game.'

'Nah,' said Driscoll. The 'Great Game', a Kipling fiction, like le Carré's 'moles'. The game didn't seem so great once you saw it from the point of view of its innocent victims: suicidal ten-year-olds in desert island hellholes, blips dissolving off the radar, faces slipping beneath the waves.

Rain pounded them off the Southern Ocean. The plan was to make Port Melbourne in time for the early-morning sailing to Tasmania. Cash again. Aunty had supplied a bag full of the stuff. She hadn't fully made her mind up about Willie Mason, wasn't sure why she'd chosen to trust him. Left it to Driscoll to form his own judgement.

'How'd you learn about this death list?' Driscoll said.

'Tipped off by an old mate in BIN.' Mason paused. 'Indonesian intelligence.'

'Yeah, I know.' A scrape and rustle in the back. Mira waking up. 'And?'

'Somebody was offering him the contract. He didn't need the money. Warned me instead. We go back a bit.'

'Who was the somebody?'

'He didn't know. A tough guy, ex-Kopassus special forces, now a Jakarta bagman. Whatever.'

'All sounds a bit vague.' Driscoll slowed for a bounding roo. 'You believed your BIN mate?'

'I do now. He sent me the list plus whatever else he'd picked up. Then he was found chopped up in a restaurant skip in Sunda Kelapa a few days ago.'

Sunda Kelapa, the old port of Jakarta. Sailing ships and bustling stevedores, skipping down narrow bending planks from ship to shore. Sweat. Spice. Kreteks. Half-close your eyes, allow yourself to daydream, and you could be in port after weeks on the high seas with Joseph Conrad.

'I don't understand why you need me. You seem resourceful and capable enough.'

'You come highly recommended. Besides, you're on the list too.' Mason thumbed over his shoulder to the back seat. 'Safety in numbers.

We all look after each other, we all might get through this. Otherwise they'll pick us off, one by one.' He turned in his seat, chuckling. 'That right, Brian?'

Brian roused himself. 'I'm getting sick of you and your jokes, Mason.'

Driscoll checked out the angry eyes in the rear-view. No love lost between the two blokes. 'You could have just placed yourself in police or spook custody for the duration.'

Mason barked out a laugh. 'I heard you went soft when you left the Job. I thought they meant soft and flabby in the gut. Not the head.'

A staying hand on the shoulder. 'Willie. We need him on our side. Be nice.'

Driscoll checked the rear-view again. Found Mira staring at him.

***

Cato was up at dawn and on the road south to Bunbury. Over a double-shot coffee at Settlers Roadhouse he browsed the case notes on his iPad as the sun rose and the crows and galahs did vocal battle among the gums. Another pensioner, a man in his seventies, bludgeoned to death, eyes scooped out with a spoon and left on display. In the age of internet-inspired thrill killers there seemed little left to shock or disturb any more. Was he becoming desensitised? He believed not; it wasn't so long ago he was on the verge of quitting because he felt hypersensitised to the suffering around him. Especially when it came close to home. So why was he still in the game? Was this all he knew? How flimsy his sense of self must be, propped up by pills. No, he was good at this. Top Gun. DI Pavlou's go-to guy. Cato screwed the lid back on his keep cup and headed for the car. Coming your way, you murdering motherfuckers.

The house was out near the beach at Hungry Hollow, south of the port area. A squat brick place with blue Colorbond roof and fence and a dog yapping next door. Over the road, the Indian Ocean foamed under a brisk south-westerly and sand blew into the front yard. The crime scene had been examined and cleared but the cordon tape was still in place and a uniform on duty. Cato showed his ID and was waved through once he'd suited up. Stepping plates led along the hall into a spacious and blood-spattered kitchen with a view onto a recently-mown back lawn and two raised vegie beds permanently netted against the birds. There was a large black-brown smudge on the jarrah floorboards where the body had lain. Dark red streaks and whiplash traces on the walls. The number tags remained in place. Cato could smell the forensic chemicals, imagine the shufflings and camera flashes as if the team was still there working around a newly discovered corpse. There were photos of adult offspring and grandkids on the fridge door and some plastic magnetised letters – happy birthday, Granda. A framed photo on the wall: Granda and his long-deceased wife on their fortieth wedding anniversary.

On the dining table, a plastic marker where the cereal bowl had been left with Bevan Drummond's eyes sitting in it. Some murmurings and a shadow moving down the hall. A woman appeared in the doorway – about Cato's height, dark hair cut short, detective's lanyard.

'Don't think we've met?' She held out a hand for shaking. 'Nikki Earle.'

Cato introduced himself. 'You've been running things?'

'Until now, yeah.'

She didn't seem defensive or put out. Major Crime stepping in was a given, particularly on a gruesome case like this, no point making a fuss. 'Where're you at?'

'Post-mortem and crime scene reports are on file. Door-to-doors and other enquiries progressing. Same with family, friends, financials, phone, computer.'

'All in hand, then. Anything of interest so far?'

She thumbed over her shoulder. 'You'll have seen the burnout marks outside on the road?'

'Yep.'

'Neighbour down the street, has history for cutting whippies. Drummond had dobbed him in, took photos on his phone to prove it.'

'And you reckon this neighbour beat him to death and spooned his eyes out for that?'

A grimace. 'One theory, anyway.'

'You've talked to him?'

'Not yet. We can't find him.'

'Let me know when you do.' Cato waved his hand at the scene. 'Want to walk me through it?'

'It's all on the database.'

'Humour me.'

She smiled. 'Sure.'

No forced entry. Body discovered by a daughter who usually called around every other day to check on him. No signs of struggle anywhere except here in the kitchen. Bloody footprints of one other person, size ten Target own-brand cheapo trainers, leading out to a side patio and away up to the front gate. Believed to have all happened around ten or eleven at night. The night before Doug Peters was found chopped up in suburban Fremantle.

'Nothing seen or heard?'

'Neighbour heard a car start up and drive away around then – she was calling her dog in from the backyard for the night. Thought nothing of it at the time.'

'Why did it register with her later?'

'Crunched gears, some swearing. She doesn't like that kind of thing.'

'No sounds of struggle, cries, nothing? Nobody saw the car?'

'Nah.' They'd done a circuit of the kitchen, then out to the side patio, back in around the house, peeked in some other rooms. 'Seen enough for now?'

'S'pose so.'

They adjourned to the Hollow Beach cafe down the road and Earle brought Cato up to speed on every aspect of the investigation. So far she was doing exactly what he and a thousand others would have done. Out on the water a handful of hardy souls tried to surf whatever was going but the conditions weren't right and it all looked pretty messy.

'Apart from a psychopathic hoon neighbour, do you have any other theories?' Cato sipped some flat white. Like the ocean today, too much froth.

Earle appraised him over the rim of her long mac. 'Ask me again when we've found the neighbour.'

'You don't seem convinced.'

'I haven't worked as many murders as you. Couple of domestics, nothing complicated. Usually wrapped up in a few days. This kid we're after has a bad temper, we know that from his record.'

'But?'

'The eyes thing is pretty weird. This boy doesn't do weird, he does stupid.'

'Maybe he saw something in a film? Thought it might be cool?'

'Maybe.' Her phone burbled. A few monosyllables later, she put it down. Earle necked her coffee and nodded at Cato. 'Let's ask him, he's waiting for us at the station.'

***

Ryan Hodgson was in a cocky and combative mood: clear complexion, blond frullet and well-fitting clothes. He could probably make something of himself if he could ever be arsed. He'd brought a lawyer when he voluntarily presented for questioning at Bunbury cop shop. The lawyer's name was Frances Cleary and she looked too expensive for Legal Aid. Maybe Ryan's mum and dad were paying. Cato watched on the video link, insufficiently prepared to be in that room himself. Earle and a male colleague were running the show.

She announced herself for the recording – Detective Senior Constable Earle. 'Thank you for coming in to see us, Mr Hodgson.' She gave him a welcoming smile. 'Or is it okay to call you Ryan?'

'No worries.' Hodgson focused on the male detective. 'Which one of you's in charge?'

'Both of us, mate. We're a team.' He handed a business card over. 'Call me José if you like.'

'José Carrascalao,' Hodgson read, awkwardly. 'Where'd you get a name like that?'

'Brazil. I was born there. Never know it from my accent, would you?' A glance at his watch. 'My colleague has some questions for you.'

Cleary checked the business card and underlined José's name on her yellow legal pad. 'You acknowledge that my client has presented himself voluntarily, is not under arrest, can refuse to answer any questions, and may leave at any time?'

'We appreciate the cooperation,' said Earle. 'Where've you been the last few days, Ryan?'

'Mates. Dunsborough.' A holiday spot fifty k's south and west.

A couple of names, addresses and contact numbers were noted. He went there the morning after the old man's murder and just got back today. Hadn't heard what had happened, hadn't been checking his phone, came in as soon as he realised he was a person of interest. Shocking, he said. How can I help?

'Maybe you could account for your movements that previous evening.

Let's say from about seven through to when you left for Dunsborough the following morning.'

Thinking face. 'Had me dinner. Watched some TV but it was shit. Went on me phone for a while. Listened to some music. Went to sleep. Woke up, had a coffee, went to Dunsborough.'

'Quiet night in, then?' said José.

'Pretty much.'

More noting of details. Mum made his dinner, some vegetarian curry crap, then went off to her book club. Dad around? Nah, fucked off years ago. Brothers or sisters? Just me, only child. Sad, eh? What was on the box? I'm a boring third-rate celebrity fuckwit get me out of here. On the phone? Tinder. Snapchat. Instagram. Facebook. The music? Can't remember, usual stuff. In the morning? Mum went to work before he woke up.

'So nobody to vouch for you,' noted Earle.

'The phone use and location can be verified.' Cleary clicked her biro. 'Is that it?'

No, it wasn't. 'We need access to your car, Ryan.'

'You've got it already. Impounded last week.'

Earle exchanged a glance with José – why didn't they already know that? 'And your phone.'

He slid it across the desk. 'Help yourself. I'll need a receipt though.'

'Computer?'

'Don't have one. Just use me phone.'

After some to-and-fro, Hodgson was persuaded to give them the required pin number and passwords. Earle tilted her head. 'Ryan, did you kill Bevan Drummond?'

'Me?' A snort. 'Nah, why would I?'

'He dobbed you in. You lost your car because of him.'

'Nah, mate. I lost my car because of my own irresponsible behaviour. I'm prepared to take the consequences. Man up, like, you know?'

Cleary started packing stuff away. 'I think my client has given you the information you require. If you have any further questions down the track he'll be happy to help. Right, Ryan?'

A big grin. 'Sure.'

Earle nodded. 'Are you happy to submit to a DNA sample?'

The grin subsided. He glanced at the lawyer. Her face said get it over with, it'll happen sooner or later. 'Okay.'

José took Hodgson off to do the business under the watchful eye of the lawyer. Earle signalled Cato through the video link to join her in the interview room. 'Any thoughts?'

'He seemed to be enjoying himself until the end there.'

'Reckon he's the eyeball-spooning type?'

'No.'

'What about the DNA pout?'

'Maybe he's done something else that'll be used against him. Murder? I don't see it.'

'I'll let you know how the tests go. You heading home now?'

Cato nodded. 'Not even sure why I came here in the first place. When you've got more on Drummond's background, or anything else of interest, can you zap it through? Unless my boss wants a full-scale takeover, I'm not going to hang around looking over your shoulder.'

'Why so shy?'

He might have talked about how he was paying out unnecessary childcare costs to be here for no good reason. About how there was already enough pressure on his family life without being sent to Bunbury to micromanage a perfectly competent fellow officer. About all sorts of things. 'I've been where you are now. We've all had the same training. Some of us apply it more than others. Some of us are smarter and less lazy than others. The floor is yours unless and until you hear otherwise.'

'What if I'd prefer somebody else took this over?'

'Shout out if that's the case.'

Earle paused. 'Okay.' She shook his hand. 'Safe drive home.'

5

Tuesday 24th April

It was a rough crossing. Brian had spent most of the time in the toilets as the ferry rolled and his stomach rolled with it. Mason and Mira sat, heads close, at a table near the cafe. She, intense and nervous. He, watchful and faintly amused. Driscoll was wondering whether he should leave them and go and check on Brian. If anything happened, Mason was probably capable of handling it at least until he got back. A tap on the shoulder. Driscoll jerked, unaware of just how tightly strung he was.

'Do you play?'

A little old man in a brown cardigan. He was seated along the bench from Driscoll, setting out pieces on a chessboard. They must have been magnetic, unaffected by the big broadside waves rolling through Bass Strait.

'No, sorry,' Driscoll lied. This wasn't the time to allow himself to be distracted. Where was Brian? He'd been in the dunny over ten minutes now.

'You were watching my last game. You seemed to know what you were watching.'

Driscoll had been an idiot. How many times had Brian disappeared into the bogs? He'd given up counting, given up caring and watching. But who wants to hang out in a stinking vomity toilet cubicle? They'd have known that. Waited. Picked their moment. Was this guy with the chessboard part of the operation? 'Sorry, mate. I need to check on a friend.'

'There he is. He looks a bit better, you think?'

True enough. Brian was back, and some colour other than green had returned to his face. He took a seat at the table with Mason and Mira, who broke off whatever it was they were talking about.

'So. A game?' The old bloke was persistent. Is this what retirement is like? Grim, clinging determination. His accent, Eastern European maybe? Eyes dancing with intelligence, and need. Driscoll nodded acquiescence and the old man's face lit up. 'Black or white?'

'I'm easy.'

'I'm Yakov.' The man extended his hand and Driscoll shook it. 'You can be white as I'm the one inviting you to play.'

'I'm Rory.' Driscoll finished lining up the pieces and made the first move. 'That accent. Polish?'

'You mean I don't sound dinky-di, after all these years?' The man chuckled. 'Yes, I suppose you could say I'm Polish although I insist I came from nowhere. I was stateless for the first few years of my life. No passport at all. We came to Australia when I was five. My parents never let me out of their sight until I was ten. They homeschooled me. All we spoke around the house when I was a child was Polish, Polish, Polish.'

Already Driscoll had lost a pawn and a bishop and was vulnerable on the left. How did that happen? 'Your parents taught you chess?'

'My father. He was a grandmaster. It helped keep him alive when he should have died many times.'

Driscoll nodded. Waited for more but it didn't come. 'Where were you born, Warsaw?'

'Our family were from Danzig, what is now Gdańsk, in Poland but claimed then by Germany for their *Lebensraum*. My mother was pregnant when she was arrested. I was born in Ravensbrück, in northern Germany.'

Ravensbrück. One of the Nazi concentration camps. Driscoll didn't know the details. It was just one of many names of such places that evoked an unknowable nightmare. Imagine being born into that kind of horror. Spending your first years behind the wire. 'It's a miracle you survived.'

'Yes,' said Yakov. 'It is. In his camp, my father would teach the Commander to play better chess. In Ravensbrück my mother gave herself first to the officers and then to the scientists who wanted her body for different reasons. I suppose you could call it a miracle.'

The guy didn't hold back. Maybe he'd told the story so many times he'd lost sense of its impact.

'Sorry,' said Driscoll.

Yakov took one of Driscoll's knights. 'Don't be. I hardly remember it. It's all over now and it wasn't your fault.'

Driscoll changed the subject. 'You live in Tasmania or just visiting?'

'Blackmans Bay, just south of Hobart. You know it?' No, Driscoll didn't. The old man smiled. 'Lots of retirees. Plenty of restful activities. A place to go and die in peace.'

Driscoll could see now he was two moves off checkmate and couldn't do a damn thing about it. 'I think you've got me.' He made to lay down his king but Yakov stopped him.

'No need to submit.' They shook hands. 'Look after your friends. They need you.' He lifted his chin in the direction of Mason. 'Even the tough guy.' He half-folded the board and slid the pieces back into the box. 'There are many ways to survive. But you don't need me to tell you that.' He pushed a scrap of paper with a phone number Driscoll's way. 'Drop by if you ever want a return match. I think the result flattered me. I'm sure you can do better.'

***

Cato got home in time for dinner. He'd been thinking about eyes in a bowl and an ear in a plastic tub. All it needed now was some false teeth on a pillow and the 'see/hear/speak no evil' triptych would be complete. Were the two murders linked? There was enough time between one and the other for the same person to have done it. Two old men, mutilated: one a former cop, the other a retired science teacher. No evidence they knew each other. Besides, they had somebody for Peters – an old score settled from his turbulent days in Meekatharra. The two murders were coincidental. End of.

'You're back early.' Sharon kissed him and offered some gnocchi from the end of her spoon. 'Does that taste ready to you?'

He'd texted ahead so Sharon knew not to book Julie in again for the night. 'It didn't warrant a sleepover. She has it all in hand.'

'She?'

'Detective Senior Constable Nikki Earle. Bunbury's finest.'

'Finest? Sounds like she impressed you. How old is she and what does she look like?'

'An old hag, must be forty at least, bad breath, and this yucky huge yellow-headed wart on her nose.'

'Just your type. I better watch myself.'

'Are you going in tonight?'

'Yep. Go and say goodnight to your daughter before she forgets you. That's her bellowing, second room on the left. Remember?'

Ella demanded three stories before she deigned to fall asleep. A very hungry caterpillar and two Mem Foxes later, Cato hoed into his gnocchi while Sharon readied herself for airport duty. 'Anything special on, or just routine?'

'Routine. With any luck I should be home by three.'

'Feel free to wake me.'

'Always do.' Her mobile beeped and she checked the message. Frowned.

'What is it?'

'They want me over at Qantas Domestic. Fracas on an incoming from Darwin.'

'AFP matter?'

'Assume so. They're pretty insistent.' She gave him a brief businesslike hug. 'See you in a few hours.'

Cato stacked the dishwasher, looked in on Ella, answered some emails and watched TV. It sounded like a grown-up version of Ryan Hodgson's night in. The lad seemed sure of himself. Cato still didn't see him as an eyeball popper and guessed the DNA reticence was down to some other malfeasance he might be pegged for. Hodgson's history of violence was typical spoilt brat anger mismanagement stuff. Punching or kicking out in a temper when he didn't get his way: road rage, parking rage, taxi rank rage, girlfriend leaving him rage, mummy not making his favourite meal rage. People had ended up in hospital and permanently scarred because of his sense of entitlement. All nasty enough but lacking the sadistic finesse of deliberate mutilation. The same could be said of Lenny Jacobs, the bloke they had in the frame for Peters – an angry man, for different reasons maybe, but not a sadist. The mutilations in both cases were sending a message to someone beyond the victim. This was cold violence, not hot. Peters. Drummond. Yes, the more he thought about it, the more Cato was persuaded the two murders might be linked after all.

***

They decided to hole up for the night in a motel in Burnie, fifty klicks west of the Devonport ferry terminal on the north Tassie coast. The young woman on duty at reception was iffy about the lack of a credit card for surety and kept casting nervous glances at Mira and at each of the middle-aged men in her company. What did these blokes have in mind with her?

'Four separate rooms,' said Driscoll. 'And we'll put a cash deposit on each if you like. Fifty per room?'

'Make it a hundred. Each.' The cash was folded into her purse. 'ID?' she insisted.

Driscoll pulled a spare driver's licence out of his wallet. 'Sure.'

She examined it. 'David Palmer?' she read. 'Rockhampton?'

'That's me.'

'But you haven't got a credit card? None of you?'

'Level with her, mate.' Mason nudged Driscoll. 'She's not stupid.'

Driscoll sighed. 'Me and my colleague here,' he nodded towards Mason. 'We're AFP. These two with us are protected witnesses.' He tapped a nostril with his finger. 'Drugs. Bikies. Queensland, Gold Coast thing. We need to keep them off the grid because we think there's been a leak. Can we count on you to help us out?' He examined her name badge. 'Aysha?'

She stiffened. 'Okay. They're not going to come here and kill everyone are they?'

'Not if we can do all this on cash.'

Tick. Sorted. 'And you're leaving first thing, right?'

'Absolutely.'

'Good. Just leave the keys in the rooms and go.'

'Will do. Um, the deposits?'

'Will be returned once my boss has inspected the rooms.' A thin smile. 'Just leave your bank details and a contact number?'

They drove around to the units at the rear. Mason grinned, 'Good work, maestro. She saw you coming. Bankrupt by Friday at this rate.'

***

He felt Sharon slip into bed, wrap her cold arms around him and snuggle in.

'You awake?'

'I am now.'

'Work was weird tonight.'

'I'm all ears,' Cato mumbled.

'Bloke from the Darwin flight. Off his face with medication and grog. The crew and a few passengers had to restrain him. Tied him to the seat and gagged him. Not sure they're allowed to but, whatever.'

'Is that a federal matter?'

'Interstate flight, grey area. Couple of local uniforms and me to cover the bases. All I did was follow him in the ambulance to the mental health unit at Fiona Stanley Hospital. He was still gibbering when I left him. They'll probably let him go once he's dried out and come down. The local plods will charge him with being a dickhead and move on.'

'Thin blue line, love.'

'Poor bastard. Shouldn't mix Jack D with pills. He was beside himself. Seeing things, they're gonna kill me, blah-blah-blah.' She squeezed Cato. 'Might have to leave the ravishing till another night. Bit stuffed.'

'No worries.'

6

Wednesday 25th April

There was an unseasonal dusting of snow atop Mount Wellington and a cruel wind barrelling along the streets of Hobart. Kunanyi, Driscoll recalled now, the local mob name for the mountain. They'd parked down at the waterfront and now sat in a cafe sipping hot drinks and not saying much. Driscoll wasn't cut out for nursemaiding. It was all too passive. If you're not in the thick of things you may as well be fishing – at least that had purpose.

Mason seemed to read his thoughts. 'Two weeks, mate. Then you're done.'

The big red *Aurora Australis* nudged its way to the nearby dock. Driscoll had read somewhere it was set for retirement soon. He wondered what it would be like pushing through an icy, crushing sea thousands of kilometres away from help, utterly at the mercy of forces beyond your control. He looked at Mason, cool bravado masking a tight knot of fear in the clenched jaw. At Mira, picking at a loose stitch on her pullover, trying not to unravel. Brian, as always, gloomy and fatalistic – staring into his coffee foam. What were their real stories? If life was so shit for them, they could just retract their testimony, go home and forget all about it. Who were they saving anyway? What point were they making? Driscoll could have asked all that of himself too. Was it enough that Aunty would be channelling a swag of currency into an offshore trust fund for him? Perhaps that was all he'd ever been – a mercenary. But the biggest question of all – who exactly were those people who wanted to silence them all?

'Are we staying here?' Brian pushed his mug away. 'In Hobart, I mean.'

Driscoll nodded. 'More chance of being anonymous here. Just another bunch of tourists on the Apple Isle.' Aunty had given him an address in Fern Tree in the shadow of the mountain: a friend's weekender-cum-retirement bolthole. It was an Airbnb until today: vacated, cleaned and available from two p.m. Luckily they didn't have to go through the usual ID rigmarole as it was now blocked out for the owners' personal use for the next two weeks.

Mason was suddenly more alert. Driscoll followed his gaze: a bloke in uniform approaching them – stocky, thirties, a swirl of tattoo creeping up from his shirt collar.

'Hi,' said Driscoll.

'That white Landcruiser belong to you?' The man nodded towards the window.

Driscoll stood up, looked that way. 'Lots of white Landcruisers around, mate. Which one do you mean?'

Derwent Security Services. Name badge, Brett. 'The one over there on the left. Lights on. Blocking access to the admin building.'

'No,' said Driscoll. 'That's not us.'

'No worries,' said Brett. 'Have a good day.' He gave them all a nod and smile and went away.

'Let's get moving,' said Driscoll. He left a twenty at the cash till as he headed for the door.

'What's the hurry?' grumbled Brian, struggling to catch up.

'They're onto us.' Mason held the door open for Mira and Brian. 'Bretty-baby was checking us out, up close, making sure we fit the description.'

'The Landcruiser?' said Brian.

'Was bullshit.' Driscoll zapped the locks and they clambered in. He scanned the car park. They'd have been watched as they left the cafe. Would they be blocked in and dealt with here? Plenty of witnesses, middle of the day. Not necessarily a problem. Any mayhem could be spun as bikie gang warfare or drug stuff. No point speculating, they had to get out of there. 'Buckle up.'

He took off out of the parking space and gunned for the exit. A ute reversed into his path and he swerved to avoid it, bouncing over a concrete kerb into an adjoining car park. The exit to this one was further away and he could see people and vehicles moving into position. He swung back over the concrete separator and there was Brett standing in the road with a shotgun raised.

'Get down!' Driscoll accelerated and everybody ducked as the windscreen shattered. Brett jumped to one side as they raced through the exit, narrowly missing another approaching vehicle. Driscoll checked the rear-view. As far as he could tell, nobody in hot pursuit. He took a winding back route through the sedate waterside enclaves of Sandy Bay and Taroona, checking all the way. Nobody.

'We better get that windscreen fixed.' Mason brushed some glass from his sweatshirt. Turned his head. 'Everybody okay back there?' They were. A friendly grip on Driscoll's shoulder. 'Legendary, comrade. Legendary.'

Driscoll said nothing and kept his eyes on the road. How could they know? Even Aunty didn't know exactly where they were. Off the grid, nobody should have known. Had somebody in this car tipped them off?

***

DI Pavlou was unimpressed that Cato was back so soon from Bunbury.

'If you don't believe it was this Hodgson kid, isn't that all the more reason for you to stay there? We had you a room booked at the Koombana Bay motel and everything. Quest. Not cheap.'

'Earle is doing a good job. If things change, or if she calls for help, we can be down there quick enough. It's a two-hour drive. I'm not needed in Bunbury, I am needed at home.'

Pavlou sniffed. 'We've got a day or two, I suppose. People back from leave by then. You're right, we need a reliable steady hand on the tiller, no point rushing things.'

Cato didn't bother replying. Returning to his desk he found Deb Hassan and Chris Thornton hovering. 'Miss me?'

'Achingly,' said Thornton.

'Nah, not really,' said Hassan. 'Got a mo?'

Cato looked at them. 'Different matters or the same?'

'Same,' said Thornton.

'Me first.' Hassan dragged up a chair. 'Got a dental appointment at half-past.' Her outside-enquiries doorknocking team had thrown up more damning evidence on Lenny Jacobs.

'Thrill me,' said Cato.

'We have three sightings of him in the vicinity of the crime scene early that morning.'

'Vicinity?'

'A radius of two hundred metres.'

'Time?'

'Around six a.m.' She slid a tablet across the desk: on the screen a timeline plus the recorded sightings overlaid on a map. 'He's heading south and east away from the property.'

'On foot.'

'Yes.'

'Demeanour?'

'Nothing suspicious. No mentions of furtive, or agitated, or nervous, anything like that.'

'Anything else?'

Thornton leaned in. 'He'd switched his phone off and removed the battery six hours before that and back on an hour later. The last signal before the sighting was downtown Fremantle. The next time we pick him up he's obviously driving along Leach doing his job, given the timings and locations of the mobile tower pings.'

'So the phone goes off-grid for nearly eight hours during which he's near the crime scene.' Cato wiped his smudgy specs on his shirt. 'Funny how not being trackable is suspicious these days. I'm sure there'll be a good explanation.'

'There usually is,' said Hassan. 'But in the body of other evidence it all helps.'

Cato nodded. 'Any other developments?'

'Still waiting for word back on that Peters offshore trust account,' said Thornton. 'They're in no hurry to be helpful. Oh, and the ALS lawyer has been ringing.' He grinned. 'Keen to chat.'

'I bet he is.'

'He's downstairs in the interview room with Lenny. Whenever you're ready.'

***

The house in Fern Tree was a timber two-storey on a sloping five-acre block. It faced north-east and enjoyed sunlight for a good part of the day. A picture window, occupying most of one wall, looked out on raised vegie gardens fenced and netted against birds, possums and wallabies.

Eucalyptus gums lined the perimeter of the property and shielded them from neighbours. The house was tastefully and expensively decorated without being ostentatious. Paintings, textile wall hangings, vases, and sculptures hinted at wanderings in the souks and casbahs of other worlds. Probably some retired spook or diplomatic mate of Aunty's.

'Nice,' said Mason. 'Bags the room with the ensuite.'

'Already taken,' said Mira. 'Sorry.'

They'd stopped off in Kingston to get the windscreen replaced. Another chunk out of Aunty's cash stack. Driscoll was feeling the strain but not yet ready to relax. He took the room next to where Brian had parked his bag. The suburban lawyer was edging towards a crack-up. True, the incident in the car park at the waterfront would have shaken most people, but Brian really was ready to pop: his face tight and pale, eyes unfocused, breathing shallow.

'You okay there, mate?'

A jolt back into the here and now. 'Yeah, yeah. Might take a lie down for a while.'

'Good idea,' said Driscoll. 'Chill. I'll give you a call later when dinner's ready.'

'Thanks.' Brian closed his bedroom door with a feeble smile.

Mason and Mira were unpacking groceries in the kitchen. Driscoll busied himself checking locks on windows and doors, assessing weak spots, areas of threat, escape routes. The place was peaceful and secluded, but that could work against them. It wouldn't be hard, overtly or covertly, to seal this place off and kill them all while they slept. If one among them was a leaker then the bad guys already knew where to come looking. It was just a matter of time.

'Coffee?' said Mason, flicking on the kettle.

'Sure. Thanks.'

Mira declined. She was going to take a shower in the ensuite and then catch up on sleep.

'Just you and me, bro.' Mason spooned some Colombian into the plunger.

What was it they said? Don't 'bro' me if you don't know me. Even after just a couple of days, Mason's faux familiarity was grating: a power play, putting Driscoll in his place. 'What's going on here, Willie?'

'Que?'

'Why are we all here?'

The plunger went down and the coffee got poured. 'Didn't Pauline explain?'

Aunty. Pauline. Her real name sounded strange in Driscoll's ears. Once, after a severe telling off the likes of which he hadn't experienced since he was a boy, he'd called her Aunty as a joke and it stuck. 'Only the bare bones. I need to hear it from you.'

'Oil.' Mason passed Driscoll a mug. 'You'll have heard of the Timor Gap and negotiations between Australia and East Timor over who controls the oil deposits off their coast.'

'Hasn't that all been signed, sealed and delivered years ago? Controversy over, friends again.'

'Australia would like to think so, but for one reason or another it's not. I won't give you the tortured history, but the nub of why we're all here in this house fearing for our lives is that I was involved in bugging the Timorese delegation during the negotiations back in the day, as was a former diplomatic colleague, now deceased, who left her diary and other incriminating evidence with the family solicitor – Brian. Mira got wind and has been writing articles about it.'

'Bugging the Timorese to what effect?'

'Read their minds. Get the upper hand.'

'And that's enough to get you all on a death list?'

'We're talking squillions of petrodollars here. If, or when, this conciliation committee from The Hague hears and reads the evidence, they're likely to nullify the existing treaties and start over from scratch. They don't like cheats.'

'So how does eliminating you solve the problem?'

'ASIO have raided Brian and Mira's offices and removed their documents. The Hague has ordered that they be sealed and protected until the hearing but there's every chance they'll be destroyed, if that hasn't already happened. All that would leave is our testimony. Meanwhile we're also, all three of us, about to be charged under certain Official Secrets laws for blowing the whistle on the activities of our secret agents. Twenty years in the slammer. If we survive the next two weeks.'

'Is it spooks we've got on our tails? Brett and his shottie?'

'Can't see it. More likely some subcontractors working at long arm's-length from Big Oil.'

'And where do I come in?'

Mason grinned. 'I was hoping you'd tell me. C'mon mate, spill.'

Driscoll really didn't have a clue. 'This list was supplied by your Indonesian intelligence buddy who later died?'

'Horribly.'

'And Aunt – and Pauline set all this up on the strength of that?'

'Naturally. She was my supervisor at the time. She knows I'm not lying.'

No, thought Driscoll. She doesn't. She might have given you your orders back then but she doesn't know what game you're playing now. 'Those jokers this morning. How do you think they knew?'

Mason shrugged. 'Tipped off, we assume.'

'Who by? We've been off-grid since you guys left Canberra. Only Pauline knows we're here, but she wouldn't have known we were in that waterfront cafe at that precise time.'

'That leaves Brian, Mira, me.' Mason drained his coffee. 'You.'

'Either somebody among us is working for the other side ...'

'Or they're not sticking to the agreement to stay off the phone.'

'Or both,' said Driscoll.

'Some people, huh?' Mason stood and held out his hand for Driscoll's mug. 'Top-up?'

***

Lenny Jacobs was due to have his charges upgraded to murder today and then, following a Magistrates Court appearance late afternoon, he would be shipped back to the remand centre at Hakea, all things being equal. Bob, his lawyer, had clearly given him a serious talking to.

'I wanted that money he'd been saving up. Peters.'

Cato exchanged a sideways glance with Thornton. 'What money?'

'He'd been putting it aside for Connie's kids, for when they turned eighteen. Some trust account in, I don't know, overseas. Bahamas, Switzerland, wherever.'

'Channel Islands,' said Thornton. 'Jersey.'

'Where?'

'Never mind,' said Cato. 'What did you want it for?'

'Connie's oldest, Kane. He's seventeen. He needs it now.'

'Why?'

'Stupid little prick has been dealing. He lost it all in a traffic stop from one of your blokes. The suppliers still want their money.'

'Who are we talking about?' asked Thornton. 'Which suppliers?'

'Mate, please.'

'Doug Peters said no, so you killed him?'

'How's that going to get me the money?'

Fair point. 'You lost that famous bad temper of yours,' said Cato. 'All logic went out the window. You just let rip.'

'No,' said Jacobs. 'I didn't.'

'You walked away? Thanks anyway, Mr Peters. Hope you didn't mind me asking. That how it was?'

'We argued but I didn't kill him.'

'All the available evidence suggests you did. You even turned your phone off during that time to make it harder for us to trace your movements.' Cato leaned back in his chair. 'And now we have an additional and compelling motive.'

Jacobs turned to his lawyer. 'Brilliant advice, Bob. Cheers.'

Bob put his pen down. 'My client has now given you an account of why he was in Mr Peters' house and thus how forensic traces of him could have got there. Not being traceable through your own phone is not a criminal offence. He maintains that he never attacked or killed Mr Peters.'

'Yeah,' said Jacobs. 'That's right.'

'Tell it to the jury.' Cato stood. 'Chris, can you take a full statement from Mr Jacobs regarding the new information. I'll send Deb Hassan in to work with you on the details.'

'Sir.'

Cato looked at Jacobs. He was going to have to formally charge the man once they had that statement. Too much pointed in his direction and Cato couldn't be seen to ignore it.

**

'I need to go through your room and things and search you too.'

'You think I'm your mole?' Mason stood up, lifted his hands from his sides. 'Go for your life.'

Driscoll patted him down. Nothing. 'Want to show me your bag?'

They went into Mason's room: a queen single bed, formerly a teenager's den maybe? The walls had been painted over but the faint grease spots of old Blu Tack remained. In military fashion Mason was unpacked and neatly folded away. Driscoll rummaged through the empty holdall, the drawers, the hangers, the toiletry bag. Again nothing.

'I've got a flick knife under the pillow.' Mason lifted it to show him. 'I handed my phone to Pauline in Canberra, as did Mira and Brian.'

'You could have a spare and you'd know where to hide one.'

'You want to spend the next few hours searching, be my guest.' He checked his watch. 'I'll start chopping vegies. Chicken risotto do you?' Mason left Driscoll to his thoughts and headed out to the kitchen.

Driscoll lifted the mattress, checked other possibilities, but after a few more minutes gave up. It would have been a miracle if he found anything. A disappointment even. Mason was too well-trained to give the game away that easily. The other two were sleeping. He'd need to go through the same routine with them later. He went outside and gave the car a thorough search, again to no avail. Mason could have chucked his phone into nearby undergrowth, letting it beep away its secrets to whoever was listening. He took a walk around the perimeter, sizing up the likely approaches, trying to foresee the dangers. It was useless. If they were coming, there was nothing he could do about it. And he wasn't even armed. How did he let himself be talked into this? These last eighteen months had sent him soft in the head like Mason said. Back to the house, lights on now in the main living area. The sun had dropped behind the trees on the western boundary and he suddenly felt colder. A scraping behind him, he tensed.

'It's beautiful here, isn't it?' Mira Soares lit a cigarette and blew some smoke skywards.

It was until the air lost its freshness. 'Yeah. Peaceful, eh.'

She offered the packet. 'You smoke?'

'No.'

'Do you mind me smoking?'

'No, outside is fine.'

'Willie said you want to search me.' A smile. 'He said you're the boss.'

'Yes, on both counts.' A kookaburra cackled and in a dim corner of the paddock two wallabies appeared. 'You slept well?'

'I did. Thank you.' She flicked some ash. 'You think I would betray us all?'

'I need to check. Due diligence.'

'Due diligence. Lawyer's words. Have you been to Timor, Rory?'

'Many years ago.'

'Speak Tetun?'

'I used to. Bit rusty now.'

'*Ita sei la sai atan.*'

'You are no longer a slave?'

'Near enough. Not so rusty after all.' She stubbed out her cigarette. 'I think dinner is ready.'

***

By home time, Jacobs had been charged with murder and packed off to Hakea in a Securimat private prison van lit up by paparazzi flashes. Major Crime had cracked open a slab or two, fished the sav blanc out of the fridge, and those who needed it nursed the odd glass of the hard stuff. Pavlou had offered a quick well done to the team, taken a couple of slurps of SSB and made her excuses. Tonight was swimming night with her Masters squad over at Beatty Park.

'Good work, Sarge.' Thornton clinked his stubbie with Cato's.

'Yeah, cheers.'

'You've got that look on your face: glass half-empty.'

'Default. You should know that by now.'

'There's enough there for a jury. Surely.'

'That's not the same as the truth though.'

A sigh and a barely audible 'Fuck's sake.'

Cato gave him a look. 'Been possessed by the ghost of DI Hutchens?'

'We've got Jacobs in the house around the time of the murder and with the motive. The man's got a history with Peters and record of a violent temper and it's proved his undoing. It's a solid result.'

Cato checked the clock on the wall. He needed to be making tracks. Sharon was on duty and would need to leave home in another hour. The traffic on the freeway should have eased by now. 'You guys pushing on for a feed?'

'Probably,' said Thornton. 'Joining us?'

'Better not. Need to mind the home fort. See you in the morning.'

'No worries. Tomorrow's another day, eh?'

Cato nudged his way through the crowd, receiving the slaps on the shoulders and good wishes. Apologising for piking out. Over in the corner Hassan caught his eye with a farewell wink. She was conspiratorially close to the new bloke who'd joined from over East. Rumour was her marriage was on the skids. Another statistic. At the multistorey, Cato zapped the locks on his new car, a Subaru – the Volvo had finally given up the ghost – and chucked his backpack on the passenger seat. His phone went. A message: probably from Sharon wondering where he was. He opened it.

Nice. Tidy. Wrong.

Whoever they were, they were bang up to date.

***

Mason's chicken risotto went down well. He was a man of many talents. Driscoll had loaded the dishwasher and wiped down the table and benchtop. Now it was time to search Mira's room and belongings. She sat on the bed, eyes big and bright, acting the coquette.

'Willie said you are good at what you do.'

'Willie says this, Willie says that. You guys get on well together.'

'Jealous?'

'Curious.' Nothing in her suitcase. No secret compartments. Driscoll rummaged through the hangers, patting down pockets. Zilch. He opened the top drawer of a dresser. Mira's underwear and other woman's stuff. He lifted and patted.

'Having fun?'

'Oodles.' A lower drawer. Shirts and such. He finished and stood straight.

'Want to search me now?'

The jeans and top she was wearing were tight-fitting. It would be hard not to notice anything amiss. 'No,' he said. 'You're fine.'

'You sure?' A playful pout. 'You really think I would do something to endanger my own life?'

'Deals can be made, trade-offs. I don't assume anything.'

'I know the value of a Timorese life. I also know the value of a man's word in a so-called deal. Both are worth very little when it comes down to it.'

'Very prudent. Keep that in mind in your dealings with Willie Mason.'

'You are jealous.' A chuckle. 'I knew it.'

'The stories you wrote. The articles. Mason was your source?' She said nothing but clearly the answer was yes. 'Did you find him or did he find you?'

'He found me.' She leaned forward on the bed, cleavage on display. 'Why? Does it matter?'

Driscoll shook his head. 'I don't know what your angle is but you don't need to play the femme fatale with me. If I feel I'm being messed around I'm just as likely to up sticks and take care of myself. No skin off my nose.'

The mask slipped for a moment. She was afraid. Didn't know who to trust, didn't know what to do, or how this might end. She recomposed herself. 'You should go and check Mr Brian now. Maybe he is your traitor.'

***

As she kissed Cato goodbye for another shift at the airport, Sharon sniffed his beery breath. 'We should crack a few stubbies together one of these fine days.'

'Maybe I'll crank up the barbie at the weekend. The weather forecast is good for the foreseeable.'

'It's a date.' Another kiss. 'See you in the middle of the night.'

Ella was already asleep but he looked in on her to check. He put his backpack on the kitchen table, set the kettle boiling, and plugged in his laptop. His mobile sat malevolently off to one side. Who was sending those messages and why couldn't they just front up and get to the point? The answer had to be that the inside knowledge they possessed must also incriminate them in some way. So why not just keep schtum? They wanted the right thing done, he assumed, they wanted redemption. Who better as a vehicle for proxy redemption than Philip 'Cato' Kwong? The prospector's phone being lost in Meekatharra had been a diversion. It turned out the prospector wasn't that sure he'd lost it in Meeka anyway. He'd been drinking heavily in Midland on the way out and back. Maybe it was there and then? Thornton had also checked on officers stationed there with Peters at the time to see if any were now in the fold here in Perth. Nothing.

Pending the next instalment from mystery man or woman, Cato logged on to the police database. He wasn't convinced by how neat and tidy the Peters case was, he didn't buy Lenny Jacobs as a deranged bloodthirsty nemesis. But if the two mutilations were linked, then what did the victims have in common?

Douglas Peters. Ex-cop. Private security. Widower.

Bevan Drummond. Retired science teacher. Widower.

What connected them apart from, possibly, their killer? Age? Widowhood?

Drummond hadn't had any run-ins with, or cause to contact, the police. Lucky man hadn't been burgled, or vandalised, or assaulted, had a car accident, a speeding ticket, a lost wallet, a found wallet, a noise complaint by him or against him. Nor had Mr Drummond taught science to any of Douglas Peters' children or grandchildren given that he had spent all his teaching life in Bunbury and that was one place Peters hadn't lived during his regional postings. After a couple of hours of flipping between case files looking in vain for areas of crossover, Cato gave up and went to bed.

7

Thursday 26th April

The floorboard creaked. Driscoll checked the time on his watch. Four ten a.m. He reached under the pillow for the kitchen knife. The bathroom was across the hall. It might just be Brian answering the call of nature. He'd barely eaten at dinnertime nor spoken a word. He'd assented when Driscoll demanded a search of his room and bags for a rogue mobile phone. Lifted his arms in submission for a pat down. His body sour with fear and anxiety.

'Try a shower, mate.' Driscoll had said. 'Feels heaps better for it, trust me.'

Brian hadn't taken his advice, closing the door on Driscoll's fruitless retreat. If any of them did have a phone it was well hidden, perhaps outside somewhere on the property. The floorboard creaked again, further away. Down the hall linking into the living area. Driscoll slipped out of bed, pulled on his jeans and a T-shirt, and tiptoed to the door, gently turned the handle. Light was coming from the kitchen. It could be an innocent middle-of-the-night snack. Or maybe not. He padded softly down the hall in bare feet. Drawers were being opened, cutlery rummaged. Whoever it was didn't care who heard.

'Peckish?'

Brian jumped. Driscoll wondered if there was some medication at work here. He hadn't found any during the search but the man seemed wired and his face was bathed in sweat. 'I'm fine. I'll take care of it. Go back to sleep.'

'Need a glass of water myself.' Driscoll laid his kitchen knife on the table and picked up a glass from the counter. 'Want one?'

'No. Yes. Thanks.'

Driscoll filled two and handed one over. 'Not what you expected from life, was it? All this drama.'

A bitter snort. 'Not wrong.'

'Why are you involved? They've confiscated your paperwork. You're not obliged to be a witness to this committee. Walk away if it's all too much grief.'

'I can't unknow something. They know I read those documents. They know I did that, whether I testify or not.'

'Who are they?'

'That's the whole stupid point. The names are in code, it's a piece of fiction. I don't know who the fuck is who. I'm absolutely no danger to them at all.' Brian grabbed a block of cheese out of the fridge door, hacked at it like it was his enemy, hauled a loaf of wholemeal out of the bread box and slapped some cheese between two dry slices. 'But how do I tell them that? Who do I tell?'

Driscoll was feeling suggestibly peckish and made himself a sandwich too but added in heart-tick marge and some chutney. Chutney? Who thinks to buy chutney in a crisis? Mason, he thought. Had to be. The food seemed to be doing Brian some good. Less twitchy all over. Driscoll took another bite of his sanger. They chewed and swallowed in companionable silence for a while. 'The people who came to your office to confiscate your files,' said Driscoll. 'Did they leave business cards?'

'No. Just flashed some ID. Said they were ASIO and asked where everything was. They told me to get out of the way, loaded the stuff into a couple of archive boxes and pissed off.'

'Your client, deceased, is that right?'

'Car crash. Two months ago.'

'Suspicious?'

'I wouldn't know. Happened in New Zealand. Kiwis, they can be a bit reckless and impatient on those mountain passes.'

'You said there was a couple of archive boxes worth. When did she put them in your care?'

'Just before she went on her hols to Middle Earth.'

'And you read it all?'

'Some of it. There were diaries, some letters and photos. A manuscript. "I know I can rely on your discretion, Brian." She was interested in my take on her novel. Her baby, she called it. Looking for a five-star review, maybe. Authors, fragile lot.'

'What was your impression?'

A snort. 'Two stars at most. Maybe three for the sex scenes. Very *Fifty Shades*.'

'Nothing controversial? Worth killing for, being jailed for?'

'Grammar and punctuation needed a look.'

Driscoll wiped a dropped smudge of chutney off his lap. 'Want me to check up on those ASIO guys? Maybe get them to pass the word on that you're harmless?'

'You think they're involved with these death-list people?'

'Not beyond the bounds of possibility.'

Brian shook his head, beyond caring. 'By the way they weren't guys; both women. Scary, like the aquafit sheila at the pool.'

'Leave it with me,' said Driscoll.

***

Sharon was late. She should have been back by about four at the latest but it was nudging six now. Ella was already firing on all cylinders – it was often that way on day-care day. She had marched into the bedroom just after five announcing 'Awake! Awake!', and demanded milk and stories. Cato poured himself another coffee while Ella interrogated the saucepan cupboard. His phone buzzed.

On my way see you in 15

Ella decided she wanted to make porridge in the pans so Cato poured oats and water and got stirring. The table was set and a fresh pot of coffee awaited Sharon as she came through the door. She looked troubled.

'Big night?'

'Quiet for most of it. Then just before I was due to come off duty we got a call from Freo police.'

'Fremantle?'

She took a long appreciative slurp of coffee. Ella was busy drawing honey swirls on the table top with her fingers. 'The guy off the Darwin flight the day before?' Cato nodded. 'Found hanging under the railway bridge in the early hours.'

'I thought he was at Fiona Stanley Hospital?'

'Once he'd dried out, they assessed him as fit for release.'

Cato spooned some porridge into Ella. 'Suicide?'

'Seems it.'

'So why the troubled look? Just another day in the Job, right?'

'He had a slip of paper in his pocket with your name and number on it. Being Freo cops, they recognised it.'

'But they called you instead of me?'

'Weird, huh?'

Cato dropped by Freo cop shop on his way to work. He'd called ahead to check the responding officers from the bridge suicide were still on duty. It felt strange wandering the corridors of his old workplace. There were nods of recognition and the odd handshake along the way. He found who he was looking for in the canteen rec room.

'Interesting night I hear?'

The more senior of the two gestured for him to pull up a seat. Her name badge said Jennings; vaguely familiar as a passing face in the hallways over the years. She had a boyish haircut and the hint of a tattoo up her left sleeve. 'I usually answer to Trish.'

Her colleague looked fresh out of the Academy but he would hate anybody to think so. 'Bryce.' He shook Cato's hand.

'Yeah, big night,' said Trish. 'You heard about our swinger then?'

'He has a name?'

Bryce flipped open his notebook. 'Paul Reinado. Age thirty-nine. Darwin resident, according to his driver's licence.'

'Married? Job?'

'Yes to both,' said Trish. 'Got a six-year-old son. Shame, eh? Employed as an electrician. Subcontractor. Does a fair bit of fly-in fly-out.'

'And he had my name and number?'

'That's right,' said Trish.

'But you phoned Agent Wang from the AFP instead?'

'Yeah, her name was on the file from the airport arrest the previous day.'

Sharon had kept her own name after their marriage, maybe they didn't know the connection. 'Do you have the bit of paper?'

Trish shook her head. 'It's in an evidence bag in the system by now. Handed it over to the techs.'

'Anything you noticed about the scene?'

'Lonely, cold and sad.' Bryce drained his cuppa. 'Poor bastard.'

'Who found him?'

'Nobody,' said Trish. 'Anonymous call from a public booth beside the town hall.'

'That's a couple of kilometres away.'

She shrugged. 'People today don't want to get involved. Some don't even bother making the call. Just go home and let somebody else find him.'

Cato left them his card. 'If anything comes to mind, give me a bell.'

Trish spun it on the table top with her fingers. 'You're not the investigating officer. You're Major Crime now. It's probably down to the local team to look at why he had your name.' A pause. 'Isn't it?'

'Fair enough,' said Cato. 'Thanks for your time.'

'No worries,' said Trish. 'Regards to your wife.'

***

So far, so good. They hadn't been slaughtered in their beds yet. A good night's sleep had done them all the world of good. Even Brian seemed chirpier this morning. Driscoll left them to their toast, cereal and coffee and did a circuit of the property on the lookout for any signs of overnight intrusion or for a secreted mobile phone. The sun was yet to breach the top of the trees and there was a chill in the air. In the gloomier pockets of the perimeter, where the sun rarely shone, vivid green moss clung to the tree trunks. There was a damp rich smell like a bag of ageing mushrooms; a grey wallaby peeking from behind a bush, and wattle birds darting around. It was peaceful here, like his place over near Warrnambool. Seclusion had come surprisingly easy to him. After all those years in the bland concrete of Canberra, the steaming metropoles of Asia, the deceptive desert island idylls, he'd wondered if he would be able to stand it in the back blocks. The answer was yes and yes again.

Why walk away? He was still good at his job. There was no shortage of missions to keep on accomplishing. No shortage of dragons to slay, demons to vanquish, even the odd maiden to rescue. Mira came to mind. Did she need rescuing? There was a moment when her vulnerability showed and he felt that old stab of remorse, of responsibility. But if she did need rescuing, he guessed it was more from herself than from anything else. Why walk away? Because he'd lost sight of right and wrong, and which side he was really on. How did that come about? His masters had read the ugly mood of the electorate, had embraced that flag with its sharp cutting stars, its desperate grip on the vestige of Empire, its cold dark ocean of life-sucking blue. Why walk away? Maybe he'd walked away from a mirage. That world he thought he inhabited had never been his. He was part of the team as long as he kept on kicking goals and taking marks. He'd been quietly proud of his 'Fighting Gunditjmara' heritage. But lift your shirt to remind them of the colour of your skin? No, they claimed that privilege as exclusively theirs.

Aunty had tried to persuade him to change his mind. To stick the course.

'These muppets won't be around forever, Rory. The voters have already had enough. People don't like being taken for granted. This mob might well feed the national blood lust but they're too chained to the top end of town, sharing tax avoidance scams in the club while the au pair minds the brats. Ordinary Aussies don't like that shit.'

'Drop over any time you like. I'll take you out in the boat. Catch a few snapper, eh?'

She'd teared up. 'Rory, if you go we'll be left with a squad of blond, skinny, monoglossic Hitler Youth sneaking around the tropical fleshpots in designer sunnies, getting us into more trouble than we budgeted for. Please, mate. Don't do this to me.'

Aunty resigned not long after but she obviously still kept her hand in – the temptation to remain in the Great Game would be too much. Still, the money and lifestyle would have been hard to give away and she'd invested unwisely in some expensive Sydney apartments that were sitting empty and developing cracks in the brickwork. Rory made his way back towards the house. Mira and Mason were out on the balcony having a smoke and another cup of coffee. He came looking for her, she'd said, with the scoop of her career. How did Mason know where to find her? Why her? Any number of high-profile scribes would have chewed his hand off for a story like that and would have had the clout to make sure it saw the light of day. They looked cosy up there on that balcony, the sun now high enough to warm their skin. They made a handsome couple, an advertisement for a romantic autumn break on the Apple Isle; murder and skulduggery banished to the shadows for the moment. Mira caught Driscoll's eye and gave him a wave. He waved back.

***

The Freo D's didn't take long to follow up on the hanging man. DI Paddy McMahon, Hutchens' successor, did the honours himself. 'This Paul Reinado bloke, he a mate of yours?'

Cato resisted the urge to hold the phone away from his ear. McMahon seemed to have a permanent cold and the virus could have been worming its way through the ether. 'No.'

'He has your name and number.'

'So I'm told.'

'You're not being very forthcoming, mate.'

'I don't know him, Paddy. Haven't a clue why he has my contact details. What do you know about him?'

'Not sure I can say right now. Might be a conflict.' A pause and some rustling. 'Says here your missus was involved?'

'Agent Wang assisted at the initial airport incident and as her name was in the system the attending uniforms called her when the body was discovered.'

'So it's just a funny coincidence then?'

'One way of putting it. Look, Paddy, I've got nothing to hide. As soon as you know more I'll be happy to assist.' A half-grunt, half-sniff in reply. 'Sharon – Agent Wang mentioned he was in a bit of a state when he came off that plane. Drugs and booze, symptoms of paranoia and delusion. Believed people were after him. That's as much as I know. The attending officers said he was a fly-in fly-out sparkie. Married with a kid.'

'Nice.'

'What?'

'Pillow talk. I always wondered what AFP liaison officers did.'

'With respect, Paddy, go fuck yourself.' Cato closed the call. The hanging man could wait. He sought out Chris Thornton and found him studying the chocolate in the vending machine. 'You'll get fat.'

'I was thinking about one of those healthy muesli energy bars down the bottom but you've convinced me now. Mars it is. Want one?'

Cato declined. 'Busy?'

'Dotting some t's on Lenny Jacobs for the prosecution brief. There's been a domestic in the northern suburbs we'll probably catch, and a suspicious suicide down at Fremantle.' The chocolate bar dropped into the serving tray.

Cato played dumb. 'What's suspicious about it?'

'According to the local D's, the height he was dangling from, the dodgy call-in.' Thornton tore the wrapping and took a bite. 'And your name and number in his daks.' A grin. 'That what you wanted to talk to me about?'

'No, as a matter of fact. Can you call Nikki Earle in Bunbury and get her to formally link you in to her homicide files down there?'

'Sure, but I thought we were letting her run it with her team?'

'Protocol. Tell her I just want to review the case against similar up here.'

'Can't you do that anyway? Direct.'

'Like I said, protocol. Don't want her to think I'm checking up on her or going behind her back.'

'Heaven forbid.'

'I'll probably be quarantined from the Freo suicide until they work out what's going on. But feel free to informally give me the odd heads-up around the vending machine now and then.'

'It'll cost you.' Another chomp. 'A Mars a day.'

***

Driscoll wondered whether he should just ditch the lot of them and look after number one. He needed to talk to Aunty. She knew more than she was letting on and, though it wasn't out of character, it was out of order. He'd given the job away and she needed him, not the other way round. And why was any of this Aunty's business anyway? She was semi-retired and running her tainted celeb consultancy. Aunty didn't need this shit any more than he did. She should have advised Mira and Brian to take a long holiday overseas ahead of The Hague committee hearing and told Mason where to shove his death list. And she should have left Driscoll in peace to do his fishing and brooding. Instead here he was perched in the shadow of a big, cold, dark hill in Tasmania waiting for death to come visiting, babysitting a neurotic, terrified suburban lawyer, a wannabe journalist playing Mata Hari, and Willie Mason, who surely was big and ugly enough to look after himself.

Driscoll set off on another circuit of the property. This whole thing was bullshit. Mason's pitch was that Driscoll was the key to their survival – if he got through this they all would. But Driscoll didn't even know why he was on this supposed death list in the first place.

'Cuppa?' Mason was on the deck, holding a mug up in question.

Driscoll nodded. 'Coffee, thanks. Milk and none. Bring it down to the shed there.' He intended to have words. Mason needed to show good cause why Driscoll shouldn't just bugger off out of here. The shed was unlocked. Half the size of his bedroom, it was storage for garden implements, tools, potting mix, spare plant pots, seeds. A moss-coated cracked pane of glass let the weak light in. Driscoll couldn't stand completely straight in it and was reminded of a Kimberley police lockup he'd once spent the night in as a young bloke. He rummaged around but to no avail.

'Find it yet?' Mason handed Driscoll his beverage. 'The phone?'

'Nah.' Driscoll nodded for them to step back outside, he was feeling cooped up.

Mason took a sip. 'You wanted a word?'

'What's the score with you and the journo? You're thick as thieves.'

'We get on. That a problem?'

'Where did you find her?'

'Through the Timorese expat community in Melbourne.'

'Why choose her for your big scoop? She's an online activist, easy to ignore, easy to dismiss. The story you had needed clout: *Guardian*, ABC, people like that.'

'Think so?'

Driscoll wasn't enjoying his coffee. 'But then a properly trained journalist might ask questions you don't want to answer. Show some initiative. Was that it?'

Mason grinned. 'Hole in one.' He glanced up to where Mira was leaning over the balcony rail, chucking food scraps to the birds and wildlife. 'And you've got to admit she's easy on the eye.'

'She won't be when they've finished with her. Whoever they are.' He drained his coffee, bitter as it was. 'You've put her in harm's way. She doesn't realise what she's got herself into does she?'

'Sir Galahad. You underestimate her. You don't grow up under Indonesian occupation and see family and friends raped and slaughtered without getting some idea about what a bad world it can be. Give her some credit.'

'You could take care of these guys all by yourself. You don't need me.'

'All for one?'

'I'm no Musketeer. I'll take my chances out on my own. You guys have a story to tell, or to kill, I don't. I'm not testifying. I don't know what I'm here for.'

'You're on the list.'

'So you keep saying but I don't believe you. Maybe it's mistaken identity.' Driscoll chucked his dregs onto the hard ground. 'Maybe you could call them on that hidden mobile of yours and explain.'

'I don't have a phone and, to the best of my knowledge, neither has Mira.'

'Maybe the safest thing for everybody is to split up and look after number one. Then nobody needs to worry about traitors in our midst.'

'So you're leaving?'

'Soon as I've packed my bag. I'll walk into town. You guys keep the car.'

'Pauline will be disappointed.'

'Aunty?' said Driscoll. 'I've been a constant source of disappointment to her since we met.'

***

The northern suburbs domestic had been given to another team and was already pretty much solved. The husband's DNA was all over the scene and the victims. He'd shot his wife and their four-year-old son with his legally licensed hunting rifle. All that remained now was to locate the man and bring him and his gun into custody. 'He never seemed the type,' said the neighbours. 'We never thought ...' But evidently he'd made little secret of his intentions on social media and to his workmates. As expected, another team was given the task of looking into the suspicious suicide of Paul Reinado, with Chris Thornton seconded to the enquiry as information manager. Which left Cato temporarily twiddling his thumbs.

'Maybe we can get you back down to Bunbury.' DI Pavlou perched on the edge of his desk, arms folded. 'DSC Earle hasn't had any dramatic breakthroughs. How's your childcare situation looking? Reckon you could manage it?'

'I don't have a magic wand.'

'For childcare or the Bunbury murder?'

'Either. How about I review the case files and liaise with Earle by remote for the time being?' He headed off Pavlou's frown. 'If anything jumps out, or things change, or she's clearly not up to it, I'll be down there in a flash.'

'There's no substitute for the real thing, Philip. Sometimes our very presence can be inspiring and change the course of an investigation.'

Yes, thought Cato. There were a couple of wrongly imprisoned blokes in Casuarina who'd probably attest to that and were seeking leave to appeal. 'I'll get right on to that case review, boss.'

'Great. Keep me in the loop.'

He called Earle. 'How's it going?'

'Slowly, but you know that already. You've been looking over my shoulder, plus you've got that colleague of yours checking on me too.'

'He's only obeying orders, as am I.'

'No dramas. If you want to take over, just get on with it. No need for all this skulking around.'

'It's looking increasingly likely. For now, though, no news, nothing at all?'

'Ryan Hodgson's DNA links to an unsolved pack-rape case from a couple of years ago. That's what he was worried about.'

'Good result though?'

'Not really. It was a dark, drunk, druggy, confusing night. The victim's memory of precisely what happened is murky. Consent is an idealised notion that the lawyers love to toss around. There's more than half a chance he'll walk.'

'Shame.'

'Isn't it just. Otherwise he still has no solid alibi for the Drummond killing, but my expectations are low. Nasty as he is, I just don't think he's our boy.'

'You've looked further into Drummond's life and times?'

'Yep, it's on the database, help yourself. You and your buddy Thornton are now official keyholders. Just log in the usual way.'

'If anything jumps out I'll give you a buzz. What's your next move?'

'Revisit doorknocks and CCTV. Maybe a media appeal in the next twenty-four hours. Drum up the crazies. You never know, we might get lucky.'

'Stay in touch.' Cato closed the call and logged on.

Bevan Drummond, aged seventy-two. He worked as a science teacher at the same Catholic college his whole career. Saw principals come and go, colleagues come and go, teaching fads and whiz-bang equipment come and go. Stayed on top of it all and taught three generations of Catholic schoolboys from Bunbury and surrounding districts all he thought they needed to know about science. No disciplinary slurs on his employment record. No hints of scandal. He was well liked and respected. He played golf and swam with a local Polar Bears swimming group, a stalwart of the open-water season. He did good works, was a member of the Rotary Club, and helped maintain a section of the Bibbulmun walk track every now and then. Salt of the earth and pillar of the community. A beacon of goodness. How on earth did this man's life end in such darkness?

He buzzed Chris Thornton. 'You were running a check on similar MOs, mutilations and stuff. How's that going?'

'Not pleasant. It's remarkable how common it seems to be. Ear-choppings and eye-gougings are a dollar-a-dozen across this wide brown land.'

'How about the display element? Ears in food containers, eyes in bowls. Less common I would expect?'

The sound of fingers tapping a keyboard. 'There was a bloke got his wedding tackle chopped off and artfully arranged on his chest post-mortem.'

'Where and when?'

'Just told you. Chest, after death.'

'Funny. Location, date.'

'About six months ago in Melbourne. I'll send you the gory details if you like but it's already solved – a scorned girlfriend. If I find any more cases I'll let you know.'

'Cheers.'

Cato flicked over to the Douglas Peters files. It was less difficult to see how his life could have ended in such darkness. He'd been a custody sergeant in the outback. Bad things happened in small town country lockups: an officer with a mean streak and a grudge, a young bloke who'd lost the will to go on, a woman with a pre-existing medical condition whose complaints and cries for help fell on deaf ears. And if it turned out not to be Lenny Jacobs exacting revenge for his sister's death, just look at what else Peters did with his life. A turnkey in one of the government's immigration hellholes: again, a similar fatal concoction – cries for medical help unheeded, despair and cruelty by the odd one who went at his task with relish. Did Peters also choose to walk in these Gethsemanes and follow the path of evil? People said not. Professor McKenzie and ex-DI Hutchens recalled a man wracked with guilt and remorse for something that wasn't even directly his fault. He'd established a trust fund for Connie Jacobs' kids. He didn't seem the type to have suddenly become Mr Cruel in the immigration detention centres. But he did do his work in sad and damaged places filled with sad and damaged people. Maybe that was all he knew?

It would be diligent to pursue Cormann Protective Services for the details of Peters' career in the border control regime, however frustrating or fruitless under the existing secretive legislation. He doubted DI Pavlou would be up for such a fight given that Lenny Jacobs sat nicely in the frame for the murder. Why waste time, energy and resources, she would say. Why indeed. Back to the task at hand – review the Bunbury case and offer Nikki Earle any pointers that came to mind. He reopened the Drummond file. Another scan before lunch.

***

Driscoll had his holdall packed and he was ready to go. Out in the living area he could hear murmuring. All three were out there discussing him. Was he doing the right thing? He didn't know. Mira stood by the window, Mason slouched on the couch. It was Brian who blocked Driscoll's path as he edged his way through.

'You can't go.'

'I can, mate. Watch me.'

'We'll die.' A staying hand on Driscoll's arm.

Driscoll removed it. 'My advice to you all is to split up and go as far away as possible from here and from each other. One of you is a fool or a dog, but either way the phone you have is alerting the bad guys where to find you. Us.' He studied their faces. Blank. 'You know who you are. As for me, I'm not sitting around waiting for them to come.'

'We can't go far away,' Brian insisted. 'They'll be watching the ports and airports.'

'So get yourself into protective custody and make a big song and dance about it to the media. Get yourself noticed, get some insurance.'

A miserable, tense, prolonged silence.

'It's me,' said Brian, finally. 'My phone.'

Mason lunged at him. 'You stupid prick.'

Driscoll stood between them. Turned to Brian. 'Why?'

His eyes teared up. 'My wife has cancer. Not long left. And here I am running away, scared. It's wrong.'

'Where's the phone?' Brian retrieved it from a recently cut hole down the interior of the couch. Driscoll took out the battery and SIM. 'I'll dump this on my travels. If I were you guys I wouldn't be hanging around.'

'Too late.' Mira stepped back from the window. 'They're here.'

8

On Cato's return from lunch, there was a message waiting to ring Paddy McMahon at Freo D's. He'd left the phone switched off deliberately. Selfish, he knew; Sharon might have wanted to get hold of him, or colleagues, or his son Jake. But sometimes you just need to not be instantly available. People managed it in days of yore and the sky didn't fall in. He rang the number.

'Paddy?'

'G'day mate. I've forgiven you for telling me to go fuck myself.'

'You're a saint.'

'The suicide's widow.'

'Mrs Reinado?'

'That'd be her. Jessica, it says here. She reckons he wasn't paranoid. People really were out to get him.' Apparently there had been anonymous phone calls in the middle of the night, dog shit in the letterbox, their car vandalised, their cat disappeared, unauthorised deliveries of pizzas, funeral flowers, even whitegoods.

'They reported this to police at the time?'

'Tried to but were fobbed off. Told it was probably just kids. An Asian family in a mainly white enclave, maybe they were made to feel unwelcome.'

'Asian?'

'Timorese,' said McMahon. 'From Timor I guess.'

'East Timor?'

'Timor-Leste as they call it now.' Cato complimented Paddy on his research. 'Thanks, mate. Means a lot.'

'Racist neighbours? Or somebody didn't appreciate his rewiring.'

'Or maybe some trouble from the old country.' McMahon drew in a breath. 'Timor-Leste has had its fair share of grief in recent years. Lot of bad blood.'

'Mate, you're growing into this job.'

'That could sound patronising to some ears but I'll take it in the spirit it's intended. Now then, my question to you is, do you still maintain you haven't had anything to do with this Reinado character?'

'To the best of my knowledge, unless he's an old arrest who's decided to fixate on me.'

'Bingo.'

'What?'

'You arrested him four years ago over a serious assault in Fremantle.'

'And?'

'And according to the widow you made quite an impression on the man.'

'What, I didn't beat him up or try to frame him?'

'Tsk-tsk. It seems you, quote, "listened to him and showed him some respect".'

'Sounds like the kind of thing I might do,' admitted Cato.

'Shit like that always comes back to bite you, mate. Mark my words.'

***

They were indeed here. Three white four-wheel drives, one blocking the entry track on the far edge of the property and two parked directly outside the house. The occupants were still in the vehicles, nobody was moving.

'What are they up to?' Mason's cigarette breath over Driscoll's left shoulder.

'Waiting for instructions?'

'Oh my god,' said Brian. 'I'm sorry.'

'Bit fucken late for that.' Mason stepped back from the window as the driver of one of the cars ducked his head to peer up at them. He turned to Driscoll. 'What now, maestro?'

Boiling oil? They only had the one bottle of Extra Virgin. It was useless even to lock the doors and arm themselves with, what, knives? The situation was out of their control. Or was it? He put the SIM and battery back into Brian's phone and handed it to Mason. 'Call the local police.

We have trespassers on the property, possibly armed. We need someone here urgently.'

Mason did it. He knew how to sound convincing and scared. Driscoll drew a knife from the kitchen wall magnet and shoved it up his sleeve. 'I'll go and see what they want.' He gestured at the phone in Mason's hand. 'Maybe get fire and ambulance here too. The more the merrier. News too, all stations, get the choppers out. RSPCA. Everybody.' Driscoll told Brian and Mira to stay away from the windows, maybe busy themselves packing. Whatever happened, nobody was staying here beyond today. He went downstairs and opened the front door. Found a smile and pasted it on. 'Can I help you?'

They didn't move from the vehicles. Didn't respond.

'You guys lost?'

He stepped towards the nearest car. Noticed the tensing inside. Some words exchanged between front passenger and driver. The passenger opened his door and got out. Driscoll took another few steps forward and held out his hand. 'Rory. And you are?'

The bloke lifted his hands. 'That's close enough.'

'Sorry?' Driscoll kept going.

'Stop there.' He was reaching inside his bomber jacket.

'I don't understand?' Driscoll was just a few paces off now. Arms outstretched in a harmless gesture. 'What's going on?'

Then the knife was out of his sleeve and he was on to Bomber Jacket. Headlocked, knife on the carotid, gun removed from holster and chucked in the bush in a series of smooth swift movements. Driscoll hauled him back to a spot where he had better vision of all the vehicles. The two nearest had emptied now: four passengers each. All military-style men with handguns pointing at Driscoll and his prisoner.

'I'm guessing you guys are not the mercenaries. Waiting for instructions, keeping to some rules. You're not the crazies from the waterfront yesterday.'

'Let him go.' One of the men had stepped forward and assumed the leadership role. 'Now.'

Bomber Jacket probably wanted to struggle and kick up a fuss. Be more manly. But too much jerking around and his carotid would puncture, leaving him dead in a minute.

'Nah, mate.' Driscoll could hear sirens, helicopters in the distance. 'So why are you here?'

'We want you to come with us.'

'Why?'

'For your protection.'

'You don't seem very nice.'

'Stop fucking around and do as you're told.'

A chopper hovered over the property. Channel 7? Another close behind. Channel 9. A quiet news day in Tassie. The four-wheel drive blocking the entry track rolled forward to admit a mini-convoy of police vehicles and an ambulance. With no sign of smoke, the fire engine was happy to rest at the perimeter until and unless needed. Driscoll patted the inside of his prisoner's jacket for any evidence of ID. He found none and guessed the others would be the same. By the time the lead police car had pulled up, guns had been lowered and put away and Driscoll had released his prisoner.

'What's going on?' The young female officer's hand hovered over her Glock. Her name badge read Chaudhury. 'We had a report of armed trespassers.' Her colleague had joined her; he seemed to know one of the guys from the four-wheel drive.

'Misunderstanding,' said Driscoll. 'These blokes were just after directions.'

'Yeah?' Chaudhury turned her attention to Bomber Jacket. 'You look like you've been fighting. All red and that.'

'Hot flush.'

His boss waved everybody back inside their vehicles. 'Thanks for those directions, buddy. Really appreciate it. Know exactly where we're headed now.'

Chaudhury held up her hand. 'Hang on.' Back to Driscoll. 'Who made the emergency call?'

He nodded up to the balcony, to Mason. 'My mate, there. Got the wrong end of the stick.'

'Sorry,' said Mason.

'There's a penalty for wasting police time. You know that?'

'My mistake.' Mason looked sheepish. 'Happy to give you my ID and contacts if there's any follow-up required.'

Her colleague tapped her on the shoulder and took her a few steps away for a whisper. He'd been given the nod by his pal from the four-wheel drive. After a few moments Chaudhury returned.

'Everything looks in order here.' She took Mason's details anyway. 'We'll be in touch if we want to pursue the time-wasting matter. Chaudhury offered a tight smile to the blokes in the four-wheel drives. 'After you, guys. We'll escort you back to the main road so you don't get lost again.'

'No need,' said Bomber Jacket's boss.

'No really,' said Chaudhury. 'I insist.'

***

Cato found nothing on the Bunbury case files that galvanised him. He messaged Earle to that effect and looked forward to her next update. Next, he pulled up the old Paul Reinado arrest on the system to reacquaint himself. One summer night four years ago a man by the name of Dutton had been found kicked unconscious in the laneway behind the TAFE centre on the corner of Norfolk and South in downtown Fremantle. Mobile CCTV cameras stationed outside the Norfolk Hotel had caught the attack and two men were apprehended within twelve hours: Paul Reinado and Christo Gutierrez. Their command of English was adequate, Cato dimly recalled, and they each had a Legal Aid lawyer. Cato and Deb Hassan had dealt with Gutierrez first then Reinado. Yes, both men agreed, that was them on camera – hard to deny after all as they'd been captured full face. They'd argued with Dutton in the Norfolk. All were the worse for drink but Dutton had that insistence some people get on the grog. He didn't want to let it go. What had they argued about? Some bullshit, both said. They couldn't remember the details. They fessed up. Yep, we gave him a smack. Do your worst. Dutton, it turned out, had links to far-right groups and a record for arson, criminal damage, and assault. He loved getting into a blue with a foreigner and posting it on Facebook Live. Closer examination of the council CCTV, backed up by a private camera from the rear of a restaurant, showed Dutton getting up not long after the beating, staggering, then hitting his head on the corner of a wall as he fell. An own goal. He'd knocked himself unconscious, albeit rendered unsteady following the beating. The charge remained though. With no previous convictions the men served six months and were out after four. Cato didn't recall being especially solicitous with Reinado. He'd just asked questions to ascertain the truth. End of story. Except, it seems, it wasn't.

Maybe Deb Hassan would remember more. He lifted his eyes from the screen. Outside, the day was closing in, shadows long across the rooftops of Northbridge. He missed working in Fremantle. Here in the city everything seemed to be greyer, dirtier, more confined. Fremantle air carried the salt of the sea and the sky reached to the horizon. Could he hack it here? No shortage of meaty cases, so to speak. And while Pavlou's demanding management style occasionally rubbed him up the wrong way, it had often been thus with his old boss, Hutchens. Which brought his mind back to the mystery text messages: *I know more than you,* was the gist – *you've got it wrong.* Who was it and what business was it of theirs?

He needed to get home: Sharon was on duty in a couple of hours. It would be nice to have some quality time between Ella going down and Sharon leaving. Besides, he'd like to quiz her further on her brief dealings with Paul Reinado. Pillow talk, McMahon had called it. Chance would be a fine thing. Ships in the night. Maybe one day they'd joyfully collide.

'Got a sec?' Chris Thornton was swigging a can of Mother. He crushed it and lobbed it into the recycling bin on the other side of the room. 'Bullseye. Yessss.'

'A quick one, sure.'

'Might have found a link between your Bunbury case and Doug Peters.'

'Go on.'

'Christmas Island. Both vics were there at the same time. Peters working in the detention centre, Drummond on secondment to the local high school. Our Education Department supplies teachers to the illustrious territory.'

'When was this?'

'Six years ago.'

'Wasn't Drummond in the Catholic system rather than state?'

'Retired? Semi-retired by then? Maybe you keep your options open when there's a junket on offer. Experienced science teacher, he'd be sought after I suppose.'

'How'd you find all this out? CPS is keeping Doug Peters' history under lock and key.'

'Tell that to the local newspaper.' Thornton slid his iPad across the desk.

Cato spun it around. 'Charity evening raises over ten thousand dollars.' A quiz night auction and raffle organised by the high school P & C to help fund a trip to Canberra by year nine students. Various photographs from the evening included one of Mr Douglas Peters who, on behalf of detention centre staff, had donated an auction prize of a day out sea fishing on a local charter boat with a gourmet lunch included. Winner – Mr Bevan Drummond, visiting science teacher. Cato looked up at Thornton. 'How do you find this stuff?'

He tapped his nose. 'Algorithms and alchemy.'

'Our psycho is a Christmas Islander?'

'Maybe he was the next lowest bidder in the auction.'

'And harboured that grudge for six years before exploding.'

Thornton shrugged. 'You wanted a link, I found you one.'

'Ever get the feeling we're tilting at windmills?'

'Who's we?'

***

'So who were they?' Brian couldn't tear himself away from the window even though, with the light fading rapidly, he was unlikely to see anything for much longer.

'Believe it or not, they might have even been the good guys.' Driscoll paced the room, checking nobody had left anything. 'Or at least the not-quite-so-bad guys, lesser of two evils, if you like.' He suspected a power play in Canberra and discerned Aunty's hand in it. Either way there would be more where that came from. 'Everybody ready?'

They trooped downstairs, threw their bags in the back and climbed into the Toyota. Driscoll, driving, had retrieved Bomber Jacket's Glock from the bushes and given it to Mason in the front passenger seat. On one of his walks, Driscoll had discovered a conservation maintenance track threading out the rear of the property and linking to the many trails leading up and around Mount Wellington – designed for quad bikes and the like, not Aunty's Prado. By the time they got out, she'd be in need of a radical respray on the paintwork. He kept the headlights off as they bumped and scratched their way through the undergrowth.

'Thank you for not leaving us,' said Mira from the back seat.

'Yet,' said Driscoll, catching her eye in the rear-view.

'Thank you anyway.'

After the afternoon visit he couldn't abandon them so abruptly. There was a brief window now where they all had a chance to get away without being tracked by Brian's stupid phone. Driscoll had no doubt that the spooks would return this evening, and he still wasn't totally convinced of the relative probity of their mission. Maybe they were, after all, simple assassins.

Simple assassins. Nice and uncomplicated.

'What was that?' Mason tensed, leaning forward, eyes scanning the dim bush ahead.

'Lights.' Driscoll had spotted them too. Two flashes and then out, ahead and just to the right. Maybe a hundred metres? He stopped and turned off the ignition.

'That a good idea?' asked Mason.

'I don't know.'

'Oh God,' groaned Brian from the back.

'It could be nothing.' Mason checked the Glock. 'Hikers, kids, hunters, drug deal, whatever.'

The lights again. Two even-paced flashes. Driscoll restarted the engine and rolled forward. 'Everybody buckled in?'

No denials.

If he tried crashing through he was just as likely to crash. He was keeping the headlights off and had earlier temporarily disabled the brake lights. The track was narrow and winding and there were plenty of solid trees to permanently halt his progress. At that point they'd be sitting ducks. Yet somebody was waiting ahead and maybe they were already sitting ducks.

'Mira, Brian, stay low. On the floor is best.' A sideways glance to Mason. 'Ready?'

'As I'll ever be.'

Driscoll increased the speed but not too much. He estimated less than fifty metres now to where the flashes came from. Branches against the windscreen, a wing mirror snapped from its mount, jagged tearing down the side panel. A thump against the front left. 'Wallaby,' said Mason. 'You got him.'

To hell with it. Driscoll turned the headlights on full beam and accelerated. The track widened, cleared, wallabies and possums scattered. He braced himself for the fusillade. Would have squeezed his eyes shut if he could. They broke out onto a gravel road and swerved left to head down the hill. The Prado fishtailed then steadied. Still nothing. No shots. Picked up speed. Nobody in the rear-view, nobody ahead. The gravel road became bitumen. Streetlights and houses. Mira and Brian had already taken the initiative and climbed up into their seats. Willie Mason sat back, surveying the peaceful suburban scene. Easy to forget for a moment that it was still early evening. Back there creeping through the bush it felt like midnight.

'Anybody fancy a feed?' said Driscoll. 'Calm the nerves.'

9

Friday 27th April

Sharon checked the time on the dashboard: just gone three thirty. It had been a quiet night on duty. A minor kerfuffle when the Singapore flight arrived and a young Italian woman was found to not have the right visa. She had a Latin temper and high expectations of being treated as a special case. She showed them the letter from her prospective employer – CEO of a property development empire, well-known local socialite and LNP donor. The photo of the two blond, overfed brats she was to nanny. That's not the point, Sharon had explained, when summoned by passport control. You still have the wrong visa. The Border Force blackshirts took over, and Sharon had gone back to her office to scroll through emails. It was nice to have that brief catch-up with Phil before she left for work. Ella asleep, they'd cuddled up on the couch, she with a fortifying coffee and he with a glass of red. Nice. Until the talk turned to shop.

'That Paul Reinado guy at the airport. Do you remember what he was raving about?'

'People out to get him. Kill him. Nobody listening, nobody believing him.'

'Did he say who? Why?'

'Yep,' said Sharon. 'I wrote it all down. Just in case you asked.'

'Sorry,' he'd said. There followed a few pathetic attempts to shift the conversation but Sharon preferred shop over domestic to-do lists.

'Sometimes he spoke another language.'

'Reinado. Spanish? Portuguese?'

'No, I don't think it was either of those. More an islander language. He was from Timor-Leste originally so maybe it was whatever they speak. Tetun?'

'Any of it recorded?'

'Probably. He was interviewed in a side room for about quarter of an hour until we realised it was a waste of time.'

'The recordings?'

'Fremantle D's will have them by now, or at least a copy of them.'

'What's the chance …?'

'Zero. Lovely as this brief interlude of quality time is, I need to get ready for work.'

And that had been it. During the quiet hours on duty she'd toyed with the idea of downloading the interview to a thumb drive but decided against it. Job's worth. It wasn't as if it was a matter of life and death, it was a matter of Phil's needling curiosity. Still, plenty of ways to skin a cat.

The wanker in the car behind. A ute. Lights on full beam. Dickhead. Leach Highway was dead at this time of night. Sharon squinted against the glare. She didn't need this. Pull over and let the jerk go ahead. She slowed and signalled. And he did too.

Uh-oh. Nah.

She kept going. Was it a creep playing mind games? Somebody needing help? Mick from *Wolf Creek*? She was in Myaree. Not that far to go. She accelerated. He did too. Maybe best not to go home but shoot straight through to the Freo cop shop. Phone ahead and have them waiting. The car behind was gaining on her, like he'd read her mind. He sat off the rear bumper, less than two metres gap. If she slammed on her brakes he would pile into her.

No thanks.

She floored it and pulled away from him, a good fifty over the limit. The car was at a speed where it would be easy to lose control. Ahead, the lights at North Lake Road. He was pulling out to overtake now. Parallel. She didn't dare look his way. At this speed she needed to keep her eyes on the road ahead. What the fuck was this? Nutcase. She slammed on her brakes at the intersection as he shot ahead. A hand appeared from his driver-side window. Middle finger raised.

Sharon took a few deep breaths and continued on her way home. She forgot to even note the make or rego.

***

After grabbing Chinese takeaway in Margate, twenty k's south of Hobart, they'd holed up at the car park at Kettering further south, sleeping in their seats, and taking the first ferry of the day over to Bruny Island. There was the odd raised eyebrow at the state of their vehicle, but curiosity was muted that early in the day. If they were twigged here they really were fucked: nowhere to run, only one way on or off the island, unless they swam. Brian's tainted mobile had been jettisoned en route. Driscoll scanned the surrounds as they unpacked the car and took up residence in adjacent caravan/chalets at the Captain Cook Holiday Park, Adventure Bay. It was a pretty spot: ocean flat, sunny day. Idyllic. Twelve days to go to the hearing. Aunty said he had to deliver them to Darwin by Monday May seventh at the latest. Preferably by the previous Friday, or at least over that weekend, so they could prepare themselves. Okay, maybe nine or ten more days. If they were anything like the first two or three it was going to be a bumpy ride. Two parties: the cowboys at the waterfront in Hobart, and the more disciplined spooks in the white four-wheel drives. Did each have the same end in mind? Open season on Driscoll and his companions.

'Be nice to rest up here for the duration, eh?' Mason slung his holdall into the shack he would share with Driscoll. 'Spot of fishing. I hear you're an expert.'

'Yeah?'

'Pauline mentioned you ran a charter business. Doing well for yourself.'

'Can't complain.'

Mira emerged from the cabin she'd be sharing with Brian. She didn't seem happy at the prospect. 'How long will we stay here?'

Driscoll shrugged. 'A few days, maybe more, maybe less. Can't predict.'

'He snores. Did you hear him in the car?'

Brian was over at the shower block abluting.

'I'm happy to swap with him,' said Mason. 'I don't snore.'

Maybe it wasn't a bad idea. One capable person per dwelling should the worst happen. It made sense but Driscoll had a nagging feeling about Mira and Mason's partnership. Was that good enough reason to go against defensive logic? He was overtired, making hasty judgements without thinking things through. 'Okay,' he relented.

Mira beamed. Mason looked chuffed too.

The bags were swapped and Brian returned damp-haired and refreshed from the shower block with no strong views on where he should sleep.

'Leave the lovebirds to it, eh?' he said charitably.

Driscoll needed two things, well, three, if you counted a solid night's sleep: communication with Aunty and another gun so he and Mason would have one each. 'Everybody rest up for a few hours. If you want to explore, don't go far and don't go alone.'

'You?' said Mason.

'Got a few things to do.' He hopped in the car. 'Back in a while.'

***

Cato was shaken by Sharon's account of her drive home. He had arrived at work late, having stayed back longer to look after Ella while Sharon caught up on some sleep. Was it just a fuckwit hoon? The middle finger at the end suggested so. More food for thought was the audio file on Sharon's phone. She hadn't been prepared to download the Reinado interview in full, but she did discreetly have her phone recording on the desk while she replayed the interview to help her complete her report on the incident. If things ever got sticky it could still get her into trouble. But now he had a sample of the language Reinado had been speaking.

'Tetum,' said Sharon, sleepily. 'Or Tetun. Both work. I googled it.'

Midmorning. Cato unscrewed the lid of his keep cup and had it filled with flat white in the cafe down the road before he swiped his card at the cop shop door. As he walked down the corridor, DI Pavlou poked her head out of her doorway.

'A word?'

'Sure.' Cato sipped from his coffee and crossed the threshold. There was a bloke slouching in a chair in jeans, hoodie and trainers. Crew cut, narrow face. Maybe Regional Crime Squad?

'Guthrie, Geoff Guthrie.' He stood up and offered a hand. 'ASIO.'

'Hi,' said Cato.

'I understand you know a Mr Paul Reinado?'

'No,' said Cato. 'I don't. But I was on an assault case involving him a few years ago, and he has since been found dead with my name and number in his pocket.'

'Correct,' said Guthrie.

'Thanks.' Cato took the spare seat as Pavlou closed her office door behind them. 'Was he a spy or something?'

'Not as such.'

'What does that mean?'

'Not on the payroll. Well the official one anyway.'

Cato smiled patiently like he had all the time in the world. He suspected Guthrie hadn't anticipated being the one to be questioned. 'A mole, an asset. A joe?' He clicked his fingers. 'Tinker, tailor, soldier … Help me out here.'

'You're a hoot, mate.'

Cato shook his head. 'What can I do for you?'

'Why'd he have your contact details?'

'Apparently he held me in high regard after I interviewed him all those years ago. Must have thought I could help him out in some way.'

'Specifically how did he have your mobile number?'

'I must have given it to him at the time.'

'Why would you do that?'

Cato shrugged. 'A swapping of numbers in case I needed to question him further or in case he thought of anything new that I should know.'

'Cosy.'

'Accessibility. It's an investigative technique I've picked up along the way. Served me well, for the most part.'

'And you'd heard nothing from him since that incident all those years ago?'

'Correct.'

'And he kept your name and number close to his heart all that time?'

'So it seems.' Cato leaned back in. 'What kind of trouble was he in that he'd be clutching at a straw like me?'

'Don't know,' said Guthrie.

Yes you do, thought Cato. 'So he has had dealings with ASIO in the past. In what capacity?'

'Can't say. It's a secret.'

'So I can't tell you anything and you won't tell me anything. Stalemate?'

'You could be compelled,' said Guthrie quietly.

'What, the rack? Thumbscrews? Waterboarding?'

'Philip.' Pavlou cast him a warning glance.

Cato was having none of it. 'This guy knows more than any of us about how and why Reinado died. All he wants from me is enough to help him tie off loose ends and close it all down.' Cato stood to leave. 'Demand his cooperation or give him his marching orders.'

Pavlou turned her gaze to Guthrie. 'Detective Kwong has a point.'

***

Driscoll made his first call over a beer at the Oyster Cove Inn, across the water at Kettering.

'What the fuck's going on, Aunty?' He'd stolen a phone from a tourist at Hotel Bruny while they were absorbed in the cider-making tour. He'd snaffled another from an open backpack hanging on a chair beside the pokie machine. Aunty had a spare number, presumably untracked, for emergencies. Driscoll had given her the abridged version of the last few days.

'I might ask you the same thing, Rory. Jesus, that Brian, what a dickhead.'

'The guys in the white four-wheel drives. Whose side are they on?'

'Ostensibly ours but they'd still like to lock Mason and Brian up for life given the chance. Rendition to some third-world dungeon or something.'

'What about the journalist? And me?'

'They could limit the fallout with her: manipulated by Mason, naïve idealist, obscure website that nobody reads, et cetera. She neglected to take up citizenship, she's only a permanent resident. They could send her back to Timor if necessary. You? Well, what to say?'

'Try.'

'You sure you don't know what it is you know?'

'Absolutely.'

'Better work it out quickly, my lad. You're causing gloomy faces around Canberra.'

'What about the cowboys? Who are they and who's paying them?'

'An eclectic and erratic bunch of goons from the Eastern States underbelly. It's a straightforward contract – somebody wants you all dead. We suspect a minor partner in one of the oil conglomerates with interests in the Timor Gap. They no doubt want an end to investor uncertainty.'

'Bit extreme.'

'My dear, these people were prepared to encourage Indonesia to invade Timor and slaughter a quarter of the population to end investor uncertainty. You are petty cash.'

'So how do we get them off our backs?'

'By all turning up at that Hague subcommittee meeting on May seventh in one piece. See if you can work out your part in this by then. Look after yourselves. Must dash.'

'Not so fast. I want you to send me whatever files and background you can. I'm working blind on this and that's a recipe for disaster.' He gave her his newly created email and Facebook contacts plus another mobile number safe for one call or message. Assuming she had the means to send the stuff untracked, then he could read up in an internet cafe – if such things still existed these days. Rory downed his drink, left the bar and tossed the mobile into the tray of a northbound ute. He still had a spare. Phones sorted. Now he needed a gun.

***

Something was brewing in Cato's mind. Like many cops he wasn't a great believer in coincidences. Such as? Such as Paul Reinado having a paranoid psycho fit at Perth Airport, committing suicide a day later, having Cato's contact details on his person and being involved with Australian spooks. Throw in Sharon's happenstance involvement, and it's *The Wonderful World of Disney*. Other coincidences. Two old men in WA die within twenty-four hours of each other and are grotesquely mutilated post-mortem. And guess what? They met each other on Christmas Island six years ago. Australia and Christmas Island, Australia and Timor-Leste, maybe even those other islands where CPS had business interests like Nauru and Manus. Was that the heart of this mystery – Australia and its relationship with the archipelago strung out to the north and east? Did CPS have interests in Timor? No immigration detention camps there, but this was a multinational company with a diverse portfolio.

He googled them. Latest news on their home page was that they had just secured a big contract from Canberra to manage the interface between key government departments and Joe Public, in effect running the call centres for the ATO and Centrelink among others. Nice. Back through the archives. Yes, right there under the umbrella of the parent

Cormann Logistics Group, CLG – installation of a network of solar panels and mobile phone towers across Timor-Leste to link up remote communities providing low-cost and reliable power sources, and access to telecommunications. Funded by AusAID. Cato studied it further: a puff piece with a pic of the CEO Graham Winter, Cormann's son-in-law, shaking hands with a Timorese government minister. So what? Were the secretive CPS and ASIO in cahoots in some way? When it came to the dark artistry of Australian border control, it seemed not unlikely. Were those two ill-fated old men caught up in that in some way? What about that other 'coincidence'? Cato did one more search. Yes, CPS/CLG also had projects in Darwin. An oil refinery linked to the proposed Timor pipeline: an aerial shot of the site, and a group pic of some business blokes trying to reconcile their shirts and ties with fluoro and hard hats. Maybe Paul Reinado did subcontract electrical work there? He could imagine DI Pavlou loving this little train of thought. She wouldn't entertain it for a second. CPS and ASIO? He may as well wear a tinfoil hat and rave on about aircraft vapour trails. Even if there was anything in it he wouldn't be allowed anywhere near: official secrets and border control laws – two great big brick walls to bang his head against.

But maybe he could burrow away at the foundations.

Cato picked up the phone. 'Nikki? DS Kwong – Major Crime. I think it's time I paid you guys another visit. Monday suit you?'

***

Driscoll felt guilty about the thefts but his needs were greater and more immediate: two mobile phones and now two more guns. He'd broken into a house on a five-acre block on Nicholls Rivulet Road just north of Kettering. He guessed, rightly, that they would keep firearms for pest control and had been doing his third drive-by when he noticed the old bloke leaving in his ute. Fifteen minutes later Driscoll was in and out of there with a shotgun, an old twenty-two rifle, and a box of shells for each. Another twenty minutes and he was on the ferry back over to Bruny. Light was fading as he pulled up beside the two cabins. Mason and Mira had cranked up one of the nearby communal barbies and meat sizzled in a spicy marinade.

'Smells great,' said Driscoll.

They both turned and smiled. Something about them suggested, if it hadn't already happened earlier, they were now an item. She early thirties, him nudging fifty: that was some daddy complex. Or, for him, Lolita complex. Driscoll shook the thought away. It was his upbringing: Australia's hard man Mr Fixit in the Asia-Pacific all those years – ruthless, resourceful – but a judgmental, prudish, puritan streak ran through him. His mum's influence, no doubt – that mission upbringing of hers.

'Where's Brian?'

Mira wiped her hands on a cloth. 'He went for a walk over to the beach about half an hour ago.'

Driscoll shook his head. 'I thought I said no wandering off alone.'

'It's been thirty minutes. Heard no gunshots or bloodcurdling cries.' Mason turned a sausage. 'Chill, mate. Go and give him a call if you like. Grub's just about up.'

Driscoll jogged across the road and followed the short path down to the beach. The breeze rippled the surface of the water. He looked up and down the bay and couldn't see Brian anywhere. He called his name. Listened. Nothing.

At the south end of the bay the sheer cliffs of the fluted cape rose from the water. The packed white sand squeaked beneath his feet.

'Brian?' A gust of wind shook the eucalypts. Then he heard it. Quiet sobbing, over to the right, back in the trees. He strolled over. Brian was sitting on the sand, his back against an old gum. Tears streamed down his face but he wiped them as Driscoll approached. 'You okay?' Stupid question.

'Yeah, just needed some time on my own.'

'Tough gig this, eh? Always on the move, looking over our shoulders.' Driscoll sat down beside him. 'Just need to hold it together another week or so.'

'Then what?'

'Then you say your piece at the hearing.'

'And then the committee fucks off back to Holland and throws us under a bus.'

Driscoll stared out towards the horizon. Closer in, a seagull wheeling, gliding, then settling on the water. 'I'd be a fool to suggest otherwise and you'd be a fool to believe me. But from what I can gather, you're only currency while the bad guys think they can stop you testifying, stop the committee from having a different view. Once the decision is made there's no point in pursuing you.'

'What about revenge, or setting an example to others for the future?'

'Fair point. But what's your alternative? Go off on your own and try to disappear and you'll be looking over your shoulder anyway. Go public at the right time and you have a few extra people looking out for you. These people don't like that kind of scrutiny.'

A bitter laugh. 'That's probably what they told those Russian dissidents over the years. Then a decade later your soup tastes funny, and bang.'

'Rock and a hard place, mate.'

'And I still don't understand what it is I'm meant to testify to. The diary papers were coded. They were gibberish. The manuscript was airport trash.'

Driscoll let a handful of sand run through his fingers. A wave broke softly on the shore. 'Maybe all you're meant to say is that they were real, they were left in your care by that person. Just confirm their authenticity and providence.'

'Like a valuable antique or artwork.' Brian drew a handkerchief from his pocket and blew into it. 'My wife is living out her last days alone and I'm here. She doesn't deserve this, neither do I.'

Driscoll sighed. 'Dinner's ready.'

'Those two are giving me the shits as well. Grunting and groaning. Giggling like it's fucking leavers week. Jesus.'

Driscoll stood and offered Brian a hand up. 'Hang in there, mate. It'll be over soon.'

'Yeah, one way or another.'

10

Saturday 28th – Sunday 29th April

Two full days together as a family. What could be better? Ella was in full throttle. She wanted to dip her hand in the honey pot and smear it on the table, floor and around the walls. Cato didn't want her to, although he was less insistent than Sharon. Ella was bellowing fit to burst because the honey pot had just been removed and put up high out of reach.

'Enough,' snapped Sharon. 'No more honey. No more screaming and shouting.'

Ella wailed, heartbroken both at the thought of not getting what she wanted and at the very idea of being disapproved of.

Cato busied himself wiping up the honey smears. 'Maybe we should go out somewhere,' he said. 'Get her running around a park or along a beach. Use up some energy.'

'No,' screamed Ella, as if she'd understood every word, tossing a plastic telephone across the room for emphasis.

Sharon lifted her up and carried her to her room. 'Stay there and don't come out until you can be a good girl.'

'What do you think?' said Cato on her return against a backdrop of distant yelling and sobbing.

'Swing by the orphanage on the way. Strap her to the foundling wheel.'

Cato took that as a yes and set about packing the necessities into the car. Where to go? Wide open space seemed like a good idea, a beach or a park maybe, but ones that didn't allow dogs so they could have one less worry about letting Ella off the leash. No dogs. That eliminated Fremantle. A playground with a fence and a soft landing. And a coffee van not too far away. Back to Freo then? They settled for Cottesloe, which had a beach, coffee, swings and soft landings but was hell for parking on a Saturday midmorning. Thankfully, by the time they were ready to leave, Ella had moved on from her tantrum and was now all sweetness and light.

While Cato pushed Ella on the swing, Sharon nipped across the road for some takeaway coffees. In their haste they'd forgotten their keep cups. Would they be struck by retributive lightning? Once again, the ocean was blue and endless, with Rottnest shimmering on the horizon.

'Higher!' said Ella, showing off for Mum's return.

'How long do you intend to be in Bunbury then?' Sharon eyed him over the rim of her latte.

'A few days?'

'We need more precision if we're booking a live-in nanny.'

'Maybe book the week and if I'm back earlier we'll keep the nanny on and treat it as respite. We might even get out for dinner or lunch together?'

She smiled for what seemed like the first time in ages. Noticing it, Ella's face lit up too. Sharon studied him. 'I thought you said everything was under control down there?'

'It's ticking along but not progressing. Needs a shake.'

'This Nikki whatshername not living up to expectations?'

Cato took the bait. 'Just needs a helping hand,' he said. 'The benefit of my experience.'

'Wanker.' Sharon laughed and chucked her empty cup in a bin.

Ella beamed. 'Wanka, wanka,' she roared, as the swing took her up high.

***

Driscoll was up at dawn. He'd slept badly. Yes, Brian did indeed snore. And a half. The bumps and groans from next door didn't help either. Mira was already up, sitting at a nearby picnic bench with a cigarette and a mug of tea. She blew out some smoke and pointed to the gas ring on the communal barbecue. 'Kettle's just boiled.'

It was peaceful, no one about. Early birds squawked and screeched in the trees and waves lapped gently at the shore. Driscoll poured himself a cuppa and stood upwind of Mira's cigarette smoke. 'You're up early.'

'I needed some air.'

'You and Will seem to be getting along well.'

She smiled. 'Does it bother you?'

'None of my business.'

'That's right.'

Driscoll took the seat opposite her. 'None of this is a game.'

'I know that.'

'The articles you wrote. Nobody is particularly interested. Do you know why?'

'Conspiracy of silence?'

'That's one theory. But you'd imagine Australian dirty tricks in the oil negotiations would be more newsworthy, wouldn't you? Spies. Lies. Intrigue. That the bigger outlets would have picked it up and run with it.'

She nodded. 'Yes, you would imagine.'

'Which suggests to me that they've been warned off.'

'Like I said, conspiracy of silence.'

'Or those doing the warning have something which discredits your source and therefore your story.'

'Like what?'

A footfall close behind. 'Yeah, mate,' said Mason. 'Like what?'

Mira made room for him on her bench. Their shoulders touched. 'Well?' she said.

'Why are you blowing the whistle, Willie? You don't strike me as a bloke overly burdened by conscience.'

'I'm hurt.'

'So you helped bug some meeting rooms that gave the Aussies an unfair advantage in the carve-up. You helped us win. Some would call that patriotic. It's like one of our bowlers sandpapering the ball. Tsk-tsk, but it's not life and death is it?'

Mira stubbed out her cigarette. 'That oil is ours by right, not as a gift or charitable donation from you. Stealing it is stealing our country's wealth, to build hospitals, provide safe, clean water. It is exactly about life and death.'

'How much of it would end up benefitting ordinary Timorese?' Driscoll shook his head. 'Already there are stories of the proceeds being siphoned off to the old cadres.'

'So Australia will look after it for us, is that right? Give it away in handouts to your tax-dodging corporations maybe? Pay for your politicians' helicopters to attend family weddings? We do not need any lectures on corruption from Australia, thank you very much.'

Mason sniggered, took a sip of Mira's tea. 'Owned there, mate.'

'You haven't answered my question, Willie. Why are you blowing the whistle?'

'It's the right thing.'

'Bullshit. It's either payback or insurance. They have something on you and this is your leverage. Your get-out-of-jail card.'

'Not true. But even if it was, what's your point? There's a fancy committee coming all the way from Europe to listen to our story and it might well change the course of the boundary negotiations for good. Taking billions from the oil barons and Australian government royalties and putting it into the coffers of Timor-Leste.' Mason took Mira's hand and squeezed it. 'That is real and a fact, and whatever motivation for arriving there is irrelevant. The people who want to harm us are focused on that, not on my personal reasons for doing this. It changes nothing.'

'But if all we are is leverage, and then you change your mind about testifying, the whole thing falls apart and we're left in the lurch.' Driscoll glanced at Mira. 'And Timor gets nothing.'

'Is that true?' she asked Mason, sliding her hand out from under his.

'No, babe.' He glared at Driscoll. 'It's bullshit. All of it.'

'Tick, tock.' Driscoll slung his dregs into the gravel and headed for the shower block.

He wasn't sure why he'd done that. Mason's motivations were a mystery but there was no evidence that he was just using them all as leverage. This probably wasn't the best time to be driving a wedge into team relationships. Or perhaps it was – Mira and Mason were too cosy, and that could lead to presumptions and misguided loyalties. Everybody looking after number one was an easier prospect to manage – it had a bottom line: survival. Alliances, caucusing, too much of that shit and before you know it you're getting voted off the island. Driscoll shoved his coin in the box and started the shower. The warm jet felt good, cleansing. His troubled, disturbed sleep sluiced down the plughole. He didn't know how they were going to while away the time until they had to move again. They were already on edge. There was Pictionary in the games room, a TV, cards. Maybe he and Brian could play chess or draughts while the other two fucked themselves silly.

The shower block door squeaked on neglected hinges and snapped shut on an over-sprung slide-track arm. Whistling, tap running, and some throat and nose clearing. The morning chorus of a holiday camp.

'You there, Rory, mate?' Mason, through a mouthful of toothpaste.

'Yep.'

'That was a bit of a dog act.'

'Too close to home?'

'You've got her worried now. There was no need for that.'

'Wasn't there?'

'We need to stick together, mate.' Rinse and spit. 'United we stand?'

'I'm still here, aren't I?'

'Me too. And I'll be there for that hearing. Come what may.'

'We're all good then.'

'Yeah.' The tap stopped running. 'A word to the wise?'

'I'm listening.'

'Before you cast aspersions, maybe you should have a long hard think about why you're on that list.' The door creaked open. 'Pot. Kettle. Black. No offence.'

***

Sunday night saw Cato with a holdall packed ready for an early getaway. He debated taking his emergency supply of antidepressants with him. He wasn't due for his next weekly dose until Wednesday but he hadn't felt the need of them so much lately. Was that all it took? Keep busy and interested? A quiet word with yourself? In the end he packed them. Just in case.

After the playground yesterday, Ella had slept off her morning blues and woken midafternoon with a new batch of traumas focused on what jumper she should wear next. In the end they'd succumbed to temptation and streamed *Bluey* for her on TV while they prepared an early dinner. Today had been a repeat. Ups and downs. Ella had copied some of Sharon's yoga poses with good humour, a tutu and fairy wings. Midday nap. An afternoon drinking endless cups of play tea in the cubby. Ella's rules this time. She made up for her loss of power over the honey thing yesterday by insisting that Dada take his shirt off in her cubby and wear one of her penne necklaces. Then early dinner, bath and bed. Sharon looked exhausted and no doubt jealous of his forthcoming child-free days in Bunbury.

'I'll miss you,' he said.

'Liar.' She continued packing the dishwasher.

'No, really.'

She shook her head. 'You really believe the Reinado thing and the murders of these two old men are linked? It's a long bow to draw.'

'I think CPS is the common denominator but I don't know why yet. Would the Feds have anything on them?'

'If they do, you'll have to go through official channels to get it.'

'Fair enough.'

'I'm serious. Don't drag me into your … speculations.'

'I won't.' He changed the subject. 'When's Julie coming over?'

'Lunchtime tomorrow. Gives me a chance to catch up on some sleep before the night shift.'

'Anything special on the horizon at work this week?'

'Not so far.'

Cato yawned. 'Might turn in. Early start tomorrow.'

'Every day's an early start for some of us. Remember?'

Trumped by the Ella card. 'I'll get back soon as I can. Maybe we can have a boozy lunch later in the week and a raunchy afternoon in the sack?'

Sharon twirled a tea towel and playfully flicked him with it. 'Why wait?'

11

Monday 30th April

Driscoll was once again on the road, having taken the early morning ferry after a text from Aunty's secure phone told him to check his emails. He'd dropped his spare burner over the side of the boat into the D'Entrecasteaux Channel, mildly guilty at polluting the waterways but promising to karmically make it up somehow. He'd spent most of the weekend brooding about his part in all this and still hadn't fathomed it out. He'd worked in the Dili embassy for eighteen months on a joint AFP and Timor police development and support program. With structures based on the old colonial Portuguese policing system, a training manual in a language that few ordinary Timor cops spoke, massively under-resourced, ill-managed and prone to corruption, the fledgling Timor national police force had its work cut out. Driscoll had been part of a team of logistics, IT, beancounters, intelligence and management consultants sent to lay the groundwork for a long-term program to try and deal with some of these exacting issues. To the best of his knowledge he hadn't broken any rules, trod on any toes, seen or heard anything he shouldn't. It had been an uneventful posting. But the truth was in there somewhere, it seemed.

Relations were strained between Mira and Mason and that was fine by Driscoll. By comparison Brian seemed downright chirpy. Maybe the cry had done him good. Driscoll had left them all, yet again, under instructions to look out for each other and not go off alone.

'Where are you off to this time?' Mason had asked.

'Best not to know.'

'Is it?'

'It's about keeping us all alive. Trust me.'

'Guess we'll have to, huh?'

He took the winding long way north up the commuter-busy Channel Highway through Margate, west along Sandfly Road past the hobby farms, left on to Huon Highway and down through the valley into Huonville, where a low thick mist hung over the river. Pulling the peak of his baseball cap lower, he grabbed a steak pie at Banjo's, scarfed it, stole somebody's phone, then headed for the library and logged on. Aunty had been busy. She'd sent him a zip folder with backgrounders on each of his travelling companions, their preliminary statements of evidence to The Hague subcommittee, background on the mysterious client of the suburban lawyer Brian, and one simply titled 'Misc'. Where to start? There were only two computers available for public use; everybody tended to access the wi-fi through their own equipment these days. Driscoll had this machine booked for the maximum allowed half hour, and already he was aware of a bloke hovering impatiently over his left shoulder. This wasn't conducive to examining top secret government documents.

'Mate?' Driscoll turned in his seat to address the waiting man. 'I need some privacy here.' He winked. 'Top secret government business. Can you give me a few minutes?'

The bloke chuckled. 'No probs. Enjoy the twerking cats.'

Driscoll used the stolen phone to photograph each page from the screen of the computer. Eighteen in all. Then he logged out and made himself scarce. As he walked back to the library car park a brisk wind shook the trees. The library was adjacent to a government services building which offered everything from Medicare reimbursements through Centrelink applications to licence renewals and driving tests. A chubby teenage girl sat sobbing in the driving seat of her L-plate Hyundai. A couple of scrawny young blokes in beanies smoked ciggies and drank cans of V at a nearby bench. Huonville was one of those little country towns where the hipster foodie marketing gurus have one thing in mind and the defiant local population another.

He'd parked strategically to minimise the chances of being crept up on and to maximise his lines of sight. He figured he was safe to turn the stolen phone on in reading mode – for a short while at least – and disabled as much of its connectivity as possible. The battery level showed half. He would have to prioritise his reading list. The submissions to The Hague subcommittee could wait, he was interested in the people themselves. Mira Soares, thirty-four, had arrived in Australia at the age of fifteen. Orphaned. Her parents had been killed the previous year by pro-Indonesian militia in the immediate aftermath of the independence referendum in Timor. There had been a massacre in a small town outside of Dili, and Mira had survived it. Airlifted to Darwin, she had been brought up by Timorese expatriate relatives. Driscoll checked the dates – something didn't fit. Airlifted to Darwin in July 2000. The massacre which left her orphaned occurred in September the previous year. Quite a delay, nearly a year. Refugees. Australia. Nothing unusual there, he supposed. He read on. She had done well at school and at university and was now based in Melbourne working as a journalist and blogger for a left-leaning news website. Her stories on the Australian bugging of the Timorese delegation offices during the maritime boundary negotiations had caused an initial flurry of excitement from other media outlets and had outraged activists and politicians. But it had fizzled out surprisingly quickly. Such is the news cycle, thought Rory. Affairs, scandals, disasters, murders, bogeymen – there's a lot of competition out there.

Or maybe it had something to do with her source. William Mason, fifty-one: veteran of Australian military adventures in Iraq, East Timor, Afghanistan. Moved into the intelligence services, principally ASIS, with stints in Indonesia, Timor, Malaysia, PNG. Divorced with two adult offspring. Spoke fluent Bahasa and had a fair command of Portuguese, Tetun, Arabic, Farsi and Dari: an earlier model Rory Driscoll but with military training. In recent years Mason had returned to the domestic arena with ASIO, monitoring returned ISIS Jihadis, but had resigned about nine months previously to tell his story to Mira Soares. Nine months to spill your guts to a journo? What else had he been doing all that time? An international man of action and mystery taking such a long sabbatical? Rory might ask himself the same question.

The phone battery level was down to a quarter. Brian Simmonds – funny how his surname had just got lost in the Brian-ness of him. Fifty-eight, going on seventy-two. Family solicitor based in rural Victoria down by the Dandenong Ranges and servicing clients primarily from the Mornington Peninsula – a specialist in real-estate settlements, wills and trusts, family law, and occasional dabbler in accident compensation and petty criminal matters. Married with three adult offspring. His life looked pretty unremarkable on the face of it. What was so special about Brian Simmonds was the manuscript lodged with him by a client, since deceased in a car accident on one of those treacherous narrow winding roads around New Zealand's South Island. The manuscript, an intended novel, was a semi-autobiographical and semi-fictional account of diplomacy, spies, dirty tricks, coups, murder, blackmail and sexual escapades during three decades of service as an Australian diplomat working the Asia-Pacific. Of particular interest was the chapter on Timor entitled 'Crocodile Tears'. Names and dates were changed, but it seemed this account went a long way to backing up Willie Mason's factual accounts of the bugging operation as reported by Mira Soares. The deceased author of this racy potboiler was one Deborah Chan who had a long and distinguished career as a diplomat before banging her head on the glass ceiling one too many times and quitting in disgust. The manuscript alone, fiction as it was, could have been dismissed, but the accompanying two dozen volumes of diaries covering most of the years in question sealed it. Annotated with codes and initials that would make no sense to the casual reader, like Brian Simmonds, it was extracts from this that compelled The Hague investigators to take heed.

The manuscript and diaries had since been seized in an ASIO raid and were being held somewhere secret pending the outcome of The Hague deliberations. The Hague had issued an order for the documents to be sealed and held in protective custody in the meantime but it was unclear whether Australia would take any notice. All interesting enough, but hardly revelatory for Driscoll's purposes. For the most part it was extra flesh on the bones of stuff he already knew or had guessed. The phone battery had given a ten per cent warning beep. Having decided to skip the evidence testimonials for now, all that was left was Aunty's single page 'Misc' file. The subject was Willie Mason. It appeared to be the smoking gun.

***

Cato had been given the desk opposite Nikki Earle. He'd hit the road early and breakfasted at a cafe in town. Bunbury was characteristically bright and sunny and the ocean at Koombana Bay had been mirror flat. Dolphins surfaced in welcome as he drove past. He could almost be on holiday.

For a murder room, the place lacked urgency. People chatted, checked their phones, stared into space. Maybe DI Pavlou was right and Major Crime should have taken over before the rot set in.

'Coffee?' enquired Earle. 'José's doing a run, it's his turn. They also do a mean hedgehog over there.'

'Sure,' said Cato. 'Flat white, no froth or sugar, and a hedgehog.' He handed over his keep cup and rummaged in his pocket for money.

'My shout,' said Earle. 'So,' she folded her arms and leaned against a partition. 'What do you want to do?'

'Your Bevan Drummond and my Douglas Peters met each other on Christmas Island six years ago.' Cato showed her the photos on his iPad. 'We need to be talking to the other people who were there at that time, colleagues at the school, et cetera, and we want to know if there's been any subsequent contact between the two.' He lifted his gaze. 'Maybe you can get your team to hit the phones. Then over a nice cup of coffee and a hedgehog, you can tell me about the clubs and community groups Drummond was involved with.'

Earle called the room together, gave Cato the floor as he explained the Christmas Island connection, and people set to following it up. Earle and Cato took their coffees and slices with them as they drove out of the police compound with the local golf club, swimming pool and Rotary Club on their agenda.

'Where are we at with Ryan Hodgson?' said Cato through a mouthful of chocolatey slice.

'Nowhere, really.'

'We should be nicer to him. Maybe he saw something that can help us.'

'Like what?'

'We won't know unless we ask him. He's a neighbour. If what he says was true, and he stayed home all night before travelling to Dunsborough the following morning, then maybe he heard or saw something in the street.'

'We already asked him.'

'Nicely? He was identified as a ratbag and suspect early on and treated as such. Maybe he needs to know what it feels like to be an asset, an upstanding member of society, a possible hero.'

'I'll get José onto it.'

'Good choice.'

They pulled up at Black Swan Golf Club overlooking the Leschenault Inlet. Like many such clubs it had a beautiful setting: bush, greenery, water. Peaceful and rarified, a privileged space where it would be easy to feel like you didn't really belong. The car park was packed and the only available slot was reserved for the Assistant Lady Vice-Captain. They took it, knowing full well there would be possible hell to pay.

Unfortunately for Bevan Drummond, it turned out that he was a pretty average player and didn't go to the club that often or kowtow to the caste system so nobody took much notice of him. He hadn't particularly come to the attention of any of the captains, vice-captains, or their assistants, and the bar staff and groundsmen had no significant recollection of him either.

'What about this bloke?' Cato showed them a picture of Doug Peters.

'No,' said all the club officials. 'Sorry.'

'Maybe,' said Babs, from behind the bar. 'Once or twice.'

'When?'

'Month ago. Two maybe? Midweek evening.' That accent. Straight out of *Coronation Street*.

'Why do you remember him?' asked Cato.

'I don't think he was a golfer, or a golf club type.'

'How do you mean?'

She dipped her head and dropped her voice to a stage whisper. 'Not a snooty boring tosser.'

'Was he with anybody?'

'He'd have to be signed in. Now you mention it, he was a guest of Bevan's, I remember now.'

'Is there any way of narrowing down the time frame?' Earle checked walls and ceiling. 'CCTV, till receipts, guest sign-in book, anything?'

All of those, apparently, but receipts or EFTPOS only if either of them used a card. Babs brightened. 'It'll have been either a Wednesday or Thursday because Tuesdays I have yoga and I don't do weekends or Mondays.' She tapped a glittery fingernail absent-mindedly on the bar top. 'And it was after Easter because I'd been to see my sister in

Broome and I must have been wearing my new top I bought up there. He complimented me on it.' So April then, in the fortnight or so before they died, thought Cato. Babs lowered her voice again. 'I reckon it was me tits I was being complimented on.' She chuckled. 'Yeah, cop, you can tell them a mile off. Flirty but harmless, not a sleazebag. Bevan looked embarrassed though. Not the company he normally kept I expect.'

Earle phoned back to base and arranged a couple of minions to come to the golf club for the necessary follow-ups on CCTV and such, and a statement from Babs. Then it was on to the pool at the South West Sports Centre just south of the city centre.

'Bevan?' said the manager on being shown the photo. 'He sometimes swims ...' A pained look. 'Swam, with the morning crew. Monday, Wednesday, Saturday. You should have been here at six this morning, you would have met them. I've got a mobile number for one of them if you like.'

'Yes,' said Earle. 'Thanks.'

The manager didn't recognise the photo of Doug Peters as someone who might have dropped by, nor did any of his staff. It was heading for lunchtime so they adjourned to the sports centre cafe for a coffee and pie. While they were waiting for their order, Earle phoned the mobile number the centre manager had provided and arranged a catch-up for later that afternoon with the swimming stalwart.

Cato fiddled with his phone. 'I wonder where Peters stayed when he was in town.'

'With Bevan?'

Their lunch was ready. Cato collected it from the counter. 'You'll need to revisit the neighbours, see if anyone recalls any visitors staying over about then. The usual accommodation outlets too.'

'There's no record of any telecommunications between the two. Your geeks checked.'

'Maybe they had burner phones – not hard for an ex-cop to organise.' Cato took a bite of pie and chewed a while. 'If so, they were already being careful – scared of someone or something.'

'You've got a bloke in prison for the Peters killing, right?'

Cato nodded. 'And he was seen in Fremantle around the same time as Drummond was meeting his maker here in Bunbury.' Not impossible that there were two killers but, without doubt, they needed to re-examine the case against Lenny Jacobs. He'd call later and give DI Pavlou the happy news.

***

There was a rap on the driver-side window. Driscoll jumped; he'd been absorbed in his reading. Two uniformed cops, one bending and gesturing for him to get out of the car.

'Is this your vehicle, sir?'

'No. Belongs to a friend.'

'ACT plates. It's a long way from home.'

'That's right.'

The second officer went back to the cop wagon to run the rego. Meanwhile the talker, an earthy type whose name badge read Marsh, asked Driscoll for some ID.

'Don't have any on me.'

'What, no driver's licence, bank card, library card. Nothing?'

'Sorry. Back in the caravan probably.'

'Tell me anyway.' Driscoll gave him a name and some contact details and Marsh wrote them down. The colleague returned to declare the car belonged to Mrs Pauline Blasey from Canberra.

'Give her a call,' said Driscoll. 'See what she says.'

Marsh rang the number the database gave him and Aunty answered. Some preliminaries to confirm she was the right person then they got down to business. 'I have a bloke here, David Palmer, who says you loaned him your car?'

Describe him, she must have said, enjoying the moment.

'Just over six foot tall. Yes, madam, that's around one point eight five metres. Age around fortyish. Aboriginal.' A quick check with Driscoll. 'That right, sir?'

'Yeah, mate.'

Handsome? she would have said.

'To some, I guess.' More chat. Marsh turned to Driscoll. 'Can you roll up your trouser leg and show me your left knee, David?' Driscoll did. 'Yes, madam, there is a scar there. I think we can leave it at that, cheers.'

'All good?'

'Yes, sir. Sorry to bother you. We had a report of a stolen phone just around the corner and of people acting suspiciously.'

And I was the first Indigenous person you came across, thought Driscoll. 'Tsk. Nothing's safe these days, eh?'

'Make sure you always carry your licence while you're driving in Tassie. Have a good day, sir.'

'Yeah, you too.' How long, he wondered, before that minor incident report was logged and triggered alarm bells somewhere?

***

The Polar Bears swimming woman didn't add much to the picture. Bevan Drummond had been a keen and regular swimmer, even in the winter months, and often won his age group in the open water meets in summer. Usually preferred the ocean to the pool but sometimes did a few laps just for the company. Hung around for a coffee some mornings. Nice enough bloke but hardly the life and soul. Anything unusual about him lately? Worried, distracted, whatever? Nothing stood out. The photo of Doug Peters didn't register either. They'd left their business cards with her just in case anything came to mind. Next port of call was the council offices where the duty JP was wrapping up for the day. He was a short rotund man with thick eyebrows and an expression somewhere between laughing and indigestion.

'Martin Zelic?' Yes, he nodded, he was. Cato and Earle introduced themselves and the nature of their business. 'I understand Mr Drummond was a member of the Rotary Club?'

'Yes, a very active member.'

'In what way?'

Zelic invited them to take a seat and turned the sign on his door to *Closed*. Anybody needing documents witnessed would have to come back tomorrow. 'Bevan was a good fundraiser, organised lots of events. Very civic-minded. But then again, we all are, I suppose. That's the point of being a Rotarian.'

Cato slid a photo of Doug Peters across the desk. 'Recognise him at all?'

'Doug, yes. He came along to one of our socials.'

'When was this?'

'Early April? Just after Easter, I think.'

'Doug, you called him. Know him well?'

'Not especially. He was something of a hail-fellow-well-met, that evening anyway. I think he might have tucked a few away earlier before he joined us.'

'And he was a friend of Bevan's?' asked Earle.

'More an acquaintance, I think.'

'Why do you say that?'

Zelic shrugged. 'Bevan didn't seem that comfortable in his company. They didn't act like old pals.'

'How did they know each other? Did they say?'

'They'd both worked as volunteers on some aid project a few years ago. Water wells, building renovation, that kind of thing. Rotary International is very supportive in that regard.'

'Do you know where the aid project was?' asked Cato, already guessing the answer.

'East Timor, I'm pretty sure. Although they call it something else now, don't they?'

'Timor-Leste,' said Cato. 'Do you recall anything unusual from that trip?'

'Like what?'

'Any accidents, mishaps, reports of any trouble. Mr Drummond didn't mention anything?'

'It was a long time ago.' He gave it some thought. 'Sorry, nothing comes to mind.'

'Was that the only trip Mr Drummond made to Timor?'

'With us, yes, as far as I know.' A pause. 'I suppose that was quite unusual. Most of our oldies jump at the chance of return trips to projects. Makes a nice change from the bowls club or whatever. Bevan would have been offered such a chance but never did take it up.'

***

Driscoll got back over to Bruny Island by late afternoon. He'd deleted the incriminating material from the stolen phone and left it, the smashed battery and SIM card in different locations along the Huon Highway. The ferryman was getting to know his face.

'Busy day?'

'Always,' said Driscoll.

'Live on Bruny?'

'Nah, just visiting.'

'Lot of coming and going.'

'Yeah, I've still got work to do. My wife's a poet. This is her annual retreat.'

'Pay well, the poetry?'

Driscoll laughed. 'One day, maybe. Meantime, I'll keep on bringing home the bacon.'

'Diamond, mate.'

Driscoll wasn't sure what he'd find when he got back to the holiday park at Adventure Bay. Would Mason have made his move? As he pulled up to the cabins it was clear there was no one around. Driscoll stepped out of the vehicle.

'Brian?' He went over to next door. 'Willie? Mira?'

Nothing.

He'd told them to stay together. Maybe they'd heeded him and gone for a walk, a companionable threesome. Then he noticed the blood. A couple of splashes to the right of the door on a slab of concrete paving and a smear on the wall of the shack. Driscoll pressed his face to the window. 'Willie? Mira?' Back to the other shack. 'Brian?'

The stolen shottie and twenty-two were in the four-wheel drive but Mason still had Bomber Jacket's Glock, and of course the flick knife. Why the hell had he trusted Mason with a gun? Answer – he had no real choice at the time. Aunty's 'Misc' email file identified Mason as being under internal investigation immediately before he quit his ASIO post. An allegation had surfaced from within the expatriate Timorese community in Darwin that he had been recognised as the foreigner people had seen in the company of pro-Indonesian militia and Indonesian army units involved in atrocities around the time of the independence referendum. Not long after the accusation surfaced, Mason had blown the whistle on the oil treaty bugging operation. A subsequent email from Mason to the powers-that-be explicitly stated that he would be happy to recant his bugging story if the war crimes enquiry was buried. Clearly Mason was using Mira to serve his own agenda. Brian Simmonds was a different matter. He was the keeper of independent corroboration of the bugging claims in the form of Deborah Chan's diplomatic diaries and racy manuscript. He strengthened Mason's hand in the negotiations but left him little room to move if he wanted to backtrack should the atrocity thing be shelved. At any point Brian might find himself surplus to requirements.

Driscoll studied the blood spatter. Was that what just happened?

12

Tuesday 1st May

Things developed swiftly overnight. CCTV and the guest book confirmed Douglas Peters' presence in the Black Swan Golf Club bar on Tuesday the third of April between six thirty and eight fifteen. He had been signed in by Bevan Drummond. The two victims knew each other then, had met previously on Christmas Island six years earlier and, according to immigration, Rotary International and other travel records chased down by Chris Thornton, both men had been part of a volunteer team working in Timor in the mid-2000s on various irrigation and building renovation schemes in and around Dili. In between those times there was little evidence of contact between the two men. They couldn't be described as old mates. Their paths crossed only now and then.

Cato had phoned Sharon around breakfast time. She sounded tired but working the red-eye shift at the airport would do that to you. In the background Ella was yelling and banging something on the table while Julie's dulcet Yorkshire tones endeavoured in vain to get her to 'Shush now, love'.

'How's the enquiry going?' Sharon had asked through a yawn.

'Progress. More evidence of a connection between the two victims. Timor seems to be looming large.'

'And your colleague. How's she shaping up?'

'Very well.'

'Bastard.' But there was half a smile in her voice.

'How about you? Any gossip?'

'Might be moving on from the airport gig back into Investigations.'

'Great,' said Cato, instinctively.

'Is it? The duties out there might be dull but it is predictable.' Ella shouted out a big 'No!' to a murmured request from Julie. 'And predictable is kind of important with a two-year-old.'

'Do you have any say in the move?'

'It's an offer I'm allowed to refuse. They need to know by early next week.'

'Sleep on it.'

'Good idea,' she yawned again. 'Hurry back. I'd prefer to sleep on you.'

He'd then phoned DI Pavlou who'd already got wind of developments from Chris Thornton and was sanguine under the circumstances. They would need to revisit the Jacobs arrest. 'It's what you do, Philip. You're known for it. That's why you're such an ass … et.'

Earle and José were hovering. 'Ryan Hodgson responds well to positivity and encouragement.' Earle handed Cato his keep cup from the coffee run. 'He thinks he might have seen something the night of the Drummond murder.'

'Go on.'

José pulled up a chair and offered it to Earle who shook her head. He sat down. 'Hodgson reckons he was out in the front yard with a spliff around midnight when he saw somebody walking away from the Drummond property.'

'Didn't find it worth mentioning previously?'

'Didn't expect to be believed, didn't want to admit to the spliff, and wasn't entirely sure they were actually walking away from the Drummond property. Could have been any of two or three other houses.'

'Description?'

'Average height, stocky build, male.'

That could have been half the blokes in Bunbury. 'Old or young?'

'Not sure, the back was turned. Not young was as far as he'd go.'

'Walking normal, or in a hurry?'

'Normal.'

'And no vehicle?'

'No, but he heard one start up about a minute later around the corner.'

Cato turned to Earle. 'You're following it up?'

'Of course.'

Back to José. 'You believe him?'

He nodded. 'Hodgson's not used to being taken seriously except by his mum who he doesn't respect.'

José went about his business and Cato turned his attention back to Earle. 'Did you manage to get on to that request at the end of yesterday?'

She grimaced. 'He wasn't overly keen but he did it anyway.'

Cato had asked Earle to get her boss, the district superintendent, to formally request that CPS open their files to the enquiry given the link to the Drummond case via Peters and Christmas Island. It was likely to rattle Pavlou's cage but it had to be done. CPS were at the heart of this and Cato didn't have the patience to let them hide behind spurious operational secrecy rules. They were investigating a homicide, for fuck's sake.

'Tell that to the blokes who copped it on Manus and Nauru,' Earle had said, picking up the phone to her boss.

'Are CPS going to cooperate?'

'They're considering the matter.'

Cato shook his head.

'Chin up,' said Earle. 'The minister assisting happens to be the local member down here. Wheels within wheels. As long as the information doesn't pertain to something awful being done to a foreigner you'll probably be given access, albeit redacted here and there.'

'Fingers crossed.' Cato studied the photos of the two dead men. 'I think there's a case for merging the enquiries now.'

'Your call,' she said. 'Boss.'

***

'I slipped and fell.'

Brian had a split lip and grazes on his knuckles. Mason just had the grazes on his knuckles. They'd returned as it was getting dark. Earlier, Driscoll had taken a drive up and down the road adjacent to the beach but there'd been no sign of them. He'd set about preparing a barbie, and if they hadn't shown for dinner he was going to call Aunty and abort the whole thing, go into protective custody with whoever seemed the least dangerous.

'Went for a walk up the fluted cape,' said Mason. 'Beautiful.'

Driscoll pointed at Mason's knuckles. 'You fall over as well?'

'Gets steep up there. Took a tumble on the way down.' He nudged Mira. 'That right, babe?'

'Yes,' she said, eyes downcast.

There'd obviously been a fight and Mason, predictably, came off best.

'Who started it?' said Driscoll shovelling meat onto plates. 'What was it about?'

'Nothing,' said Brian.

'Water under the bridge, mate.' Mason helped himself to some salad.

'Eat up.' Driscoll turned to Mason. 'You and me need to have a talk after your feed.'

'Too easy.'

The meal was eaten in sullen silence. Mason had attempted small talk but he too gave up after a short while. Brian and Mira set about clearing up, and Driscoll nodded for Mason to join him in a walk.

'So,' he said, once they were out of earshot. 'You going to tell me what the fight was about?'

Mason chuckled. 'Prick was looking funny at Mira. I told him to stop perving. He took a couple of swings. Even connected with one. I swung back, harder and on target.'

'That's it?'

'Yep.'

'What were you doing hanging out with the Timorese militias back in ninety-nine?'

Mason stopped. 'Been googling me? I thought we were staying off-grid?'

'Answer the question.'

'Obeying orders.'

'Whose?'

'The Dark Lords'. Look mate, you've obviously read the charge sheet and it's nonsense. No detail, no dates even. I wasn't the only *malae* in town then. Somebody's trying to set me up.'

'Why?'

'Why do you think? That's what we're doing here, isn't it?'

Driscoll shook his head. 'The accusations predate your whistleblowing.'

'It's still bullshit.'

'Does Mira know about the militias link?'

'No.'

'How's the trade-off going? Will they drop it in return for you keeping schtum on the bugging?'

'Still under consideration.'

'And if you get your way? Where does that leave us?'

'I'll give you a heads-up in good time.'

'Not that simple though, is it? Brian complicates things.'

'Not really. His documents have been seized; they can just disappear when it comes down to it. He can be discredited, not that he seems to know or understand anything anyway.'

'And Mira?'

'Was lied to by a deluded fantasist rogue agent with a grudge.'

'Which leaves only me,' said Driscoll. 'And I still haven't worked out who I'm dangerous to and why.'

Mason grinned. 'Better get your thinking cap on, then, eh? You don't want to die not knowing.'

And now here they were the next morning packed up again to move on. Driscoll had explained the encounter with the local cops in Huonville and how that might trigger alarm bells for those tapped into state police computer systems. Mason and Mira sat in the back holding hands – sweet, creepy, or pathetic depending on your world view. Brian sat in front, nursing his grazed knuckles and picking absent-mindedly at the scab forming on his split lip. He seemed relieved to be on the road again.

'Buckle up everybody,' said Driscoll.

***

Exhausted as she was, Sharon couldn't sleep. Something about Phil's phone call and his words 'Timor is looming large'. It bothered her. That demented, terrified man they'd taken off the plane from Darwin one night. The next: a deflated and dispirited body swinging in the breeze under the bridge, haloed by the crane lights from the harbour. Something nagged at her about the way the events unfolded over those two days; about her involvement, about Phil's. What was it? Outside she could hear Ella laughing, telling Julie to push her higher on the garden swing. As a family, they'd come a long way in the last year or so. Phil had hit rock bottom after the attack on his son Jake and it nearly finished them all. But they'd clawed their way back. True, both of them trying to hold down jobs such as theirs put them under the kind of renewed pressure they could do without. But, for the most part, it worked. Another triumphant yell from outside. So far, Ella didn't seem to be overly affected by it, but with Sharon moving back into Investigations – would that tip the balance?

She'd lost her train of thought. Timor. That bloke Reinado. Something didn't fit. She was all set for a quiet night in International and then they got a call from Qantas Domestic about a disruptive passenger on the incoming Darwin flight. The local uniforms would meet him and deal with it, she was told. Her job was oversight and liaison. He was a mess. Red-faced, snotty, crying, yelling, hair dishevelled, clothes torn. In the zeal to restrain him some fellow passengers, or crew, had taken the opportunity to smack him around a bit. There was a graze on his cheek below the left eye and his lips were puffed.

While the uniforms attended to Reinado, Sharon had got the lowdown from Greg, the hostie-in-charge of the cabin crew. 'He'd been drinking before he got on at Darwin but it was high-spirits tipsy back then. We all agreed to monitor and limit his intake if necessary. Unfortunately, there were also stops in Kununurra and Broome where he had the opportunity to reload out of our supervision. An hour out of Broome he started to get stroppy.'

'Stroppy?'

'Arguing with passengers around him, demanding more drink, which we refused. Abusing cabin staff when we asked him to calm down and behave.'

'At what point did you feel the need to get serious?'

'He settled for a while after the initial telling. Dropped off to sleep. Then we hit turbulence over the Gascoyne, and he jumped up in the aisle, ignored the seatbelt sign and refused our instructions to be seated.' Greg sighed. 'A couple of his neighbours in adjacent seats and rows were telling him to sit down, and after that it all kicked off. On for young and old.'

'So up to that point he's drunk and belligerent.' Sharon had gestured towards the figure being cuffed and led away. 'By the time he gets here he's a blubbering mess.'

Greg nodded. 'Didn't like being restrained that's for sure. Something clicked inside when he was being held down by so many.' An almost visible shudder. 'Primeval stuff. Groaning, wailing. Horrible. Upset a few kids. Few adults too, come to that.'

'Thanks.' Sharon had taken contact details. Somebody would follow up with Greg and the rest of the crew for detailed statements.

'For all his aggro manner, I still think he didn't actually mean any harm.'

'What makes you say that?'

Greg shrugged. 'Hostie's intuition?'

They'd driven in convoy to Fiona Stanley Hospital and Sharon observed the booking-in procedure. They'd all swapped contact details and gone their separate ways. Reinado could be heard jabbering away – they'll kill me, they won't stop, you need to keep those doors and windows locked. On a loop, variations on the theme interspersed with sobbing and angry yelling in his mother tongue. The shift from tipsy drunk to troublesome drunk made sense; it was a standard through-line. But the meltdown to paranoid terrified wreck suggested a cocktail of medication or other drugs in the mix. That was the assumption but when they'd checked him in and emptied his pockets there was nothing. The luggage? She should follow that up. If there was nothing on his person, then what did he take and when?

It was a state investigation now. Fremantle Detectives, Phil's old colleagues. Funny nobody had given her a call yet to ask her what she knew. She jerked fully awake now. She had remembered another thing. That slip of paper with Phil's name and number wasn't there when they got Reinado to empty his pockets at the hospital. He'd obtained it sometime in the next twenty-four hours before he died.

***

Driscoll couldn't see much point staying in Tasmania. The enemy, both camps, already knew they were here courtesy of Brian's phone. It may as well be Devil's Island. Maybe Bomber Jacket and friends had already effectively closed the airports and the ferry terminal at Devonport. Either way, they had to get back to the mainland, to bigger population centres where they could more easily be anonymous. Besides, they had to be up in Darwin by the weekend. They needed to start driving now, but therein lay another problem. There were only so many roads in and out of Darwin and they could easily be monitored. Cross that bridge later. In the meantime, he was hightailing it for Devonport and the night ferry back to Melbourne. If that was a no-go they might need to find a friendly boatman to do the job from somewhere else on the north coast.

It occurred to him that they, whoever they were, would be smarter to let them get on the ferry rather than cause a fuss at the dock. Once on board they'd be even more vulnerable and with nowhere to run. It was a risk they might be obliged to take.

'So we're leaving Tasmania?' Brian pulled a bag of party mix lollies out of the glove box and offered them around.

Driscoll took a few. 'That's the idea.'

'Makes sense.'

'Glad you agree.' They'd only just lunched in Launceston and more food was the last thing he needed right now but the afternoon slump had kicked in.

'Happy to give you a break from driving there, mate.' Mason leaned forward and plunged his hand into the lolly bag.

'I'm good,' said Driscoll. 'Cheers.'

'They will be waiting for us.' Mira shook her head. 'It is useless. We should never have come here in the first place.'

'A lot of people say that about Tassie.' Mason chuckled. 'Bit harsh, though.'

'Not everything is a joke.'

'Sorry, babe.'

'Don't call me that.'

Driscoll watched her in the rear-view. It was like some weird game of musical nervous breakdowns. Brian had his turn. Now Mira seemed to be heading the same way. Face pinched, eyes red, nerves pulsing in her neck and at her temple. He tugged his water bottle out from its slot and passed it back. 'Have a drink.'

'I don't need one.'

'Yes, you do.' He explained his thinking. If it looked like the ferry port was being monitored, and he would hopefully spot the signs, they could try and get a boat somewhere else on the north coast and ditch the four-wheel drive. But if it all looked clear they'd drive on the ferry and hope for the best.

'What if that's exactly what they want?' said Mason. 'Fish in a barrel.'

Cheers, thanks for that. 'Then we'll take our chances and make sure we're always in the public eye. Keep them accountable.'

'Sounds like a plan,' said Mason, insincerely.

Driscoll hoped so. He really bloody hoped so.

'Another?' Brian rumpled the lolly bag in Mason's direction. 'There's a snake left in there with your name on it.'

***

Cato received a batch of stuff about Doug Peters' career at CPS in his inbox around midafternoon. Yes, large parts of it did seem to be redacted. There were the digital equivalents of black marker pen through whole lines, usually to blank out the names of other people: colleagues, inmates, whomever. But for now it was all he was going to get, so it would have to do. The file was flimsy, running to no more than four pages. It included basic information like Peters' date of birth, tax file number, salary level, nominated super fund and job description. All of that on page one. The rest, just short of three pages, listed his postings and any incident reports involving him. After a one-month induction period including visits to other CPS-managed facilities in the Eastern States and at Yongah Hill in Northam, north-east of Perth, he was given his one and only posting lasting two years at the North West Point Immigration Detention Centre on Christmas Island. There, after the first six months in the general admissions and receptions section, Peters moved two more times, supervising specific blocks or areas of the detention facility which seemed to be colour-coded red, gold, white and green.

At this stage it looked like there were about forty male asylum seekers mixed in with around two hundred men who had served time in Australian prisons and were awaiting deportation to their country of origin. The latter group, nicknamed 501s as a reference to their visa status, comprised men mainly of New Zealand or UK extraction. Australia was re-transporting its convicts. So the asylum seekers were vastly outnumbered by a lot of hard, angry blokes and that was without even counting the guards. Doug Peters would have found himself in a tense and volatile situation and earning every cent of his hundred and thirty thousand–plus salary. The report redactions were so numerous towards the last page the pattern resembled a Rorschach inkblot test. The designated area of operations Peters supervised during this final nine month period in 2013 was called White 1 – the punishment and isolation block.

It looked like there were six reports featuring Peters and unnamed others. There had been a number of 'Code Black' incidents which Cato presumed was some sort of emergency, like a fight or a meltdown. These had necessitated intervention by the ERT – Emergency Response Team – comprising several censored names. The outcome and timing of each incident was noted – so-and-so pacified and placed in isolation, calm and order restored, certain minor injuries requiring medical attention by the FIFO nurse or doctor. Cuts, broken noses, lost teeth, dislocated and broken fingers or wrists or ankles. Concussion, cracked ribs. Sometimes the injuries looked like they could have been inflicted by the 501s and other times by the ERT. But the final incident report went a step further. The only word visible in a sea of black redactions was the word 'deceased'. Once again, it seemed, somebody had died in custody on Doug Peters' watch.

***

Driscoll didn't like what he saw. They'd parked up the road from the Devonport ferry terminal on a rising side street offering a view of the approach to the boarding ramp and the docked ship *Spirit of Tasmania*. It was dark, just gone six thirty, and the boat was due to depart for its overnight sailing an hour from now. He'd bought a set of binoculars during the lunch stop in Launceston. They weren't the best but they would do. It being a midweek out-of-season overnight sailing, the traffic was light but progress still seemed painfully slow. With each vehicle required to have its boarding passes on the dash, there should have been randomly selected checks and a lot more waved through to keep the flow going. There was an enlarged police presence too – four or five extra uniforms standing around and a vanload parked just off-ramp behind a container.

'Not fancy it?' Mason had just got back in the vehicle after a smoke break. He brought the smell of it with him.

'No.'

'So?'

Brian wrinkled his nose and wound his window down. 'We have no choice. We need to be in Darwin by the weekend, and if we're driving all the way we need to keep moving.'

'Keen as mustard,' said Mason. 'Eh, mate.'

'The sooner this is all over, the better.'

Driscoll was glad to see this new-found gung-ho resolve of Brian's but it needed to be tempered. 'It will be over even sooner if we go on that boat tonight.'

'So?' said Mason again.

Driscoll didn't know. Why the hell had he brought them here in the first place? It had been Aunty's idea; she had this friend with a house in Hobart, she said. And who would expect them to head south instead of north? Maybe without Brian's treacherous phone it might have worked. Now it had just led them into a trap. They didn't need to be killed or locked up. They just needed to be stopped from leaving Tasmania until The Hague committee had been and gone – self-imposed exile to Van Diemen's Land.

Driscoll started the engine. 'Let's go.'

'Where?' said Mira. 'Not on that ship, surely?'

'No. Not on the ship.'

Brian shook his head. 'This is turning into a bad joke.'

'I'll get you to Darwin,' said Driscoll. 'Trust me.'

13

Wednesday 2nd May

Cato woke refreshed. This thing, ever so slowly, was coming together. His room at the motel had a view out over Koombana Bay and a balcony where he now sat with his room-service delivery of coffee, cereal and toast. The ocean was once again autumn-flat and two swimmers carved their way across the surface. A short way out from them a dolphin rode shotgun. DI Pavlou had agreed, the two enquiries should now be merged. She hadn't even kicked up a fuss about him going behind her back with the CPS thing. Admitting she was wrong might not be on the cards but neither was getting stuck into Cato. It would be good to know who the deceased was in the Christmas Island incident report though. For all they knew, that person's friends or relatives might have had some unfinished business with Peters. Or perhaps CPS colleagues from the ERT who'd maybe been heavy-handed and decided to make Peters their enemy. Who could say? Only CPS probably, and their censor-in-chief behind the redactor pen.

He'd also had a late-night chat with Sharon during one of her breaks at the airport. More food for thought. How had that slip of paper found its way into Paul Reinado's pocket in the twenty-four hours between being taken off the Darwin flight and ending up swinging under a bridge in Fremantle? Sharon would enquire further as it was in her remit.

'So if the enquiry is to be merged you can do some delegating and get yourself home, right?'

'Yeah, I think Pavlou's examining the logistics in the morning.'

'Great. I'll see you sometime tomorrow then?'

'Hopefully.' Cato had detected an extra lightness in her tone which, in his experience, often masked an underlying disturbance. 'I'll keep you posted.'

They'd chatted on further about the stuff of life and then her break was over. 'Love you,' Sharon had said, closing the call. 'You know that, don't you?'

Yes, he'd said. He did. 'Love you back.'

So what would he be doing in Bunbury today? Nikki Earle had her team following up the new leads – the club connections, Ryan Hodgson's sighting of somebody possibly walking away from the death house and a car starting up around the corner a minute later. Chris Thornton, in consultation with his Bunbury counterpart, had taken a look at Bevan Drummond's telco and financial records and was sending through his observations this morning. Cato decided to read that before making his next move, be it homeward bound or not.

On cue, a call came through from Nikki Earle. 'You were right about the burners. A neighbour of Drummond, over his back fence, found a mobile in her garden this morning.'

'She only found it now?'

'She keeps chooks. Free range. They scratch, kick shit around, dig. She found it when she locked them in to do some watering and weeding in peace.'

'How did it get there?'

'Maybe he chucked it over when he heard death come knocking.'

'Anything on it?'

'Messages and calls, all to and from the one number – Peters, we assume. Want to come and have a look?'

'Shower and brekky. See you in half an hour.'

***

Cato made it in twenty-five minutes. Earle handed him a five-page printout – the first two were records of the call times, and the last three were the actual messages. His primary interest was the latter. He accepted a mug of tea and they adjourned to a side room.

'The calls and messages don't go back beyond early March.' Earle dragged up a chair in the cramped room and they sat knee to knee poring over the paperwork. 'We're following up on the numbers, looks like prepaids with Vodafone.'

The first one. **Testing testing** from Peters.

All good. Smiley face from Drummond.

A couple of jokes about Drummond's familiarity with emoticons. **I was a high school teacher**, he explains.

Then nothing for a couple of weeks save for the odd check-in message back and forth. **Any news? All good?** The room was getting stuffy so Earle opened the door. José cast a glance their way through the gap and smiled to himself. 'Third week in March,' noted Cato. 'Thursday the twenty-second. Look.'

She slid back into her seat. 'Peters: "Had a break-in at my place while I was out this morning. Nothing taken but left a mess." And this wasn't reported?' asked Earle.

'Not to my knowledge,' said Cato. 'I'll get Thornton to check.' He knocked off a text to that effect.

'Drummond: "Did they find it?" No, comes the reply. Smiley face.'

'Find what?' wondered Cato aloud. 'We need to follow that up at both ends.'

'Noted.' Earle pointed to the next message.

We need to tell someone. 'Drummond's getting jumpy.'

Tell who? Peters responds. **Nobody will believe us.**

We can't just do nothing.

Calm down. Let me think.

They read on. Nothing for over a week taking them through the Easter long weekend. Then from Peters on April second. **Coming your way soon. Got a spare room?** And on Sunday eighth again from Peters. **There by 5. Meet in Hungry Hollow Tav**

'I'll get that followed up,' said Earle. 'CCTV, et cetera.'

'No more messages after that,' noted Cato. 'Until the day they died.'

***

Driscoll won the next game but wondered if the old man had let him.

'More coffee?' said Yakov, clearing away the chess pieces.

'Great.' Their view from the balcony overlooking Blackmans Bay was stunning: tree-clad hills tumbling to a plate glass sea. He could see Mason and Mira walking along the sand, his arm protectively draped over her shoulder, her arm encircling his hips. He was a calming influence on her, Driscoll had to admit. She'd been close to cracking up when he told them about his plan to drive all the way back south of Hobart to take Yakov up on his offer. The old man had been relaxed about the emergency request to house four almost-strangers. But maybe being born in a concentration camp gives you a different perspective on life.

'Strangers?' he'd said. 'But you and I have played chess together. Sailed together.' Yakov returned to the balcony with a fresh plunger of coffee. He nodded back at the couch inside. 'Brian sleeps late. It's nearly ten o'clock.'

'I think he was awake a lot in the night. He worries.'

'Yes,' said Yakov. 'I noticed that.'

Driscoll hadn't told the old man why they were there and the old man hadn't asked. For him it was enough that they needed help and that he was able to offer it by way of a spare room and couches in his spacious widower's apartment.

'We really appreciate this.'

'My pleasure, really.'

'May I?' Driscoll gestured towards Yakov's dusty old laptop and his mobile.

'Of course.' The man knew only that Driscoll and his friends were in some kind of danger and needed to avoid being tracked. 'Help yourself. The computer I keep mainly for an online chess group.' He smiled. 'I'm in the middle of a very intriguing game with the former Venezuelan grandmaster. The phone?' He waved his hand dismissively. 'My daughter tries to keep me on a leash all the way from Melbourne.'

First Driscoll logged into his new email account. Nothing from Aunty. Already the spammers had found him with job offers in India, a massive inheritance from Zambia and an offer of marriage from the Ukraine; plus some Viagra if he needed it. He logged off and picked up Yakov's old Nokia to phone Aunty's secure number.

'Where are you?'

'It's a secret.'

'Rory, mate. This is serious.'

'You don't need to tell me. Look, the gorillas who called at the house, supposedly for our own protection. Are they still in play?'

'Yes.'

'They make it complicated, Aunty. How about they back off for a while?'

'They're there as a favour, you know.'

Some favour. 'Let us get to Darwin with just the one set of problems to worry about. If they want to step in on our arrival, so be it. I'm juggling too many balls right now.'

'I'll see what I can do.' Then he told her about the lockdown at Devonport and probably the airports at Hobart and Launceston too. No doubt that would have been officially sanctioned. 'I won't be able to get that lifted, Rory.'

Inside, Brian was stirring, shuffling sleepy-eyed to the kitchen to flick on the kettle.

'Leave it in place as a diversion. If they think we're still on the island, that gives us some time and space. Meantime, do you know anybody who can get us on a boat or private plane out of here? Time's running out for the Darwin road trip.'

Once again, she'd see what she could do. 'What do you make of the stuff I sent you?'

'Mason's playing us, especially Mira. He's got her wrapped around his little finger.'

'If an accident happened to him, a lot of this would go away.'

Brian rapped a knuckle on the balcony window and made the sign for tea. Driscoll shook his head and mouthed no thanks. 'What are you saying, Aunty?'

'You heard.'

***

Cato looked again at those last text messages that had passed between Peters and Drummond in the hours before they met their terrible deaths. They saw it coming, he realised. Earle had left him alone in the room while she arranged various follow-ups including the new leads from the remaining SMSs.

Drummond, the afternoon of his murder. **Followed all way 2 shops and back**

Peters. **Description?**

Drummond. **White saloon. Commodore? Middle-aged, brown hair,**

bland. And a rego that Earle was having traced.

Peters. **Still around?**

Drummond. No

Peters. **Keep me posted**

Peters. Early evening. **All good?**

Peters. At ten fifty. Bev. **Tried calling. All OK?**

Peters. At eleven. **FFS, call me, mate. Getting worried**

By now Drummond was most likely dead.

Peters. **Twenty to midnight. Bev R U OK?**

White saloon. Commodore? Middle-aged, brown hair, bland. 'Got that rego,' said Earle. 'Hire car booked at Perth Airport using ID of a person who doesn't seem to exist.'

'CCTV at hire desk?'

'On its way.'

'That car's been driven down from Perth and then back up for the Peters murder. Send the details through to Thornton for tracking.'

'Already done.'

In the meantime, Thornton had sent through his analysis of Drummond's email and internet traffic along with his ordinary mobile phone and landline use. But this was only for the last six months. They'd need to go further back. Much, much further. Along with the time spent on secondment to Christmas Island six years earlier and the trip to East Timor another seven years before that. Doing a search of the previous six months, Thornton had found no connection with Doug Peters which, if they had innocently renewed their old acquaintance over the years, should have been evident before Peters obtained those burner phones in March. Surely the caution wasn't necessary from day one. Or was it? The same applied to the mobile and landline – Doug Peters' official number never featured. This six-month period contained some work emails, he was still doing casual teaching, along with other stuff relating to family and friends mainly through the clubs and groups he was a member of. Cato decided to focus on the Rotary Club connection in lieu of older records becoming available but there was nothing of interest except for an email notification from Australia Post the Wednesday following the Easter long weekend. Apparently, his parcel would be delivered that day. That was definitely worth a follow-up. Otherwise, it was less than slim pickings. Impatient, Cato got on the phone to Thornton.

'This Drummond telco stuff is next to useless. We need everything back to around two thousand and five or six, at least.'

'That's huge.'

'It's what we need. Make it a priority.'

'Along with all the others,' grumbled Thornton.

Cato bit his tongue. 'Thanks, Chris. Love your work.'

Thornton grunted. 'While you're waiting, check out his internet use for February and March. Might make you happier.' The phone went dead.

Cato did as he was told. Thornton was right. It did make him happier.

***

Driscoll got word from Aunty late that afternoon. A plane could fly them out of the George Town private aerodrome up on the north coast the following day. With a few hops it would take them all the way to an airstrip at Noonamah just outside Darwin.

'You need to be at George Town no later than four tomorrow arvo.' She gave him a name and mobile. 'Tell them Pauline sent you.'

'Thanks, Aunty.'

'Leave the vehicle with him. He'll burn it.'

'Shame, it drives nicely.' He didn't mention the numerous scratches and broken wing mirror. Driscoll shivered, eager to get back indoors. He could see his fellow travellers through the window of the Salty Dog restaurant at Kingston Beach, next bay round the headland from Blackmans: Mason, Mira, Brian and Yakov, all studying menus while they awaited his return. In truth, it would have been safer to stay home but Driscoll wanted to do something nice for old Yakov. Besides, bad guys out and about on a cold Wednesday night in Kingston? You'd have to be unlucky.

'Worked out what to do with Willie?' said Aunty in passing.

'Sabotage his parachute?'

'It doesn't need to be so final.' A pause. 'Or maybe it does.'

'I'm not convinced,' said Driscoll. 'Maybe it's my parachute that needs snipping. I can't see where I fit in, but perhaps you can do some digging?'

'There's definitely nothing stands out from your time there?'

'I wasn't much more than a beancounter, logistics nerd. You were right to snap me up at the end of that gig. I was going stir crazy, would have joined any passing circus.'

'Thanks, Rory.' The sound of a cigarette lighter flicking and a big inhalation. 'Maybe it's personal rather than professional. You didn't have a fling with anybody, did you? Break a heart here and there? You used to have a reputation.'

Used to. Touché. 'I'm sure I was an absolute gentleman at all times.'

A dragon's snort. 'I'll make some enquiries. Make sure you're at the aerodrome on time. And if you need to kill or maim Willie Mason en route, you have my blessing. Even if he isn't the key to this, he was always a pain in the arse.'

'Slash and burn – the Aussie management style.' Driscoll hung up and joined the others for an early dinner.

Mason asked for an update so Driscoll gave him one, minus the Aunty recommendations. He whistled appreciatively. 'Flying all the way. Sweet. Bit over the old road trip TBH.'

'So we'll definitely get there on time?' Brian's spirits too were raised.

'All things being equal.'

Mira took a sip of her Coke and said nothing.

Yakov lifted his wine glass in salute. 'I will be sorry to see you all go so soon, but good luck and safe journey.'

'Cheers,' they all clinked glasses.

***

In mid-February, Bevan Drummond had suddenly taken a great interest in Timor-Leste and, in particular, the events around the 1999 independence plebiscite. He'd spent best part of a weekend trawling firstly through stories of atrocities by the Indonesian military in concert with allied Timorese militiamen, then homing in on those featuring one militia group in particular. He had downloaded dozens of articles and photographs plus reports by human rights groups, the UN, even one by an Australian embassy political analyst stationed in Dili at the time. Cato, as he retraced those steps through the search engine, felt the darkness closing in. He'd called Sharon and said he'd be in Bunbury at least one more night.

'Pity,' she'd said. 'Something come up?'

'Possibly. Hopefully.'

It had been a stilted, awkward call and they both put it down to exhaustion and stress. He'd returned to the motel, ordered a room-service dinner of pizza and beer and logged on to follow the trail Bevan Drummond had taken. Events in Timor twenty years earlier were clearly the key to the deaths of Drummond, Peters and Paul Reinado. But among all the blood and horror of these images on his screen, what precisely had occurred to visit similar carnage upon these old men in suburban WA all this time later?

Drummond's focus seemed to be on a massacre of around two hundred people that had occurred just a week after the referendum. It had been in a church in a small town west of Dili: a familiar tale of terrified civilians – men, women and children – seeking their last refuge in a House of God and it counting for nothing. The church had been set alight and tear gas lobbed through broken windows, and when the occupants fled they were shot and stabbed by members of the surrounding militia with the Indonesian army looking on. Those who survived had been trucked over the border into West Timor, forced to remain with Indonesia despite the referendum result. Some returned in later years, some didn't. To the best of Cato's knowledge, all this happened at least five or six years before Drummond and Peters had set foot in the country on their Rotarian charity work. Why would Bevan's attention be drawn to an incident, horrific as it was, which predated his involvement in Timor?

The internet search had focused on one name: João Ximenes, leader of the militia in that area. A barrel-chested man with a mischievous smile and an unfashionable mullet, according to the photos Drummond downloaded. He had a fearsome reputation which would grow with the savage and systematic violence unleashed in the few months after the population voted for freedom and before the international peacekeeping force arrived. His militia came to define the terror behind that very Indonesian of terms – to run amok. And how he loved the attention, holding the foreign media crews in his charismatic thrall. Then, just as quickly as he rose to infamy, he seemed to disappear from view. After retreating to the border territories following the intervention of the Australia-led military task force, he doesn't appear in Drummond's search until two years later in the inner circle of an Indonesian presidential candidate. Nothing again until around two thousand and five, when he is part of an Indonesian delegation to a petrochemical conference in Darwin. Then quiet again for over a decade until this February's oil and gas industry conference in Perth where he is pictured at an opening night cocktail party in the company of leading players from state and federal parliament, and oil company bigwigs – familiar faces among them. Twenty years on, his barrel chest has flattened out as his stomach has grown to meet it. The hair is short, businesslike and grey. But the infectious smile remains.

It's him, thought Cato – João Ximenes. He is the man behind the slaughter and mutilation of the two pensioners and the stringing up of Paul Reinado.

But why?

**

Mira and Mason had retired to the spare bedroom and Brian was curled up on the couch staring vacantly at some trash on TV. Yakov and Driscoll had retreated to the balcony with the chessboard and a glass of whisky each. They were rugged up against the cold with extra jumpers and beanies and a doona for Yakov.

For all that, the old man was bright-eyed in readiness for their final game. 'The decider.' Yakov took a sip of his whisky and eyed Driscoll as he did the same. 'You like it?'

'The taste of peat, smoke and a cold river somewhere in Scotland. What's not to like?'

'Expensive, but I'm allowed to indulge myself at my age. White. Your move.'

It was a companionable silence. The sipping of whisky, a breeze off the Channel, the occasional passing car, and the click and clack of pieces moving on the wooden board. Driscoll detected a hint of melancholy in the old man. He said as much.

'You think so?'

'None of my business,' said Driscoll. 'It's the whisky talking.'

'Don't blame the whisky.' Yakov plucked one of Driscoll's bishops out of the game. 'It's a strange situation. I've taken on my parents' philosophy all my life – live life to the full, survive, defy those who would try to take it from you.' A sip of the amber fluid and a deliberately expressive smacking of lips. 'And so you survive and thrive and become old enough to be invisible.'

'Check,' said Driscoll.

The old man blocked it with a pawn. 'There was a time I would have been curious and wanted to know more about the trouble you're in. Perhaps thrown my lot in with you, made you my cause.'

'Best not to. I'm not worth it.'

Yakov shrugged and took one of Driscoll's pawns out of play. 'It wouldn't have mattered, then or now, whether you judged it a good idea or not. It would have been my decision to man the barricades. Check.'

Driscoll leaned in and saw that he was three moves off being beaten. Again he was ready to tip his king and concede but remembered the old man didn't like that. 'You've got me.'

'See it through to the end, though.'

He did and it played out as expected. 'Congratulations, champ.' They shook hands.

'One day you must tell me the full story of how and why we met, including the ending.' Yakov swallowed the rest of his whisky and blinked against the fiery taste. 'You promise?'

'I promise.'

14

Thursday 3rd May

Cato was headed back up the Forrest Highway to Perth after an early breakfast at the motel. He would probably cross paths with a couple of southbound cars full of Major Crime D's sent by Pavlou to muscle in on the Bunbury end of what was now a double murder enquiry. It was not inconceivable that Fremantle's Reinado case too would be brought under their remit. The irony wasn't lost on Cato after all those years as a Fremantle detective trying to keep Major Crime at bay. Last night Thornton had run João Ximenes through the system and it turned out he'd flown into and out of Darwin, with connections to Perth, in the days preceding and following the deaths of Drummond, Peters and Reinado. As far as anybody knew, he was now based back in Dili and rehabilitated in the new united Timor-Leste. The bad old days were, it seemed, all just bloodstained water under the bridge.

This update was courtesy of the former Australian embassy political analyst who now lectured at UWA. Associate Professor Steven Brown was an acclaimed expert on the Timorese and Indonesian militias and was very much looking forward to meeting Cato for lunch at the University Club to enlighten him further.

'Fascinating,' Brown had said. 'Can't wait.'

To Cato's relief they didn't meet upstairs in the rarefied atmosphere of the members' dining room – it would have been like gatecrashing a golf club. It was a sunny, wind-free day so they adjourned to the outside area of the downstairs cafe with the plebs. Steven Brown sported jeans and a checked shirt and his grey hair was close-cropped. He had the wiry physique of a competitive cyclist. They both ordered pasta. Cato briefly outlined his interest, skirting around the issues which might be legally problematic should Brown ever be called to testify. 'You were in Dili during the INTERFET mission, right?'

'Indeed,' nodded Brown. 'And just as you've just danced around a couple of sensitive issues on your agenda I might have to do the same. But somehow we'll get there, eh?'

Cato described the murders he was investigating. 'The bodies were mutilated, although I can't go into detail.'

Their pastas arrived and Brown twirled some fettucine on his fork. 'A display element? It was a common signature of the militias, the taking of heads, fomenting terror.'

'A warning to others?'

'Exactly. There's a misconception that the militias were the bastard child of Indonesian military brought into being just to try and cow the independence vote. But there's a longer history going way back through the colonial days under Portugal. We're talking hundreds of years of local warlords and gangster fiefdoms. The Indonesians just used the existing tools at hand.'

Cato didn't get the significance of that and said so.

'The significance is that if you understand where your man Ximenes came from, then you understand where he is today, and why.' Ximenes, he explained, was from a long and proud line of *liurai* or lords of that district and they survived and prospered over many generations because they had learned how to deal with the occupier or coloniser.

'Collaborators?'

Brown chided Cato for his oversimplification but conceded the basic premise. 'They might take up arms against the oppressors as they sometimes did under Portuguese rule. Locally they would be seen as heroes for standing up for the people. Likewise, if they found a way of minimising the harm to the local population, and perhaps scoring points against rivals, they might cooperate as happened under Japanese occupation in World War Two.' Timor, like most nations, he explained, is a country of social divisions, petty jealousies, and festering feuds held together by a vulnerable and fragile ideal of a unified homeland or *patria*. The Easterners and the Westerners don't like or trust each other, city versus country, old versus young. 'It's the same class and geographical divisions you might get in Australia, France, UK, USA or anywhere. And as in all these places the local lord, strong man or whatever, is often what people know and understand and come to rely on for better or worse.'

'And Ximenes, for all he was on the wrong side of history at referendum time and probably guilty of atrocities, is now back in the fold?'

'He did a very public *mea culpa* a few years ago as part of a staged national reconciliation process. Shed some crocodile tears for the TV cameras, donated bigly, as they say these days, to some charities and political coffers, visited orphanages. Made amends.'

'Why?'

'He wasn't prospering in Indonesia. They'd said they would look after him but governments and favourites change. The reconstruction and nation-building back in Timor offered lucrative returns for a man such as him.'

'Is he capable of murder, or arranging a murder?'

Brown pushed his plate away and chuckled. 'You kidding?' He took out his phone, scrolled through until he found what he was after, and handed it over to Cato. 'I dug this out this morning.'

An archive photo of a grinning Ximenes, holding up a severed head which was missing the ears and eyes.

***

Driscoll buckled himself in, checked his fellow passengers in the seats behind, and gave the thumbs-up to the pilot. The propellers roared into action and the six-seater Cessna taxied towards take-off. The pilot was called Charlie. She was in her late sixties, early seventies maybe, grey hair tied back in a ponytail. She reminded Driscoll of a teacher he once had at primary school, focused so much on the task at hand that you may as well not have been there. That suited him. Clouds had crept in during the day and the wind was strengthening. Crossing Bass Strait on a big ferry could be hairy enough in bad weather. In a small plane? He turned his mind to other things as the aircraft climbed into a bumpy, darkening sky.

Yakov had clearly been sad to see them go. Yes, he was starved of company but there was something else at play. A sense of foreboding like he believed they would never see each other again. Not just because they were mere acquaintances passing briefly through each other's lives.

'Remember your promise?' he'd said as he shook Driscoll's hand one last time. 'I want to know the whole story one day.'

'You will.' Driscoll had placed his hand on the old man's shoulder. 'Make sure you're here to hear it when I return.' When a Nazi death camp survivor displays a sense of foreboding, it's worth heeding. Driscoll tucked the thought away in a safe compartment way back in his head.

The drive from Hobart back up to the north coast aerodrome had been uneventful. They'd left the four-wheel drive in the care of Charlie's boss, an old contact of Aunty's, who would keep it undercover for a few days then leave it burning somewhere where it would easily be found to sow confusion and buy time. Driscoll hadn't taken Aunty's advice to hurt Mason and put him out of the game. Given how close Mason and Mira had become it would only complicate things further – she'd want to be wherever he was. No, he'd deliver them all to Darwin and whatever came up, he'd deal with it there.

The journey to Darwin would be about fifteen to twenty hours of actual flying time. Charlie needed rest and replenishment, they all needed food and toilet stops, and the idea was to do some zigzagging so that the logged flight plan wouldn't give them away too early. It was now Thursday afternoon and it could take right up until sometime Saturday before they rocked up in the Territory. Aunty had organised another safe house there so they wouldn't attract attention by checking into a hotel. The Hague subcommittee would be holding their week-long hearings in the Supreme Court building in Darwin following in the footsteps of Lindy Chamberlain, and of Bradley John Murdoch, who'd killed an English backpacker to achieve his fifteen minutes of infamy. Darwin court house was the home of iconic Aussie crime and punishment, and a fitting place to deliberate upon whether or not Australia had committed grand larceny with the oil reserves of a tiny neighbouring fledgling nation state.

Wind and rain buffeted the Cessna. Driscoll had the sensation of being a cork in a washing machine. 'You do this a lot?' he asked Charlie.

'Flying? Well yes, you see I'm a pilot. It's my job.'

'Sorry,' said Driscoll. 'Stupid question.' Another broadside slap of wind and his knuckles whitened on the cissy handle. 'Been doing it a while?'

'Forty years – although I took thirty out to have a family. Once they left and my husband died I decided to take up where I left off.' She gave him a sideways glance. 'I usually know who I'm taking and precisely where and why, and I tend to take the most direct line.' She flicked some switches on the dashboard, cutting off the headsets of those in the back. 'How about you?'

'Me?'

'Yes, do you do this a lot?'

'Not as much as I used to.'

'And you usually know who you're taking and precisely where and why, and you tend to take the most direct line.' She grinned. 'But not this time, huh?'

'Looks like we're in the same boat. Or plane.'

'Bad weather aside, how dangerous might this get?'

Driscoll shrugged. 'Don't know. Hopefully it's just a delivery and, after that, home you go.'

'A simple delivery? Not with a shottie, a twenty-two and a pistol in play.' Driscoll didn't respond. 'I weighed the bags and checked inside them as is my prerogative.'

'Just a precaution,' he said.

'Fair enough. I'm paid well, although not that well, and I've done a few ghost runs here and there that nobody was meant to know about. But just so you know, I'm in charge in this plane and on this journey. Okay?'

Up to a point, he thought. 'Sure.'

***

It had been a quiet night in Terminal One so far. A group of Poms pre-loading in the bar ahead of their non-stop to London had been paid a visit by uniforms and told to shush and behave or else. Sharon was glad not to be sharing a seventeen-hour flight with them. There were inbounds from Singapore, KL and Hong Kong due around midnight but there was no specific intelligence of miscreants. She had a couple of hours to kill and that suited her fine; she needed the time and space to do some thinking. By the time Phil had got home from his Bunbury trip, she was getting ready to leave for work, and Julie the nanny was reading bedtime stories to Ella. He had good news and bad news. The good? Day off tomorrow. How about a long leisurely romantic lunch out while Julie looks after Ella? Great. The bad?

'I need to go to Timor-Leste.'

'When?'

'In the next few days, soon as we can set a few things up.'

'Like what?'

'Local liaison, checking the rules of engagement, organising interpreter and guide. Stuff like that.'

It brought back memories. They'd met under similar circumstances in Shanghai. That had been the upside but the China trip had also cost his colleague her life. 'How dangerous is this bloke you want to talk to?'

'Fairly.'

'Anybody going with you?'

'This guy José, a D from Bunbury. He speaks Portuguese.' He'd lifted the lid of the upright Kawai. Tinkled absent-mindedly on the piano keys.

'Haven't heard you play for a long while.'

He'd smiled, sadly it seemed. 'Lost touch. Must get back to it one of these days.'

And so Sharon had arrived at work, a tightness in the pit of her stomach, leaving Phil in that distracted state of nervous energy she'd come to recognise when he was deep into a case. To keep her anxieties at bay, she focused on the two things she wanted to know about Paul Reinado: how Phil's number got into his possession, and who gave him the drugs that turned him from drunk to psychotic on that Darwin flight. She checked the time. Approaching ten o'clock. Made the call.

'Patrick McMahon. Fremantle Detectives.'

Sharon introduced herself and told him she had a few loose ends on the Reinado matter.

'Loose ends? At this time of night?' She explained about the slip of paper and the drugs. 'You call them loose ends?'

'Anomalies,' said Sharon. 'Whatever.'

'He could have written down the contact details himself during the time he was released from hospital and found under the bridge. He could have bought a bad batch of chemicals from some sleaze in the Broome departure lounge bar in between flights. Hardly rocket science is it, Agent Wang?'

'How are your enquiries progressing, DI McMahon?'

'Steadily.'

'Have you been able to map out his movements after he left hospital? Established a timeline?'

'Telling me how to do my job?'

'I wouldn't presume. Ease up, mate.'

A sigh. 'We tracked him via his phone which he was given back when he was checked out of Fiona Stanley. He put his travel bag from the plane into a luggage storage place just over the road from the railway station.'

'Did you get it off them?'

'Yep. Nothing of interest. He then wandered around Freo, had a late brekkie on the Strip, sat on the CAT bus for a couple of circuits. Then he hung out in the mall area for a while, then in the library. After that we lost him.'

'What time was this?'

'Late afternoon. His phone went off the system. He was seen leaving the library in the company of another bloke; shorter than him, medium build. There's CCTV but the bloke is aware of it and keeps his head down.'

'Still thinking suicide?'

'Not beyond the bounds.'

'But?'

'But we've had a call from Major Crime and it looks like your hubby is taking an unhealthy interest. Doing a bit of empire-building? Maybe you can pass on a message from me next time you see him?'

'If it's a work matter you can do it yourself.'

'I don't dislike the man. We got on famously last case we worked. But he shouldn't take me for granted.'

'Is that it?'

'I run a tighter ship than he gives me credit for and I've got a few loose ends of my own that need some attention. He's one of them.'

'So you'll look into those anomalies I mentioned then?'

'Think you're smart, don't you?'

Sharon bristled. 'Ever come across a guy called Guthrie?'

'No.'

'Here's some more pillow talk for you. He's a spook and he reckons Reinado was on his payroll.'

'Brilliant, all we need.'

'I'll leave it in your capable hands, DI McMahon.'

***

Cato lay awake wondering about João Ximenes. There was no extradition treaty between the two countries. Timor could choose to assist but was not obliged and any moves to extradite him could end up in a protracted court battle. Besides, as of now, there was insufficient evidence for arrest.

'Have a chat,' Pavlou had said. 'Even if we can't bring him back you might at least get closer to the truth and then we can leave it to the lawyers.'

'What if he doesn't agree to an interview?'

'Then his name, photo and history will be all over the Australian media as a person of interest, and that will ruffle feathers in Canberra and Dili.' Cato liked the sound of that and it showed. 'You see, Philip. You don't always need to go behind my back to get results. Sometimes you just need to do more to convince me.'

'Point taken.'

'Good.'

As anticipated, Sharon had been underwhelmed by the idea of him disappearing yet again. 'How long this time?'

A shrug. 'Few days? Week at most?'

'Maybe I'll take that posting in Investigations after all.'

Revenge? Perhaps, but she had a point. He was going about his business as usual and expecting her to hold the fort. What if she had such a job that demanded likewise?

'Busted,' was all he could say. 'Sorry.'

'No, you're not.'

Hopefully the long luxurious lunch would soften the blow. He'd keep his phone turned off, quarantine the quality time. She'd gone off to work not obviously in a bad mood but troubled all the same. Maybe she was remembering the scene at Shanghai airport and Lara Sumich in her arms, bleeding out on the floor of the departure terminal. That was the last time he'd ventured overseas on a case and back then he'd found himself at times way out of his depth.

Would Timor be the same?

João Ximenes: a man with a fearsome reputation and the means to deal with the likes of Cato without breaking a sweat. Twenty years after his prime, he would be in his mid-fifties by now, and still capable of taking care of things with his own hands or, no doubt, rich and powerful enough to get others to do it for him. There was a contingent of both AFP and Australian military advisors stationed there at the moment. Could Cato count on them for protection? He could always hole up in the embassy if things got too hot. In the next room he heard Ella stir and was about to get up to her when he heard Julie's footsteps padding down the hall. They were lucky their combined wages covered this kind of eventuality. If Sharon did take up that job in Investigations that would be yet more pressure.

First-world problems. He was beginning to finally drift off to sleep when his phone lit up on the bedside table. Nikki Earle? He checked the time: heading for one thirty. What now?

'Ryan Hodgson,' she said. 'Found an hour ago in a builder's skip with his throat cut.'

15

Friday 4ᵗʰ May

The next hop would take them to Oodnadatta, south of Alice Springs, after a couple of refuel stops. Their overnighter in country Victoria, down by the Otways, had been uneventful but, after being tossed around in a stormy sky on the way over, that came as some relief. A night in a plain motel, early breakfast on the run at a roadhouse courtesy of the driver arranged by Charlie's boss, and they were back in the air by eight. The further north they flew, the clearer the sky, the redder the earth, and the warmer it got.

'Nice the weather's picked up,' said Driscoll by way of conversation.

'Yep,' said Charlie. She flicked a switch to isolate the headphones again. 'Got a text from my boss. You're to call Mrs Blasey from the next stop. You can use my phone.'

'Something come up?'

She shook her head. 'He didn't say.'

Aunty had been the one to suggest radio silence at least until they got to Darwin. Something must have happened. He felt a tap on the shoulder, Mason leaning in.

'What's up?' he shouted above the plane noise.

Charlie flicked all the headphones back into connection.

'Nothing,' said Driscoll. 'Just working out the next stop.'

'She keeps cutting us off before she has some quiet words with you. Doesn't inspire confidence and trust.'

'Charlie's the boss,' said Driscoll. 'Her plane, her rules.'

A confirmatory nod from the pilot seat.

'So you're not holding back anything?'

'Getting uptight the closer we draw, huh, Willie? What happened to that sangfroid of yours?'

'Don't mind me, mate.' He grinned and sat back in his seat. Laid his hand proprietorially on Mira's thigh and winked at Driscoll.

Mira removed the hand and kept staring down at the red earth.

Behind her, Brian took everything in, making his entries in a mental ledger. When Driscoll caught his eye he looked away.

***

Whoever had cut Ryan Hodgson's throat had very nearly taken his head off, according to Earle. He'd been found by a bloke walking home late from drinking with a mate and decided to have a piss against the builder's skip. After unzipping and doing the business he'd looked up to find he was eyeball to eyeball with hell itself.

'Any leads?' asked Cato with his phone tucked into his chin while he fed porridge to Ella. Sharon was catching up on post-work sleep, as was Julie after a wakeful night with Ella. Cato had volunteered for the breakfast shift.

'The knife was found nearby, big sharp bastard as you might imagine. No real attempt to hide it. No fingerprints though.'

'Nothing seen or heard in the lead-up?'

'Not so far. We're canvassing this morning, checking CCTV in the area, the usual.'

'Did he have his phone with him?'

'No. His mum said he left it in his room.'

'Unusual for somebody like him.' Ella was drawing honey rings on the table again. Cato let it go.

'My thoughts too.'

'Any theories?'

'Heaps but I'm happy to let your A-team run with it. May or may not be linked. We'll see.'

'José got his bags packed?'

'Not yet,' said Earle. 'Still in the thick of things down here. Don't worry, he'll make that flight in the morning.' In the background somebody was claiming her attention. 'That level of violence isn't coincidental, is it?'

'No,' said Cato. 'I doubt it.'

'But if your bloke is back in Timor it couldn't have been him.'

'I suspect he'll have people doing his bidding. He's a born leader.'

'Be careful up there.'

'Yes,' said Cato. 'I will.' The call ended and Cato found himself staring at Ella without really seeing her.

***

'You been following those murders in WA?'

No, Driscoll hadn't. 'What murders, Aunty?' They'd landed somewhere hot with lots of dust and flies and while Charlie refuelled the plane, the others sought shade in a tin shed by the roadside. The sky was cloudless, the wind had disappeared and the temperature had climbed fifteen degrees. The landscape blurred and melted in the distance. Charlie had phoned ahead for a delivery of water bottles, fruit and sandwiches before handing him the phone.

'Two old blokes got mutilated.'

'What about them?'

'There's been a request through diplomatic channels. The investigators want to talk to a certain João Ximenes in Dili.'

'Isn't he ...'

'Yep. The head of the same militia Willie Mason is accused of being over-friendly with back in the day.'

Driscoll waved a cloud of flies from his face. 'Is their enquiry a problem for us?'

'It might be. It's caused some ripples on the pond.'

'Spit it out, Aunty.'

'Ximenes is one of ours.'

'We were paying a militia leader?'

'Not back then. But since. It seems he proved useful in the oil negotiations, and when he was based in Indonesia he helped us out with the people-smuggling ops.'

The jigsaw clicked into place. Sweat ran down his neck. 'Is that why I'm on the death list?'

'Operation Sovereign Borders?' A pause and the sound of a lighter clicking. 'Never thought of that.'

I bet you didn't. 'Ximenes is in the thick of this, isn't he?'

'For better or worse, yeah.'

'So what now?'

'I suggest you hightail it to Darwin, drop off your cargo of the Damned, then get over to Dili and make sure this police enquiry goes our way.'

"Our" way? 'Why not let justice run its course? If he's behind these WA murders, he deserves to be behind bars. To hell with whose side he was on back then, or now.'

'If they put the squeeze on him, his only current bargaining power is Willie Mason. If he blabs about any of that, it all gets very murky and uncomfortable.'

'What do we care, Aunty? We're retired, out of the game.'

'Timor. Stop the Boats. All the dirty tricks we were part of. Do you really want your name all over the internet, Rory? How would that affect your nice quiet life as old salty sea dog?'

Driscoll glanced upwards. A couple of dark wedgetails circling lazily. 'I did nothing in Timor to be ashamed of. What anybody else did is their problem.'

'Stop the Boats? Your hands weren't so clean there.'

'Were anybody's? Anyway, it won't be reported. It'll be an official secret.'

'In Canberra they pick and choose which secrets are worth keeping and when. There are noses out of joint because you and I are known to be chaperoning the Timor Gang of Three. Four if we include you.'

One of the wedgetails swooped and carried off a tiny critter. 'So remind me. Why the fuck are we doing this again? On the one hand you want me to valiantly guard these whistleblowers so the truth will out and justice be done. On the other you want me to close down the WA cops to keep the truth buried.'

'Spooks. We're a weird mob, eh?'

Driscoll sighed. 'Do we have any names for these cops?'

'The lead investigator is a certain Kwong. DS Philip Kwong. Ring any bells?'

Driscoll grimaced. Yes. It did.

PART TWO

16

Kupang, Indonesia. November 2013

The car had finally stopped doing the tortuous circuits of the last two hours and, as darkness closed in, headed into the hills behind Kupang.

Abdullah. The penny dropped for Driscoll.

According to the intelligence files, Abdullah Hamady, originally from Iraq, came a close second to the local kingpin Ali and had seemed content to wait his turn or just simply accept his lesser share of the people-smuggling business. Hamady and Ali had reached an understanding, even cooperating in recent months to jointly fund and fill boats as business tightened in the face of the changing political environment in Australia. It seemed that the *entente cordiale* was now over. Rolling into the driveway of Abdullah's hilltop villa, Driscoll had a sense that events were ahead of him – something he wasn't used to.

Abdullah presented as slight and scholarly: he could have been a poet or an academic, a doting grandfather. His greeting was warm.

'John. Is that right?'

'Yes.' The goons had faded away into the shadows. Only the lieutenant, Wayan, remained – watchful, obedient, double-dealing. Somehow different from his persona with Ali: here a disciple rather than an ambitious punk.

Abdullah smiled. 'Welcome to my home, John.' Driscoll followed him past a fountain and lush foliage in a cool courtyard through into a large, airy room with rugs, cushions, carved mahogany chairs, art on the walls and books on shelves. 'Please, sit down.'

Drinks were ordered, green tea all round. Driscoll admired the decor. 'An oasis. It must be hard to leave this place.' Insects clicked, geckos burped.

'I cannot complain.' The tea arrived and Abdullah poured. 'These are interesting times.'

'Indeed.'

'You are Australian.' Not a question. 'Aboriginal?'

'Yes.'

'And you work for the government.'

'That's right.'

Abdullah nodded, appraising Driscoll a while longer. He gestured to Driscoll's confiscated briefcase sitting at Wayan's feet. 'They provided this money.'

'Yes.'

'With a promise of more.'

'Yes.'

Abdullah took a sip of tea. 'Explain it to me, please.' A nod in Wayan's direction. 'My young friend already tried and it sounded,' he searched for the right word, 'fanciful.'

So Driscoll did.

Abdullah nodded pensively at the end. 'The Australian government will match, dollar for dollar, if we just take the clients somewhere else, or even bring them back here to Indonesia?'

'Yes.'

'Paying us to traffic these poor souls elsewhere?'

'If you like.'

'Is that not illegal?'

'Not in Indonesia.' Driscoll shrugged. 'Anyway, who is going to prosecute?'

'It could be very expensive for you.'

'Less expensive than the detention centres and the navy.'

'Accepting these people into Australia would also be less expensive than the detention centres and the navy.'

'But it sends the wrong message.'

'We cannot have that.' Abdullah signalled for a refilling of the pot. 'In the short-term it would be lucrative for us but, as you say, it sends the wrong message.'

'To?'

'To our customers. They need us. To some extent we rely on our reputation, our ability to deliver an outcome. A successful outcome. They need to be able to trust us.'

'How's that going, right now?'

A furrowing of the brow. Driscoll wondered if he'd gone too far. Too direct, too brusque, too soon.

'Have you ever been driven from your land, John? Have you ever feared for the safety of your family? Been so desperate to protect them that you will do anything?'

'No.' Maybe if you'd asked a century or so back.

'I arrived in Indonesia nineteen years ago.'

Driscoll knew the story from the file: imprisoned in Abu Ghraib and tortured under Sadaam Hussein's regime. Wife and two sons killed. A surviving daughter who had made the journey with him. A thumbnail sketch from the database now brought to life vividly through the quietly spoken words. The horror, tragedy, frustration and sheer strength of will mesmerising between sedate sips of green tea.

'You chose not to continue on to Australia?'

'We were due to get on a boat but my daughter had another one of her breakdowns. She suffered, still does, from anxiety. Crippling. We missed the sailing.'

Again, bland words on the database: 2001. SIEV-X. Three hundred and fifty-three lives lost at sea, just south of Java, in a zone under constant surveillance by Australian and Indonesian military.

'We were lucky,' Abdullah said. 'God delivered us. It was a sign.'

Lucky. 'So you made a life here in Indonesia. A successful one, it would seem.'

'In many ways, yes, but I never forget the journey which brought me here.'

'And my proposal will ensure continued success for you in these troubled times.'

Abdullah nodded. 'I suppose it will.'

'But?'

'But I fear that others will no longer be prepared to share. To cooperate.'

'Ali?'

Abdullah stood, summoned for Driscoll to follow him. They went along a dimly lit corridor towards the back of the villa, down some steps and across another courtyard to an outhouse. Wayan stepped forward to open the door for them. Rory smelled the scene before it was revealed to him. Metallic, gamey. A slaughterhouse.

There was a man strapped to a chair in the centre of what seemed to be a toolshed. It looked like some of those tools had been used on him. An ear missing, an eye gouged, terrible gaping wounds.

'He is still alive,' murmured Abdullah.

There was a small video camera on a tripod a few metres in front of the man. 'Who is he?' said Driscoll. 'Not Ali.'

'An informant, a traitor.' Abdullah handed a knife to Driscoll. 'You can end his misery.'

Driscoll shook his head. 'Your business, mate. Not mine.'

'I insist,' said Abdullah. 'If we are to go into business together I require an article of faith.'

'No.' Driscoll dropped the knife on the floor. 'Leave me out of it.'

'Good faith, John,' urged Abdullah. 'I need a sample of your good faith.'

Wayan had edged closer, a pistol loosely at his side. Driscoll shrugged. 'Sorry, bro. Not the way I do business.'

'You would be doing him a favour, John. He needs to be released from his torment.'

Driscoll looked the man in his remaining good eye. Saw a pleading there. Maybe Abdullah was right. An article of faith.

17

Saturday 5th May – Sunday 6th May

Charlie dropped them at the Noonamah airstrip on the distant outskirts of Darwin and didn't hang about. After refuelling, she'd taken off again immediately, as if aiming to put as much distance as possible between her and them.

'Cheers,' she'd said. 'Good luck.'

It was late afternoon, still warm, and Driscoll lifted a hand in salute as the Cessna taxied away. He surveyed the scenery: dry, red-brown dirt and tired-looking trees. The sky heading for purple in the east. Shadows long, insects clicking in the soft breeze.

'Somebody's coming,' said Mason.

A cloud of dust in the distance. 'Our ride into town. I hope.'

The four of them stood, bags at their feet, watching the dust cloud draw nearer. Mira Soares had opened up a gap between herself and Mason. She no longer needed him, no longer trusted him. And yet, there was still a longing there. Brian remained chipper; the end in sight. 'D'you reckon this place'll have a pool?'

Driscoll didn't reply. The vehicle was turning through the gate into the airfield. It was a minibus, the type used to transport backpackers around Top End tourist hotspots. It even had the hostel name on the side in graffiti-style lettering – *The Hungry Croc* – plus a cartoon of said smiley beast wearing a cork hat and waving a tinnie of XXXX. The van pulled up a few metres from them.

'G'day.' The driver was a statuesque, middle-aged woman in stubbies, a singlet and Blundies. Red-grey hair cropped close, freckles on every bit of exposed flesh. A firm handshake. 'Jill. Good trip?'

'Good as can be expected.' They loaded their bags into the back and took their seats. Driscoll hopped in front with Jill. 'Friend of Pauline's?'

'Who?' she said, crunching gravel.

The drive into the city took the best part of an hour. Driscoll suspected some meandering and doubling back along the way, and by the time they hit the CBD it was dark. It had been a wordless journey. Jill didn't do small talk and everybody seemed locked in their own thoughts. Darwin had grown since Driscoll was last here, more high-rises and generally a fattening and spreading out like a complacent middle manager. The oil and gas boom, he guessed. And tourists. And US military rotations. They pulled into the courtyard of The Hungry Croc.

'This where we're staying?' said Mason. 'Seriously?'

'Closed for renos.' Jill lifted the back van door so they could get their bags. 'Should be nice and peaceful. A room each.' She eyed Mason and Mira. 'If that's what suits.'

Driscoll had spent the journey speculating on how much Jill knew and what her relationship was to Aunty. She'd given nothing away and parried any attempts at conversation. Something about her said ex-military. Right now, it didn't matter; a closed-down backpacker hostel was as good a cover as any. They took up residence, Mira rebuffing Mason's suggestion of a shared room. Brian said something under his breath and chuckled. Mason was on him, pinning him against the wall with an arm across the throat.

'Say that again, fuckface.'

Brian was going red but merriment danced in his eyes. 'I said she no love you long time no more.'

If Driscoll had been on the receiving end he would probably have taken Mason's view. As it was, things needed calming down. 'Mate,' he said to Mason. 'Leave it. It's not worth it.'

Mason eased off and Brian straightened himself out. Mira had already disappeared into her room and was unaware of the slur. Mason and Brian went to their doors, gave each other a parting glare and disappeared.

'Roll on Monday, eh?' said Jill, showing Driscoll his room. 'Tea, coffee and breakfast stuff in the kitchen.' She handed him the keys to the minivan. 'The fridge is stocked. Make yourselves at home. Sweet dreams.'

But Driscoll, tired as he was, knew he wouldn't sleep. After months of peace in his isolated coastal hideaway, the ghosts had found him once again.

***

Cato looked out the window as the plane made its descent: the dry green hills rising steeply to the east and then, crossing the north coast, the sparkling bright blue ocean. It reminded him of the Top End, the Kimberley in particular, the same hues and haze as if viewed through a lace curtain. From the air, Dili looked small. It could have been Bunbury, or any reasonably sized city in regional Australia. Instead it was the capital of this tiny young nation.

José Carrascalao stirred beside him. He'd slept most of the journey, seemingly unfazed by pastures new. 'That's it, eh?' He brought his seat back upright and breathed his sleep-fug into their shared space.

At the top of the steps leading down to the tarmac they were met by a wall of heat. The terminal, again reminiscent of a regional airport but perhaps darker and dingier, bore signs welcoming them to Timor-Leste. *Bem vindo*. About to queue up to pay for their visas, they were waved aside. Two people awaited them, a white man aged somewhere in his thirties and wearing shorts and a polo shirt with the crest of the joint Australian–Timorese Police Development Program. With him, a Timorese woman of similar age. Both were short but had big smiles.

'Sam McGuiness. AFP,' said the bloke shaking hands.

'Rosa,' said the woman doing the same. 'Rosa Domingos.'

José matched their welcoming smiles and said something to Rosa.

'Sorry,' she said. 'I do not speak Portuguese.'

'Really?' said José.

She lifted her hands in supplication. 'I am from the west.'

'I said it is an honour to visit your beautiful country.'

He received another smile in reply but no words.

Bags collected, formalities cleared, they were driven out of the airport, past a large statue of a Falintil resistance fighter and along a busy avenue towards the centre. They passed a newly built shopping mall and the ostentatious white confection of a government building.

'Presidential Palace,' said Sam. 'Nice, huh?'

At the roadside, hawkers sold coconuts and trussed chickens in rusty cages. Some buildings were burned-out shells. They looked like they hadn't been touched in years. The light was fading and the heat with it. Mopeds and minibuses weaved beside them, occasionally a flash four-wheel drive bearing the insignia of an international NGO. They pulled into the forecourt of Hotel Timor, across the road from the port and the ocean. A man dressed in a gold and burgundy bellboy suit opened doors for them while another carried their bags.

'Rest up for the night,' said Sam. 'We'll pick you up in the morning and take it from there.'

'Is Ximenes expecting us?'

'Probably.'

More shaking of hands and they left. 'What did you make of her, then?' said José as he took his passport back from the receptionist.

'Rosa?' Cato shrugged. 'Seemed nice enough.'

'Put me in my place, that's for sure.'

'How?'

'She understood Portuguese, she just chooses not to speak it.'

Cato shrugged. 'Her country, I suppose.'

'Tits on a bull.'

'What?'

'That's how useful I'll be if they're all like her. Could've stayed home.'

'Chin up,' said Cato. 'Tomorrow's another day.'

***

As predicted, Driscoll's sleep had been fitful and plagued by old demons. A bloody figure strapped to a chair in a cellar. A formless mass huddled on a beach at night shepherded towards an already overfull boat. People bobbing in the ocean beside a sinking vessel, waving, crying out, observed remotely through a drone camera. He surveyed the faces around him at the breakfast table and guessed the others had also had a rough night. Mira seemed stretched tight as a drum. She'd completed her high-schooling in Darwin, it should be familiar territory, but that didn't necessarily equate with home-ground advantage. This would have been where she gradually recovered from the trauma of the massacre that killed her parents – or more accurately, her mother. A closer read of her file showed that it was just her mother who died in the massacre; her father had been killed a few years earlier in an Indonesian reprisal raid on their village. The family were known independence activists and their cards had been marked by the Indonesian authorities. Orphaned in her early teens, Mira was brought here to Darwin to live with strangers, learn a new language and way of life, enter a new school where she was an outsider. Then to face the onslaught that teenage years bring to any Aussie kid. Mason meanwhile was moping. He was losing face in the eyes of Mira and of Brian, who no longer seemed to fear him. His day of reckoning was at hand: his gambles, his bluffs, all about to be called. Brian, by contrast, was refreshed from an early morning dip in the pool, fizzing with bright nervous energy. He flicked on the kettle.

'Anyone need a top-up?'

Neither Mason nor Mira replied. Driscoll held up his full mug in answer.

'Going to be another hot one.' Brian spooned some instant into his cup. 'Then again, we are in the tropics, eh?' He rubbed his hands together like Superdad on holiday. 'So what will we do today?'

'Maybe shut the fuck up?' said Mason.

'I'll go out and make contact with the tribunal,' said Driscoll. 'You all need to stay here and stay nice.'

'Today is their last chance, isn't it?' Mira drew a cigarette from a packet and lit it. 'Today and early tomorrow. If they mean to stop us.'

'Depends who we mean by them.' Mason lifted his gaze to Driscoll. 'This is where it all falls apart, doesn't it? Where's the protection and security to get us into that tribunal? What happens when we come out? Who do we trust?' He drained his coffee mug. 'You?'

Driscoll twirled the van keys on the table top. 'You invited me in to this, remember? You said I was the only one who could get you through it.'

'You've worked out why you're on that list?' Mason grabbed the cigarette packet. 'Care to share?'

'You already know. You've known all along.' He flicked his fingers at the assembled company. 'We're all here because of you. And tomorrow you find out whether or not you win.'

Mason didn't answer.

'Trust me, you'll make that tribunal.' Driscoll stood and pocketed the keys. 'Then we can all go home.'

***

Their first stop would be the Australian Embassy for a briefing. Sam and Rosa rocked up on the dot at nine in the same black four-wheel drive with the joint police cooperation program logo on the doors. Cato observed that aid and development four-wheel drives seemed to be more common than taxis in Dili. The previous evening he'd taken an early dinner, skyped Sharon on the slow unstable hotel wi-fi, and succumbed to sleep. José had gone his own way too. Next morning, after a dip in the hotel pool, the country cop had helped himself to a heaped plate from the cooked breakfast buffet. Cato had been more modest with fruit and cereal but he was pleasantly surprised by the smooth Timorese coffee.

'We'll go the scenic route,' said Sam as they pulled out of the hotel driveway. 'Rosa insists.'

It being a Sunday morning, there was less traffic around than usual but still enough to make a noise. They crossed over to the port road and followed the coast. 'The wharf behind that building?' Rosa nodded her head in that direction. 'That is where the Indonesians killed many people when they first arrived in nineteen seventy-five, and again just before they left in ninety-nine. Shot them, stabbed them, threw them in the water. The crocodiles ate well.'

'Going to be one of those days,' muttered José under his breath.

'That's right,' said Rosa into the rear-view. 'It is.' The sun glinted off the ocean to their right. To the left, a row of old colonial villas which, according to the signage, now housed the NGOs. 'The Indonesian military officers used to live there,' said Rosa. 'My uncle was tortured to death in that outhouse down the side.' She pointed. 'That one, there. See it?' A grey cinder-block building not much bigger than a garden shed.

'When was this?' asked Cato.

'Nineteen seventy-eight. I wasn't born then, but my mother told me. She wanted me to know what they did to her little brother.' She eyed the rear-view again. 'Now you know too.'

'Terrible times,' said José. 'Good job that's all over now, eh?'

'Yes.' Driving past the embassies: each competing to be the biggest, securest, most imposing. It was a close race between the Americans and the Chinese. Across the road, that sparkling ocean and a statue of one young man cradling another who was obviously dying. 'The massacre at Santa Cruz cemetery. Nineteen ninety-one. Around three hundred died. You remember that? Saw it on the TV, maybe?'

Yes, they recalled. They did. Wailing sirens, chaos, gunfire, panicked crowd.

'Good place for a statue,' said Rosa, proudly. 'The ambassadors are reminded every day of our recent history when they try to enjoy the ocean view. So they never forget our sacrifice.'

They turned into side streets – narrower, poorer, graffiti on the walls. Abandoned buildings.

'The Australian Embassy?' asked Cato.

'Back near the main drag,' said Sam. 'But with the one-way system it's just as easy to come along this way and give you the history lesson.'

'Cheers,' said José. 'Appreciate it.'

'The numbers,' said Cato, nodding towards the graffiti. 'Seventy-seven?'

'One of the more well-known gangs.' Sam signalled a turn left through some high automatic gates above which flew the Aussie flag. 'They have links to our friend Ximenes.'

IDs checked, they parked up and were led into a boardroom on the second floor by a blonde flunky who reminded Cato of Jacinta the CPS PR guru. 'Mark will be with you in five minutes. Anyone for coffee, tea, anything?'

They all agreed on coffee.

Mark made them wait ten minutes then breezed through the door and handed out his business cards. He looked like he spent a lot of time in the gym.

Colonel Mark Rintoul. 'Military attaché?' said Cato, examining the card.

'That's right,' said Mark. 'Enjoying the local coffee?'

'Great,' said José.

'Special stuff, strained through the arse of a civet cat up in the hills, so they say. Not cheap.'

'You'll know why we're here,' said Cato, getting down to business.

'To rock the boat, I'm guessing.'

Cato explained their presence for the record. The flunky, whose name was Maddie, took notes and he expected that they were also being taped. 'So,' he said in conclusion, 'we're hoping an interview with Mr Ximenes might clarify a few matters.'

'What if he says no?'

'Then we'll have wasted our journey.'

'Any whispers?'

'Just pillow talk, Rory.'

'I meant about the opposition.'

'Oh, right. Well, as you might expect, they're in town and looking for you.'

'Both camps?'

'Yes.'

'Mason brought me on board to deliver up to them, didn't he?'

'Looking like it, yes. Our spooks aren't particularly interested in you, except as a barrier to be removed between them and your companions.'

'So it's the cowboys who want me. The ones who shot at us down at the Hobart waterfront.'

'Yes.'

'They're not Big Oil mercenaries if their interest is me. I'm irrelevant. They're from somewhere else.'

'S'pose so,' said Aunty.

'You knew Mason was setting me up, didn't you?'

'We had an inkling.'

'We? So you're back in the fold.'

'We've been trying to flush out these people for a while. Now it's game on.'

'With me as the Sherrin? Thanks, Aunty.'

'Fair go, Rory. You get to lay some ghosts to rest too.'

'How's that?'

'Operation Sovereign Borders. The same guys who stiffed you then are behind the Timor business and behind all this now: the nut-job Neanderthal flat-earthers. It's a turf war and we need to turf them out and get this country back on track.'

'Very patriotic.'

'Fuck off, Rory. You know what I mean.'

'So what about tomorrow?'

'Tomorrow belongs to us, Rory, mate.'

Then she'd told him the plan and given him the name of The Hague committee fixer, a certain Jens from Denmark who, she said, looked divine and whose English was impeccable. They were to meet today for a briefing at the Boatshed Coffee House down at the waterfront: big, open, popular and public. That suited Driscoll just fine. He ordered a coffee and waited at an outside table. It didn't take him long to spot the activity: private security, white shirts, some with fluoro vests. Walkie-talkies, shifting position to close in and close him off. Had he been rumbled that quickly? His coffee arrived, and with it a security guard by the name of Martin. He had an English accent.

'Morning, mate. Everything good?' Northern, trouble-at-mill dialect.

'Yep, cheers.' Driscoll looked around for weapons. There was a knife on an uncleared breakfast plate at the adjacent table. Not sharp, but enough to do some damage in his trained hands.

'Want to change that for a takeaway?'

Driscoll examined his latte. 'It just arrived. So did I. I'm meeting somebody.'

'Haven't seen you around here, have I?'

'I'm a tourist. Just got in yesterday.'

'Got any ID?'

'Not for you, no.' A lift of Martin's head and a wink and a few of his colleagues moved closer. Driscoll knew what was going on now. It wasn't the bad guys, he hadn't been rumbled. He raised his voice a notch. 'Are you wanting me to leave because I'm Aboriginal?'

Sly smirk. 'Not at all, mate. It's just there's a dress code here.'

Driscoll looked around. Everybody was wearing shorts, T-shirts, thongs or sandals. Just like him. He made a come-closer gesture to Martin. 'I'm not going to shout and scream and make a scene because I know that's what you want. But I promise you, brother. If you and your mates don't get out of my face right now, you're going to be permanently scarred.' A sip of latte as he stared at Martin. 'You, mate. Just you.'

Martin straightened up. Kept his eyes on Driscoll's. Seemed to come to a decision. 'Behave yourself or we'll be back.'

'Yeah, cuz. Off you go.'

Jens appeared. Glasses, Hawaiian shirt, iPhone held up in Martin's face. 'Smile, you're on Facebook Live.' He pumped Driscoll's hand. 'John! So good to see you again! How was London?' He turned to Martin. 'Two more coffees please and can you wipe down the tables?'

***

'So are we heading off to see Ximenes now?' said Cato.

'No,' said Rosa. 'Now you get to meet my boss and go through the same thing we just experienced with Colonel Mark. Only perhaps less rude.'

José groaned.

'Protocol, mate.' Sam laid a brotherly mitt on his shoulder. 'Makes the world go around.'

'Will the lovely Maddie be there?' José enquired.

'Not if she has half a brain. I expect she'll be waiting outside when we're done.'

They swung through the gates into the compound of the national police headquarters. As the day wore on, the heat was building. Already Cato's shirt stuck to him. The compound resembled more a used-car lot than a police HQ. Not even that, a car graveyard: row upon row of dusty vehicles, mopeds, motorbikes, buses, minivans, four-wheel drives.

'Confiscated,' explained Sam. 'Or recovered from accidents or crime scenes.'

'Some look like they've been here for years,' said Cato.

'They have, but nobody's worked out what to do with them yet.' Sam sighed. 'That's why I'm here. Get some systems in place, particularly the ones from the crime scenes. Sitting out in the elements, they're forensically useless by now.'

'They haven't been dabbed yet?' José looked incredulous.

'That bus over there?' Rosa pointed to a wreck sitting on flat tyres and rusty wheels. 'A Japanese girl was gang-raped in there five years ago. The forensic specimens have to be sent to Lisbon. It's very expensive. The manuals? Instructions are all in Portuguese which very few of us ordinary Timorese speak or read.' A sideways glance at José. 'So nothing has been progressed, even though we're pretty sure we know who did it.'

'Those people are still walking the streets?' asked Cato.

'Not all,' said Rosa with grim satisfaction. 'Accidents happen.'

'Postcolonial detecting in Timor-Leste,' said Sam. 'A work in progress.'

Rosa's boss, Captain Saldanha, was far less brash and obnoxious than Colonel Mark. In fact, not at all. They all shook hands, he welcomed them, offered coffee and gave his fullest cooperation.

'That went well,' said Cato on their way out.

'We'll see,' said Sam.

Rosa had been asked to stay behind for a few minutes. Maybe that was where the truth lay.

'Can we go and see Ximenes soon?' said Cato.

'Just one more thing.' Sam led them to a fenced-off compound in the central courtyard. It looked like a large ornamental fish pond.

'Fuck me,' said José as they drew closer. A huge saltwater crocodile basked in the fierce sunlight. Half in, half out of the pond. 'Does he have a name?'

'Either Maria or Antonio,' said Sam. 'Nobody's been game to check, although the odds are on Antonio, given the size.'

'I like it,' said José. 'Makes a nice change from telephone directories to the kidneys, or being pushed down the stairs.'

'The crocodile is our totem,' explained Rosa, joining them. '*Lafaek* is also known as our grandfather, he protects us, brings us luck. He judges without prejudice, eats only the guilty.'

José nodded. 'Like I said.'

'I'll explain some other time maybe.' Rosa turned her attention to Cato. 'So, shall we pay a visit to Mr Ximenes?'

***

Jens was enjoying his Australian junket. 'The bright colours, the weather, the food, the beaches, the crazy dangerous wildlife, everything,' he enthused loudly. 'It's beautiful. The history, the culture ...'

'Glad you like it,' said Driscoll. The guy's voice was as loud as his shirt. People who were looking away while Driscoll had been in danger of being moved on by security were now openly staring at the odd couple. This was no way to be discreet. The coffees arrived and Jens took a brief pause to sip.

'Even the coffee. Fantastic.'

'Mate, I'm on a schedule.' The second coffee was making Driscoll buzz like a toaster in a bathtub. 'Tell me, what's the plan for tomorrow?'

The voice dropped an octave or two. 'The tribunal meets at nine sharp. They will hear submissions from government lawyers, from technical experts, from the oil and gas companies. It will take all day. Maybe two, three.'

'Why could that not be done in The Hague?'

'Hearts and minds,' Jens said wearily. 'Glasnost. Transparency. Accessibility. Call it what you will.'

'And our witnesses?'

'Will be heard in camera before the tribunal sits. Seven a.m. Get them to the door at the rear of the courthouse at six thirty. We'll take it from there.'

'What about when it's over?'

Under the sun-ruddied complexion and flowery island shirt, a Scandinavian chill had settled in. 'That's your problem. Not ours.'

'They'll be hung out to dry.'

'The tribunal hears evidence on maritime boundary disputes. It is not a war crimes trial. It does not do witness protection. That is the work of your security services.'

'They are the very people implicated.'

'An unusual situation,' Jens admitted. 'But beyond our remit.'

'Fair enough,' said Driscoll.

Suddenly quiet, a hardness came into Jens' eyes. 'That car has done three circuits now. They're not searching for a parking space. They've stared at us, every time.'

A white Toyota, hire stickers on the rear window. Two men. Driscoll looked without looking. Over Jens' shoulder, two more blokes who didn't seem to fit the ambience of the cafe. 'Did you drive here?'

'Moped,' said Jens. 'Ever been on a Vespa?'

'Probably best if we split up.' Driscoll spotted a mountain bike unsecured against a railing. The Toyota had commenced another circuit. It was a one-way system, they wouldn't be able to get back around in front of the cafe for a minute and a half at best. He reached across to the neighbouring table and swiped their metal stand with the order number. 'Mind if I borrow this a sec?' He tested the weight of the base in his palm. It would do. To Jens, quietly. 'I'll take care of these two at table thirteen. Careful on the moped, see you tomorrow.'

Jens nodded and reverted to his loud voice. 'And Kakadu. Man, Kakadu. Phenomenal.'

Driscoll stood, holding up the order number, looking for a waiter. 'Mate, mate? Been waiting half an hour for my pancakes. Jeez.' In three long strides he was on the men who didn't suit the ambience, swinging the base of the stand into the teeth of one and then down on the skull of the other. The second was out cold. The first he finished off with two punches and a head bang on the table top. He checked, yes, both were armed. Their pistols were lobbed into nearby bushes then he vaulted over the railing and hopped on the bike.

'Hey!' said the bike owner and a waiter together.

Driscoll pointed to Jens. 'He'll take care of it.'

Jens grinned and pulled out his wallet. 'Darwin. Man, I just love Darwin.'

***

João Ximenes lived in a villa up in the hills behind Dili. He wasn't that far from Xanana Gusmão's place according to Sam. Xanana – Timor's Che Guevara, now comfortably semi-retired. Far below them, the city sat hunched on the shore, shrouded in a light sea mist.

'My parents came up here in nineteen seventy-five,' said Rosa. 'They watched the Indonesian ships bombard the city. Saw the paratroopers floating out of the sky. Watched our homes burn.'

'Does anywhere in this country not have a history lesson attached to it?' wondered José.

'Nowhere,' said Rosa. She looked ahead. 'Next left. The high gate and the guard dogs.' There was an intercom at the gate, she spoke into it: a brief exchange with a man's voice. Rosa's tone became terse then the gate slid open.

'He's home?' asked Cato.

'And happy to chat,' said Sam. 'He's always been a publicity tart. Puts out a press release when he takes a dump.'

That fitted with the brief internet search Cato had conducted. The man enjoyed the limelight. Maybe he felt untouchable and maybe he was right. Or maybe it would be his undoing. They drove up a steep driveway past two chained and barking Dobermans. Another fifty metres or so on and the vegetation was more lush, well-watered and tended. Some vivid tropical flowers, the kind that might eat a small animal. Ximenes himself was there to greet them at the top of the drive accompanied by a young woman in a bikini. He was wearing sunnies, dressed in shorts, thongs and a Bintang singlet, holding a machete.

'That for us?' whispered José.

'It's his trademark, what he's famous for,' said Sam. 'Think Clint Eastwood and his Magnum, Gary Ablett and a Sherrin.'

'We'll do the talking,' said Rosa. 'Don't speak until we tell you.'

They all shook hands. While Rosa and Sam explained their business in more detail, Cato took stock. Ximenes looked all of his fifty-odd years. Since the last business photo Cato had seen of Ximenes at the oil and gas conference in Perth, the hair had been allowed to grow out again, covering his ears and creeping down the neck in reminiscence of his famed mullet of twenty years ago. There was grey at the temples and in his unshaven stubble. A man on the slide, or just on holiday? The once gym-honed body had paunched out but still looked like it harboured great strength. The sunglasses turned out to be self-tinting prescription spectacles. He kept them on as he invited them all inside and back through to the rear patio and pool.

They took their seats at a poolside table and the young woman in the bikini went to bring some refreshments.

'Her name is Felicity,' said Ximenes, noting José's appreciative gaze. 'So,' he turned to Cato, 'You have questions for me? Ask away, my English is very good.'

'Thank you for taking the time to see us,' said Cato.

He beamed. 'Australia is a good friend of Timor-Leste. I am happy to help.'

Rosa showed great interest in the tiling around the pool.

A bank of dark clouds had appeared in the western sky and a cool, refreshing breeze swept the patio. Felicity returned with drinks and snacks, shivered, made her excuses and went indoors.

'Douglas Peters and Bevan Drummond.' Cato laid photos on the table, weighed them against the wind with his glass of Sprite. 'Do you know them?'

Ximenes examined the faces. 'No,' he said. 'I don't think so.'

'You sure?' said José.

'Two old Australian men. Why would I?'

'One of them was very interested in you. He'd been searching you on the internet.' Cato took the photos back and returned them to his file. 'Any ideas why?'

'Maybe he is, what do you call it, a history buff. Or a fan.' He smiled. 'I have many. I'm quite famous.'

'I don't think he was a fan. He seemed afraid of you.'

Ximenes nodded and sipped from his cocktail. 'Some people are.'

'According to our records, you were in Perth at the time these two men died.'

'They died? Terrible. How?'

Cato described how. 'Can you account for your movements while you were in Perth?'

'Business meetings, some tourism. I can check my appointments calendar if you like, but it won't be a complete picture.' He dropped some names of influential people in Australian business and politics. Mentioned classy expensive restaurants. Wineries. As the sky darkened further, the tint lifted on Ximenes' spectacles. Cato could see now that one eye didn't move. It was false. Ximenes noted Cato's close attention. 'You seem to be implying that I was involved in some way?'

'Were you?'

'No.'

Rosa and Sam were getting restless. Cato sensed that things might be drawing to a close. Inside, a buzzer sounded. Felicity came to the French windows, a kimono over her bikini. 'Jo-Jo?' Some words in Tetun then Cato discerned the name of Madeleine from the Australian embassy.

'Shit,' said Sam. 'She's here.'

Ximenes nodded affably. 'Send her in, Felicity. The more the merrier.'

Cato downed his Sprite. 'Those men were here in Timor many years ago. They know something about you. They have proof of it and I think that is why they died.'

Ximenes turned to Sam. 'Your Chinese friend has quite an imagination. Does he not know what happens to the likes of him in Indonesia when people get upset?'

'We're not in Indonesia any more, mate.'

Maddie's voice at the front door, urgent and commanding.

'I'm a history buff, too.' Cato stood to leave. 'I'll be having a good look around while I'm here.'

'Enjoy your stay, Mr Kwong. Timor has a lot to offer.' Ximenes smiled. 'We like to think it is the best kept secret in the region.'

It was as Ximenes stood and turned his head to greet the rapidly approaching Maddie that Cato noticed the man's left ear and the surrounding skin graft scars. It was almost perfect – too good to be true.

So perfect it might have been the work of a very good plastic surgeon.

The first fat heavy raindrops started to fall and the heavens opened.

***

It was midafternoon by the time Driscoll returned to The Hungry Croc. On the stolen bike he'd zipped through pedestrian malls and down narrow laneways and alleys to avoid being followed. He returned to the parked hostel van over an hour later, leaving the bike back at the Boatshed cafe to be reunited with its owner. He'd received an SMS from Jens to say he was okay. No surprise, their priority would have been Driscoll, not some UN flunky. How had they known to find him at the cafe? Had he been followed? Maybe they were already at the hostel finishing the rest of the job. Pulling into the driveway, he saw no sign of visitors or of any activity.

The street was Sunday quiet. The footy would be on TV. Across the road the deli disgorged a couple of kids and their lollies. A car rolled by, a battered Datsun with stickers against uranium mining and US bases, and for the Greens. Some bird squawked on the telephone wires. A dog barked over the fence next door. A muffled command: 'Shut it, you mongrel.'

Driscoll went inside. 'Get the kettle on, Daddy's home.'

Silence.

He went through to the kitchen. No one around. Plates left unwashed. Unusual. Mason, he knew, was a stickler for cleanliness and order. 'Willie? Mira? Brian?'

Nothing.

Through to the residents lounge.

Empty.

Upstairs to the bedrooms. Driscoll beginning to wonder if he should have had the Glock with him, or kept those he took off the guys in the cafe.

A rustling, a squeak, coming from Mira's room. He went through the door. 'Mira?'

She was handcuffed to the bed. Mouth gagged, tears streaming down her face. Whoever had done it had thoughtfully left the key on the desk by the door. Well out of Mira's reach but available for whoever found her. Driscoll did the honours.

A wail escaped her as the gag came off. 'They took them.'

'Who?'

'Those men who came to the house in Tasmania. They took Willie and Brian.'

The spooks. The news might not be as grim as he feared. They were supposedly the not-so-bad guys. Mason and Brian were their priority – they were threatening to blow state secrets – now they were in protective custody. Or so the theory went. He checked Mira was unscathed, helped her clean up, tried to reassure and calm her. Then he called Aunty.

'They've got Mason and Simmonds.'

'I know.'

'You know? Fuck, Aunty. What the hell's going on?'

'Mason was going to serve you up to Ximenes. You and Mira.'

'Mira?'

'Unfinished business we can only guess at. It was Mason who tipped off the guys at the cafe.'

'They belong to Ximenes.' Driscoll nodded. 'Anything you're not two steps ahead of me on?'

'Doubt it. The lesser of two evils was to neutralise Mason with our team, but that meant giving them Brian too.'

'What will happen to them?'

'They'll be charged under our draconian laws and released on bail for a year or two while the lawyers argue it out.'

'Me and Mira?'

'Are not needed anymore. Not by our side anyway.'

'The Hague tribunal?'

'Has been notified and will adjust their timetable accordingly.'

'So the truth no longer matters and the last ten days or so has been a massive waste of time and money.'

'Not totally.' Aunty chuckled and it turned into a cough. 'The culture wars in Canberra have taken a new turn. But I suggest you and Mira get out of Darwin quick smart.'

'And go where? Ximenes isn't finished, is he?'

'Maybe you should go and help out your detective mate from the west. Kwong, was it?'

'Dili? With Mira? You have to be joking.'

'The lion's den, Rory. Tends to bring out the best in you. It's the last place they'd expect you to go. If you hightail it to the airport you'll make the late afternoon flight. There's tickets for you both and a green light through the border formalities. I've booked you into the Hotel Timor. Separate rooms, of course.'

'And the plan is?'

'Cry havoc and let slip the dogs of war. It's game on, Rory. Get a good night's sleep and await my instructions.'

'And what if I just say get fucked and I go back to my fishing shack?'

'Sure, Rory. And sit and wait for Ximenes and his men to come looking? You know that's not your style. Besides you now have a damsel in distress to rescue.'

Driscoll cast a sideways glance at Mira. A new sharp light had come into her eyes at the mention of Dili. It looked like she relished the prospect. 'Talk in the morning, Aunty.'

18

Monday 7ᵗʰ May

Cato had sat quietly through the bollocking from Maddie back at the embassy. She wasn't happy that they hadn't waited for her before interviewing Ximenes. She could bluster all she liked and Rosa and Sam were obliged to duck and weave – they had to live and work here for the foreseeable. Cato was on borrowed time and didn't give a stuff what she thought. Ximenes was his man, he was sure of that, and even if he could not be brought back to Perth to face justice, then Cato at least wanted to know the truth of the matter.

'Are you even listening?' Maddie had asked.

Rain pounded the boardroom window. 'Honest answer?' said Cato.

'You realise I can have you on the next plane out. You understand that?'

'Embassy Official Blocks Police Probe into Slain Aussie Pensioners.' Cato unhooked his finger quotes. 'Wouldn't look good, would it?'

'You don't know who you're messing with. Chum.'

Chum. Half a syllable off 'chink' and they both knew it. 'The sooner I get my answers, the sooner I'll be gone.'

Maddie had pointed out that, following her conversation with Ximenes after their departure, it seemed unlikely he would be granting them any further audiences. 'So there are no more answers for you to get.'

'More than one way to skin a cat,' said Cato. 'I won't bother him anymore, and you won't need to give up your desk job to chaperone me.'

'The rain is set to clear overnight. Enjoy the sights.' Maddie had shuffled some papers in a file and signalled their dismissal. 'Then catch the afternoon plane home tomorrow.'

'I'll sleep on it,' he'd replied. 'The idea, not the plane.'

José returned to the table, his breakfast plate laden. 'I take it we're not checking out today?'

'No. Can you do me a favour?'

'Sure.'

'When Sam and Rosa come to pick us up, can you keep Sam occupied? Tell him our victims went to a girly bar when they were here. You need to check it out.'

'Are there girly bars in Dili?'

'They're well hidden if there are. I noticed a sports bar along the seafront, Scottie's. Not quite the same but it'll do.'

'You want the lovely Rosa all to yourself, eh?'

'See,' said Cato. 'Getting into the pervy expat mindset already. You're a natural, mate.'

And so they went their separate ways: Rosa and Cato keeping the company car while José and Sam took a stroll along the seafront to Scottie's.

'What are you up to?' said Rosa as they edged out into the Monday morning traffic.

'Tell me what you know, and what you think, about João Ximenes.'

'He's dangerous.'

'I'd gathered that. Why is he tolerated here, now?' He cracked the window open. The air was fresher after yesterday's downpour and a brisk but warm wind whipped off the sea.

'Reconciliation,' said Rosa. The word seemed to leave a bad taste in her mouth. They were heading past the embassies again, past that statue of the fallen at the Santa Cruz cemetery massacre.

'You don't agree?'

She shrugged. 'I do my job. I don't get paid to have an opinion.'

'You're one of the very few women investigators in the national police. I would have thought you'd already given your opinion many times.'

'Not on politics.'

'On criminals, then,' said Cato. 'Ximenes, for instance.'

'A thug. He should be in jail. Or dead.'

'He is a *liurai*?'

'Where did you learn such a word?'

'From a professor in Perth. *Liurai*. Some kind of lord, is that right?'

'Petty king might be closer.'

Cato nodded; he preferred that interpretation. 'Can we go to his, what, petty kingdom? His district?'

'What do you hope to learn?'

'I don't know.'

Rosa shrugged. 'Madeleine won't be happy.'

'I can live with that. It's Ximenes I'm really hoping to upset.'

***

Driscoll had watched from his hotel window as Kwong left. He was looking older, carrying a little bit more weight, had some grey at the temples. Join the club. The other one he assumed was Kwong's offsider from the WA police. Bulky, back turned. He'd gone off with the AFP guy while Kwong had got in the four-wheel drive with the woman from PNTL. With the coast clear, Driscoll joined Mira for breakfast. Their flight over had been uneventful; nobody trailed them to the airport. As promised, they sailed through immigration and security at both ends. Hotel reception had been suspicious of him checking in with Mira but held their tongues once it was clarified she had her own room several doors away from his. Await instructions, Aunty had said. So he waited.

'Is this the first time you've been back?' he asked Mira.

'Yes.' She nibbled on a chunk of pineapple. 'How about you?'

'First time since two thousand and six.'

'Why were you here?'

'Like Willie, I worked at the embassy.'

'Secret agent.'

'Fledgling.'

Her eyes filled. 'I was wrong to trust him, wasn't I?'

'Probably.'

'What will they do to him?'

'Charge him, warn him, let him go. Maybe there'll be a trial sometime in the future.'

She snorted. 'A show trial.'

'Hardly,' said Driscoll. 'It will be held in secret. A kangaroo court might be a better way to describe it.'

'Brian too? A civilian? They can do that?'

'Yes.'

Mira glanced out of the window at the sunshine, hazy blue sky, hooting traffic. 'Maybe this is the best place for me now. Maybe I can do more for Timor if I come home to *patria*.'

'Maybe,' said Driscoll. His phone sounded. Aunty. She wanted to know if he'd made contact with Kwong yet. 'No, I was awaiting instructions. Remember?'

'Looks like he's already stirring the pot. Ximenes is jumping up and down, wanting something done about him.'

'I'm not inclined to help Ximenes out right now.'

'A deft touch is what we're after, Rory, dear.'

'Your idea of deft often ends in tears.'

'I suggest you drop by the embassy and say hello. We'll do a teleconference so we're all on the same page.'

'And Kwong?'

'Might be just the fall guy we're looking for.'

***

Sharon couldn't make sense of it. She'd run another check on Paul Reinado and kept getting blocked. The spook Guthrie had told Phil that Reinado had been on their books. Fair enough, some stuff would be classified. But suddenly even files she had access to a few days ago were now closed to her. Reinado was dissolving like a body in a barrel of acid. Meanwhile the reports from McMahon in Fremantle Detectives were that 'enquiries were progressing' – which meant they were stuck and seriously tempted to run with the suicide theory so they could all get on with their lives. So behind the scenes there was increased activity to ensure that, out front, the curtain came down early. Why was she interested? What did it matter for Phil up there in Timor?

She tried running a trace on Guthrie but there was little after his graduation from uni: ANU, class of ninety-nine, politics and international relations, first-class honours. Then postgrad languages: Mandarin, Bahasa, Spanish, French. Then a big fat nothing, no social media profile, zero. ANU postgraduate class photo two years later: there he is back row, third from left, bland nonentity then, as he no doubt is now. Two rows directly in front, a familiar face. She'd last worked with him in China. He'd muscled in when Phil had come to Shanghai on police business.

Rory Driscoll didn't belong to any particular department, she recalled – a freelance troubleshooter with high-level clearance. It didn't surprise her that he and Guthrie would be contemporaries, the spooks drew their recruits from a shallow and murky gene pool. Driscoll. In at the flowering of her relationship with Phil. She wondered where he was now. Maybe he could help clear up a few matters?

Did she still have his number? She scrolled through her phone. All she had was a China-based mobile; he would probably have moved on long since. She tried it anyway and was surprised to find it still active. It went to messagebank so she left one, in Mandarin. Sharon checked the time: seven thirty. She'd managed to wangle the six-to-two shift while Phil was overseas. It meant she could get some quality time with Ella in the afternoon before the holy hour of dinner, bath and bedtime. Julie was getting antsy with the extra childcare demands. No way this was going to be sustainable over the longer term. Sharon back in Investigations? Dream on.

Her phone buzzed.

'*Ni hao*. Howdy stranger.' Driscoll.

'You're still in China?'

'Call forwarding. Then I filter them. You got lucky.' Cocky as ever and probably lying.

'So where are you?'

'It's a secret. What can I do for you?'

She told him.

'Paul Reinado? Never heard of him. Why the interest?'

'He was found dead in Fremantle recently. I was tangentially involved in the investigation.'

'Tangentially?'

'Yes. He's a Timorese national, now Aussie citizen. I'm reliably informed via hearsay that he was on the payroll of Australian security services.'

'Who were you reliably informed via hearsay by?'

'I could say it's a secret but I won't. A certain Geoff Guthrie. Know him?'

'Don't think I do, no.'

'You went to ANU together. Modern languages, postgrad.'

'Did we?'

'Stop fucking around, Rory. Can you find out whatever you can about Reinado and get back to me?'

'I'm retired now, a simple fisherman out Woop Woop.'

'Those car and moped horns in the background don't make me think Woop Woop.'

'Holiday.'

'So can you help me?'

'I'll see what I can do. But you haven't really answered my question. Why the tangential interest?'

Should she come clean? Appeal to his better nature? 'It concerns my husband. I'm worried he might be in danger.'

'The lecturer?'

'No, I remarried. Remember Philip Kwong, the cop who came to Shanghai?'

Was it her imagination or had the line suddenly gone quieter?

'Yeah,' said Driscoll. 'I think I remember the guy.'

***

Paul Reinado. Aunty hadn't mentioned him, only these two pensioners who'd died in WA. It was Aunty who tipped him off to Sharon's call, his old phone monitored by a tech unit in Canberra in case any China issues resurfaced. So, Kwong and Sharon. Well, well. He hadn't heard, but then again why would he? Not long after the Shanghai affair he'd joined Operation Sovereign Borders, and that had consumed him for the following three years. Maybe still did. Mira was looking at him expectantly.

'Who was that?'

'A colleague from way back.'

'That name you mentioned, Paul Reinado. What about him?'

'Why?'

'The family who looked after me in Darwin. Their name was Reinado. They had a son, maybe five years older than me. His name was Paul.' Her lower lip trembled. 'He was like an older brother. Is it him? What has happened?'

His face gave it away. 'He's dead. He was found hanged in Fremantle.'

Tears ran down her face. 'Suicide?'

'As far as they know.' Ximenes, thought Driscoll. Has to be. 'When did you last see Paul?'

'Nah,' said Mark. 'We've checked you out, mate. You never go quietly. Maddie?'

Maddie scrolled through her tablet. 'Twenty-thirteen. Shanghai. You caused no end of trouble there.' Clearly Maddie was no lackey; she was the resident spook. Those bright friendly secretary eyes had chilled and locked onto Cato's. 'That isn't going to happen here.'

'If Ximenes refuses an interview, I can hardly compel him.'

'He's a very well-connected bloke. You know that?' Mark paused to glance at Rosa. 'You look like you lost a dollar and found a cent. Something I said?'

Rosa didn't reply.

Mark turned his attention to Sam. 'The joint Timor-Australian police cooperation program is about exactly that. Cooperation. Got it?'

'Absolutely,' said Sam. 'Sir.'

'The past is past. Water under the bridge.'

'Our interest isn't in history,' said Cato. 'These murders occurred just last month. This is very much a live and current enquiry.'

'Maddie will be point of contact while you're here. If she chooses to accompany you at any time she absolutely will. If we don't like the way things are going, we'll pull the plug and ship you out. Understood?'

'Yes,' said Cato. 'We get the picture.'

***

The initial impression of a Darwin boom was undercut by the empty shopfronts in the CBD. Another mirage? The heat bounced off the concrete, steel and glass and any pedestrians hugged whatever shade they could find. Even Driscoll, who'd grown accustomed to such a climate in his years in the job, found himself struggling. A fucking tree would be nice, he thought. He'd called into Vodafone and bought himself a prepaid with false ID, shielding himself from the CCTV with a large-peaked baseball cap pulled low. He'd called Aunty's secure line.

'We're here.'

'I know. The pilot sent word yesterday. As did Jilly.'

'Jilly?'

'An old friend. We shared a swag for a while on a delightful trek in the Flinders Ranges.'

She shrugged. 'Three, maybe four years ago. A family Christmas. He seemed happy. New family. Good job.'

'And you hadn't heard about his death?'

Mira shook her head. 'I've heard nothing since we turned our phones off and gave them to Mrs Blasey, back in Canberra.' A pleading look. 'I need to talk to his parents, they will be wondering. They will think I don't care.'

'Their phones will probably be monitored.'

'Who cares! Your people already have Willie and Brian. They will know where we are.'

'It's Ximenes and whoever is helping him that concerns me now. Maybe Paul's death was a message to you. Do you want that for his parents too?'

She slumped. 'So what do we do now?'

'The embassy. We'll go there first.'

'Can we trust them?'

'I don't know.'

***

The road was rough, skirting a hill scarred by repeated and unrepaired landslips. Out to their right the sea shimmered. In the distance a large mountainous island loomed out of the mist.

'Atauro,' said Rosa. 'You should visit if you get the chance. It's beautiful.'

Tourism, thought Cato. The next frontier. Could such a poor country with such a bloody and sad history take that path and make it work? If Cambodia can do it, he supposed, anybody can. The wind was hot now and offered no real relief. Along the way, signs warned them not to swim in the ocean because of crocodiles. Here and there people ignored the warnings.

Rosa noted his interest. 'In the last ten years there has been a huge increase in the number of attacks. It now averages one a month. Some say there are extra crocodiles coming from Australia. Making trouble.'

'That's what, six hundred kilometres away?'

She shrugged. 'Habitat encroachment. It's a theory the scientists have.'

'And it's only the Australian ones who make trouble?'

'Of course. Timorese crocodiles only attack people who deserve it.'

'Tell me about the Timorese crocodiles,' said Cato. 'They sound so wise.'

'Are you sitting comfortably?' Rosa smiled. 'Then I will begin. Many years ago, a small crocodile, what we call *lafaek*, lived in a swamp. The small crocodile had dreams of becoming a big crocodile but, in that faraway place, food was scarce. Day by day, the small crocodile grew weaker and sadder, until he had to leave the swamp in search of the open sea, where he might find food. But the seashore was a long way away and the day was hot. The crocodile, so far from water, could go no further, and lay down to die.'

'Not sounding good,' said Cato.

'Shush and listen,' said Rosa. 'A small boy came across *Lafaek* and carried him to the sea. In return for saving his life, the grateful crocodile told him that if he could ever help the boy, he would. Years passed. The small boy, now a big boy, called the crocodile, who himself had grown big and strong. "*Lafaek*," the boy said, "I too have a dream. I want to see the world." The crocodile told the boy to climb on his back. "Where shall we go?" he asked the boy. "Towards the sun, brother crocodile," the boy replied.'

Cato found himself lulled by the honey warmth of her voice. Or maybe it was the heat of the day.

'The boy and *Lafaek* together travelled the oceans for years. But there came a day when the crocodile had grown old and he said to the boy, who was now a man, "The time has come for me to die." Then, in memory of the boy's kindness, *Lafaek* turned himself into a beautiful island. "Here," he said, "you and your children can live until the sun sinks in the sea." Then the crocodile died, and his back, with its ridges, became the mountains and his scales the hills of Timor.' Rosa waved a hand at the towards the sea. 'Now when the people of Timor-Leste swim in the ocean, they enter the water saying "Don't eat me, *maun alin*, I am your relative".'

Cato nodded. 'A creation story.'

'A little like your country's Dreamtime maybe?'

'Something like that, I suppose. And Antonio, the pet at HQ ...'

'Is not a pet, he is our guardian, our protector.'

'Is it not cruel to keep him captive?'

'Maybe,' said Rosa. 'There has been so much cruelty and captivity already in Timor.' She smiled. 'Maybe you can liberate Antonio next time you meet him.' Her eyes clouded. 'Now we are in the Petty Kingdom of Mr Ximenes. I will take you to the place that made him famous.'

Ahead of them a handpainted sign – *Massacre Church, Right 300m.*

'It helps the tourists find it,' said Rosa. 'They read about it in *Lonely Planet* or some such and want to see for themselves.' She indicated right and they bumped down a rutted track nudging carefully through flocks of chickens and the odd goat.

They pulled up outside a church that you might see in any Australian suburb. Cato had been expecting an old, ornate Portuguese style colonial-era building. Instead it was a design that he would have more readily associated with the sixties: straight lines, sharp angles, defiantly modernist. It wasn't how he imagined a massacre site should look.

'September sixth, a few days after the independence vote.'

Cato nodded. 'Around two hundred people, I read somewhere.'

'That's right. Hacked, shot. By Ximenes and his men, and by Indonesian soldiers.'

'You would have been very young?'

'Thank you for the compliment, I am older than I look. I was seventeen at the time. Luckily I and my family were not here that day. We took refuge in the hills immediately after my parents voted. Others, not so lucky.'

'Nobody was held responsible later? Surely there was an enquiry?'

'Indictments, findings, yes, but nothing came of it.'

They walked around the outside of the building, looked in through the glass doors at the empty pews. Silent. Peaceful. Nearby a goat bleated.

'I can't imagine ...' Cato began.

'No,' said Rosa. 'I don't suppose you can.' She shook her head. 'For some, death might have been the best thing.'

'Why?'

'The survivors were forced onto trucks by the militia and taken across the border. Many have still not returned. Some were killed. Some were forced to serve the militias. I have some friends from school who I have not seen since then.'

'Serve the militias?'

'Become their slaves, their property, their hostages against war crimes investigations.' She turned to Cato. 'You wanted to know why I am so cynical about reconciliation.'

'Ximenes might be the petty king here, but what do his subjects think of him, after all this?'

'Look around you.' Rosa smiled sadly. 'We are only one hour from Dili by road but we may as well be on a distant hill down by the border. Life is basic here. It has always been about survival. Tyrants and oppressors come and go. Politics and ambition are what happens in the city. Here we live every day with the power of the natural world: the sun, the earth, the storms, the ocean. The *liurai*.

Cato recalled Rosa's story. Those words of the little boy: "Don't eat me, *maun alin*, I am your relative".

They drove away from the empty church. At the gravel turn-off as they eased back onto the bitumen road, a battered ute cruised slowly past them.

***

Mark and Maddie were back on duty in the embassy boardroom with Driscoll and Mira.

'Busy, busy, busy,' said Colonel Mark. 'All this attention, downright flattering.'

'Is the video link with Canberra set to go?' How many times had he sat in such a room? Another embassy, another day. Driscoll no longer had the patience for the conga line of foppish ex-private school boys he'd had to endure along the way. He had an urge to slap Mark's entitled gubba smirk.

'You there, Pauline?' Maddie peered irritably at the snowy wall-mounted screen until Aunty morphed into existence.

'Maddie, my dear. Long time, no see. You're obviously going from strength to strength. Who's that with you?'

'The name's Mark,' said Mark, sourly.

'And Rory and Mira. How are you, dears?'

'Great,' said Rory. 'So what's the plan?'

'Never were one for small talk, were you?'

'Things to do, Mrs Blasey. Places to go, people to see.'

'Fine, fine.' A brief had been sent down the line to Mark and Maddie. Assuming they'd read it, they should be up to speed. 'Ximenes might have been an asset once but he's just a huge fucking liability now. We need him out of action.'

'The Timorese are never going to hand him over,' said Mark. 'However badly he behaved in the past, he's one of theirs. This is an issue of sovereignty.'

'Got any eggs for me to suck?' said Aunty.

'He's hardwired into the economy now.' Maddie shook her head. 'He's behind the government push to buy out those multinationals wavering on their Timor Gap commitments. Backchannelling on the pipeline options too. Pretty soon he'll have us surrounded and under siege.'

'Like peasants cowering in a church,' said Aunty. 'Maybe it's now in our national interest to take him down?'

'He's tried to kill us,' said Driscoll. 'He's been a piece of crap from day one.'

'Yes, Rory, but he was our piece of crap.'

Mira and Driscoll contained their disgust but a gleam had appeared in Maddie's eye. 'We'd need to keep it arm's-length.'

Aunty nodded. 'That's where Detective Kwong comes in.'

'Arm's-length, my arse.' Colonel Mark looked like he would love to pound the table but it might appear a trifle *trop*. A glance at Driscoll. 'Your Chinese chum from Perth hasn't got any solid evidence and there's no extradition treaty. Ximenes isn't going anywhere.'

'So we need to give this Kwong chap all the help he needs.' Aunty was fiddling with her lighter. 'And if that doesn't do enough to budge the powers-that-be in Dili then we'll have to think more creatively about how to take Ximenes out of play.'

'Does that mean what I think it means?'

'Rory,' she beamed. 'So you were paying attention after all.'

Maddie glanced at Mira and then back at the screen. 'Maybe we need to have the civilians out of the room before we discuss matters further?'

'What do you reckon, Mira?' Aunty couldn't wait. She lit up and blew a plume of smoke at them. 'Reckon you can keep a secret? Because if you can't, we'll lock you up for twenty years. Look at poor Brian and Willie.'

'In this case,' said Mira. 'The enemy of my enemy is my friend.'

Aunty looked puzzled. 'Was that a yes?'

***

Rosa had spotted the ute as it U-turned in her rear-view mirror to tail them. She'd alerted Cato immediately. The ute hung back, maybe two hundred metres, following them all the way to the big house where generations of the Ximenes family had lived. Recently the house had been converted into a restaurant and boasted a million dollar view over a foaming ocean. The wind was strong but still offered no cool relief.

'Let's see what happens now.' Rosa checked her pistol, straightened her uniform, and led them into the restaurant. She chose a seat on the balcony facing inwards towards the doorway they'd just walked through. Below them a sheer cliff and crocodile-infested waves. There was nowhere to run if anybody came for them. Rosa studied the menu. 'I doubt they will come in. Too public, and they probably don't have the money. I'm guessing they're just watching and reporting, nothing more.'

'I hope you're right.'

'You were the one who wanted to ruffle the man's feathers. Is that the term?'

'Yes,' said Cato. 'Your English is very good.'

'Thank you. Your Tetun, Portuguese and Bahasa are terrible.'

'Touché.'

'But your French is better.'

They ordered Diet Cokes and, as it was nearly lunchtime, some food. There were others there: a Timorese family – relatively affluent if their clothes, the car outside, and the food orders were anything to go by. Visiting expats, guessed Cato. Further down the balcony two old men played a game of chess and, just beyond them, sat a table of four backpackers. They looked and sounded European, scandi maybe. 'The Ximenes family no longer owns this land?'

Some eyes darted his way. The waiters were on alert now. 'Voice down, please.' She smiled reassuringly at the staff and said something to them in Tetun. 'I told them you are a historian, that you write dusty books about dusty history. They believe me. You must look the part.'

'Sorry,' said Cato, *sotto voce*. 'So. Do they?'

'Yes, he still owns it. He collects the rent but now will only visit on special days. His life and his business are in Dili and elsewhere.'

'You know a lot about him. You take a particular interest?'

The Cokes arrived and she sipped hers. 'He is my *liurai*, my Petty King.'

'Are you a loyal subject?'

She shrugged. 'Loyalty.'

It was no real answer. 'You were born near here?'

'Yes, near that church I showed you.'

'Were any of your relatives …'

'All of these questions. Ah,' she smiled. 'The food, at last.'

They ate in silence. The warm wind stuck the shirt to Cato's back. The only coolness was in Rosa's distracted gaze. After a while they finished and left. Rosa decided it was time to confront the men in the ute.

'Is that a good idea?'

She turned. 'You want to shake them up. This is your chance.' They marched up to the ute and Rosa tore open the driver's door, shouting something in Tetun. The driver and his companion stepped out and leaned over the bonnet, hands on head. 'You search him, I will do this one.'

'I'm not sure I have the authority.'

'They don't know that,' she snapped. 'Just do it.'

Neither was armed and both seemed bemused by the reaction. Rosa told him to watch over them while she did a quick search of the ute cabin and tray. She came back with a mobile phone from the passenger side. Scrolling through, she found what she was looking for. Her thumbs were furiously active on the buttons then she threw the phone over the cliff into the sea. The man protested and she hissed at him.

'You sent a message to Ximenes?' asked Cato.

'Oh, yes. I sure did.'

***

Driscoll was waiting in hotel reception when Kwong returned.

'G'day mate. Drink?' He gestured towards the bar. 'My shout.'

The woman Timorese cop eyed him warily, made her excuses and left. Kwong shook his head like nothing surprised him anymore. They took some seats and ordered a couple of Tigers.

'Congratulations on the nuptials,' said Driscoll, chucking down a handful of peanuts and clinking glasses. 'Sharon told me the good news.'

'Thanks. Let me guess, our meeting here is not a happy accident?'

'Astute as ever.'

'Ximenes?' A nod in reply. 'You want me to leave him alone?'

'*Au contraire*, I'm at your disposal.'

Kwong sipped his beer. 'Have you told the embassy? They seem to take a different view.'

'Not any more. We're all singing from the same songbook.'

'Even Maddie?'

'Especially Maddie, she's a pragmatist.' And one of Aunty's protégés, Driscoll guessed. He could see Mira heading their way. He stood to welcome her, made the introductions. 'Philip is the detective I was telling you about. The guy from Perth.'

'Hi,' she said.

'You're colleagues?' Kwong was sizing her up, trying to work her out.

'Of sorts,' said Driscoll. 'How are your enquiries progressing?'

'Slowly. Ximenes blanked me. I'm aware he just needs to sit put until I fly out. But he's my man, I'm sure of it.'

'When do you fly out? What's your plan?'

'Look for evidence. Shake the tree. See what happens.'

'Bit loose as plans go.'

Kwong conceded the point. 'I'm on borrowed time. Life and the Job goes on. Maybe this will have to take a few visits. Months, years even. A patient build. Some diplomacy.'

'Patience and diplomacy? You?'

'Any other ideas?'

'One or two.' Driscoll gave him a brief summary. 'But we'll have to keep the locals out of it – the PNTL and the AFP liaison guy.'

'Rosa and Sam.'

'Right.' Kwong's colleague had come through the lobby doors, looked their way and headed upstairs without saying hello. 'And your offsider – we might need to keep him out of it too, for his own good.'

'José.'

'José, right. So how about we meet at reception after dinner? Just you and me.' Kwong nodded his assent. They parted ways and Driscoll got on his phone. The last time he'd seen 'José', that hadn't been his name.

19

Driscoll in Dili. Why did that not surprise him? Could the man be trusted? No, not entirely, although Cato thought he detected a certain mellowing with age, nothing specific, but not quite the man he recalled. He knew from experience there was a line Driscoll wouldn't cross. It was just a lot further away than Cato's. In Shanghai, the wanker had left him at the mercy of a vicious local gangster longer than was necessary, and his misreading of the situation led indirectly to the death of Cato's colleague. Fair appraisal? Who knew, but Cato once again found himself playing away from home and reliant on local help, which he would need if he had any chance of getting a result. Could Rosa deliver that? She said she had sent a message to Ximenes which hopefully would spark a reaction. Now the embassy and its spooks had come in on his side. The timing was suspicious to say the least. He looked out of his hotel room window at the port across the road and the crane unloading containers from a docked ship. It was midafternoon. José should have returned by now from his visit to Scottie's sports bar. Cato had no expectations of a report or update. It was solely a diversion to keep AFP Sam occupied.

A knock at the door. Speak of the devil. 'How was Scottie's?'

José smiled grimly. 'A non-event, but then we knew it would be. Sam wasn't too worried by the waste of time. Had an extended lunch, steak and chips and a few beers. Happy as.' He took the only available seat at the desk by the window. 'You?'

'Had a look around Ximenes' territory, some church where they had a massacre. Got tailed by a couple of his men for a while.'

'Any trouble?'

'No, Rosa had it all under control.'

'Formidable woman.'

'She'd have to be, I expect.'

José tapped his fingers on the desk. 'We're wasting our time on Ximenes, aren't we? The bloke isn't going to fess up and we don't have enough on him. What's the point of us being here?'

Cato shrugged. 'Get closer to the truth? It might not be the same as a result but it might eliminate some lines of enquiry.'

'Truth? An expensive exercise.'

'Didn't know you'd gone over to the beancounters, José.'

A grunt. 'Did I see you chatting with some punters in the bar earlier?'

'Yeah, you should have come over and introduced yourself.' Cato recalled Driscoll's plea for discretion. 'People from one of the NGOs, forget which. Seemed nice enough.'

'Right,' said José. 'So what's the plan from here?'

'Can you liaise with Earle, get an update from her end of things? I'll do likewise with Perth Homicide. Regroup in an hour?'

'Sure.'

'And talk to AFP Sam. Get him to dig whatever he can on Ximenes. Rumour, tittle-tattle, whatever.'

'That'll rattle the embassy cage.'

'Apparently not. They're coming around to our way of thinking.'

'Really? How'd you hear that?'

Too long a pause and Cato realised he'd been caught out. 'A phone chat with Madeleine earlier.' He dug himself deeper. 'There's been a thaw.'

'Interesting.' José nodded, let his eyes drift away. 'Right, better get onto it then.'

Cato had just lied to his colleague and it was clear he had been busted. José no longer trusted him. That could be fatal when they were in an unfamiliar and potentially dangerous place and needed to count on each other. A wedge. Had that been Rory Driscoll's intent?

Played. Like a fucking piano.

***

Sharon was beginning to get worried. Driscoll hadn't returned any of her calls since that initial contact. She'd run a check with Border Control to find out where the hell he was in the world so she could try and track him down through the relevant embassy. He'd flown out of Darwin that weekend headed for, of course, Timor-Leste. Wherever Driscoll was, trouble followed. It was no coincidence. Whatever path Phil's investigation took now had Driscoll's imprint on it. She checked the time, it would be late afternoon in Dili. She made the call.

'Hi.' Phil failed to hide the surprise in his voice. 'Everything okay?'

'Yeah,' she said, artificially bright. 'Just fancied a chat. Got time?'

'Sure. How's it going back there?'

'Same old. I think Julie's losing her mojo with Ella.'

'I better get back there quick. Give her a break.'

'Julie or Ella?'

'Both,' he chuckled. 'Hey, never guess who I caught up with today.'

'Rory Driscoll?'

The line went silent for a moment. 'You *were* speaking to him? I thought he was just messing with my mind.'

'This morning,' she confirmed. 'I'd been looking at Paul Reinado. He's being wiped from the record. I took a closer squiz at that spook you met, Guthrie, and saw a link between him and Driscoll. I phoned Rory to see if he could check stuff out for me. Didn't realise he was already in Dili.'

'Small world.'

'Is he there to help or hinder?'

'Help, he says.'

'In what way?'

'Cage-rattling. It's his speciality.'

'Anything specific?'

'Not yet. So what's with the Reinado case?'

'I think your old friend DI McMahon is looking to ditch it. Call it suicide.'

'Major Crime hasn't taken over? Pavlou was meant to move on it by now.'

'Maybe you should phone the office, find out what's going on.' Sharon could feel the call slipping away from her. This was shop talk. She was happy to help out, be a pro, but to hell with it. 'Be careful, Phil. Don't trust Driscoll, the embassy, any of them. There's something going on behind the scenes. Bigger than your murder enquiry.'

'I'll be careful.'

'I'll keep looking into Reinado before he disappears completely.'

'Thanks.' A pause. 'Love you.'

'Take care.' Sharon closed the call. And then made another.

***

Cato got onto Thornton.

'How are the mojitos up there in the tropics?'

'Bitey,' said Cato. 'But I've got repellent. What's going on?'

'As in?'

'What's the status of the Reinado case? Aren't we taking that over?'

'Evidently not. It's being left in the capable hands of DI McMahon. Resources issue according to the boss.'

'Any outside pressure?'

'Above my pay grade. Gossip like that you'll have to get direct from the horse's mouth. In other news today, we have possible witness IDs on a car in the vicinity of both the murders and it matches with the hire car Ximenes had during his time in Perth – down to the make, colour, and part of the rego number.'

This was good news. It strengthened his case for an extradition request. Cato asked Thornton to send the details through in a formal report. 'Anything else?'

'The body in the skip, Ryan Hodgson? The boss is looking at keeping that separate too.'

'Why?'

'It obviously doesn't link directly to Ximenes because the guy was out of the country by then. And it's a sufficiently different MO. Could be drugs. Could be revenge for his part in that pack-rape a few years ago. Whole bunch of alternative scenarios being mooted.'

Cato didn't buy it but had no choice. 'So who's covering it?'

'Earle has taken that over and handed Bevan Drummond to our crew. Pavlou's mantra of the day is focus. Focus, team. Focus,' he said in passable imitation of Pavlou's tobacco-coarsened tones.

'Is she around?'

'Budgets, efficiency dividends and KPIs at HQ. Out for the day.'

'Cheers, Chris. Keep on at the hire car thing. If we can have Ximenes in that vehicle at those places and those times it'd be great.'

'The man's DNA would be good too. Any chance of a sample? Just asking for a friend.'

'I'll see what I can do.'

***

Driscoll met Kwong in reception after an early dinner as planned. There was still a glimmer of orange in the western sky, but it would be gone soon. The embassy had loaned him a gun and a car, those they used for just such a purpose as tonight: unofficial, untraceable, slightly battered. Not unlike himself. The gun was on Driscoll's hip and the car was parked across the road. They dodged the mopeds and headed that way. Kwong looked his usual worried self.

'All good?' asked Driscoll.

'The jury's out. I had a word with Sharon earlier. She told me not to trust you.'

'I thought Shaz and me got on well back in Shanghai. Something I said?'

'Tell me about Paul Reinado.'

Driscoll palmed a dollar into the hand of the car park attendant, exchanged some words of Tetun and eased out into the traffic. He swung an immediate left at the lights onto the port road that would take them past the embassies. 'Reinado?' He made a show of trying to remember an unfamiliar name.

'You're not as cocky or convincing as you used to be. Bit rusty or just jack of the job?'

Driscoll appraised Kwong. 'And you're not as sweet and innocent as you used to be.'

'So. Reinado?'

Driscoll recounted what he'd read in the summary Aunty sent him. 'Timorese expat. Family moved to Darwin immediately after the referendum. They were on a hit list. His dad was a leading light in Fretilin from way back. Price on his head. Paulho, as he was known then, was a student activist in the last years before the Indonesians got kicked out.'

'Who killed him and why?'

'I heard it was suicide. Drugs and alcohol, unbalanced mind.'

'He'd been under threat in the weeks preceding. Like my two old men in Freo and Bunbury.' Kwong shook his head. 'The hanging theory is problematic.'

Driscoll kept his eyes on the road ahead. 'Not according to the local plods.'

'You're well informed.'

'It's my job to be.'

'Your mate Guthrie told me Reinado was working for you.'

'Not me. I've been …' Driscoll checked himself.

'Out of the game?' Kwong smiled. 'Guessed as much. So what brought you back in? Something personal?' A nod to himself. 'Unfinished business.' He settled back into his seat. 'Now we're getting somewhere.'

'Really?' They were skirting back inland now, starting the climb into the hills to Dare.

'Sure. Me? I'm just doing my job. I can walk away from this if it gets too hard.' Kwong drummed his fingers on the door handle. 'You? You have a problem that needs solving, a problem close to home. You're committed. That means you need me more than I need you.'

'You're wasted as a cop. This ability to look into the souls of men.'

'If we're both after the same guy then fine, let's make this work. But don't take me for granted.'

Driscoll changed gears as the climb got steeper. The Ximenes place was just around the next bend. 'Perish the thought, mate.'

**

Sharon hadn't been able to get hold of Paul Reinado's widow until she was driving back from work late afternoon. Jessica Reinado had a Territorian drawl that must have taken root in the DNA at least four generations ago. She'd been out making funeral arrangements but was yet to be told when the body would be released.

'I'll try and find out if you like?' said Sharon.

'Could you?' A crack in the dry-creek voice. 'I want to be able to give him a proper send-off. It's doing our heads in. Me. The kid. His folks.'

'You mentioned to one of my colleagues that there had been some strange stuff in the lead-up. Do you mind telling me again?'

'There'd been phone calls at all hours. Sometimes nothing on the other end when I answered, other times when Paul answered there would be threats. Vandalism: our car was damaged, scratched, tyres punctured. We had a cat. It disappeared for a few days then was found up the road in the gutter like it had been run over.' A sigh. 'Shit in the mailbox. There were reports of a van and some bloke taking photos of the kids in the school yard at recess but that might just have been standard Darwin pervs.'

'You don't know who was doing this or why? Paul didn't?'

A hesitation. 'Paul suspected it was something to do with what his dad was involved in.'

'His dad?'

'An activist in the Timorese community. Been at it for yonks. The war's never over for those people.'

Hence Paul's usefulness to ASIO. Sharon wondered how he'd been recruited – reward or threat? Both probably. Wondered how much Jessica knew about her husband. 'Anything specific?'

'Some bloke had been recognised on the streets of Darwin. He'd been involved in some massacres back in the day. They don't forget that shit, do they? Paul's dad was making noise about it to whoever would listen.'

'When was this?' Jessica gave an approximate date. 'March? But that was months ago.'

'Yeah, funny that. I said to Paulie it didn't make sense, but he was convinced. He reckoned it had taken that long for his dad's noise to get through to somebody that mattered.'

'So this person who was recognised, accused of being involved in these atrocities, he was part of the Timorese community?'

'Nah, nah. That's why it caused so much fuss. This bloke was an Aussie, true blue.'

***

They parked a hundred metres down the hill and walked the rest of the way. The wind had dropped. Insects ticked in the undergrowth where the road ended. Odours of overripe fruit, frying chicken, sewerage. Way below them Dili twinkled in the distance and a half moon hung over the sea. Cato felt clammy and unfit trying to keep up with Driscoll's long stride. He could see now the bulge at the hip. Driscoll had come armed.

'I thought we were just here to talk, do some winding up?'

Driscoll shushed him with a finger to the lips. 'Insurance. That's all.'

They strolled up to the reinforced two metre high gates and Driscoll pressed the intercom button. A crackly voice answered and Driscoll spoke to it in Tetun. The reply to Driscoll's request seemed to be negative.

Then he said something else. Almost immediately the gates swung open and four men came out and surrounded them, machetes raised.

'What did you say?' said Cato, holding his hands high in surrender.

'I reminded Ximenes of exactly who I was and the last time we met.'

Each of them was patted down. 'There goes the insurance,' noted Cato as the gun was confiscated, along with their phones and the car keys. Machete blades prodded them through the gates.

Driscoll offered a reassuring grin. 'All going to plan, so far.'

'I'd hate to be with you when things go wrong. Oh, wait ... there was that time.'

'Faith, brother.'

They were ushered into an empty room down some stairs below the main house. It would be pretty well soundproofed if that was your intent. The door closed behind them.

'This doesn't look good,' said Cato.

'Mind games. Trust me.'

The door slammed open, bouncing off the wall. In came Ximenes and the same four men from earlier. He marched straight up to Driscoll and stood chest to chest. Shorter, by maybe ten centimetres, he lifted his gaze in examination. 'It really is you.'

Driscoll said something to him in Tetun.

'No. English is fine. We want your colleague to be able to understand.'

'They patched you up well, João. The ear especially, you'd have to look closely. The eye is still a little obvious. Hence the shades, huh?'

One of the henchmen stepped in from the side and king hit Driscoll. He dropped like a stone. Cato wondered if he'd killed him. Two of the others stood in front of Cato in case he thought of getting involved. Unlikely, unless it really was a last resort. After a moment Driscoll stirred, blood pouring from smashed lips. He climbed painfully to his feet, shook his head to clear it, and almost collapsed again.

'You blame me for what Abdullah Hamady did to you. Understandable, I guess.' He wiped his mouth with the back of his hand. 'You put my name on that death list that found its way from BIN into Willie Mason's hands. You wanted me involved, out in the open.'

'Loyalty is important to me,' said Ximenes. 'Mateship, you call it. A good Aussie looks after his mates.' He turned to Cato. 'That right, Chinaman?'

'I guess.'

'You people are living a lie. Australians? Treacherous and self-serving one minute, sentimental and smug the next.'

'Don't beat around the bush, mate.' Driscoll looked unsteady on his feet. 'Say what you mean.'

'They stole your land from you, and then they go and make their borders into something rigid and sacred against any other foreigners. Except for our oil reserves of course, where your border is as elastic as a Dali clock.' He nodded. 'Yes, I too have had an education.' He was enjoying himself, once again in charge. 'All the things you do in the name of your plastic empire. Hypocrites.'

'Look I'm sorry I gave you up to the people smugglers. But all's fair in love and ...'

Ximenes prodded Driscoll in the chest. 'And you're the biggest fool. Thinking they would ever accept you. They used you like they used me.'

'So we're brothers, right?'

'When they find your corpse in the gutter tomorrow, they'll walk past it. A troublesome black, that's all you ever were.'

Cato was sick of the sideshow. 'Why did you kill the old men in Perth?'

'Old men? What do I want with old men in Perth?'

'You were there recently. Your hire vehicle was in the area of each murder at the time. One of them was researching you. They had links with Timor. They had been here.'

'You are wasting your time. And mine.' At a nod from Ximenes, the henchmen wrestled Driscoll to the floor. Spread out his arms, hands, fingers. Another stood ready with the machete. 'Abdullah's men spent hours with me. Took their time. Shall I accord you the same privilege?'

Driscoll spat some words of Tetun.

Ximenes cupped his false ear. 'What was that?' Then he took the machete into his own hands and raised it.

***

Driscoll had miscalculated. Had he even calculated in the first place? He was losing it, he realised. Even mild-mannered Kwong had wrong-footed him on the journey here, changed the balance of power. Now Ximenes had him at his mercy, just like he too had been all those years before, back in Abdullah's basement in Kupang.

'You should have killed me when you had the chance.' Ximenes had his mouth close to Driscoll's ear. 'Put me out of my misery, instead of leaving me to them.' His hand clamped Driscoll's wrist and he lifted the machete.

'Enough!'

'Shut the Chinaman up.' Ximenes turned and pointed the machete at Kwong. 'You are next.'

'I have told my colleagues in Perth where I was going. If they do not hear from me there will be police here and you will be arrested. We will bring you to Australia and charge you with murder.'

'What police? PNTL?' A snort. 'Nobody will touch me.'

'Are you telling the truth about the old men? They are nothing to you?'

'Yes.'

'Then somebody is trying to set you up. You must have a very powerful enemy in Western Australia, where you do so much business. They know your movements. They know all about you, your history. They want to eliminate you.'

Ximenes held his grip on Driscoll's wrist. Turned his gaze away from Kwong.

'Don't you want to know who it is?'

The machete slowly came down. 'Do you know?'

'I think I do, yes.' Kwong pressed his point. 'There must be a lot of money at stake. Oil, gas money. Yes?'

'You will trade me this person for your miserable lives?'

'Yes,' said Kwong. 'Of course.'

'Like I said before,' Ximenes put down the machete. 'You Australians – self-serving and treacherous, all of you.'

20

Tuesday 8th May

Cato woke sweating and reached instinctively for his pills. The old dreams were back and mixed in with some new ones: a white lake with blood rippling outwards, fireworks and a knife tearing at his gut, darkness and sump oil and relentless pain, a black tunnel and weight pressing down on his shoulders, machetes raised over helpless limbs. He hadn't felt like he needed his medication for some time. The focus and the drive of an investigation was drug enough it seemed. But those moments when you stopped and thought. Cactus. You were done for. That's when he craved chemical help. He was due his weekly slow-release dose tomorrow. Could he hold out until then? No. He swallowed two of his emergency stash pills with a swig from his water bottle. After a while the palpitations settled, his chest loosened, breathing returned to normal.

Ximenes had chosen to believe Cato's lie. There had been something in his expression. Relief? Choosing to believe Cato allowed him to save face. Did he, after so many years bathed in blood, no longer have the heart to spill more? Cato doubted it. Did Ximenes fear the repercussions if he carried through his threat on Driscoll? More likely. Maybe the dark forces that had lifted him up in recent decades were about to tear him down again. The vulnerability of the hard man – the harder they fall, it is said. But before that they lash out, they weep and wail and claim victimhood, they cajole and manipulate. Still they cannot forestall the inevitable. Or was that wishful thinking? Some despots stay in charge for decades before retiring in luxury only to die peacefully in their sleep. Ximenes had a brush with mortality. This Abdullah bloke, a people smuggler, had dealt him the terrible mutilations replicated in the deaths of the two old men in WA. But Ximenes denied all knowledge of those old men, and Cato leaned towards accepting that denial. If that was the case, then somebody seemed to be setting Ximenes up for those murders. Who and why? This was the basis of their life and face-saving bargain. All Cato had to do now was deliver.

Or what? Or Ximenes would come looking for him – he made that very clear.

'Quick thinking, mate, I'm impressed. I thought I was a goner there.' Ushered out of the gate, Driscoll had shivered like he'd just been told a ghost story. 'D'you reckon I'm past it?'

'Yes,' said Cato. 'You're a liability.'

'Still,' he'd said, reaching into the boot of the embassy car for a clean plastic bag to wrap around his wrist – the one Ximenes had grabbed with the aim of chopping off some fingers. 'Maybe you can drive back?' Lifting the hand. 'That DNA sample you wanted.'

In theory Cato should just leave Timor if Ximenes really wasn't the culprit. But not before the DNA tests had been done. And, he suspected, Driscoll still had unfinished business that might be worth hanging around for. Cato swung his legs out of the bed, shook his head to clear it. The sky was growing light outside the hotel and already the street traffic was building. For a small city on a sleepy island that time forgot, there seemed to be a lot of throbbing undercurrents. Today he would visit the aid projects undertaken by the WA Rotarians all those years ago. Just because Ximenes claimed no knowledge of the old men, that didn't mean they weren't connected in some way.

***

Driscoll woke with a start. He sleepily surveyed his surroundings, allowed memories to take shape. Had he really just come within cooee of losing some of his extremities? One thing was for sure, he hadn't been adequately prepared – he'd miscalculated, big-time. The Ximenes DNA sample on Driscoll's wrist hadn't been part of the plan, it was a consolation prize. Rosa, the Timorese investigator who seemed to have taken Kwong under her wing, had assumed responsibility for the swabs and the dispatch direct to labs in Darwin and Perth rather than Lisbon where they were usually obliged to send forensic samples. She'd been unfazed by their late night call and shown no hint of surprise or disapproval when learning of their visit to Ximenes and what had ensued. She'd been impossible to read. He couldn't tell whose side she was on.

'And he let you both go unharmed?' she'd asked. 'Why?'

Kwong had explained the theory of the Ximenes frame-up and Rosa didn't look like she'd bought it. Join the queue. The important thing was that Ximenes himself bought it. He had no need to, he was in no great danger of extradition. Something obviously rang true about the idea that somebody was out to set him up, to destroy him. Somebody who knew all about him and favoured this complex roundabout method of character assassination over the brute force of a machete to the skull. Who and why? The question occupied Driscoll too. It had spooks written all over it – but whose?

'So if you think he is innocent, you have no need to be here, do you?' Rosa had looked at them both. 'Either of you.'

'We need to crosscheck a few things first.' Kwong had glanced at Driscoll for support.

'Right,' he'd said.

Rosa had packed away her forensic utensils. 'Our job is hard enough without people coming here to cause even more trouble.' She'd looked at Kwong and said something cryptic about Australian crocodiles.

Kwong had acquiesced, offered an apology of sorts. Keeping his options open, no doubt. All Driscoll knew was that Kwong's intervention had saved his skin and for that he owed him. He doused himself under a cold shower, towelled off and checked his phone. Three messages and missed calls, all from Mira. He listened in, growing cold as he did so. He ran down the corridor to her room.

The door was ajar, the room was wrecked, and she was gone.

***

Cato was sitting across from José at the breakfast table when Driscoll burst in.

'Mira. She's disappeared.'

'Who?' said José.

Driscoll barely spared him a glance. He focused on Cato. 'Will you help?'

'Sure.'

While Driscoll went off to interrogate hotel staff and request any CCTV, Cato called Rosa and AFP Sam, who came straight round from HQ just a few streets away. Ten minutes later they all gathered in the foyer and occupied the leather couches.

Driscoll looked tight as a drum. 'She was seen leaving around sunrise in the company of two young men.'

'Voluntarily?' José picked at his teeth to remove some breakfast remnant.

'Not relaxed, was as much as I could glean.' He studied José. 'ABIN, right?' For the benefit of everybody else. 'Agência Brasileira de Inteligência. And you aren't no José, either.'

This was, of course, news to Cato. He examined his partner for signs of mistaken identity or busted imposter panic. Not a peep.

'I am now. I left, changed my name.'

'Why?' asked Cato.

'None of your business.' José smiled at Driscoll. 'Good memory you have there.'

Driscoll nodded. 'A CIA training course, two thousand nine or ten. The class buffoon.'

'Bit harsh, mate.'

'You'll keep.' Driscoll turned his attention back to everybody else. 'The doorman reckons they had tattoos from the local seventy-seven gang.'

'CCTV?' enquired Sam.

'Doing a thumb drive for me now and a print off of some close-ups.' These were promptly delivered by one of the women from reception. Driscoll handed out copies.

Rosa and Sam exchanged glances. They recognised the faces. 'We know where they live.' Sam keyed a number into his phone. 'UIR,' he explained. 'Riot squad.'

Driscoll shook his head. 'No need for that. Just take me to them.'

Sam looked troubled but Rosa acquiesced. 'We'll have the squad on standby around the corner. Just in case.'

Driscoll lifted his chin towards Sam. 'I'll come with you. Hey, José,' he gave the name added emphasis to underline the lie of it. 'Join us. We can reminisce along the way.' Back to Cato. 'Maybe you can keep Rosa company?'

That was fine by him although he would have loved to hear the José backstory. Maybe later. Meanwhile Rosa was studying the CCTV photograph.

'Mira Soares?' She looked up at the departing Driscoll.

'Yes.' He caught the strange expression on her face. 'Why?'

'Seventy-seven first. Then we'll talk.'

***

While Sam did the driving, Driscoll reacquainted himself with the guy who was now José. Turning round in the front passenger seat, he observed a man absolutely at ease with the course of events. 'Been a while, Rodrigo,' he said. 'What's new? Apart from the name?'

'I kept the surname. José was my middle name.'

'And you're no stranger to Timor.'

'It shows?'

'Still in the game?'

José shook his head. 'Nah, finished with all that. Came back home to Oz. Just a country copper these days. Surfing, barbies, footy. Collect the pension in a few years. Sweet.'

'Kwong know your history?'

'I'm guessing his curiosity will be piqued now.'

'Can I trust you?'

'Up to you, mate. No skin off mine.'

'Whose idea was it to send you here with Kwong?'

José shrugged. 'Ours not to reason who or why.'

Driscoll didn't believe him. Brazilian intelligence would have recruited him from his adopted Aussie homeland because of his language skills and his ability to lie like a pig in shit – like all good spooks. Was his presence tied to unfolding events or a coincidental sideshow? Brazil had legitimate interests in Timor as a fellow lusophone country and had committed big time to aid and development assistance programs. Driscoll glanced out the window. They were nearing their destination. Whatever game José/Rodrigo was playing, or not, would have to wait.

The jeep pulled up beside an old shipping container partly blocking an alley that led into the winding lanes of the barrios beyond. On the side of the container some old graffiti: the number '77' plus a crude drawing of a thieving kangaroo carrying the Aussie flag and hopping away with a bucket of oil, leaving behind an angry crocodile under a Timorese flag.

'This is the place?' Driscoll received nodded assurance from Sam. The second jeep rolled up with Kwong and Rosa, their faces unreadable. Timor, reflected Driscoll – a nest of fucking spies. He checked his Glock and placed it back in the holster.

'You got permission to have that?' Sam had just confirmed the riot squad were in position not too far away.

'Of course.' Onlookers were already gathering. Mobiles raised to take photos or make calls. They didn't have long to do this. 'So,' he acknowledged Rosa's approach. 'After you.'

In they went. Down a dry rutted lane past shacks and stalls, chooks in cages and roaming free, a skinny dog scavenging from a pile of garbage, a snotty toddler running along in a disposable nappy and a Wiggles T-shirt.

'This way.' Rosa took them left into a narrower, gloomier alley where the breeze didn't venture. The smell of fried chicken and old cooking oil. People saw them coming and backed into dark doorways as they passed. Turn right and much of the same. Left again.

Driscoll felt the heat, the sweat on his torso, the tightness in his chest and gut. He checked behind him. Yes, Kwong and José were there, looking like he felt. A bottle sailed through the air, catching the sunlight and shattering at their feet. Driscoll looked back to see where it came from. Nobody in sight. Another, not lobbed but barrelling hard and fast. Kwong ducked just in time.

Rosa took out her gun and yelled warnings in Tetun. 'Do that again and we burn this whole place down.' She turned and kicked in the nearest door, stalking in, with her gun arm outstretched, telling them who she was and for everybody to lie down flat on the floor. 'Agora!'

Driscoll was right behind her, followed by Kwong and José. Sam stayed at the door – guarding against ambush, on the phone summoning the riot squad closer and into readiness. Four young men lay facedown, hands behind heads, in a room littered with ashtrays and Coke cans. The place smelled of adolescent sweat and cigarettes. Maybe some ganja in there too. Driscoll studied the men closer, two of them were from the hotel CCTV leading Mira out through the lobby. Rosa ordered them to their feet and signalled for Driscoll to take over. He reached deep for his rusty Tetun.

'Where is she?'

The oldest and most confident of the two, with the '77' tattooed on his neck, wrist and bicep, addressed himself to Rosa. 'Why did you bring the *malae* here?'

Driscoll repeated the question.

'*Fila fali, malae.*' Go home, foreigner.

Driscoll took out his gun and placed it against the youth's head. 'Last time.'

Rosa explained. They were dealing with a powerful, crazy *malae* who had protection from high-up. Where was the woman? Answer the question. Gone, he said.

'Dead?'

A laugh. 'Not yet.'

There was a sharp crack outside and Driscoll heard Sam yelp and curse. He came through the doorway, blood pouring from a wound in his upper arm. 'Fucking *rakitan*.'

A homemade gun, popular in the independence upheaval, the word taken from Bahasa, *senjata rakitan*: a crude concoction of steel pipes and taped pistol grips. To the untrained eye and ear, they recalled the flint-locks of old and skirmishes with the Portuguese colonists. The *rakitans* were as much a trademark of the militias as the machete, each inspiring fear and awe in their crudeness. Its use now was a message.

The youth laughed, as did his comrades, emboldened.

'We need to go,' said Rosa. 'Mira is not here. They are itching for a fight.'

Driscoll turned back to the youth. 'Ximenes? Is that where she is?'

The reply in English. 'Fuck you, *malae*.'

They left.

***

They had delivered Sam to the hospital and proceeded in convoy, two jeeps up the hill to Dare and Villa Ximenes: José and Driscoll in one vehicle, Cato and Rosa in the other. Followed by a minibus full of riot squad.

'Will Sam be okay?'

'He should be,' said Rosa. 'It will hurt for a while and they will need to dig around for shrapnel. It will leave an ugly but heroic scar to remind him of his time in Dili. Something to show off at Aussie barbecues.'

Cato was still jittery after the encounter. 'You're a tough woman, Rosa.'

'It's called survival.'

'You know this woman, don't you? This Mira Soares.'

Rosa nodded. As they rounded a bend the low afternoon sun blinded them momentarily. 'I thought she had died in the massacre or soon after.'

'The church you showed me?'

'Yes.' She braked suddenly, narrowly missing a little boy who had run onto the road. The mother dragged him back to their gate, casting an accusing glare at the jeep. 'She was a year or two younger than me, more. She would have been fourteen maybe?'

'You were friends?'

'Not really. But it was not a big town. We all knew each other.'

'She has been living in Australia for many years now. She's a journalist.'

'Really?'

'What would Ximenes want with her?'

Rosa pursed her lips. 'Maybe she knows something about him. Something he fears.'

'A witness to the massacre?'

'Possibly, but there are already photographs and testimonials placing him there. Old news. Nobody is interested anymore.'

'They always say to follow the money, don't they?'

'Do they? A balancing of the ledger. I guess that is really what they mean by reconciliation.'

Cato nodded. 'Reconciliation.' Up ahead he could see Driscoll in the lead vehicle slowing to the gates of the villa. 'Maybe we will find out now.'

Rosa brought the car to a halt and checked her pistol. 'Maybe.'

***

The gate was untended and unlocked. No dogs barking.

'Scarpered?' wondered José aloud.

Driscoll noticed a middle-aged man waving at them from his folding chair a little way up the road. He had the obligatory pile of coconuts and a couple of cages of trussed chooks beside him. Driscoll told the others to stay at the gate while he took a walk.

'*Maun boot,*' he greeted the man in Tetun. 'You wanted to talk to me, big brother?'

'You were here yesterday. Australian, yes?'

'That's right.' He introduced himself and they shook hands. The man was missing two fingers on his right hand.

'Your friend, the Chinese?'

Driscoll nodded back towards the gate. 'Yes. You keep an eye on everything here, *maun boot*? Nothing escapes you.'

A nod. 'Soldiers.'

'Soldiers?'

'Two trucks. This morning.'

'What time?' The man told him. 'Shooting?'

'A little. Muffled. Only the dogs, I expect. No more barking since then. A good thing, too. They were crazy, vicious.'

'They arrested the people?'

'I don't know. The trucks went through the gates, there was shooting, then they came out again.'

'Did anybody leave or arrive since then?'

'Only you.'

'You didn't look?'

'None of my business.'

Since when, thought Driscoll. 'Thank you, *maun boot.*' He gestured at the chickens. 'How much?'

The man shook his head and laughed. 'No need to buy them. Go and do your work. If the soldiers haven't already killed or arrested that bastard, maybe you can do it now.'

'Ximenes?'

'Who else?'

Driscoll returned to the gate and told them what he'd learned.

'Soldiers?' said Rosa. She took out her phone, stepped away a few paces and made a call. Returning, she shook her head. 'Not ours, or not officially anyway. Nobody has heard of an operation.'

'Would they?' asked Driscoll.

'My contact would, yes.'

'Let's take a look.' Driscoll ratcheted his Glock and went through the gates.

Rosa directed the riot squad to stand guard and caught up with him after a moment. The driveway banked and turned steeply. Shadow crept across the gravel, birds and rodents darted in the bushes. By the time they got to the house, it was clear something bad had happened.

***

The first two bodies were just outside the front door. Cato recognised them from previous visits: Ximenes' henchmen, their chests raked open by automatic gunfire. Near to them lay the dogs.

'Fuck,' said José. 'These people don't mess around.'

In the hallway, a middle-aged woman and a man in his twenties, servants maybe. Facedown, blood had spread and darkened beneath them. Flies already on the scene and, in the heat of the afternoon, a ripe gamey smell. An open door, splintered hinges and lock, a bedroom. Felicity, the girlfriend, must have heard the commotion, tried to save herself by locking the door. She was slumped against a wall, face obliterated and a bloom of crimson above her head. The last time Cato had seen this level of wholesale carnage had been in a McMansion in Port Coogee – a whole family slaughtered.

'In here,' said Driscoll.

The kitchen had been the scene of Ximenes' last stand. Or rather that of his remaining bodyguards. Here two soldiers had also died: one with a knife in his chest and the other shot, possibly with his own gun, up through the jaw in what must have been a hand-to-hand struggle.

'Soldiers don't usually leave their own behind,' observed José. 'Interesting.'

'No insignia on the uniforms,' noted Cato. The faces and bodies, even in death, had a hard, chiselled look about them. They weren't baby-faced conscripts. 'Special forces? Mercenaries? Gangsters in khaki?'

'Whatever,' said Driscoll. 'Some high-level clearance for this. Had to be if they get to use official Timor army trucks.'

'But no sign of Ximenes,' said Cato. 'Or Mira.'

José was crouching down in the doorway of a walk-in storage pantry. 'Over here. I heard something.' He rapped lightly on a panel low down. 'Hello? Anyone home?'

The panel slid open. A panic room. Ximenes emerged, shaken, angry, the stench of fear in his sweat. After him came Mira Soares, a triumphant gleam in her eye. She didn't seem to be his prisoner. If anything, he could have been hers.

***

Sharon had just got Ella off to sleep when her phone buzzed. It was Jessica Reinado.

'I remembered something.'

In the background Sharon could hear a TV blaring and canned laughter. The high volume forced hilarity seemed jarring under the circumstances. 'Yes?'

'About two months before he … before …' Jessica choked up.

'Go on,' said Sharon, gently.

'Paul was arguing on the phone with somebody. In his own language.'

'Timorese?'

'No, not Tetun. I can recognise that these days. Even know a few words for when we go to the expat gatherings. No, it was Portuguese I think. He was brought up speaking both.'

'Do you know what was being said?'

'No, but it definitely sounded like an argument. When it was over, Paul was angry, upset.'

'Did he tell you what it was about?'

'No, I tried asking but he just said it was nothing. Community stuff, politics.'

'And this was when?'

'Early March. I remember because …' again the voice cracked. 'It was Carlo's birthday a couple of days later and he couldn't work out why his dad was so low, so down. He thought he'd been naughty, done something wrong.'

'Did the call come in on Paul's mobile or a landline?'

'Our landline.'

'So the police will have a record of it, I assume.'

'S'pose so.'

'Why did this particular thing jump out for you, Jessica?'

'I don't know. The Portuguese language maybe? He usually avoided speaking it, even though he was fluent.'

'Why did he avoid speaking it?'

'Dunno, something to do with community politics again. Anyway, that was when all the weird shit started happening. The harassment, the vandalism.'

'You've mentioned this all to the investigating officers from Fremantle?'

'Yeah, they sent a couple of blokes round from NT police to ask some questions on their behalf. They were going to send off a report and the interview recording.'

'No follow-up questions?'

'Not so far. No.'

Was this the time to broach the subject? 'Do you know of a bloke called Guthrie, or Geoff? Did Paul ever mention anything?'

'No. Who is he?'

'He works for ASIO.'

'Oh, them. There's always somebody like them hanging around, trying to snoop on the community. Spot them a mile off.'

'Would Paul have had anything to do with them?'

'Don't know, maybe. His dad was always playing games with them. He'd use them to score points against old rivals back home. Settle accounts. Make stuff up.'

And maybe that game turned bad, thought Sharon. 'Anything else come to mind?'

'No,' said Jessica. 'That's it.'

'I'll follow up with the investigators. See if they can track down the number that called Paul. Do you remember what day it was, and round about what time?' After some brain-racking and prompting they narrowed it down to a Thursday at the beginning of March, early evening. 'Thanks, Jessica. How's it going, do you have somebody around to help out, to talk to?'

'Yeah, my mum. It's ... we'll get through.'

'Call me if anything else comes to mind.'

'He didn't kill himself, you know. He wouldn't. He wouldn't abandon us like that. He'd got himself together after ...' More snuffling.

'After what, Jessica?'

'He was only a kid, a teenager. The Indonesians took him to this house. Did terrible things to him. When I heard about what happened on the plane that night from Darwin, all those people holding him down.' A choking sob. 'It must have brought it all back.'

***

Driscoll pulled Mira aside for a quiet chat. 'What's going on?'

'Did you send those soldiers in to kill us?'

'No.'

'Him?' She nodded towards Kwong. 'Was it him?'

'None of us. We don't know who is behind it. What happened?' He touched her arm. 'Those guys from the gang, and Ximenes. Did they harm you?'

'No, they just delivered me to him. As I asked.'

'What?'

'I will explain later. Not here.'

Ximenes meanwhile was kicking up a fuss, prodding a stubby finger into Kwong's chest, breathing fire into his face. 'I should have known not to trust you.'

'You're talking to the wrong guy.' Kwong swatted the finger away.

'Am I? I don't think so.'

Driscoll stepped in. 'Whoever is behind it, they're not finished. They know by now that they failed to get you. That means they're still looking and might be back here soon. How about we make tracks now and recriminate later?'

'Where do you propose to take me?'

In other circumstances the embassy might have been the logical place, but what if Colonel Mark was behind this? The joint military program. It made sense. Canberra cabals. Power plays. A private shadow army. Forces way beyond his control. Driscoll was lost for ideas. It was a new sensation for him.

'How about your district?' said Kwong. 'Surely you would be safe in your own Petty Kingdom?'

Ximenes laughed. 'I'll be fine,' he said. 'Not so sure about you.'

Kwong turned to Driscoll. 'Thoughts?'

He shrugged. 'It gives us breathing space. Time to regroup.'

Rosa shook her head. 'Police custody. It's my duty. We need to keep this official.'

Ximenes took a step toward her. '*Hatene ó-nia fatin!*'

Know your place.

Rosa lifted her chin. 'Respect must be earned.'

Mira gently laid a hand on Rosa's arm. 'Please, sister, a little more time.' She started towards the door. 'Let's go. We can take refuge in the church there.' She eyed Ximenes. 'What could be safer?'

21

Wednesday 9th May

There would be little sleep in the night. They'd split up, taken divergent and circuitous routes, stopped for food along the way, arriving in the district just before midnight. The riot squad had been sent back to barracks. Ximenes had travelled with Driscoll and José, while Mira went with Rosa and Cato. The two women had spoken quietly in Tetun for most of the journey and Cato sat in the back none the wiser. All he could pick up was that they did not dislike each other, even shared the odd joke, and some tears. As they bumped down that last gravel lane towards the church, Cato discerned the atmosphere in the car had become electric. It was as if they had collectively breathed in and didn't dare expel. The place was deserted, as hoped and expected. The other car had arrived ahead of them; maybe Ximenes had warned off any curious souls. In fact they didn't stay in the church; the priest gave up his adjoining house and went somewhere else. Such was the power of the returning *liurai*. Ximenes had taken the best and biggest room for himself, the women shared another, while the *malae* men elected to take turns on sentry duty and use whatever beds or couches remained.

Cato and Driscoll had taken the first watch while José grabbed a nap.

'So,' said Cato. 'You have your breathing space, some time bought. What's the plan?'

'Ask me in the morning.'

'Reckon we'll make it that far?'

'We'll get plenty of warning if they come here. Ximenes has seen to that.'

The vehicles were parked at the rear, out of sight, and all house lights extinguished. They sat on a front porch in pale moonlight, slapping at mosquitoes, Cato mindful that malaria and dengue fever were still a big issue here. Driscoll cradled a semiautomatic assault rifle commandeered from the riot squad. He'd given Cato the embassy Glock. By now it was heading for three in the morning. A dog howled nearby then settled after a curse from its owner.

'Did you get the story from Mira yet?' Cato asked.

'No.' Driscoll yawned. 'She said nothing in the car with you?'

'She and Rosa spoke Tetun the whole time. What does Ximenes say about all this?'

'Raging bull. He doesn't know who to blame first.'

'How about you?' Cato straightened in his seat, stretching out a sore back. 'Do you know who to blame?'

'I'm leaning towards Mark from the embassy,' said Driscoll. 'The joint military program.'

Cato frowned. 'He's not a charming bloke. But murder? Why? Who for?'

'I've got one or two ideas, but they'll keep.'

'What are we going to do with Ximenes?'

Driscoll's fingers drummed lightly on the gun. 'If we hand him over, your enquiry comes to a dead end.'

'I sense that's not a priority for you.'

'My boss has you lined up as a fall guy.'

'Really?' Cato frowned. 'Should you be telling me this?'

'Probably not, I think it might be an official secret.'

'So how does it work, this fall-guy thing? What am I meant to do?'

'Not sure yet. We still haven't worked out whether Ximenes is worth more dead or alive.'

'Keep me posted.'

Driscoll chuckled. 'I will. Meanwhile, your mate José. What do you know about him?'

'Not much. He works for Bunbury D's and was born in Brazil, speaks Portuguese. You have history, I gather.'

'He used to be with Brazilian intelligence, I met him on a course a few years back. Has dual nationality. He was useful to them as a conduit to the Australians, two hats if you like.'

'Why would Brazil need a conduit to Australia?'

'Shared interests. Timor.'

'Ah.'

'José says the powers-that-be decided he should be here with you. That right?'

'Not sure where the idea came from, but he was happy enough to put up his hand.'

'Yeah. Has he proved useful so far?'

'Not very. His Portuguese hasn't helped.'

'So he didn't mention that he also speaks Tetun?'

'No.'

Driscoll smiled. 'The games spooks play.' His phone lit up with a message. Cato was surprised there was a signal out here. Maybe that was the privilege of the modern *liurai* – a phone tower wherever and whenever you needed one. Driscoll read the message and winced.

'Bad news?' enquired Cato.

'Yep.'

***

It was from Aunty. Willie Mason was dead, found hanging in the cell where they were holding him ahead of a court appearance that following day. He probably would have been released on bail. Maybe that was why he was dead. Was it at his own hand or was somebody tidying up loose ends? Driscoll would call Aunty later and find out.

In theory they should wake José now and one of them take a break but Driscoll was too wired to sleep, especially with the news about Mason. Kwong was happy to do a swap and went off to wake José. A few minutes later the man himself appeared, sleepy, night-breathy, a mug of Timor coffee in each hand. He passed one to Driscoll.

'No zombies so far?'

'Nothing. All quiet on the Western Front.'

'Sweet.'

'Sleep well?'

'Like a baby.'

They sipped their coffees in silence for a while, slapping at the occasional insect. Finally Driscoll put down his mug. 'What are you really doing here, Rodrigo?'

'José.'

'Whatever. You invited yourself along, or got strings pulled to make sure it happened. What's your game?'

'I'm just a plod, mate, investigating a murder. Following orders.'

'Really? Reckon Ximenes is your man, then?'

'He'll do. Nicely.'

'Would ABIN have a stake in seeing him locked up?'

'Wouldn't know, mate. Don't work for them anymore.'

'Hypothetically speaking.'

'Hype away, buddy. It helps fill the hours.'

'The Global South, a new alignment or axis of shared interests. Brazil taking the lead among the old Portuguese colonies. Old-fashioned influence-peddling if you like.'

'Whoa, sunshine. It's a while since I was at uni. Keep it slow and simple.'

'You play the part well, Rodrigo.'

'José, please ...'

'Class buffoon, Sancho Panza to Kwong's Don Quixote.'

'Not sure he'd appreciate the comparison.'

'So Brazil is heavily involved in Timor. Aid projects, cooperation, training.' A penny dropped and Driscoll clicked his fingers. 'And Brazil trains the Timor special forces. Ain't that a coincidence?'

'Spooky.'

'What's the pay-off though? Nothing's free. A slice of the oil riches maybe? Some action for Brazilian petro-oligarchs?'

'All very interesting,' José conceded.

'Ximenes made the wrong enemies. Didn't see them coming from that direction. He would have been expecting Timor, Indonesia, Australia even.'

José picked the Glock up from the side table, tested its weight. 'You should write a book.'

'What suits you best, Ximenes dead or alive?'

He put the gun back down. 'Not my decision. Cato's in charge, not me.'

'Who?'

'Kwong. It's his nickname in the Job. Didn't he tell you? And here's me thinking you went way back.' José smiled. 'You two should talk more.'

'I could go another coffee if you're brewing.'

'Sure, mate. I'll get the kettle on.'

The eastern sky grew lighter and morning birds made their noise. Roosters yodelled and dogs set to yapping. Driscoll desperately needed to sleep but something drove him to stay awake. Fear of imminent attack? Probably. He wasn't sure whether it would come from without or within.

***

Cato woke to a commotion out in the kitchen. He went to investigate and found Mira holding a knife to Ximenes' neck. She was screeching at him in Tetun but he seemed to find it all quite funny. Rosa was trying to calm Mira down while José stood to one side peeling a boiled egg with exaggerated detachment.

'What's going on?'

'They're having a domestic.' José took a bite out of his egg.

Driscoll entered the scene, red-eyed from sleep deprivation and hair still wet from the shower. He said something to Mira in her language. She slammed the knife down on the kitchen counter and stormed out. He followed close behind.

'These peasant *maubere* girls.' Ximenes checked his neck for a smear of blood from the knife prick. 'An embarrassment.' Rosa fired off a stream of Tetun at him but he just shook his head, laughed, and pushed past her. He reached into José's personal space to grab a cup.

José's hand locked on his wrist. '*Respeto*.'

Ximenes looked at him. 'He speaks! What is your name, Australian servant boy?'

'Really, mate,' said José. 'I wouldn't.'

Ximenes turned to Cato. 'You let him speak to me like this?'

'I'm thinking we're all a bit overtired and need to calm down. You especially are under our protection. Maybe some civility would go a long way?'

'To hell with you all.' Ximenes shouted through the open door and an old woman appeared within seconds. He issued instructions and she set to making his breakfast.

Cato summoned Rosa and José outside for a chat. 'Timeout would do us all the world of good.'

Down the lane, Driscoll was in intense conversation with Mira. Cato gave Rosa a querying look. 'Care to fill me in?'

Rosa shook her head. 'It is not for me to say.'

He looked at José. 'You heard everything. And I know you speak the lingo.'

José glanced down the road at Driscoll. 'So you guys do talk to each other.' Back to Cato. 'There was a massacre here back in the day. Mira survived it. Ximenes was involved. He took her back over the border with him. Made her his "wife" for a few months then gave her back as part of a prisoner swap with the new independent Timorese regime. She's still angry about it.'

'She would have been, what …?'

'Fourteen,' said Rosa.

'What is she hoping to get from this … situation?' asked Cato.

'She wanted to confront him. Tell him the impact on her life.' A snort from José, but Rosa pressed on. 'I tried to convince her not to. She is an idealist, believes in the power of truth.'

'In this day and age?' José shook his head. 'Sheesh.'

Rosa rounded on him. 'The world needs people who are not cold and bitter and cynical like you. For some, the truth is all that is left.'

'Good luck with that.'

'That's it?' said Cato. 'She just wanted to explain herself to a man like him?'

'No "just" about it.' Rosa lifted her head. 'It was important to her.'

'If it was me I would have stabbed the fucker first chance I got,' said José.

Rosa spared him a glance. 'Maybe that is the difference between you and us. We are trying to see a way forward which doesn't involve violence. We've seen enough.'

'Self-defence, I call it.' José thumbed back inside. 'He's not going to put up with her talking to him like that for much longer. He might find it amusing right now but it'll wear off soon enough.'

'At this stage he is not completely in control of events.'

'So what next?' said Cato. 'She's said her piece and he's laughed in her face.'

'Now,' said Rosa, 'she needs to move on.'

Driscoll and Mira were on their way back. Cato didn't meet her eyes and she knew that they all now knew what had happened to her. All this knowing and still the world would turn as it always had.

***

He would deal with Ximenes later. The blow-up in the kitchen explained a lot. Did Mira know right from the start that this was where it would all lead? Doubtful. But one person who had known was Willie Mason. Why? Because he was there at the time. Driscoll still hadn't fully figured Mason out and now he never would because the bastard was dead. He took himself off for a walk down the lane and phoned Aunty.

'Tell me about Mason.'

'Good morning, Rory. How are you?' A few seconds of silence and she must have sensed this was no time for a refresher lesson in manners. 'Found hanging in his cell at North West Point last night.'

'Where?'

'Christmas Island immigration detention centre.'

'Overstayed his visa? What was he doing there?'

'Protective custody. Think about it, Rory, love. If you need a secure secret place to lock somebody up out of the public eye, where better than the immigration gulags?'

'You mentioned a court appearance due the next day?'

'Video link. He wasn't going anywhere soon.'

'Brian there too?'

'No, he got bail with lots of onerous conditions. Being an Aussie civilian, we can't be so fast and loose with his human rights, unfortunately.'

'Did Mason suicide or was there foul play?'

'Suicide as far as we can tell. Facing twenty-odd years in the slammer, you can see his point.'

'How'd he do it?'

'Torn-up bedsheets, door handle.'

'Who found him?'

'A guard doing a night check.'

'You buy it?'

'Have to, Rory.'

'What was the plan? Keep him there forever or what?'

'Until the trial at least; one maybe two years. A man of Mason's capabilities could easily disappear himself otherwise.'

'He certainly did that.' Driscoll sighed. 'It stinks, Aunty. You know it does.'

'Maybe, but it's a problem out of the way.'

He told her about what had happened at Villa Ximenes. About the personal connection between Mira and the ex-militia leader. 'Mason knew all along. He didn't just pick her as a naïve journalist he thought he might be able to manipulate. She was something to bargain with – value-added pressure to apply to Ximenes.'

'What pressure?' said Aunty. 'Sounds like Ximenes couldn't give a fuck.'

'Mason wasn't to know that.'

'Wasn't he? He got to know him pretty well during his tour of duty.'

'What were we doing cosying up to the militias anyway?'

'Playing both sides as usual, Rory. Keeping an eye on things. Right then we weren't convinced that Timorese independence was a great idea. Some people in Canberra still feel nostalgic about the good old days of Suharto and his iron fist.'

'Oil.'

'Always was, always will be.'

'So where to now? Somebody wants Ximenes dead. We're hiding out in the sticks in Timor waiting for them to come and get him. I suspect Colonel Mark from the embassy has a hand in this somewhere. Any chance you can jerk his leash?'

'Leave it with me. Meantime, keep a lid on Mira and keep everybody in order. How's that WA cop behaving?'

'So far so good. It's more his colleague that worries me.' Driscoll gave her the lowdown on José. 'Can you do some digging on him while you're on? See what ABIN's up to.'

They signed off. Driscoll started back up the lane. The wind was already hot and strong, sending dust swirling. At the bottom of the hill the sea was blue and inviting but Driscoll knew it was infested with crocs. It was hard to see a way out of all this that didn't involve more spilling of blood. He looked up. Kwong was waving to get his attention. Up on the main road a dust cloud heralded an impending arrival. Two, maybe three military vehicles.

***

'PNTL?' said Driscoll, as they rolled up. 'What?'

Rosa stepped forward, chin lifted. 'I called them.'

'But I thought we agreed.'

'We agreed nothing. This is my country. These are our laws. And he,' a thumb in the direction of Ximenes, 'is my prisoner.'

'But we can't trust PNTL.'

'Can't you? Why? So far it is you, your colleagues and possibly some rogue elements of our army special forces who have caused trouble. Not Timorese police.'

Armed police jumped down from the trucks, some in paramilitary gear despite the heat. A lot of heads. Twenty? Driscoll could see he was outnumbered and outgunned. He studied Rosa. Outplayed too, he realised. 'What are you arresting Ximenes for?'

'For war crimes, for rape, for sex trafficking.'

Driscoll looked at Mira. 'You are prepared to testify?'

'Of course.'

'And if the Timorese government and prosecutor do not wish to pursue the charges?'

Kwong raised a finger. 'Then we'd be interested in opening extradition proceedings.'

'Again, what if the government isn't interested?'

He shrugged. 'If you don't ask, you never get.'

Everybody by the fucking book. Driscoll began to wonder what he was resisting and why. Aunty and the other Canberra mandarins wanted to protect their age-old secrets. Driscoll no longer cared about that, nor was he paid to do so. Self-preservation? Let them take Ximenes and hear his stories of how both Indonesia and Australia enabled him. Let due process run its course, whatever the result. If the fucker ended up in jail, well and good. If he walked free, then back to the rules Driscoll played by. Find him and finish him off. Driscoll turned back to Rosa. 'Go for your life.' He paused. 'But give me ten minutes alone with him to ask a few questions.'

She shook her head. 'No way.'

Ximenes looked like he wasn't sure which he preferred, quality time with Driscoll or with Rosa and the PNTL. On balance the latter, probably. He had half a chance of being rescued.

'What if Kwong sits in on it?' said Driscoll. 'You trust him to do the right thing, don't you?'

Rosa glanced at Kwong, appraised him. Finally she nodded, 'Ten minutes, in the priest's house. We will have the place surrounded.' She took Driscoll's pistol off him and handed it to Kwong. 'If there is any sign of trouble shoot one of them, both of them, whatever is necessary.'

'Not sure I have the diplomatic authority,' said Kwong, weighing the pistol in his hands.

She pointed at the gun. 'I just gave it to you.'

***

They sat around the kitchen table. The room was gloomy, not cool, but a welcome relief from the searing heat outside. Driscoll and Ximenes faced each other across the table, Cato in between them with his chair pushed back a little to give him room to move quickly if needed. He suspected it wouldn't be necessary. Driscoll had an agenda and wanted some answers. Ximenes too no doubt. Maybe this was just about getting their story straight and working out some kind of deal – with Cato as a duped witness? If they spoke in Tetun, he wouldn't have a clue what was going on.

'The conversation needs to be in English.'

Driscoll smiled. 'You don't trust me, mate?'

'No.'

He looked at Ximenes. 'That suit you, João?'

'No problem.'

Flies buzzed around the uncleared breakfast plates. Cato undid a button on his shirt, peeled it from where it stuck on his torso.

'Willie Mason was here with you on the day of the massacre.' Driscoll said. It was a statement, not a question. Driscoll scratched his nose, feigning nonchalance. 'Did he play a part?'

'Did he kill anyone? No.' Ximenes seemed bored to be talking old news. 'I do not need to answer your questions. What is in this for me?'

Driscoll glanced at Cato. 'Witness protection in a third country. Immunity. New life.'

'Or maybe my friends in the Presidential Palace will protect me.'

'What friends? The tide's changing, João, you know how these things work. Elections coming up. The opposition have unfinished business. Some of them are still fighting the war. They remember whose side you were on.'

'That's a chance I can take.'

'Is it? You sure? There are people lining up to take a pop at you. My bosses could go either way right now. Big Oil doesn't like being fucked around by upstarts. The Indonesians think you've got a big mouth, even the Brazilians ...' a flicker of reaction from Ximenes. 'What'd you do to piss them all off, João?'

'So what do you want from me?'

'The truth. Did Mason play a part in the massacre?'

'No. He just watched. He was interested in our, how do you call it, our MO? I didn't want him there but the Indonesians insisted. I think they wanted to send a message to your intelligence services about what we, and they, were capable of if anyone interfered.'

'So he did nothing?'

'He helpfully pointed out survivors, people still moving. We killed them. He stopped us from killing the girl.'

'Mira Soares?'

'I never got to thank him. She made a good wife.'

Cato felt his grip tighten on the pistol.

Driscoll leaned in. 'The girl knew about his intervention?'

'No, she was too far away. His back was turned to her, he had a word in my ear.' Ximenes' hand went involuntarily to that spot. 'I still had it then.' A bitter laugh.

'What words did he use?'

'"No more killing. You've made your point." Then he glanced at the girl and said it would be a terrible waste.' A smile. 'Maybe he meant it, maybe he didn't. Maybe he was appealing to my better nature.' He sat back in his chair. 'There you have it, your truth. A small matter. I am surprised you are interested.'

'Did he know her, talk to her?'

'No, I doubt it. She was a body in the crowd, still moving. He could walk past her in the street today and not know.'

Driscoll's face registered disbelief. 'Did you send those gangsters after us in Tasmania and Darwin?'

'I don't know what you are talking about.' Truth? Lie? Again, thought Cato, a chimera floating between the two men.

'You knew Mira had returned to Timor with me?'

'I have my sources.'

A pause. 'You never had children, did you? Especially after what Abdullah did to you in his cellar in Kupang.'

Ximenes drummed the table. Cato noticed that not all the fingers were there. 'My enemies are not the only ones with unfinished business.'

Driscoll stood up, took a knife from a drawer and slid it across the table to Ximenes. 'Blame me for that? Go ahead, have a go.'

Cato figured it was time to intervene. 'Leave it where it is.'

'Or what, Chinaman. You will shoot me?'

'If I have to.'

'You don't have the guts, but don't worry.' Ximenes sneered at Driscoll. 'I will act at the time of my choosing.'

'Are we finished here?' asked Cato. 'Only I think the ten minutes is up.' As if on cue, the sound of footsteps in the hall.

Rosa came through the door. 'Time to go. The locals are gathering.'

'My people.' Ximenes laughed. 'My people.'

'They are not coming to your rescue,' said Rosa. 'Your people are happy to see the last of you. Some of them would be happy to lynch you. So let's go.'

22

They got back to Dili as the sun was going down. Rosa and the police convoy had gone ahead. Ximenes would be taken to police HQ and locked up pending a decision by the authorities as to what to do with him. While the others checked back into Hotel Timor to shower away the dust and grime, and reacquaint themselves with sleep or civilisation, Driscoll took himself off to the embassy. He wanted words with Maddie and Mark. The guy at reception wasn't sure whether to let him through or not.

'Tell them I'm here. Let them decide.'

A few minutes later he was buzzed through and told to wait in the conference room. The aircon was refreshing and after another five minutes, a soft drink arrived. Still no Maddie and Mark fifteen minutes later, and Driscoll was getting ready to trash the joint. He stood up, wondering how many doors he could get through before he was either locked out or shot. Then Maddie came into the room.

'Where's Mark?'

She checked her watch. 'Getting ready to board the evening flight to Darwin, I expect.'

'Recalled?'

'Stress leave. Extended.'

Aunty must have really put the boot in. 'How much can you tell me?'

'Not much. A call came through from Canberra this afternoon. He looked like he was going to vomit. Said he needed to spend more time with his family. I suspect you know more than me.'

'I doubt it. Surprised they didn't send him out on a Hercules?'

'They didn't think he warranted the expense. They've got him on Jetstar from Darwin all the way through to Canberra. That'll teach him.'

'Was he behind the raid on Ximenes' house in the hills?'

'He was in the supply chain. We think somebody in the Presidential

Palace gave the nod. There's jostling ahead of the elections. Could be political, could be a business fallout, or a settling of old scores.'

'Or all of the above.'

She nodded. 'I understand the PNTL have Ximenes now.'

'How's that going to play out?'

'Damned if I know.'

***

Cato had let the opportunity slip but even if he had asked, yet again, directly of Ximenes – did you kill two old men in WA? – all he would have said was no. That kitchen encounter was between him and Driscoll, and Cato was just there to spectate. Ximenes was an animal and the world wouldn't miss his passing, but there was no hard evidence linking him to the WA murders. Cato dropped his sweaty clothes on the floor and stepped into the shower. The hotel with its air-conditioning and western luxuries was a welcome relief from the brutal heat and the even more brutal history of this country. He was ready to go home but he still needed to check out the aid projects Peters and Drummond worked on back in the day. Tomorrow he'd visit them, then maybe they could take the evening flight out.

Towelling himself dry, he noticed the flashing of missed calls on his mobile. Sharon, Chris Thornton and Nikki Earle. He ordered some room-service food and returned the calls. Business first. Earle was on her way to pick up her daughter from childcare and running late.

'Got time to talk?' asked Cato.

'Sure.' The sound quality changed to that of speakerphone with traffic noise in the background. 'How's Timor?'

'Hot and hard to fathom. There's a lot of nuance up here.'

'José behaving himself?'

'So far. Did you know about his colourful history?'

'I know he's a good dancer.'

'I'll leave him to tell you.'

'What happens in Dili stays in Dili, huh?'

Your colleague's an ex-Brazilian spook, but it's a long story and I'm not sure if or where you might fit in. 'Something like that. You rang?'

'Two things. Your enquiry into that CPS mob has caused ripples. My boss has been getting antsy. He got a flea in his ear direct from their CEO and from the police commissioner.'

'If you're going to make enemies, may as well make big ones.'

'He'll get over it. Secondly, we got a call from the Rotarians, some guy who'd been up there in Timor at the same time as our two.'

'Yep?'

'He remembers they started acting funny after a few days on this well project.'

'Funny? How?'

'Secretive. Furtive. Like they knew something everybody else didn't. Before that they'd been normal, chatty. Good Rotarians, he called them. But not after that.'

'Where was this place?' She gave him the details and he wrote them down. 'We'll check it out tomorrow. Any sign of the missing Australia Post package or developments on Ryan Hodgson?'

'Nada on the package. Hodgson's phone shows calls to mates, mum and José the day he died.'

'José?'

'Maybe he'd thought of something about the person he saw the night of Drummond's murder. Tried phoning him to tell him. Pretty short call.'

'I'll ask José about it.'

They signed off and Cato got onto Thornton. After an exchange of pleasantries it emerged that Lenny Jacobs was now out of prison, kicking up a justified fuss and considering his options for redress. Cato didn't see it as his problem but thanked Thornton for the update. He gave him a list of new enquiries along with some outstanding priorities: the Australia Post package, the two men's emails and telcos going back at least to their Christmas Island reunion and further if possible. 'Can you run a backgrounder on José Carrascalao and Mira Soares too?' He supplied context.

Thornton chuckled. 'José's an ex-spy? Cool.'

'Not necessarily ex. Find out the chain of orders that put him on this trip too.'

'Will do. What's happening with this Ximenes bloke?' Cato gave him the lowdown. 'It might not be him either?' Thornton whistled. 'Pavlou's going to go ballistic.'

'I'll be back tomorrow night and in the office the day after. She can give me her two cents then.'

A grunt. 'Speaking of spies, I had this bloke Guthrie up my arse today. Know him?'

'ASIO,' said Cato. 'What did he want?'

'He wanted me to keep my nose out of Paul Reinado's financials and telecoms.'

'What'd the boss say?'

'Which one? I'm helping out Paddy McMahon who'd prefer crime to go away so he can have a beer and a party pie in peace. Pavlou? Bit distracted by HQ politics. Word is the minister and the new commissioner have fallen out and heads are due to roll.'

Cato heard the beep of an incoming call. 'Ignore Guthrie and do your job.'

'Aye, aye, Cap'n.'

Next he tried Sharon but it went through to messages. He checked the time – holy hour with Ella – probably more than enough on her mind right now. He left a message saying he'd call again later. There was a knock at the door. Room service, Cato assumed.

It was José, holding his phone up as explanation. 'Rosa wants us down at PNTL HQ. There's some trouble.' He checked out Cato's post-shower attire. 'Might need to get some strides on. I'll go and organise transport while you do.'

Rosa must have tried him while he was on the line to Thornton and opted for José when she couldn't get through.

'Great, cheers,' Cato said. 'Oh, by the way, just had a word with Nikki Earle. She mentioned you'd taken a call from Ryan Hodgson the day he died?'

'Yeah, he left a message. Bit incoherent, must have been a good spliff.'

'You didn't follow it up?'

'Nothing to follow up. I assumed he'd phone back if it was important. See you downstairs in five?'

Cato found José and Driscoll talking in the lobby.

'Transport sorted,' said José.

'What sort of trouble, did Rosa say?'

'Mira and Ximenes again.' A grim chortle. 'The mother of all domestics.'

***

Driscoll would have liked to punch José/Rodrigo; he had a bad attitude. His machismo was skin deep and very wearing after a while, plus his jokes just weren't funny. Driscoll let the tosser enjoy his own wit in the back while they raced to PNTL HQ. Kwong was in the front passenger seat, looking pensive as usual.

'Colonel Mark has been sent home.'

'Interesting,' said Kwong. 'He was behind the attack on Villa Ximenes?'

'In the food chain. I don't know why, yet.'

A pause. 'This guy Guthrie, colleague of yours, right?'

'Used to be.'

'He's interfering in our criminal investigation. Why?'

'Haven't a clue.'

'Don't believe you.'

'That's your prerogative.'

'Reinado. Paul Reinado. Your pal keeps warning us off him.'

Driscoll turned through the gates of PNTL HQ, waved through on prearrangement. 'Love to help, mate, but sorry. Keep me posted, eh?'

Kwong gave him a look, but it was nothing Driscoll hadn't encountered a thousand times before. A small crowd had gathered in the central courtyard comprising mainly police officers but also among them some of the gang members Driscoll recognised from the raid a few days earlier. Some had the homemade *rakitan* pistols held loosely at their sides or cradled in folded arms. The police officers seemed unconcerned and some hadn't bothered arming themselves. Odds-on they knew each other well, perhaps even lived in the same barrio. Beyond them were the lockups. Light was cast by weak pale lamps around which moths and other insects fluttered and died. Driscoll pushed his way through the crowd. The atmosphere was one of curiosity and spectacle rather than of agitation. At the centre of the throng he found out why.

Rosa lay facedown and still, blood seeping from a wound somewhere on her torso. Ximenes stood over her, eyes glittering with triumph, face shiny with sweat, a knife in the dust at his feet. Mira held a *rakitan* to the side of his head.

'Wife, behave yourself.' Ximenes gestured calmly with palms upturned. Some in the crowd sniggered, cops and gangsters alike. 'Know your place. My bed, my kitchen.'

Out of the corner of his eye Driscoll could see Kwong tensing, ready to do something. José was whispering to him, translating maybe, urging caution perhaps. So the dickhead was useful for something at least. 'What's going on, Mira?' Driscoll addressed her in English, trying to break the Tetun spell that Ximenes was trying to cast over the crowd.

'None of your business.'

'He is not worth it.'

'What would you know? You weren't there.' Her voice was steady. She was resolved. She clearly did not need calming like the hysteric that Ximenes portrayed.

'History,' said Ximenes. 'It is history and nobody is interested in these stories. The traitors who died, let them rot in peace. You were one of the lucky ones, chosen to be my queen. Be thankful.'

'The law will take care of him' said Driscoll. 'Let it.' Rosa was stirring. 'We need to stop this, Mira. Rosa needs to go to hospital. Do you want her on your conscience too?'

'Call your ambulance, this will be finished soon. I am sorry for her but that was his doing, he is responsible for her fate.' She pressed the *rakitan* into his ear. 'Like I am, for his.'

'You are responsible for yours too, Mira. If you kill him, he wins. His way wins.'

Some of the gang members were making kissing noises and obscene gestures. Driscoll saw that the idea was to rile Mira. The cops too were stirring into action, realising maybe it was about time they did their jobs. A bad situation was on the way to worse. Driscoll felt the weight of the Glock in his belt, knowing he would have to use it soon.

'Let *Lafaek* decide.'

They all looked around at the man who had spoken the words in English. Kwong.

Driscoll knew the crocodile origin tale from his earlier tours of duty. But Kwong? 'What do you know about *Lafaek*?'

'Rosa told me the story. Justice. He decides who is guilty, who isn't. He is the ultimate judge.'

'Mate, best you stay out of this.'

Murmurings spread through the crowd. Kwong's words translated for those who needed it. The *malae* was right. *Lafaek*, they were saying. *Lafaek*. Mira was unreadable but perhaps this was a way to save face and get what she wanted from the situation without risking her own future.

Besides, the *rakitans* were notoriously unreliable and could just as easily blow her hand off rather than his head. Ximenes, for his part, no longer seemed so sure of himself. One of the gang members – older than the rest, maybe someone in line for the Ximenes throne – was nodding. It was written all over his face: opportunity knocks.

'*Lafaek*,' he chimed, urging on his coterie. '*Lafaek*.'

Rosa was out cold now, her skin turning grey even in the weak lamplight. Driscoll weighed it all up: would the crocodile, Antonio, be the circuit-breaker they needed?

Kwong stood his ground. 'It's not for us to interfere. Let the law take its course. The law of *Lafaek*.'

'What do you think this is, fuckwit?' Driscoll growled. 'Tintin goes to Timor?' He turned and whispered in the ear of a sergeant to summon the riot squad plus an ambulance for Rosa. All that happened next would rely on perfect timing.

***

Cato wasn't usually the type for kangaroo or crocodile courts but his priority was to get Rosa the medical help she needed. Maybe it was already too late. Cato had moved closer to Mira and just out of her field of vision. José had edged around behind the crowd, strategically placing himself just behind a young gang member who seemed too caught up in the theatre of unfolding events to be alert to his own safety.

'*Lafaek*?' Ximenes was saying something in Tetun. Cato got the meaning from the man's facial expression and tone of voice. Are you fucking kidding? Driscoll had taken note of their strategic shufflings, he knew what they were doing.

'Mira,' said Driscoll, holding his hand out for her weapon. 'Enough, now.'

She shook her head. 'He killed my mother, my neighbours, my friends. He raped me for six months. Allowed his men to have me when he was finished. He is an animal. This country will not give me justice, neither will that stupid crocodile.' She told Ximenes to kneel.

'Mira,' said Driscoll. 'Please.'

The rumble of engines. Two trucks rolled into the compound. Heavily armed men in paramilitary uniforms jumped down. They barked out orders, and the gang members and uniform cops lay facedown in the dirt. Driscoll, Cato, José, Mira and her prisoner remained upright. The order came again and a machine gun was raised in warning towards Driscoll.

'It's over,' said Cato. 'Out of our hands now.'

'Always was,' said Driscoll, raising his.

He was pushed down to the ground with Cato and José following. Only Mira remained standing, with Ximenes on his knees in front of her. The order came one more time from the special forces officer.

'Mira,' Driscoll raised his head from the ground. 'Do as he says. They will kill you.'

'No.' Tears rolled down her face. 'I can't.'

The ambulance arrived. They couldn't move in to attend to Rosa until the situation with Mira and Ximenes was resolved.

Driscoll once more. 'Mira, your son needs you.'

Ximenes turned his head, looked at her. Saw in her eyes the truth of it. He laughed. 'I have a son! An heir! My own little prince! What is his name?'

Mira sobbed and pulled the trigger.

23

Thursday 10ᵗʰ May

Parts of João Ximenes would wash up over the next few days, mainly along the beach area in front of the embassies and near to the statue of the fallen in the Santa Cruz cemetery massacre. Those parts not consumed by crocodiles, that is. It seemed *Lafaek* had his say after all, just not Antonio himself. Mira's *rakitan* backfired, disintegrating in her hand and leaving her with burns and a broken trigger finger. The special forces had taken Ximenes away and word had since been passed along to the Australian embassy that he was no longer of this world – the troublesome foreigners should go home. Some said he was killed and chucked off Dili wharf like so many poor bastards before him, fed to the waiting crocs. Whatever the story, it no longer mattered. He was dead, and with him perished a whole host of truth and lies indistinguishable from each other. The latest being who it was that summoned special forces when Driscoll had clearly asked for the riot squad. The officer he'd given the instruction to pleaded ignorance. He'd done as Driscoll asked and didn't know what had happened in between. Maybe someone at the Palace got wind of it, and something was lost, or intercepted, in translation.

Rosa was recovering in intensive care from a stab wound that should have killed her. Driscoll and Kwong had visited her in hospital that afternoon on the way to the airport. Drowsy after her operation, she had reassured them she did not intend to die yet. She had squeezed Kwong's hand as he looked down at her, pale with shock.

'Take your domestic Australian dramas with you,' she'd said, 'and leave us in peace.' They'd been shepherded through customs and immigration with unseemly haste. AFP Sam, his arm in a sling, was there to see them off.

'Make sure you leave,' he'd said, only half-jokingly. 'Maddie says ditto.'

Mira had changed her mind, for the moment at least, about returning to *patria*. Hand bandaged and finger splinted, she couldn't wait to get the hell out of there. She hadn't been prepared to look Driscoll in the eye since he'd broadcast her secret in the hope of a bloodless resolution to the impasse. It had backfired, almost literally. José, meanwhile, was studying his phone, relaxed as if he was just returning from a fortnight in Bali. Only Kwong was predictably pensive. Like Driscoll, he was left with questions unanswered by the death of Ximenes. They lined up to board the plane. Mira had expressly asked for a seat nowhere near them. Driscoll found himself across the aisle from Kwong and José. Nobody was in the least bit chatty. As the aircraft climbed out over the ocean, the sun low and orange in the western sky, circling back over Dili and the mountains, it occurred to Driscoll that he'd lost, that someone out there was still at least one step ahead of him. And still he had no fucking clue as to who or why.

***

Cato looked out of the aeroplane window at the dry, hazy hills of eastern Timor where the rebels had held out under Indonesian military occupation as long as possible, and much longer than anyone expected. That ability to adapt, to survive, to exceed expectations – did he have that in him? He doubted it, as he doubted it of most of his compatriots. Australia, like many developed capitalistic nations, measured resilience in broadband speeds, aircon power outages, proximity to dog beaches – at least it seemed that way if you read the wrong newspapers. Maybe that was no bad thing when it all came down to it. A life of first-world problems was what we all aspired to, wasn't it? He had received his bollocking from Driscoll over breakfast that morning. It had been pretty quick, done in the time it took José to go up to the buffet and reload his plate.

'Let *Lafaek* decide?' Driscoll had shaken his head. 'It's not Paul the Octopus picking who gets into the quarterfinals, mate. Fuck's sake.'

'I'd been hoping a local would come up with the idea but they were neck deep in the soap opera. I thought it was pretty classy actually. Cultural, you know? Certainly a game-changer.'

'Leave the culture to me, mate.'

'Tick-tock,' said Cato.

By the time José had returned it was all over, and Driscoll was taking a call from Maddie at the embassy telling him the Timorese authorities wanted them all out on the afternoon flight. Cato waited until José went for a coffee refill before asking one final favour – could Driscoll organise a car to take him out to the site of the aid project Peters and Drummond had worked on? Driscoll had acquiesced, grudgingly, and arranged for a driver who could also translate if needed. José had been happy to hang out in his room, pack, maybe have a swim in the pool, do some internet shit. He was, in that regard at least, easy to please.

The water-well project was back in the petty kingdom of Ximenes. As a project, it was complete. Water had long since been reliably supplied to the village and, as well as the houses having it piped in, there were two community standpipes for emergencies or simply for meetings if people felt nostalgic for the old days. There was also a mobile phone relay mast on a nearby hill so that they would want for nothing. What was there for Cato to see now? The village head had taken Cato on a tour of the original diggings and, through Eurico the driver, explained how hard life was before the Aussies came to help them.

'That's great,' Cato had said, with Eurico translating. Just a short way down a rocky incline and half-hidden in undergrowth and rubbish there was a dilapidated, semi-ruined building. A collection of rubble really. It was maybe the size of Cato's old two-bedroom place in South Fremantle – the width of a garden shed, perhaps twice the depth. 'What's that?'

The old man had shaken his head and tried to lead them away but Cato was insistent.

'Nobody uses it,' explained Eurico after a brief exchange. 'From the bad times.'

And, in the telling of the story, Cato came to see why the two Australian pensioners had developed an interest, indeed a morbid fascination, in João Ximenes. His link with the horrors perpetrated in that building was clear. They must have seen those same ruins, asked around, got to thinking. It still didn't explain their deaths twelve years after they dug into a small part of this nation's history, and almost twenty years after the terrible events in question. Between leaving Rosa at the hospital and getting to the airport, he'd phoned DI Pavlou and Sharon in that order. Pavlou was upbeat.

'If there's enough on this Ximenes bloke to pin our murders on, that'd be good. No need for the weight of evidence and a trial if the crocs have eaten him.' Cato had outlined his doubts nevertheless. 'No,' Pavlou had replied acidly. 'Heaven forbid we should make life easy for ourselves.'

Sharon was just glad he was finally coming home.

Cato glanced across the aeroplane aisle to Driscoll. He wasn't the same man who'd run circles around him in Shanghai six years ago. This version was far less self-confident. What had happened in between? Cato recalled a conversation they'd had in Fremantle back then when Driscoll showed up unexpectedly to tidy up some loose ends on the Shanghai connection – entrapping an oligarch who would end up before a Chinese firing squad. Driscoll was on a fitness regime and hanging out at the SAS base at Swanbourne, training for his next job tackling the people smugglers. The incoming government was committed to stopping the boats, and Driscoll was part of their armoury. Was that the source of this new, weighed-down version of the international man of mystery?

'That mate of yours who died. Close?'

Driscoll looked at him, puzzled.

'You took a call a few days ago. Someone had died?'

Driscoll shook his head. 'No, he wasn't a mate. Just a ... colleague, I guess.'

'Sorry. You looked like it hit you hard. I just thought ...'

A shrug. 'Nah.' They were getting ready to land in Darwin: tray tables, seat backs, the usual. He gestured for Cato to lean closer, away from José's earshot. 'You and me have some unfinished business. How about we hop off at Darwin and ditch the Perth connection?' He saw Cato's confusion. 'Reinado? Wasn't he from Darwin?'

'What about Mira?'

'She can push on to Melbourne, your mate there can head back to Perth. They'll be fine.'

Cato wasn't sure they should be abandoning Mira after what she'd been through, not just these past few days but all those years ago at the hands of Ximenes.

'Mate, she's been living with that for twenty years. She's tougher than you think.'

It was time to fasten seatbelts. José nudged him. 'What were you and Austin Powers talking about?'

Cato told him about the plan for a Darwin stopover to check out the Reinado angle with Driscoll.

'Just you and Driscoll? That wise?'

'Loose ends, mate. May as well while I'm in the area.' He thumbed back in the direction of where Mira was sitting. 'Can you keep half an eye on her until she gets her onward connection? Be nice and all that?'

'Do my best.'

***

Sharon was relieved Phil was on his way home. She'd been worried about him. This time more than others? Previously she'd known him as a persistent, tenacious man. Genuine, when he wasn't lying by omission to be what he thought was protective. She'd warned him off that when they'd gone through their rough patch after the attack on his son Jake.

'Lying to protect me is still lying. Got it?' Yes, he'd nodded. 'And who says I need that kind of protection?' She'd reminded him of her AFP training and the likelihood that she could outrun and outpunch him if it came down to it. 'Capeesh?'

He'd lifted his hands in mock surrender. 'Got it.'

A persistent, tenacious man both as a husband, lover and, no doubt, as an investigator. But since the attack on Jake, something new had crept in. A dark recklessness and disregard for his own safety and survival. An impulsiveness that sometimes sparked things up in the bedroom and left her both exhilarated and unmoored. Afraid of what he might now be capable of.

Ella stirred. She'd gone down early after a big day in the park where Julie had let her run herself out. Usually it was a good strategy but now and then Ella became overtired and her sleeping patterns defied logic. Julie had slipped away back to her own place once Ella was asleep. She had been patient with the sleepover demands of Phil's absence and Sharon's work but she was ready to go back to her own life and her own personal space. Besides, she had a new boyfriend she wasn't seeing enough of. Sharon breathed her own sigh of relief. Phil would be home tonight. Things could get back to normal. Then she noticed her phone was flashing with an unread message. It must have come through when she was supervising Ella's bathtime. Phil: **Sorry. One more night. Darwin.**

Shit.

She tried to return the call and give him a piece of her mind but it went straight to messagebank. 'Fuck you,' she wanted to say. Of course she never would; what if they turned out to be the last words he ever heard from her? A ring on the doorbell. She checked her watch, nearly eight. Julie back already? A surprise visit from Jake? Another ring. Ella started crying, fully awake now.

'Coming.' She irritably flicked on the porch light, unable to remember if she'd latched the security grille. A shape beyond the glass. She opened the door.

***

Cato and Driscoll checked into a hotel near the airport. They were re-booked onto their respective connections to Perth and Melbourne for the same time the following day. Twenty-four hours to look into Paul Reinado's role in this whole sorry affair. Should they check in with Northern Territory police, for protocol's sake? It was their turf after all, only polite.

Driscoll counselled no. 'Why upset the apple cart?'

Speaking of food, they agreed to assemble in the hotel lobby after they'd dumped bags and freshened up, and then go in search of dinner. Cato had messaged Chris Thornton seeking useful local contact details and had let Sharon know about the change of plans, then turned his phone off while he grabbed a quick shower. To be honest, he was too much of a coward to face Sharon's wrath. He'd talk to her in the morning. He and Driscoll took a taxi downtown and opted for an Indian place.

Mid-evening and it was still Top End sultry. Cato welcomed the cold beer and aircon. He cracked a poppadom and dipped it in some chutney. 'So what do you know about Reinado and his link with this mate of yours, Guthrie?'

'Not much on both counts and Guthrie's a colleague, not a mate.'

'Yeah, yeah so nobody's a mate in your world, only colleagues.'

'Sound familiar? Don't tell me it isn't the same for you.'

Cato conceded the point. 'So tell me the "not much" that you do know.'

'Reinado's family took Mira in when she left Timor. Fostered her if you like. Paul would have been a de facto brother to her, maybe five years older?'

Some bhajis and samosas arrived and they tucked in. 'Did the Reinados also take in Mira's son who would be, what, twenty by now?'

Driscoll shrugged. 'Assume so.'

'And we have no idea where this son is now?'

'Gap year, travelling, according to Mira.'

'How long have you known about this?'

'Not long.'

Cato waited for more but nothing came. 'That's it?'

'I don't know the details of Paul Reinado's connection to Guthrie or to ASIO. I can only speculate that he was a source of information to us and/ or a channel of disinformation from us.'

'About what?'

'Community gossip. The Reinados are, or were, major players, connected into the old cadres back in Dili. People like Ramos-Horta, Xanana Gusmão, will often stop by on their way through to Canberra or some such. Sometimes respected expats might hear something too sensitive for ears back in the homeland. Or they could be used to funnel something useful back there.'

'Oil gossip?'

'Maybe. But that's not the only item on the agenda. Who's forming alliances with who. Who's mixing with the wrong crowd. Transnational crime. What other governments, for example China, are doing. All of that.'

'What was in it for Reinado?'

'Money? Revenge? Influence? Maybe Guthrie had something on him. Who knows?'

'Are you able to ask anybody?'

Driscoll studied him. 'I could try. Tell me your end of this first.'

'Reinado was found dead, swinging under the railway bridge in Fremantle. He had my name and phone number in his pocket.' Cato gave the background: the disturbed flight from Darwin, Sharon's involvement, the previous arrest many years earlier, the warning from Guthrie to leave well alone.

'But suicide hasn't been ruled out?'

'It's the preferred option for some. Less paperwork. But it doesn't stack up.'

'I can understand why Geoff Guthrie would prefer to keep it that way.'

The main meal arrived accompanied by naan breads. Cato tore off some garlic naan and dipped it into his lamb saag. 'So the three areas of crossover between our two agendas are Ximenes, Reinado and Guthrie. Would that be right?'

'On the face of it.'

'Old crimes, politics and spies.'

Driscoll raised his beer in grim salute. 'It's what pays our mortgages.'

'Not yours though, eh?'

'What?'

'You gave the game away. Isn't that right?'

'A simple fisherman now, like I said.'

'But you came back because Ximenes threatened it all. That night in his house when he threatened to chop you up. Those injuries of his, the eye, the ear. He blames you for it. What was the name he mentioned? Abdullah?'

'A people smuggler. My next job after Shanghai was Sovereign Borders. Ximenes had shifted to Kupang in West Timor by then. He was helping us out, although I didn't deal with him directly.'

'Do you know who did?'

'There's a couple of candidates.'

'An informer. So now there's a fourth crossover between us. Border control.' Driscoll paused, puzzled. Cato explained about Peters and CPS. 'He was a guard at Christmas Island.'

'Interesting,' said Driscoll. 'That's where Willie Mason just died.'

***

Sharon invited him in and offered him a seat. She had no real choice, he was holding a gun. In her room, Ella was screaming fit to bust.

'I need to go to her.'

'No problem,' he said.

Ella took nearly half an hour to settle again. Some milk and a song helped. All that time he stood in the doorway, watching. Just watching.

He hadn't offered a name but Sharon had recognised him immediately from the ANU class photos. Geoff Guthrie, the security services guy who had warned Phil off the Reinado case.

'Is that why you're here?' she'd asked on their return to the kitchen. 'Reinado?'

'You need to stop digging.'

'Okay, whatever, but the gun in my face is a bit of overkill.'

He held it palm upwards as if he'd forgotten it was there. 'This? I suppose so.'

'I promise I'll stop digging. So you can leave now. Or do you want me to sign something?'

He shook his head. 'No need.'

Sharon stood up. 'Well, thanks for coming.'

'Sit down.'

He had come to kill her, not just to scare her. Sharon could see that now – it was written on his face. Ella mewled softly, she was on her way to sleep. Tears ran down Sharon's face. And when her baby awoke? 'There's no need for this. I haven't learned anything, and I won't look further. Whatever your secrets, they're safe.'

Guthrie stood up suddenly, went to the kitchen counter and took one of the knives from the wall magnet. 'If we can do this quietly, it will be better for your daughter. She'll live.' He filled a glass with water. 'I can phone it in afterwards and she won't be alone for long.'

Her insides froze. 'Please.' Her voice cracked. 'You don't have to. I'll stop. Finished.'

'Some people need to be sent a strong message.' He smiled sadly. 'Two birds, one stone.'

She pushed her phone facedown across the table towards him. 'Phone Phil. He'll stop too. None of this will go any further. Believe me.'

'He has a reputation. Sorry.' Guthrie sat down again, gun in one hand, knife on the table in front of him. He placed the glass of water in front of her and pulled a foil of pills from his pocket. 'Take them,' he said. 'All of them.'

She recognised the name on the back of the foil. Opioids. Another tear slid down her face. 'No.'

'Quickly, now. It's for the best.'

'You won't get away with this.'

'You think so? Those drug mules you've been busting at the airport. Tempting to dip into the confiscated goods maybe? Or maybe you just pissed off their bosses too much. It's all spinnable if you have the connections.'

A shake of the head. 'No.'

'Ella needn't even die. She could just grow up with terrible scars. Maybe I'll put the kettle on for a nice hot drink.'

'You fucking bastard.' Sharon pressed one out of the foil, took it, swallowed some water.

'Another' he said. 'Keep going.'

Sharon did, fighting back the choking sobs.

'Nearly there. Good girl.'

Suddenly she started coughing violently as the pill stuck in her throat. She clutched at her neck, panicking, eyes wide. In that moment of his distraction, she seized the water glass and ground it into his face, with her free hand she grabbed the knife from the table top and whipped it across his throat. The red spray went across the wall. Slumped forward, head on the table, blood sluicing from a sliced carotid, he was dead within a minute. She leaned into his ear. 'You should have listened to me. I was happy to stop.'

24

Friday 11ᵗʰ May

Cato had taken the first plane out when he heard. Driscoll could look after the Reinado affair in Darwin. He got back to the house early afternoon and the crime scene team was still in place. Sharon had summoned Julie to get Ella out of there, and they had taken up residence at a neighbour's granny flat down the road. She'd undergone a preliminary interview with state cops and with AFP internal affairs. It would be the first of many. For all that, she seemed to be in good form. They sat on a bench outside the granny flat, nursing mugs of tea and enjoying the sunshine on their faces.

'He's the first person I've killed. Hopefully the last, too.'

Cato shook his head. 'I'm sorry. I've done it again.'

'What?'

'Brought danger into our home.'

'Give me some credit. Why's it always about you? I was the one investigating, digging. The one who wouldn't leave it alone. Odds-on it was me who triggered this bloke.'

'Right.'

'See that ute parked down the street? That's his. He was the one who followed me home from work that night, I'm sure of it. He's been onto me for ages.' She clinked mugs with him. 'That psycho is all my own doing, thank you very much.'

Was she putting on a brave face or was this the real kick-ass Sharon Wang he'd met and fallen in love with in Shanghai?

'Yes,' she said, seeming to read his thoughts. 'I am being brave and I probably will crack up sometime soon. But I'm also proud that

I remembered my training, kept my cool, picked my moment and defended myself and my daughter. Our daughter,' she added quickly.

'You're amazing,' he said. 'I love you.'

'Good. You can prove it later on.'

He nodded in the direction of their home up the street. 'What's happening with all that?'

'We're in a hotel tonight. Forensics are far from finished. Hopefully my phone recorded enough to back up my story. Already from internal affairs and state CIB, I get the impression of machinery working in the background to bury this whole thing.'

'Who from CIB is on it?'

'They brought some D's up from Mandurah to run it because of perceived conflicts of interest with both Fremantle and with Major Crime. You being the common denominator.' She smiled wryly. 'They'll do as they're told apparently.'

'But we'll never learn what Guthrie was up to?'

'Not through official channels, no. Heard from Rory Driscoll lately?'

'Not since I left.'

'Will he bury whatever he learns on Reinado too?'

Cato thought about it a second. 'No, I think he's become a truth-seeker of late. He's a changed man.'

'What brought that about?'

'Too many dark deeds done cheap. I think he's seeking redemption.' Cato's phone buzzed. He checked the caller ID. 'Speak of the devil. Rory?'

'Mira's missing. Again. I called to check she got home okay. No answer after several tries. Checked with her workplace. They haven't heard from her. They sent somebody around to her apartment, and they reckon from the neighbours that nobody's been there for yonks.'

'She never arrived? Have you talked to José? Did she make her connecting flight?'

'He's not answering either. And your colleagues at Bunbury D's haven't heard from him.'

***

There were any number of scenarios. Maybe the spooks had changed their minds about charging Mira and grabbed her in transit once she'd raised a flag entering Darwin. Maybe she'd just taken off to lie low, sort herself out after a traumatic few weeks. Maybe the same people who'd taken Ximenes out of the frame now had their sights set on her once she was on her own and more vulnerable. All these maybes. And maybe José had got in the way, ending up dead in a ditch somewhere. Or maybe he was more dangerous than he seemed. Once again Driscoll was stuck for ideas. Kwong could follow up some enquiries at his end; up here, Reinado still might provide some answers. He was due to meet the widow in an hour, after she'd collected the kid from school. In the meantime, he wanted to know what Aunty had to say for herself. In case she hadn't already heard, he gave her the update: Kwong's wife – the inimitable Sharon Wang – had killed Geoff Guthrie, an experienced agent who people tended not to mess with. 'What was Guthrie up to, Aunty?'

'Your guess is as good as mine.'

'I doubt it. The through-line here with Ximenes, Mason, Guthrie, Reinado, now Mira Soares is nothing to do with oil. It's all about either the referendum atrocities or something linked.'

'You think so? I'm surprised atrocities still bother people these days. The world is full of them.'

'Mira's missing. Know anything about that?'

'No, I don't.'

'You'd better start helping me soon, Aunty. Work out whose side you're on. I'm on the verge of going commando, and you can take that any way you like.'

'Either way, I'm sure it'll set the cat among the pigeons.'

'I'll take that as a green light.'

'Rory, love. So many mixed metaphors I'm getting dizzy. Go ahead, do your worst.'

Enough. He cut the call. Jessica Reinado lived in Fannie Bay, two streets back from the ocean, with her six-year-old son Carlo and a house full of memories of Paul, a husband and father. The boy looked like a mini-me of the photos stuck on the fridge door. He was planted in front of the TV watching after-school cartoons with a Milo and some rice crackers. Jessica had offered Driscoll an iced coffee and made one for herself too. The aircon was on full blast although there was enough of a breeze to do without.

'You'll be number five or six by now.'

'Sorry?' said Driscoll.

'Cops I've told my story to.'

'I'm not police.' Again he showed her some spare ID he had.

'Yeah, yeah. Territory, WA state, federal, I'm losing track. Ask away. Maybe one day I'll say something magic and something will actually happen. Not holding my breath though.'

Jessica was more petite than she sounded on the phone. Her raspy Territorian drawl had suggested someone more robust. She looked fifteen and sounded fifty, and there were dark rings under her big eyes. Driscoll got her to recount the tale she'd told all the others – the strange goings-on in the lead-up to Paul's death.

'And like I told that Sharon chick in Perth, I reckon it all started with that angry phone call back in March, the one in Portuguese.'

'And he didn't tell you what it was about?'

'No. Community stuff, he said. "Don't worry your pretty little head, Chiquita." But he was rattled, I could tell.'

'You reported the harassment, the vandalism?'

'Yep. Like I told all the other cops. Nothing happened. Just kids, they reckoned.'

This would all be on various reports which Aunty could access if necessary. Driscoll went off down a line the cops wouldn't have followed. 'Did you ever meet Mira?'

'His sister? Once or twice, family do's, Christmas and that. She lives in Melbourne. Why?'

'Were they close?'

'In earlier years, less so lately. Again, why?'

Driscoll shrugged. Took a long slurp of iced coffee, it hit the spot. 'She hasn't made contact since Paul died?'

'No. Is she okay? Does she have something to do with this?'

'She might have, not directly. Did you ever meet her son?'

'Alex? Yeah, again, family do's. Good kid. He's on gap year in Europe, isn't he?'

'Far as I know.'

'What's this about? No more answers from me until you tell me.'

'I think it's connected to what happened to Mira back in Timor.'

Jessica shook her head. 'She had a shit life, poor woman. But why would what happened back then be such an issue now, twenty years on? And what's that got to do with Paulie? There's any number of people in the Timorese expat community with stories like hers.'

But not so many featuring a central character who was hardwired into the history, economy and politics of a nation. A man with powerful friends and enemies. 'Reckon you can get me an intro to Paul's mum and dad?'

***

Cato had obtained permission to gather some essentials from his house, space-suited up and skipping across the stepping plates and back out again with a couple of suitcases and boxes. Then they'd checked into the Esplanade hotel in Fremantle awaiting clearance to return home. While Sharon and Ella took an afternoon nap, Cato got on the phone to follow up on the whereabouts of Mira Soares and José Carrascalao.

'Good news and bad news,' reported Nikki Earle from Bunbury. 'José called in sick in the last hour. Ate something dodgy in transit, too shitty to even drive down to Bunbury after he got off the plane. He's still holed up in one of those No-Tell motels on the Great Eastern Highway up in Perth.' She gave Cato the details.

'Is that the good or bad news?'

'Your colleague Thornton was in touch. The DNA sample you sent from Dili?' Ximenes, leaving his handprints and traces on Driscoll's wrist ahead of a planned amputation. 'No match to either of our crime scenes.'

'He wasn't there?'

'Or he was very careful.' A hand over the phone and a brief conversation with someone at that end. 'How are things with you? How's …?'

'Sharon? So far so good.'

'Nasty stuff, look after yourselves.'

'Cheers.' Cato closed the call and tried José. No answer. Probably incommunicado and staying close to a toilet bowl. At least Cato hoped so. He tried a few calls to Melbourne, numbers Driscoll had given him, but to no avail. Mira still hadn't been heard from. He called his counterparts in Victoria police and started the ball rolling on a preliminary missing persons enquiry.

A hand on his shoulder. 'Hard at it, still.'

'Justice never sleeps.'

Sharon bent down and brushed her lips to his neck. 'I did and I feel much better for it.'

'You bearing up okay, after ...'

'After slashing some bloke's throat and letting him bleed out all over our kitchen? Yeah, all good. I'm hungry, going to call room service. AFP's shout. Any requests?'

'Whatever you're having.'

'I should really ravish you during this brief window before Ella wakes up, but I can't be arsed and even after two showers I still don't feel clean. You okay with that?'

'I'll survive.'

'Wrong answer. You're meant to be choked with grief.'

'Right. That as well.'

'Justice never sleeps and romance isn't dead.' She picked up the room phone and ordered two toasted BLTs with fries.

***

Alexandre Reinado didn't look like a former Falintil resistance fighter. Maybe it was the wheelchair and the oxygen bottle that skewed things.

'Asbestosis,' he rasped, lifting a wasted bony hand in greeting. 'I survived a decade in the mountains with the Indonesian air raids and shelling.' Grim smile. 'Many of the buildings the militias and army destroyed when they left in ninety-nine were made from asbestos. I just went into the dusty rubble to rescue some belongings before we were evacuated.'

Filomena Reinado set down a mug of coffee for Driscoll and a glass of water for her husband. She also looked frail but it was the frailty of age and grief rather than disease. Still, for all that, there was a steeliness to her gaze. They all waited for the noise of another landing fighter jet from the nearby RAAF base to recede.

'It's busier now with the Americans using it too.' She pushed some cake towards him. 'You are the first policeman who has wanted to talk to us about Paulho.'

'Really?' Driscoll clarified, once again, his non-police investigatory status but she shrugged it away. 'Nobody has come to talk to you?'

'Nobody. Jessica maybe, but not us. Why should they? They do not suspect a crime.'

'Do you?'

She nodded. 'I wish it were not so but what else could it be? He wouldn't kill himself, he loved his family, his life, despite everything that had happened.'

'Jessica mentioned trouble in the few weeks before that?'

'Weeks? It was nearly two months.'

The coffee was good, Timorese of course. Driscoll glanced around the room, waiting for Filomena to continue. On the shelves and sideboards, pictures of the family through the recent ages, among them Mira and Paulho. Some famous faces too: Ramos-Horta, Xanana, Bishop Belo, all had passed over the Reinado threshold in suburban Darwin during the last twenty years. At a signal from her husband, Filomena went on. She was their voice now, talking would exhaust Alexandre.

'One Sunday morning, early March, Nightcliff Market. I help out at a Timorese art-and-craft stall.' She dipped her head, nibbled on a piece of cake. 'And there he was, out of nowhere, right in front of me.'

Driscoll waited. And waited.

Filomena stared at the floor. 'After all this time, we still don't know his name.'

'But you recognised him. Why do you know him?'

'He was there when they gave Paulho back to me. Leaning against the doorframe of that hell hole. Enjoying the sun on his face.'

'*Malae*?' Driscoll prompted. 'Not Indonesian or Timorese?'

She nodded. 'He looked so ordinary. Like the man who stamps your passport, or, or …'

'Tells you that you have six months to live,' offered Alexandre.

Driscoll brought up a picture of Willie Mason on his phone and showed it to her. She shook her head – not him. Maybe Guthrie? No. 'But Australian, yes?'

'Yes. He spoke English to Ximenes that day. Loudly, clearly. Like he wanted me to know.' She recounted the story. It was in the months preceding the referendum. After a demonstration in Dili by student activists, the army and militias had come to the village and taken some of the young men, among them Paulho. He had been returned to her two days later as a shell. Alexandre was still in hiding in the hills, his association with Falintil a death sentence if he was caught. Filomena had passed herself off as Paulho's aunt. If they had known who she really was she too would have been killed. Driscoll again asked her to describe the foreigner and again she failed: a man of average age, average height, average build. Hair a sandy brown nothing. Eyes blue, or maybe hazel.

'Why is he important? Surely Ximenes and his men were the ones who did the violence?'

'Paulho told us later this man had instructed them in every foul terrible thing they did. And, in the case of Paulho, he joined in.'

'And so one day this man appears in front of your market stall here in Darwin. Did he know who you were?'

A bitter laugh. 'Oh, yes.'

'Did he say anything?'

'He made a show of trying to remember where he knew me from, like we were old friends or acquaintances. But he knew I recognised him immediately.'

'Was he alone?'

'No, there was a woman with him.' Filomena described her and Driscoll made some notes. The description rang no bells, his wife maybe?

'Did he say anything else?'

Tears filled her eyes. 'He asked how Paulho was doing. Even remembered his name after all this time.'

She'd found her voice then. Raging at him in Tetun, in English, in Portuguese. Pointing him out to all those in the vicinity who might listen. Murderer, war criminal, beast, pervert. She had caused a scene. Tears flowed down her face as she recounted it. The rage and fear still hot.

'How did he react?'

'Very calm. He said he knew even back then I was Paulho's mother, not his aunt. It was not important to him then, or now. "Water under the bridge, Filomena." He knew my name too. "Cry, no more," he said. "We are all reconciled now." Then he went away with his lady friend.'

'But the strange happenings began after that?'

'Maybe a week later. I told Alexandre. I told Paulho. He wanted to forget it, move on. I insisted. We argued and finally he agreed, so we made complaints to the police that somebody should do something.'

Was this the argument Jessica overheard? Her husband Paulho rowing in Portuguese with someone? This family, he was sure, would speak it among themselves. 'But you didn't have a name. What could they do?'

'Yes,' Filomena said sadly. 'That was what the police told us.'

***

Great Eastern Highway was one of Cato's least favourite roads in the Perth metropolitan area, if not the world. The Burswood Motor Lodge had a well-provisioned mini-mart and a stunning view of the passing traffic. Was José still in situ? Duty Manager Shania checked her computer screen.

'Carrascalao. Hmmm.' A furrowing of her carefully crafted eyebrows. 'And you are?'

Cato showed her his police ID. She looked at it closely checking his face against the photo twice in case he wasn't who he claimed to be.

'Satisfied?' said Cato.

'I'll try his room,' she said, picking up the phone. After about thirty seconds she shrugged. 'Not answering. He must have gone out.'

'Which room is it?'

'Not sure I should tell you.' Cato swung her screen his way and saw the number. 'Hey!'

'Relax,' said Cato. 'Welfare call.'

The room was on the second floor along an open balcony walkway. Traffic noise bounced off the concrete. An acrid odour of exhaust fumes and a nearby fast-food joint. The Perth city skyline glinted in the distance as the sun fell. Number 218 was at the end of the walkway overlooking the pool and its surface of oily grime. A discarded can of Red Bull glinted in the bushes. The curtains were closed and, ear to the door, no sound came from inside. Cato unclipped his Glock. There was no reason to feel any threat but he felt it anyway.

He knocked. 'José? You there, mate? It's Phil. Philip Kwong.'

Nothing except the rush of traffic.

Cato took out his phone and dialled José's number. Inside he could hear the phone ringing a few times before it went to messages. If José had gone out, he'd left his phone behind. Unusual these days, but not impossible. A scrape behind him and the muzzle of a gun behind his ear.

'Hand me yours, nice and relaxed.' José's voice. Cato did as he was told.

He received the room card in return. 'Go ahead and open it. We've been expecting you.'

We?

He pressed the card into the slot and twisted the door handle when the little light flashed green. Edging over the threshold into the gloom Cato was aware of the sour smell of vomit and the rotten fruity stench of diarrhoea. 'You really were crook then.'

'Not me.' José nudged him forward with the barrel of the gun. 'Her.'

With a twist of his head Cato discerned the prone figure of Mira Soares on the bed under the covers. 'Spiked her drink at the airport bar in Darwin, changed her ticket, made up a story and flashed my cop ID.' José came around in front of Cato and flicked on a bedside lamp. 'Plain sailing.' He waved the gun. 'Want to open a few windows?'

Cato obliged. 'What's this about?'

'Sorry, mate. Not really one for explanations.' He shot the figure on the bed and then turned the gun back on Cato.

***

'He's dead.'

'Looks like it.'

'You wish.' He opened an eye and shut it again. The pain and the glare too much. He'd woken with a blinding headache and a hospital smell in his nostrils. A pistol-whipping, the doctors reckoned, from the injuries. He was content to drift in and out of consciousness.

'Been in the wars, Philip.' DI Pavlou laid a bag on his bedside table. 'Have a grape.'

Chris Thornton put a cardboard cup beside the bag. 'Flat white, no froth. Just the way you like it.'

'You're going to look like a panda for the next few days and your nose will need re-setting but otherwise the prospects are good.' Pavlou pulled up a chair. 'You should be fit to stand trial.'

'Trial?' Cato took a sip of water.

'Ms Mira Soares. Attempted murder. Charges may be upgraded later. See how the docs go over the next few hours.'

She's joking, has to be. 'It wasn't me. It was José.'

A thin smile. 'Thought that might be your story. Over to you, Chris.'

Thornton leaned against a wall and scrolled through his iPad. 'José Carrascalao. Born nineteen seventy-four, Rio in Brazil, Aussie mum and local dad. Moved to Australia at the age of three. Lived in and around Bunbury until he left school. Went to UWA, excelled in languages – Portuguese and Spanish in particular. Returned to Brazil in his early twenties for a decade or so – call of family, roots, et cetera. Plus his mum had died of breast cancer and his dad wanted to go home. Believed during this time he was recruited by ...' he paused.

'ABIN,' said Cato. 'Brazilian intelligence.'

'You know all this already?' Pavlou looked put out, as did Thornton.

'Not all. So, let's guess, he finds himself in Timor around independence referendum time, late nineties?'

'Seems so. The Brazilians and Portuguese, speaking the same language and all, were interested in staking their claim in a future free Timor.'

'Where's your info coming from? Not Google surely?'

'In part, yeah, but also been chatting to your mate Driscoll. He's on the next flight down.'

'José's our killer?'

'His DNA is on the body in the skip ...'

That last call to José's phone. 'Ryan Hodgson?'

'Yep. Maybe he was in a hurry.'

Pavlou interrupted. 'We'll put this all together in good time, but any ideas why and where he might have disappeared to?'

'Why? I'm guessing something to do with past atrocities in Timor but it seems far-fetched. Where? Some embassy or consulate? He could just go and hide under cover of whichever crew he was working for at the time. I assume you're watching the airports and such?'

'Yep, and his family and workplace.'

'DSC Nikki Earle?'

'Is in the loop.' Pavlou checked an incoming on her mobile. 'By the way have you got insurance?'

'Why?'

'He scarpered in your car.' At that moment a flustered Sharon came into the room with an excited and chatty Ella. 'We'll be in touch.' Pavlou popped a grape in her mouth. 'Get well soon. And don't leave town.'

***

Driscoll arrived in Perth around nine that evening. He collected a hire car and headed for Royal Perth Hospital. Security gave him a wary look as he approached the counter but he flashed some official-looking ID and made like a cop and they waved him through to where Kwong was resting up. The patient's black eyes had blossomed and his face was a wreck.

'Surprised you're still here, Kung Fu Panda. Didn't think a broken nose warranted a hospital bed?'

'They want to know if I've got concussion or not.'

'Fair enough. I asked at reception, they said Mira's in ICU?'

'Bullet in the chest will do that to you. They say she'll pull through. It missed the vitals.'

'Good. Any ideas where José's gone?'

'You probably know him better than we do. Or at least his likely MO.'

Driscoll shook his head. 'Kidnappings. Shootings. Half-arsed frame-ups. He's erratic. Attention-seeking secret agents tend not to last too long. Either he's forgotten his training or this is all part of the plan.'

'Maybe he's hiding in plain sight. Tell me about Darwin. Did José get a mention?'

'No. Some other foreigner is in the frame.' Driscoll filled Kwong in on what he'd learned.

'And this fearsome marketplace stranger isn't your mate, what's his name?'

'Mason. No. And I zapped Filomena a pic of José en route when I heard what happened to you. Not him either.'

'Guthrie?'

'Nah. He was never up in Timor best of my knowledge. It was before his time with the agency. We're talking at least twenty years here, Guthrie would have still been at college.'

'Do we then assume that Guthrie and José, maybe even Mason too, were all working for somebody else, our mystery man?'

'If so, this bloke's got a lot of clout.'

'And perhaps more to lose if his secret gets out?'

'A public figure.' Driscoll thought about Aunty and her PR consultancy; taking in other people's dirty laundry. 'Only people in the public eye worry that much about secrets.'

Kwong was looking weary. 'If the reason you, this Mason guy, and perhaps Mira, were in the crosshairs was nothing to do with oil, then that leaves your fourth man as the odd one out.'

'Brian Simmonds?' The suburban lawyer.

'I'll take your word for it. You haven't mentioned him much.' A foil of pills on the bedside table. Kwong popped two and took them with a swig of water. 'Headache,' he said, slipping the foil into his drawer.

'I should leave you in peace.'

'I'll be out of here in the morning.' A weak smile. 'Ding, ding, round two.'

Driscoll took his leave, musing about Kwong's medication and why he felt the need to pass it off as paracetamol.

***

Ella was asleep in the hotel-provided cot. Phil was staying in hospital but was going to be okay, so Sharon made the call. Half an hour later there was a knock at the door – one she was expecting this time. She invited Mick Hutchens over the threshold and offered him a hotel teabag and UHT milk.

'Great,' he said, settling in. 'Cheers.'

'You're looking well. Retirement agrees with you.'

'Thanks.' He took the mug offered to him. 'Cato okay?'

She nodded. 'Face like a dropped pie but he'll live.'

'And the woman?'

'Her too. More serious, but all good.'

He took a sip. 'So what's this about, Shaz?'

She gave him the story then pushed the phone across the table towards him, along with the separate battery and SIM. 'Guthrie's. I hid it before the techs arrived.'

'Why?'

'I don't trust the usual channels. Somebody out there has influence and reach. It could disappear.'

Hutchens took a pen from the inside pocket of his jacket and prodded the phone with it. 'You haven't tried turning it on yet?'

'No.'

'I thought all these *Get Smart* people spoke into their shoes.' He picked up the SIM and squinted at it, held it to the light as if it might give up its secrets there and then. 'And you want me to do something about it?'

'Can you?'

'You really don't trust your own mob? Or Chris, or Deb?'

'I want to; just playing safe I guess.'

'Right.' He frowned. 'Marj won't like it if I get spirited away to Guantanamo. She's got this holiday booked in Aix-en-Provence. Still ...' he grinned. 'Might get my exegesis finished if they put me in solitary. Leave it with me.' He pushed his cup to one side. 'You okay, after ... everything?'

'Yeah. Maybe I shouldn't be. It might hit later but, you know.'

'Fair enough. Don't bottle it up if it begins to show.'

'Not my style.' He had a look on his face. 'Spit it out.'

Hutchens leaned back in his chair. 'Has Cato ... Phil been okay these last few months?'

'Seems to be. Why?' This time the look was on her face, she couldn't hide it.

'The meds the docs put him on. Take them for too long, become dependent, and they do funny things. Had some myself after the bashing with the cricket bat. Threw them away after a few months.'

'Phil said he was gradually reducing the dosage. Weaning himself off.'

'When was this?'

'Six months ago, maybe.'

Hutchens smiled sadly. 'Believe him, Shaz?'

No, she realised. She didn't. She never had, but was content to live with the denial and focus on Ella and on her job.

'I was telling Cato. I don't miss the Job at all. Thought it would kill me being out of it.' Hutchens shook his head. 'Never looked back.'

'What are you saying?'

'I know a downward spiral when I see one. Ultimatum time. He won't take the initiative so you'll have to. The only thing that will break the circuit is fear of losing you and the bub. He needs a sabbatical for all your sakes.'

'That's pretty full-on marriage guidance advice, Mick.'

'I don't do subtlety, love. But I mean well.'

25

Saturday 12th May

Driscoll started the day by turning over Geoff Guthrie's home. It was a nondescript unit by the railway line at West Leederville, more suited to a student or somebody on welfare benefits than a bloke on a hundred-plus grand a year, not including the extra he was making from moonlighting. But it made for a good cover story. On the wall was a sun-faded poster of Anna Kournikova returning serve and revealing plenty of flesh and underwear. Furniture stained and unloved like its owner, the fug of loneliness and failure permeated the place and clung to the walls like condensation. This was a guy you'd avoid in the street and forget as soon as you met him. That would have suited Guthrie perfectly. According to the bills on the fridge and the spare ID in the bedside drawer, he was living there under the name of Owen Marshall, and he had an appointment with a social worker that coming Monday. Aunty had supplied Driscoll with the safe-house address and arranged for a key to be left under the plant pot.

'ASIO are putting some distance between themselves and him,' she'd said. 'He's gone off-piste.'

There was no laptop or tablet. Missing or never existed? His phone was missing too, although Driscoll suspected Sharon might have something to do with that. As soon as it was switched on, she'd have goons at her door, either from ASIO or from Guthrie's second job. So who else was he working for? On the fridge a photo of him, in character as Owen Marshall, in happier times with a wife and small child – a daughter. No sign of them living in this hovel. Were they part of his legend or did they really exist? Even if they did, what would they know of his secret life?

He'd shown up at police HQ openly in an official capacity to tell Kwong to back off. That must have been sanctioned. But what was the undercover nature of his work, this assumed identity and safe house? It was clearly sanctioned and resourced officially from Canberra – otherwise Aunty would not have been able to find out about it.

The phone he was carrying when he died would have been his moonlight burner. He probably had another for his official ASIO work. Maybe yet another for personal or other matters. Driscoll began a search through cupboards, drawers, air vents, loose skirting panels, toilet cistern, freezer – the usual. Nothing. The grouting in the shower cubicle was black, and the once-white tiles had turned a yellowy-grey. Down in the bottom corner, with some scraping, the tile came loose. In the recess, more false ID and cash in a plastic bag, along with a spare phone. The ID was a driving licence in yet another name, the cash amounted to five grand in fifties and twenties. Driscoll dismantled the phone and pocketed the components for further examination, along with the cash which could come in handy if he had to go rogue. He locked up, replaced the key under the plant pot and hopped on the next city-bound train out of West Leederville. En route he belled Aunty again.

'Found a spare phone and some ID. Nothing much else of interest.' He asked about the wife and daughter.

'Estranged. She took the kid back to Ireland and is now remarried to a boyhood sweetheart in the Garda.'

So the atmosphere of failure and loneliness in Guthrie's home wasn't all confected. 'Still no whispers as to who he was moonlighting for?'

'Maybe the phone will tell us.'

Driscoll kept to himself his suspicions that Sharon Wang might have the most useful one in her possession. He kept the cash stash to himself too. Why? Maybe he wasn't so sure about Aunty anymore.

***

After another head scan and a check on his blood pressure and other vital signs, Cato was discharged from the hospital and lowered himself gingerly into the passenger seat while Sharon strapped Ella into the back.

'You sure you're okay?' Sharon started the car and backed out of the parking space.

'So the doc says, and she's the expert.'

'We're in the hotel for the rest of the weekend. They're not far off finishing the forensics on our place and then the cleaners come in Monday morning. Hopefully we'll be back in there by the end of the day or early Tuesday.'

'That'd be good.'

'So what do you want to do today?'

Find José Carrascalao maybe. Dig the bullet out of Mira Soares' chest and make her well again. Undo the knife wound in Rosa Domingo's gut. Turn back time. He became aware that Sharon was looking at him out the corner of her eye while negotiating the Saturday morning traffic on South Street. 'Hmmm?'

'You're miles away.'

'Sorry.'

'I was talking to Mick Hutchens last night.'

'Really? Why?'

'Work stuff. He mentioned that medication you were on, said he'd been on it himself a while back. I told him I thought you were in the process of giving it up.' Another sideways glance. 'That's right, isn't it?'

'I'm on the slow-release weekly dose.'

She detected a "but" and articulated it.

'I have an emergency stash, a mini-stockpile. Now and then I still use them.'

'You didn't feel the need to tell me.'

'Do I need to?'

'If it affects all of us, yes.'

'Does it?'

Sharon signalled left into the forecourt of a petrol station and found a spot outside the shop. She turned off the ignition and turned to face him. 'What do you think?'

Cato didn't need this right now. 'I'm easing off. Sometimes they take the edge away. Lately it's been ...'

She grasped his hand. 'They're not the answer.'

He stared bleakly out at the sunshine and the passing traffic. 'What is?'

'This job is going to kill you, directly or indirectly.'

'I can handle it.'

'No, obviously you can't. What's your biggest fear?'

'Losing you and Ella.'

'And what would you do to prevent that?'

'Anything. Everything.'

'Prove it.'

***

Driscoll needed to find José but he also needed Guthrie's phone. Aunty was on the case with the techs looking for any evidence of communication between the two. They were also on alert for José using any known phones, credit cards, social media and email accounts, but no doubt he would be too well-trained for that. He wouldn't be found until or unless he wanted to be, or purely by chance. The priority may as well be Guthrie's missing burner phone. He rang Sharon.

'What's happening?'

'Nothing much. We're on the way home from hospital.'

'Hubby keeping well?'

A pause. 'Well as.'

'I'll get to the point. Do you have Geoff Guthrie's phone?'

'No.'

'I don't believe you.'

'Not my problem. Hang on,' said Sharon. 'I'll just put you on speaker so I don't cop a ticket.'

'How's the head, Phil?'

'All good. Found José yet?'

'No. Thought Guthrie's phone might give us some clues.' Was it Driscoll's imagination or was there friction at the other end of the line? Anything he could use to his advantage? 'You guys'll be needing some quality time I expect. Lot of pressure at the moment. Can't be good.'

'Appreciate your understanding, Rory.' Sharon had that steel in her voice he recalled from their time working together in Shanghai. 'Keep us in the loop, eh?'

'If you do come across Guthrie's phone back at your place, I'd advise you not to turn it on. Might bring a whole heap of grief back to your doorstep.' In the background a child's voice, miserable at being woken up.

'Good advice, mate. Cheers for that.'

Sharon had it, definitely, but didn't want to play ball. 'Phil? You still with us?' Affirmative. 'I still owe you for saving me in that cellar in Dili. It's a debt I take seriously, mate. Together we can crack this.'

'No worries,' said Kwong. 'All good.'

***

'What cellar?' said Sharon.

'What phone?' said Cato.

'You first,' she insisted.

So he briefly outlined the scene in Ximenes' cellar and the machete threat to Driscoll's extremities.

'Jesus, no wonder you feel the need to reach for the extra pills now and then. Bloody Driscoll! You should have let Ximenes follow through.'

'You don't mean that.'

'No,' she conceded. 'I probably don't.'

They were nearly back at the Esplanade. Across the road was the Carriage Cafe where, just the previous year, Cato had been called to investigate the third in a series of murders of Fremantle's homeless. This one an ex-soldier stomped to death. 'Do you have Guthrie's phone?'

'Mick Hutchens has it.'

They pulled into the angle parking in Essex Street and Cato unstrapped Ella while Sharon grabbed bags from the boot. 'I never saw Hutchens as a "Q" type figure.'

'He was the only person I could think of.'

'You suspect bad apples in the AFP?'

'And among WA's finest.'

'I guess that does make Hutchens the last resort.'

'I heard that.'

Cato turned and there he was. For some reason that really cheered Ella up and she beamed in adoration. 'Ganda!'

Hutchens tickled her under the chin and pulled a funny face. Looked at Cato. 'Been fighting again?' He waggled the phone. 'Somebody want to buy me a cuppa?'

'It'll have to be another hotel teabag in our room.' Sharon lifted her chin towards Ella. 'I can't see her lasting the distance in a cafe.'

'Suits me.' Hutchens unclipped his bike helmet and chained his machine to a rail. He pressed a few buttons on his wristband. 'Eighteen point four k's in fifty-five. A PB.' He noticed Cato's quizzical look. 'Did a U3A course a few months ago. "Master Your Fitbit." Never looked back.'

While Ella was distracted with a rice cracker, fruit segments and the Wiggles, Hutchens reported on Guthrie's phone. 'Three numbers he regularly rang or was called from.' He passed over a sheet of paper with the numbers handwritten. Beside each a letter: A, B, and C. 'That's what was in the contacts address book.' He handed over a second sheet, the log for the life of the phone. Just a week and totalling less than twenty calls made or received.

'How did you get this without triggering the forces of darkness?' Cato passed him a mug.

'I didn't. I went against Sharon's wishes and just asked Chris Thornton to do it. He did so in the bowels of police HQ. If the forces of darkness want to pay a visit, they've got to get past the senior constable on the front door first.' He turned to Sharon. 'Sorry Shaz, but Chris is top notch. You really can trust him.'

'Hope you're right.' She handed Ella a plate of chopped fruit. 'Did he run the numbers?'

'Prepaids, unregistered. Chris cloned the SIM and ran the phone for fingerprints and other traces before he gave it back to me. In the end though, he'd appreciate it being returned and entered into evidence.'

'Sure,' said Sharon, without conviction.

Cato scanned the log. 'Most of the calls seem to be from "A" and primarily in the three days leading up to Guthrie's death.'

'You noticed that too.' Hutchens drained his tea. 'So what are you going to do with this?'

Cato turned the phone thoughtfully in his palm. 'Call those numbers and see who comes running?'

'We don't want them running to here,' said Sharon. 'We need somewhere open, public, plenty of witnesses.'

Cato still looked like he'd just been hit by a bus. It wasn't a good idea for him to be out in public. 'How about we do it?' Hutchens grinned. 'Me and Shaz?'

'No way,' said Cato and Sharon together.

'Why not?'

'You're a civilian,' said Sharon.

'It's too dangerous,' said Cato. 'For both of you.'

'But not you?' Sharon snorted.

'If those numbers are for spooks, maybe Driscoll should be doing this. It's his world. He speaks their language, probably knows whoever is at the other end.'

'Do you trust him?' Sharon clearly didn't.

'Like he said, he owes me after the cellar.'

'What cellar?' said Hutchens.

'Long story. I think somewhere deep inside, Driscoll's a man of honour.'

'He sidelined me because he knows you're a soft touch.' Sharon stole one of Ella's apple slices while the kid was absorbed in Lachy the purple Wiggle. 'I took the initiative to keep Guthrie's phone, I should make the call.'

Hutchens frowned. 'Cato's right, Sharon. This is no time for any of us to be taking unnecessary risks. You both have a little kid to be worried about and I have to finish my thesis. Bring the spook in.'

'If the phone has been activated in police HQ they're going to know not to touch it with a barge pole.' Sharon spun it on the coffee table. 'It's a waste of time anyway.'

'Depends whether everybody is in the loop – A, B and C.' Hutchens shrugged. 'It only needs one of them not to be.'

Cato reached for his mobile. 'So, shall I call Driscoll?'

***

Mira Soares was well enough to receive visitors by early Saturday afternoon. The police guard had checked Driscoll's name against an approved visitors list and examined his ID. Driscoll would let Sharon and Kwong have their game with Guthrie's phone. At some point they'd come to their senses and realise he was on their side. He was, after all, wasn't he? José would make his next move in his own good time and that, for the moment, was outside Driscoll's control. So here he was holding Mira's cool hand, listening to the machines beep and watching the numbers on the monitor.

'Hey,' she said. 'I'm here. You're visiting me, not the machines.'

The bullet had lodged high in her chest within the pectoral muscle. It had been extracted and the internal damage repaired. Driscoll wondered why José hadn't gone for the more certain head shot to finish her. He'd have had time. Maybe he wasn't as cool-headed as he pretended. Or he didn't mean for Mira to die. Who knew? 'How are you feeling?'

'Great. Never better. Maybe we can hit the clubs tonight?' Her face was grey and drawn, but the smile was genuine. She coughed and winced with the pain. 'This would be a good time to give up smoking, you think?'

'Good idea.'

Mira shifted in the bed, trying to find some comfort. The machines didn't like it and beeped in protest. A nurse popped her head round the door briefly but didn't stay. Mira squeezed Driscoll's hand. 'Why did José do this to me? What is all this about?'

'I don't know. I thought you might. He said nothing to you?'

'I don't remember anything between Darwin and waking up here.'

'It has to be about either the past or your journalism. The oil stuff with Willie Mason maybe?'

'Then why didn't he make his move in Dili?'

Driscoll eased a kink in his neck. 'Who knows? Clearly Ximenes was part of the equation.' A pause. 'What do you recall of that day of the massacre at the church?'

She lifted her hand away from his. 'Nothing. Horror. Blood. Noise. I was terrified.'

'Do you remember seeing any Westerners that day? *Malae*?'

'No.'

'Did you know Willie Mason was there that day?'

She shook her head. 'You're lying. He wouldn't ...'

'He was.' He hadn't told her of Mason's death yet. Decided against it for now.

'No. He told me it wasn't him. Some other *malae*, but not him, not that day.'

Could that be true? Whose word did they have? Ximenes? Mason himself must have seen some truth in the allegation, and he was trying to bargain his way out of it. Was that because he was guilty or because he could feel a noose tightening around him? The noose that found him at Christmas Island. 'Did Filomena ever talk to you about the *malae* involved in Paul Reinado's arrest and interrogation?'

'His torture and rape, you mean? Yes, she did.'

'She said she saw the man again at the market in Darwin.'

'Yes.'

'It wasn't a story you wanted to write about as a journalist?'

'I did some digging but there was nothing to go on. No photograph. No name. The description of a thousand nobodies.'

'Where did you dig?'

'I can't remember.'

The nurse came back into the room. It was time for him to go. Mira was clearly tired and no longer up for this.

'Try and think,' he said. 'Please.'

His mobile buzzed. Kwong. They had finally come to their senses.

***

All of the numbers were being monitored both by WA police and by Aunty's spook contacts. Only one was active: B. Driscoll left the same message on the other two and then punched in the numbers for B.

'G'day, mate.' It was José. Of course it was. He was the only one of the three whose cover was already blown. 'What took you so long?'

'Let me guess. B for Bunbury?'

'Nah, mate, nothing so deep.'

Kwong was seated close by, taking a direct feed from the techs at HQ if they traced any of the numbers. The old guy, Hutchens, had gone his merry way and Sharon was looking after the bub. That left the two of them and where more public, open, and teeming with witnesses than Fremantle's Cappuccino Strip on a Saturday evening? It was already dark and a brisk wind shook the olive trees outside Gino's. Driscoll and Kwong made a fine pair and were already attracting their fair share of attention. For all its claim to multicultural laissez faire, Freo still wasn't ready for a bashed-up Chinaman in the company of a tall, and in this mood, dangerous-looking Aboriginal. Double takes, open staring, bouncers on alert. It all suited Driscoll just fine. If anything happened, it would be noticed. 'Thought you would have skipped town by now, José. Or holed up in a friendly consulate. Your job to take one for the team?'

'My job to pass on a message.'

'I'm listening.'

'Let it drop and walk away.'

'Just when it's getting interesting?'

'I mean it, mate. It's high stakes. You, your friends. We don't want anyone else getting hurt.'

'Bit late for that. Anyway, who's we?'

'Got a fix on my location yet?'

Driscoll checked with Kwong. 'James Street, Northbridge?'

'Yeah, mate. Probably as busy as where you are right now. Look, must dash. Don't waste your time with these numbers, they're dead from now on. Just take heed. We're done. It's all over from our end.'

'But Mira's still alive.'

'Say hello from me.'

Driscoll's screen died. He looked at Kwong. 'You got that?'

'Final warning?'

'Pretty much. He reckons they're finished, mission accomplished. Time to move on.'

'He stayed around long enough to bother saying that?'

'Nah, I don't believe him either.'

***

'José's wife and younger son flew out of Australia just over a week ago. She's originally from Brazil and has no other rellies here. They have another son travelling on a gap year in South America, no doubt planning a family reunion.' Thornton had cupped his hand over the phone to talk to whoever had come into the room. 'Their house was rented, lease prepaid to the end of July. Furniture still in situ, fridge and pantry stocked, but all personal stuff gone save a few pics on the fridge, and some books and sporting gear.'

'Brazil-bound?' said Cato.

'Yep, but who knows what *his* plans are.'

'Thanks for coming in on the weekend, Chris.'

'Got the boss, beside me. She'd like a word.'

Pavlou came on the line. 'Who's this Blasey woman from Canberra?' she asked Cato.

'That'd be Driscoll's boss.' Cato cast a glance at the man himself. They were still on the Strip, the crowds had thinned as the wind picked up and the evening wore on. The early diners had gone and the hardcore clubbers had arrived, spilling out of the Newport as they preloaded for a big night.

'Got tickets on herself. Wants me to send her everything we've got with nothing on offer in return.'

'That doesn't sound fair,' said Cato.

'Leave her to me. So was this Carrascalao a sleeper agent or something? Waiting for the call?'

'Not as *Tinker Tailor* as all that, boss. I'm guessing he was a well-placed freelancer and opportunist. I think he really was just paying the bills with his Bunbury cop job and probably just picked up the odd bit of moonlighting here and there.'

'But somebody knew where to find him. And Guthrie. What the fuck is this, like some employment agency for former spies and assassins? A spooks Silver Chain?'

'Nicely put. But yes, somebody knew where to look for him and Guthrie, and that suggests prior knowledge. Plus, something triggered all this activity over the last few months.'

Pavlou cleared her throat. 'Which takes us back to our old codgers and the Reinados in Darwin.'

'Thornton is on the case, boss.'

'I'll put him back on.'

Cato issued a fresh round of instructions and closed the call.

Driscoll looked up from his latte. 'Australia Post?'

'An old-fashioned method of communication and freight delivery quite popular in the last century.' Cato ignored Driscoll's blank stare. 'Because we haven't found the package, I'm assuming our killer has it.'

'And our prime candidate for your old men killings would be José?'

'He's up there.'

'Intercepting and disposing of some proof on behalf of his employer.'

Cato nodded. 'In a way that pointed the finger at Ximenes. All tying in to the date things started going weird up in Darwin, early March.'

'So while your bloke Thornton looks for, among other things, links between your old men and Darwin, I suggest we go after José. You never know, he might be able to tell us what was in that Australia Post parcel.'

'And where do you suggest we start looking for him?'

'Fuck knows.'

26

Sunday 13th May

Cato woke to the buzzing of his mobile. He checked the time: 4.55 a.m. Too early even for Ella. A message from a familiar number.

Time to come clean

His mystery caller since day one. José. He fit the bill, knew who'd killed Doug Peters, knew Cato was on the investigation, knew how to contact him. Of course it was him. Now they were approaching endgame, and José would be looking to pry him away from Driscoll who he no doubt judged to be more dangerous. Cato texted back. **Where and when?**

Sharon stirred. 'Who's that?'

'José.'

'What does he want?'

The mobile buzzed again and Cato checked the screen. 'A meeting. Alone.'

'Great idea. Of course.' Ella stood up in her foldaway cot and demanded milk and stories. 'Turn your phone off and attend to your daughter.'

He did. All the while thinking it through. If José had wanted Cato dead he'd have done it earlier when he had the chance, shot both Mira and him and made sure of the job. What had been his motive in sending those early messages anyway? José didn't strike him as a man who did things for the sheer hell of it. A simple hired gun would just strike his target, take the money and run. José wasn't doing that. Was there another motive to his actions? Something driving him personally? Cato had thought from early on that his mystery caller was someone who knew the truth, would be damned for his involvement in it, and sought some kind of redemption through this contact. His job wasn't finished until he'd achieved it. And the only way José could get redemption was by revealing the truth.

'I need to do this,' said Cato. He outlined his reasoning to Sharon.

'No, you don't need to do this at all. You want to, there's a difference. Maybe he didn't kill you then because the timing wasn't right. And now it is.' The toaster popped up. Sharon spread some marge and vegemite on a slice and quartered it for Ella. Ditto for the second slice which she saved for herself. 'Want some?' She dropped two more in at his nodding.

'If I don't keep this meeting he'll probably disappear into diplomatic protection and we'll never find out the truth of the matter.'

'You and your bloody truth. You pick and choose when and how much it matters to you.' Sharon licked some vegemite off the end of her finger and started a count. 'If it was an official operation, you probably won't get the truth of the matter anyway. If he was moonlighting, he won't be getting any diplomatic immunity. If he wants redemption, tell him to write up his confession and name names, sign it, and hand it and himself into police HQ. You don't need to be part of this.'

She was right. Still. 'You said yourself, whoever he's working for or protecting they possibly have enough influence to bury this, and that's why you don't entirely trust the cops, state or federal.'

Sharon shook her head. 'Take Driscoll with you.' She handed over a plate of toast. 'Things have to fucking change around here. Really.'

***

Driscoll had slept well. No ghosts had visited him in the night. A longer lie-in would have been nice, but a shower, coffee, bacon-and-egg toastie from the local deli, and a loaded gun under his armpit, and he was ready to take on the world.

Aunty had booked him into a chain motel on Canning Highway near the river. She'd been grumpy that the state cops weren't doing her bidding. 'Some prissy little arriviste called Pavlou. Quid pro quo, she says. Like we're equals or something.'

'Sounds like you've met your match.'

'That'll be the day.'

'How do you want me to handle Carrascalao?'

'I'm tempted to have him put down. Dead men tell no tales.'

'I'd like to hear his tale first.'

'Redemption?' she'd muttered. 'Is your man Kwong on something?'

'Antidepressants, I'm guessing. Makes him see the bright side.'

'José is our only lead to who's behind this, isn't he?'

'At the moment, yeah.'

'Find out what you can and we'll decide what to do with him later.'

'It's hard to imagine.'

'What?'

'That we don't already know who it is, if Mr X does have a service background like Mason and Guthrie. We must have known who we had in Timor at that time.'

'It is strange, isn't it?'

'And you won't let me look at the files from then?'

'You're no longer on the official payroll, Rory, love. You haven't got clearance.'

'You have though.'

'Not that level.'

It was then that Driscoll was convinced Aunty was lying to him. Maybe he'd suspected all along. Was she lying for a good reason and could he trust her not to sacrifice him to a higher cause? 'So if I'm not on the team as far as information-sharing, then I'm free to go my own way.'

'Always have been.' A sigh. 'Rory, I'm not your aunty. I'm a taxpayer-funded mandarin, and my job is to solve the government's secret problems and keep them secret. I use people. Always have, always will. Folks live and die because of me. Trust me as much or as little as you like. I'm not in the business of reassurance.'

That was her way of saying she wouldn't sacrifice him today. 'Hope springs, eh?' Rory said, terminating the call.

He and Kwong would rendezvous at Perth train station on the high concourse connecting Northbridge and the city, and looking down over the Armadale, Midland and Fremantle platforms. He checked the time: 9.40. Kwong was due in five minutes, José at ten. The latter was probably already here and had no doubt already spotted him. That didn't matter. José couldn't have realistically expected Kwong to run this alone. At least this way, José would know it was just going to be them and not a fifty-strong SWAT team. Still intimate enough for the sharing of secrets and the benediction of redemption. They were in a big public place in broad daylight with lots of witnesses and more CCTV cameras than you could point a stick at – what could possibly go wrong?

Driscoll ordered his third coffee of the day and took a spot at the bakery cafe. The table was near the entrance, and his seat faced out to the world. José would have his back to the crowd, a minor disadvantage. Kwong appeared at the top of the Fremantle platform escalator and made his approach. He ordered something on his way past the cafe counter, the young woman behind the cash till trying not to stare at his battered face. He flashed his cop ID and she got on with her job.

'No sign of José?' he said, scraping a chair out next to Driscoll.

'Not yet, but he'll be around. Making sure we haven't brought reinforcements.'

'Except for you.'

'He'll cope. Any updates from your mate Thornton?'

'Australia Post tracking say it was definitely delivered to the address in Bunbury. It was a standard A-five padded envelope, weighed next to nothing.'

'Thumb drive?'

'Or camera chip. Something like that.'

'Found any Darwin connections?'

'Nothing on phone or email but there were communications with Melbourne. We're filtering them, watch this space.'

'Mira?'

Kwong shrugged. 'Maybe. Also, Peters has a daughter in Melbourne. Shouldn't get ahead of ourselves.'

'Here he comes.'

José placed his order and took the remaining seat – blocked in hard against the wall with his back to the passing foot traffic. Strategically Driscoll couldn't have asked for any more. Except that if the balloon really went up, then strategic seating would count for very little. Their coffee orders arrived plus a sausage roll for José.

'*Bon appétit*,' he said, taking a bite.

'Time to come clean?' prompted Kwong. 'You sent me those text messages in the early days. Why, and why me?'

'Checked into the system. Saw you were going to be running it. I'd heard you weren't the kind of bloke to accept the bleeding obvious. Wanted to make sure you lived up to expectations.'

'Again. Why?'

'It suited me.'

'You wanted to be caught? Why not just hand yourself in?'

'Then you wouldn't have been at the centre of it. All-knowing.' He swiped some flakes of pastry from his chest. 'These are good. You should try one.'

'I'm not all-knowing yet,' said Kwong. 'Fill me in.'

José glanced at Driscoll. 'Uncharacteristically shy today, Rory?'

'I'm a gatecrasher. Here to observe, for the moment.'

A nod and another bite of sausage roll. 'I'm not a natural-born killer. Before Peters and Drummond, there must have been a good ten years or so where I never hurt a fly.'

'Congratulations,' said Kwong.

'You'll have got a taste for it in the *favelas* though, eh?' Driscoll tilted his head. 'Bit of Death Squad slum clearance in Rio to test you in your early days with ABIN?'

'Didn't think you'd hold your tongue for long, mate.'

'So it's just your job, and you don't see yourself as a bad man.' Kwong pushed his cup away; frothy dregs like a river after a chemical spill. 'But you were very convincing with Peters and Drummond, the mutilations. Laid it on thick.'

'And sent you after Ximenes as intended.'

'But Ryan Hodgson must have worked out it was you he saw that night. One of his last calls was to your phone.'

'No, he hadn't, fully. But he was on the right track. He'd have sussed it sooner or later. Smart kid, thought he was being helpful.'

'Why did you want us to target Ximenes?'

A shrug. 'Mine not to question why, mine but to do or die. Orders, mate. It was in the brief.'

'Whose orders?'

José grinned at Kwong. 'Patience, young padawan.'

'What did you do with the thumb drive?' Driscoll cricked his back, he'd need to stand up and stretch soon. 'Or camera chip. Whatever.'

'Safekeeping.'

'I'm guessing that wasn't in your brief. That was your insurance?'

'All part of the game, mate. You'd know.'

'And now that you've become disposable to your employers, you want to cash in.'

'Hole in one.'

'What is it you're after?' said Kwong. 'I'm not going to let you get away with murder.'

José shrugged. 'We can let the lawyers thrash it out.'

'No promises, no deals.'

'If so, why are we here, then? What's in it for me?'

'You can tell me who you work for, or where to go looking, and hand over the thumb drive you stole from Drummond and Peters.' Kwong glanced over his shoulder and Driscoll saw what he was looking for. Bodies taking position, a pattern in the formless crowd. Easier to discern in the Sunday morning quiet. Kwong had picked up a thing or two from Rosa the Timorese cop, taking the initiative and calling his own reinforcements.

***

Cato hadn't called in the TRG. It didn't require that kind of scene. Nor had he informed Pavlou of his intentions. Any leaks, any pressure linked to a man of influence, were likely to be focused on HQ. Instead he'd opted for a joint Bunbury and Fremantle operation. It was Nikki Earle who placed her hand on José's shoulder and leaned down with her mouth to his ear.

'Nice and calm, buddy. Keep your hands on the table where we can see them.'

Meanwhile Paddy McMahon and his minions were emptying the cafe and creating a safer and less cluttered working environment. Discouraging the almost instinctual need for some to raise their smartphones for yet another social media posting.

José shook his head. 'This isn't going to achieve anything.'

It looked like he and Driscoll agreed on that at least. 'Phil, mate, can you give us a minute?'

'You and José? Sorry, you're a civilian. Maybe you can step over there with the others, for your own safety.'

Driscoll sighed. Turned as if to join the onlookers then brought José's head down to the tabletop and prodded a gun into the man's ear. 'A minute, mate. That's all I need.'

Gasps, shrieks, a hundred smartphones clicking and flashing. Half-a-dozen cops with guns and tasers drawn. And José, chuckling. 'What the fuck?'

'You can't do that, Rory.' Cato lifted a palm in supplication. 'Gun down, hands up.'

Driscoll pressed the pistol further into José. 'Who's your boss?'

'You aren't gonna shoot me. Not with everybody watching.'

The finger tightened on the trigger. 'Last chance.'

'Blowhard. Don't start something you can't finish.'

'Rory.' Cato could see uniform cops and Transperth security heading their way. A circus forming. 'Enough.'

José's right index finger waggled in a gesture for Driscoll to come closer. He did so. 'You and Mrs Blasey need to talk more. She's playing you.' He started laughing. 'Help. Get this madman away from me. Police! Help!'

Driscoll stood up, took his gun from José's ear. That's when Nikki Earle pulled her trigger.

***

Driscoll had never been tasered before and didn't ever want to be again. He'd never felt so much pain. Intense, comprehensive, absolutely incapacitating – just as it was designed for. It felt like a violation. He'd believed his training would have enabled him to deal with it. He was wrong.

'Sorry,' said the female cop. 'I got carried away. I'm Nikki Earle.'

He'd been picked off the floor and sat in a chair. Offered a bottle of water. Not sure of the science of it, he wondered if the water would be dangerous with all that electricity in his body. José had been taken away and Kwong was talking to an older cop who kept glancing their way.

'No worries,' said Driscoll, weakly. The crowd had dispersed save for a handful of rubberneckers. Driscoll felt a weightlessness under his armpit. 'My gun?'

'Confiscated. You'll get it back once your status has been confirmed.' She had nice eyes and a ready smile.

'Status?'

'Nobody seems to know what to make of you. But I'm told you're on our side.'

Kwong returned from his powwow. 'That went well. How you feeling?'

'Outplayed, again.'

'That's what José said. Maybe he's right, maybe you and your Mrs Blasey need some quality time together.'

'I'll call her. I assume you're going to grill José and I'm not allowed anywhere near?'

'Correct. After that stunt, you're lucky not to be under arrest yourself.'

Update from Thornton: none of those Melbourne numbers connect Peters or Drummond to Mira or anyone else of consequence to our enquiries.' He patted Driscoll's shoulder. 'Maybe when you're feeling better you can pay her another visit in hospital. See if she knows anything more?'

'Will do.' Kwong left and Driscoll took another slug of water.

'Need to make tracks too.' Earle stood from her crouch, hands on hips. 'Sure you're okay?'

'Yep. Thanks.'

'Where's home?'

'Victoria. On the coast.'

'Nice?'

'Can be.'

'You'll have to show me around there one day, if I'm ever passing through.' She handed him her card. 'Mobile's on the back if you want to sue me for assault.'

'Noted.' He slipped the card into his shirt pocket and enjoyed the view as she walked away.

***

Cato and Thornton took the running on the José interview with DIs Pavlou and McMahon watching the monitor in the adjacent room. It was midafternoon. They'd needed time to prepare for the interview and to brief Pavlou so she could head off any media enquiries or flak arising from the cafe incident which was trending on Twitter. Cato had played humble and apologetic.

'Forget it,' she said drily. 'It's what I get paid all those extra bucks for. Covering your arse.'

Thornton did the preliminaries for the recording. José had declined a lawyer for the time being. Cato got him to go through the circumstances of the Drummond, Peters and Ryan Hodgson murders, the attempt on the life of Mira Soares, and the assault on Cato himself. Almost two hours later, detailed confession in the bag, Cato changed gear.

'So these murders were carried out under instructions from another person?'

'Yes.'

'Who?'

'I'm unable to say without receiving certain assurances from you.'

'You're already facing life inside. What kind of assurances are you after?'

'My own safety, that of my family. Consideration in my sentencing for cooperation. That kind of thing.'

'No,' said Cato. 'I am unable to provide any assurances.'

'Then I can't give you a name.'

'This bloke forced your hand. Made you abduct Mira Soares. Before that nobody was looking at you. He blew your cover.'

A shrug in reply.

'But, like you said, you're not a natural-born killer. Particularly once you know you've been thrown under a bus. No more cash, no more protection. There was no motivation for you to kill Soares or me. We were *his* problem from now on, not yours.'

'Fascinating.'

Cato then tried to ascertain the communication method. The receipt of instructions. The payment of expenses. Of fees for services. No comment all the way. 'This bloke has a lot of reach. Probably all the way to Brazil. You sure you want him being a threat to your family for the next twenty-odd years?'

'He will be anyway, even if he's locked up. And if he is locked up on my say-so, then he'll definitely be after revenge.'

Cato gave the time and announced a toilet and tea-break for the recording before switching it off. 'Chris, want to organise some cuppas?' He looked up at the CCTV camera. 'Make sure the boss and DI McMahon are looked after as well?'

'Sure, Sarge.' Thornton took the orders along with a whispered instruction from Cato.

The room emptied. 'Need a piss, José? I'll escort you.'

They went along the corridor, a uniform stationed outside the door, then took their places at the urinals.

'This scumbag you're protecting, I don't want to see him in prison.'

José stared at the tiled wall in front of him. 'No surprise. Got to you already, eh?'

'You miss my point. People like him, connections like that, the most he'll be done for is conspiracy. You've done all the dirty work. If he serves any time at all, it'll be a couple of years on a prison farm. Then he's free to get on with threatening you, me, anybody else in his way. The world increasingly revolves around people like him. Makes me puke.'

'Only just worked that out?'

'Yeah, but we get our noses rubbed in it every day now, eh? Just turn on the TV news.'

'So?'

'So we're not bound by the same rules as, say, Rory Driscoll.' Cato lowered his voice a notch. 'You saw him in the cafe this morning. Mad as a cut snake. Give him a name and that person's no longer anyone's problem. He's not even tied to ASIO, ASIS, whatever any more. He's out. PTSD or some such. He doesn't give a fuck about anything.'

José zipped up. 'Can't see it. If anything, they'll close ranks and look after their own.'

'That's my point.' Cato doused his hands under the tap and set the dryer roaring. 'Driscoll's outside the circle. Face doesn't fit. No family. No job. No future. Nothing to lose. And this Mr X's got *his* name on a list too.' He waited while José checked himself in the mirror. 'I've seen Rory in action in Shanghai. He doesn't mess about when somebody gets in his way. I watched him shoot a guy and tip him in the river, right in front of my eyes. Dinkum.'

José smiled. 'Got any biscuits coming with those cuppas?'

***

Driscoll had tried Aunty but she wasn't answering the phone so he'd dropped by to see Mira instead. On the way he had retrieved his gun from Kwong who'd advised him to refrain from waving it about more than was absolutely necessary. Asked how the interview was going with

José, the bloke had gone all inscrutable. It was now late afternoon and Rory was still a tad groggy from the zapping but, he reflected, if you're going to be tasered by anybody it may as well be DSC Earle. Was this the twenty-first century version of Cupid's arrow?

Mira seemed even further improved from yesterday, sitting up and with fewer tubes and wires coming off her. Her finger was still splinted from the exploded *rakitan* but otherwise. 'On the mend?' he enquired.

'So they tell me.'

'The cops have José in custody.'

'Good.'

'Did he ever say anything while you were with him? Reasons why, anything like that?'

'Nothing.'

'How about before, when he found you in the airport bar?'

'That's a blank. He spiked my drink.' She was getting upset, time to ease up.,

Driscoll glanced out the window. Clouds had built over the city with the promise of rain. Maybe winter was finally on the way. By now his shack down at Warrnambool would have felt the odd icy blast but here in WA, who knew? The sun and the blue sky seemed unrelenting. If you liked that kind of thing, it would be paradise. If, like him, you craved relief from the heat and the glare, it became a kind of hell. José Carrascalao had made this place his home, playing the part of the sleepy small-town cop, supplementing his retirement fund with the odd moonlighter, a freelance fixer not unlike Driscoll himself. It had extended to murder, visiting a nightmare on those two old men and possibly on Paul Reinado.

Or was Reinado someone else's doing? Guthrie had probably been running him. Did Reinado make the fatal mistake of trusting and confiding in his handler? My mum saw this bloke at the Darwin markets, Geoff. The one who was there when the Indos had me. Any chance you could help me put a name to him? Describe him, says Guthrie. I'll try, says Paulho, writing his own death warrant. Next time you're in Perth, we'll meet up, says Guthrie. Sort this problem of yours out, once and for all. Guthrie and José. Somebody recognised their worth and their potential and offered them a job. Somebody who either knew them, or of them. Mason too? Or was he just a handy fall guy?

'Any news of Willie?' Mira, speaking of the devil.

'No,' he lied. 'What do the docs have planned for you?'

'They say maybe I will be well enough for medical transfer home in another week.'

'Home?'

'Melbourne, I suppose.'

'You have people to look after you there?'

'Friends.' She didn't sound convinced. 'Maybe Darwin is best but Filomena already has enough to worry about with Alexandre.'

'How about your son Alex?'

'I don't want him to know. I want him to finish his travels.'

'You're in touch?'

'Facebook, Skype, email. But not since all this started.' She waved a hand uselessly at the tubes and wires.

'Where is he now?'

Her face darkened. 'I don't want to tell you.'

A simple Facebook or Google search would solve that. 'Fair enough.' Driscoll hesitated. 'I'll be heading back to Victoria soon. If you do want to return to Melbourne and there's any way I can help, I'd be happy to.'

'Thank you.' She nodded, pensive. 'Brian. Any news of him?'

'Nothing.'

'It's strange, isn't it?'

'What?'

'Such a weak man. All that crying, the weeping and wailing. His poor wife and her cancer. That's why he needed the phone that showed them where to find us. Then he cheered up and we heard no more about it.' Mira took a sip of water from the plastic cup at her bedside. 'Did you have any enquiries from her or her doctor since her husband was arrested by your security services? Did she suddenly get better?'

Or, thought Driscoll, did she ever even exist?

***

They'd been given a name from José now, but that person seemed to have disappeared off the face of the earth.

'Nothing?' said Cato.

'Nada,' confirmed Thornton. 'Maybe Carrascalao is bullshitting us.'

'Not beyond the bounds.' Cato examined an incoming text from

Sharon replying to his home ETA. She'd ended with a smiley face, so all good. 'And Driscoll's phone is still off?' Affirmative from Thornton. 'José isn't in a great position to waste our time. He's Casuarina-bound for the rest of his natural, and his only interest now is protecting his family. Jerking us around doesn't achieve anything.'

'The guy couldn't lie straight in bed. Maybe he doesn't realise he's doing it.'

'Driscoll is the shortcut to this. Keep trying.'

The name given wasn't of the man behind this whole sorry mess but of somebody in the food chain. José might not be jerking them around but he was drip-feeding. Holding out on the last name as it was all he had left, watching and waiting to see how things developed. Maybe he harboured hopes of getting away with murder. Still, they were one step closer. The name wasn't new to Cato, he'd heard mention of it from Driscoll.

Brian Simmonds. Meek suburban lawyer. Odd man out.

So far, Thornton had a last known address in regional NSW where Simmonds hadn't been seen since early April. Bank accounts, credit and Medicare cards, et cetera, hadn't been used since around the same time, likewise registered mobile phone, emails and social media. His only family was his wife who had lain in a coma in a hospital in Newcastle, NSW for the last three months – cancer of some sort. They had no children, he had no siblings, and neither had living parents. The wife had a brother overseas but they had been estranged for decades. Simmonds' name had been on that death list Driscoll had talked about, four people who ostensibly were about to blow the whistle on nefarious dealings between Australia and East Timor over oil reserves. Except that was all smoke and mirrors. The real reason seemed to be linked to atrocities in Timor's recent turbulent history. Driscoll, Mira Soares and this bloke Willie Mason had ties to the atrocities story through their connection to the militia leader Ximenes. Two of those people, Mason and Ximenes, were now dead and there had been an attempt on Mira's life. Last man standing – Driscoll. Odd man out – Simmonds. He had no apparent link to the war crimes angle and was simply the holder of some diaries and a manuscript from a former diplomat. Except he wasn't as meek, mild and innocent as he seemed.

According to José Carrascalao, Simmonds was the link man – the point of contact – for all the freelancers: Guthrie, José himself and others called in to do certain jobs for the cause. He ran the 'Spooks Silver Chain' agency. So what qualified him? Cato couldn't ask the man himself. Simmonds was either in secret service custody or flown the coop, perhaps dead – a loose end snipped off. In the absence of Driscoll, who must surely be able to answer some of these questions, the options were limited. But maybe there was somebody who could help.

***

'Brian Simmonds?' A nod. 'Yeah, I remember him.'

Associate Professor Steven Brown was keen not to miss the last of the Sunday blues sesh at Clancy's in Freo. Cato didn't fancy the noise but it was on his way home and he was, in the end, the consummate professional. In a welcome break between sets and over some gassy boutique ales, they retreated to an outside table. They had plenty of privacy for sensitive matters. Rain and a biting wind kept everyone, bar the hardened smokers, inside. Cato recalled a body found some years ago just four metres from where he was now sitting. Fremantle carried many such memories for him.

'He was at the embassy the same time as you? The INTERFET mission?'

Brown nodded. 'Bit of a nonentity. Second assistant acting pen-pusher, something like that.'

'Was he really that boring or was that good cover?'

'He certainly had me fooled.'

'You heard about Ximenes?'

'A fitting end. Must have trod on one too many toes.'

'Do you remember who, among the Australian spooks, passed through the embassy then?'

'Probably most if not all of them, I imagine. As for names, I either don't or won't recall. There are laws about that kind of thing can get you sent away for a long time.'

'Apparently Brian Simmonds was detained for exactly that.'

'Well there you go.'

'But I don't believe that's the reason he's out of circulation. I think he's either in hiding or dead.' Brown seemed unmoved by such a possibility. His new life in academia was a world away, and he no doubt preferred it like that. Cato persisted. 'What about Deborah Chan? She worked there too. Kept a diary. Spiced it up into a novel.'

Some tentative drumbeats from inside, the twang of guitar. The band was getting ready to come back on. Brown drained his drink. 'I remember Deborah. She was in the ascendancy. Keen not to rock the boat, make waves. But careful and smart too. Always observing and making notes to protect her arse. Put some noses out of joint for sure.'

'Anyone in particular?'

'The hawks. The hard-arses. Naming no names, not allowed to, but if you look closely enough you'll find them on the public record.'

'Any names you can point me to? Time is of the essence.'

'Sorry, buddy.' He waggled his glass. 'Good to talk again. Stay in touch.'

'If I found some candidates and put them before you, could you tip a wink or wiggle an earlobe or something?'

The opening bars of 'When Love Comes to Town'. Brown shuddered, perhaps because of the wind. 'Some matches are made in heaven, some in hell: Stevie Wonder and Paul McCartney, B.B. King and U2 ...'

'Deborah Chan and Brian Simmonds?'

'He definitely wouldn't have been her type. But hell hath no fury like a nonentity scorned.'

***

Near to midnight, Driscoll turned on his phone to see nine missed calls and as many messages, mostly from Kwong's offsider, the young dogsbody Thornton. They were on to the Simmonds track too. José must have coughed up the name, sending them off down the path that would hopefully lead them to Mr X but would also buy time for José to consider and develop his options. Driscoll didn't believe for a second that Brian Simmonds was being detained against his will. It was either protective custody in a safe and secret location, or down a mineshaft beyond the black stump. Far from being the terrified innocent bystander caught up in events beyond his control, he was, in fact, a key player ensuring he was at the centre of things and guiding them where he wanted. Driscoll had used a burner to phone Aunty's secure line.

'How long have you known about Simmonds?'

'Do you realise what time it is over here?'

'He was part of this cabal that you're dismantling. Him, Guthrie,

Colonel Bogey from the Dili embassy. You're getting me to flush them all out for you.'

'Only it's not our side who snatched him and Mason in Darwin.'

'But you told me it was.'

'The fog of war, Rory dear. I was misled by people I trusted. Things are only really taking shape now.'

'If it was the bad guys, wouldn't they have just killed everyone they found?'

'Maybe they're adapting, evolving. Sowing confusion instead of splashing blood.'

'Sometimes Aunty, I wonder if you're making this up as you go along. Do you even know whose side you're on?'

'Everybody's. Nobody's. Bear with me.'

'Mason wasn't lying, somebody was trying to set him up.'

'He and Ximenes both. Neither of them particularly nice blokes and all the more suitable as stooges.' The click of a lighter and a deep sucking inhalation.

'You know who's behind all this, don't you?'

'Pretty much.'

'So?'

'So it has to be an organic process, Rory. The best thing for your continued wellbeing and for that of this great nation of ours is if these people don't win and the consequences of their actions are swift and decisive.'

'You want him dead.'

'I would never suggest such a thing.'

'But you want to keep your hands clean.'

'Rory, you need a good night's sleep. It's very late.'

'I don't do that stuff anymore. We need evidence, proof, and the rule of law. I'll get Kwong onto it.'

'I took a look at his case bible today. His boss gave me a sneak peek. Tell him he's got the answer under his nose, has had from early days. Wind him up, Rory. Set him marching. Ni-night.'

27

Monday 14th May

Cato was woken early by his phone flashing and buzzing to a call from Driscoll. Really early, like pre-Ella. 'Do you realise what time it is?'

'Why does everybody think I don't know the time?'

Sharon stirred and grumpily turned away from him. 'This better be good,' said Cato.

'I need access to José. This morning. Through him, I'll get you Brian Simmonds and whoever is behind all this.'

'You got our messages then. What are you going to do, tear his fingernails off?'

'I'll meet you at, what's the remand place called? Hakea? One hour.'

Cato made it an hour-fifteen out of spite, taking time for a shower, a cuddle with Sharon and Ella, and a drive-through Muzz Buzz coffee. Magpies warbled and crows aarked. The rain had passed through and the earth and trees smelled fresh. Cato had made a few calls in transit, clearing the visit with José himself, the Hakea authorities and with DI Pavlou.

'I was talking to my spooky counterpart yesterday while you were scaring cafe patrons at Perth station,' she told Cato. 'Comparing notes on you and your mate Driscoll, we could write a book.'

'Might have to self-publish. It's pretty cutthroat out there.'

'Keep a leash on Driscoll,' she'd said. 'We're bound by rules even if he isn't.'

Cato kept schtum about his conversation with José in the toilets and the persuasiveness of Driscoll's MO. 'It feels like we're getting close.'

'Hmmm. Mrs Blasey said as much too. I gave her a squiz at the files.'

'Was that wise?'

'I'm hoping so.'

Driscoll was leaning on the bonnet of his hire car, enjoying the early morning sun and chewing on an egg and bacon toastie from the deli back down the road. It was the only place for miles and profited richly from the proceeds of crime: cops, screws, journos and social workers all needing a feed and some time to think. He crumpled up the wrapper and binned it.

'You'll need to play nice today.' Cato drained his flat white. 'Leave the gun in the car and take your manners in there with you.'

'Absolutely.'

'I'm surprised he agreed to talk to us.'

'Hope springs eternal, he's probably thinking.'

Cato filled Driscoll in on the empty promise made to José: that rogue agent Rory would be let off the leash to deal with José's enemies. 'Behave yourself. Just look like a government-paid hitman, don't act like one.'

Driscoll smiled. 'So you're using me and I'm using you. Sounds fair.'

He wouldn't elaborate, and Cato let it go.

They were signed in and checked through, anything dangerous left in a locker near the X-ray machine. Cato had lost count of the times he'd walked these corridors, smelled these sad, sour odours, shared a nod with familiar faces. José was waiting there in prison greens. He'd be in isolation given he was a cop and quite a few knew it. He could probably handle himself but one day he would be outnumbered, too slow, and his luck would run out. Even after just a day, the strain of that inevitability showed.

'How can I help?'

'We need to find Brian Simmonds,' said Cato. 'Quickly.'

'What's the rush? It's already been a while.'

'The sooner we find him and wrap this up,' a sideways glance at Driscoll was the cue for a barely perceptible assassin's nod. '... the sooner you have fewer worries.'

'What makes you think Simmonds is still of this world?'

'You gave us his name.' Driscoll stayed civil but had maintained the in-character terseness to his manner. 'You don't have time to mess about having us running around after a dead man.' He made a show of checking his watch. 'If you think you do, you're an even bigger fool than I took you for.'

'Look, your guess is as good as mine, maybe even better. We operate on a need-to-know basis. I don't need to know where he is.'

'Maybe you do, bro.' Driscoll was piling on the hard-boiled noir but José remained unimpressed.

'If I could help, I would.'

'The thumb drive,' said Cato. 'Hand that over, tell us where it is.'

'I was bluffing. I handed it over, had to so they'd pay me the next tranche.'

'No copies for your own insurance?'

'Nah.'

Cato didn't buy it. 'Your employer owes you. You didn't need to break cover if things had been better planned.'

'I doubt he sees it that way. He's the kick-down type, like most of his breed.'

'And yet you're not giving him up. Staunch, mate.' Driscoll stood and readied to leave. 'Nobody's coming to your rescue, José. No last-minute twists and turns. You're going to be buried in here, or somewhere like it, forever. The try-hards will be lining up week after week to take a pop at you, and that's without Mr X paying somebody to do the job properly.' He nodded at the guard to open the door. 'Way back in the day, during those CIA training courses, I had you marked as a lightweight, too busy providing comic relief to learn anything. Our friend saw you coming a mile off.'

José smiled. 'He saw us all coming, I reckon.'

***

It was decision day for Sharon. Ella was at day care, Julie would pick her up and be with her until Sharon got home. Phil was God knows where. This was going to be a rare nine-to-five day: meetings with the prospective boss and her investigations team. A business lunch. Sharon felt like she was being wooed and it was flattering. The disciplinary matter that had seen her sent home in disgrace from China a few years ago was a receding memory. Her conduct, reliability and occasional flair in the airport busts had been noted. Even her dispatching of a rogue spy in spectacular and bloody fashion was seen as a plus. Sharon was officially kick-ass and welcome back in the fold. Girl power. Somebody with her experience, particularly in sensitive foreign fields like Beijing, along with her language skills, made her an asset. It was now or never. There were plenty of younger and more eager colleagues lining up behind who could do the job in Investigations. But none of them were as good as her. Sharon wanted this move, she realised. She wanted it badly, and now. Could she have it all? It wasn't a question asked of men, the answer was always an assumed yes. There were precious few famous examples of women having full-on careers, fulfilling family life and a perfect partner to boot. If they did, it tended to involve bottomless wealth and an army of nannies: think royalty or Beyoncé. The only other role model was the Kiwi prime minister who managed to make motherhood and international political leadership seem natural, normal and down-to-earth. Would Phil embrace the role of stay-at-home dad? Only if Sharon put a rocket under him.

Lunch was at a posh place overlooking the Swan River. Her would-be boss was taking the measure of her. There was a hint of Norse in the cool gaze, and the confidence that comes and stays with those born tall, blonde and good-looking, and maintaining it well into middle-age. 'Senior Investigator. Team leader. It would involve the occasional interstate and overseas travel, possibly long periods away from home and often irregular hours. It's a job you could do standing on your head.' She smiled. 'But we all know that standing on your head requires a fine sense of balance.'

Her way of saying the unsayable. Can you juggle the professional and personal?

'The job is yours, Sharon, if you want it, and starts first Monday in the new financial year.' A sip of sparkling mineral water. 'So?'

Sharon glanced out across the river. A rowing duo from the uni boat club slicing the surface of the water. Precise, strong, focused. Absolutely in unison.

'Yes,' said Sharon. 'I'm in.'

***

Driscoll and Kwong had gone their separate ways for the rest of the morning. He'd passed on to Kwong the hint from Aunty that the perpetrator had been under the detective's nose from very early days.

'And you guys reckon José's a joker.' Kwong had shaken his head dismissively. 'If you know the name, spit it out. Otherwise go back to your fishing village in Victoria and let us get on with our jobs.'

'Bit harsh, mate. Just passing on a message.'

Kwong hadn't bothered replying. Understandable. Driscoll too was over the game-playing and the idea of returning to his fishing village was very appealing. Except now he did have a strong inkling of who the mystery man was. Driscoll was driving around and around, filling in time and dredging up memories.

He saw us all coming, I reckon.

José was right. He did see them coming. A winter's morning in mid-west USA in the mid-noughties. Snow halfway up the doors, minus fucksake degrees outside. Inside it was downright balmy. A talk on the technological innovations used by and against the terrorists. War on Terror this, War on Terror that. As the war dragged on in Iraq and people became more and more desensitised to the horrors on the evening news, Abu Ghraib and waterboarding wormed its way into the international imagination, a grey weariness permeated everything. Driscoll was still young and keen, making notes, making connections, exuding confidence and reliability. José/Rodrigo at the back of the class with the bad boys and girls, wisecracking and flirting. Nursing an obvious hangover. A small handful of older men and women in the group. No names or lanyards. Quiet and watchful. Recruiters and supervisors, he'd guessed. Sizing people up, talent-spotting. Writing off the blowhards. Maybe that was when José's career started its downward trajectory until he ended up a detective in regional WA, rejected by his adoptive fatherland. Or maybe that was the perfect legend. One of those watchers so grey and forgettable he might never have been there. Driscoll recalled steel-rim glasses and an English accent. Maybe that's what threw his own memory in more recent times; the assumption the guy was British and probably with MI5 or 6, and irrelevant to this unfolding story. At the end of the session, Rory had quietly asked a question of the woman who'd done the presentation, trying not to draw attention to himself, seem like an over-keen swot.

Something about the latest GPS phone-tracking capabilities. José had drifted by, cracking a joke in Portuguese about Rory the teacher's pet. The grey man in the steel-rim glasses had said something in reply to José, which wiped the smirk off his face.

He would have had ten years or so on Rory. Perhaps the same vintage as Willie Mason, early fifties by now. Could a picture be conjured out of a hazy fifteen-year-old memory? Back to the city along Perth's clogged arteries. Wispy clouds in a blue sky and a post-rain freshness and clarity. He buzzed Kwong and arranged yet another catch-up.

***

Cato had spent the morning poring over the case files looking for what was supposedly right under his nose from day one. Thornton had dropped by midmorning with an update on various matters.

'Telcom and emails for both men going back as far as their reunion on Christmas Island. I've had some of the civilian analysts trawling through earlier stuff, nothing so far but as soon as anything shows I'll let you know.'

'Any highlights?'

'Good to catch up, enjoyed the fishing, best wishes to each other's families. An exchange of happy snaps in memory of fun times in the tropics.'

Cato took a look at them. Innocuous smiling faces, beers held aloft, fish trophies, et cetera. Nothing jumped out. 'Reinado?'

'Had a spare phone, provided by Guthrie, for their communications. His number is one of those on the Guthrie phone we examined, under C. The call times and pinged location of the recipient number in Darwin corresponds to their likely timeline of dealings. The number wasn't used after Reinado's death and the actual phone hasn't been found.'

'So B is Carrascalao, C is Reinado. All we need now is A. Do we have an analysis of those calls and locations?'

'During the short period of operation since March obviously we have Guthrie mainly in Perth or surrounds, and the recipient A all over the place: Perth, Canberra, Sydney, Melbourne, Darwin, Townsville.'

'Any patterns or crossovers with say Reinado?'

'No discernible patterns with other numbers, but Guthrie made sure to report in regularly to A at least once a week.' Thornton prodded a spot on the printout. 'Monday mornings, eight forty-five, without fail.'

'Duration?'

'Varied, but not usually more than a couple of minutes.'

'So any detail was provided some other way.'

'Or via an intermediary.'

A call came through from Driscoll. Cato wasn't really in the mood for him but answered anyway.

'Got anybody there who's good at drawing?' Driscoll asked.

'Depends. What's the subject?'

'A nobody.'

***

The e-fit artist had little to work with but it gradually took shape. Steel-rimmed specs, sandy-brown hair, the facial structure of a Ken doll – and equally lifeless and plastic. To Cato's eye he looked like any of the last three or four Australian prime ministers, a man who would fail to make an impression at the world leaders photo op in the funny shirts. As Driscoll visibly strained to remember the details of a briefly encountered nobody from at least thirteen years ago, Cato found his own memory was being triggered.

'I know him. I've seen him recently.' He asked the e-fit artist to do a version with a few adjustments: a fatter and older face, the specs now dark-framed, hair more closely cropped and darker. Cato nodded. 'Graham Winter. CEO of Cormann Logistics Group.' The faceless face of a heartless organisation.

They zapped the updated e-fits off to Filomena Reinado in Darwin. Yes, came the swift reply, that's him. The timing wasn't yet right on sending Filomena real pictures of the real man. What to do, how to play it, who to trust? Driscoll wanted to run it past his Canberra boss, Mrs Blasey, but Cato persuaded him out of it.

'She's known all this time and not shared it with you, with us. Whose side is she really on?'

No need either to run it past José. As long as he held out on the missing thumb drive and on whatever else he knew, then he was no further use to them. Cato got Thornton to put together as much as he could on Winter in the next sixty minutes. They'd peruse that and make their move.

'We pull him in too soon, and without enough evidence, he'll disappear.' Pavlou was understandably nervous. 'We've got to be watertight.' On that at least, all three agreed, although Cato thought he detected in Driscoll's manner a certain impatience to expedite matters.

It was midafternoon before Thornton's profile of Graham Winter landed on Cato's desk. There was a copy too for Driscoll plus an electronic version in Pavlou's inbox. Unsurprisingly, the man didn't leave much public trace before ten years ago when he married Susan Cormann, daughter of the ailing Gregory Cormann, founder of the ever-expanding blue chip Cormann Logistics Group. CLG seemed to have a profitable hand in everything that Australia was good at: oil, gas, mineral resources, channelling aid funds to Australian businesses and locking people up. Winter, with his vague security background and experience in the Asia-Pacific region, had initially been offered a position in the protective services division and, after marrying the boss's daughter, found himself fast-tracked to head that division within a year. Post 9/11 and *Tampa*, it was boom time in the offshore caging industry. Mr and Mrs Winter were both on their second marriages and she already had two children from first time around. A further two arrived and the Cormann– Winter blended family took shape. They lived in a riverside mansion in Peppermint Grove, as befits a man on his kind of money, had a holiday home in the south-west near Dunsborough, as well as pieds-à-terre in Sydney and Melbourne.

'The Brady Bunch,' said Driscoll. 'Minted.'

Traces of Winter before that were sparse, at least in the records Thornton had access to. No doubt Driscoll and Mrs Blasey could provide a fuller picture if they chose. Winter was born in Portsmouth in the UK, where his father was a high-ranking officer in the Royal Navy, and emigrated to Australia with his parents as a teenager. They'd settled in Adelaide where Winter senior worked at the then newly established Osborne Naval Shipyard while Graham completed his schooling at Saint Ignatius' College, a prestigious Catholic establishment. He then joined the army and went through the officer training academy at Duntroon. At which point he dissolved into thin air before re-morphing two decades later in Camp Cormann, rising through the ranks to end up figurehead CEO of the whole Cormann Group – answerable to a board of venture capitalists and their avaricious shareholders. A marriage certificate dated 1994 and a 1997 decree nisi citing 'irreconcilable breakdown' are all that exist during those missing years.

'No Medicare number, no driver's licence, no passport, no bank accounts. Nothing during that time.' Cato shook his head.

'They'll have existed but under different names.' Driscoll cricked his neck; desk duties didn't suit him. 'Sure you don't want me to dig further?'

'Not yet.' They examined Winter's current social media accounts: Twitter and Facebook, essentially adjuncts to the business model with posts about the great work and fantastic people in Cormann-land. 'Probably administered by a minion.' Cato rubbed his weary eyes. 'So what's at stake that he's prepared to pull all these strings and spill all this blood to protect his secrets?'

'Hard to imagine anything big enough these days. Nothing is shocking anymore. A world leader could commit murder live on prime-time TV and his supporters just go, meh, fake news.'

'But this guy hasn't got a hardcore following. Maybe he's just used to his privacy, pulls strings because he can, and places no value on those who get in his way.'

'Like the high cadres' children in Beijing.' Driscoll nodded. 'Rough somebody up in a road rage incident, use your influence to get away with it, bump off the victim if they don't shut up.' He looked to be weighing his options – to share or not to share. 'That might apply to our man. But also he does have a hardcore following of sorts.'

Cato listened as Driscoll outlined a tale of rival cabals in the secret service, of culture wars, of lines in the sand, battles for hearts and minds, and resources. 'These wankers would do that to protect their turf? Be that destructive? Kill innocent people? That's some Canberra Bubble.'

Driscoll nodded. He had seen Aunty in full flow at times over the years, reserving most of her bile for miscreant colleagues, and she was supposedly on the side of the good guys. He had no trouble at all imagining the capabilities of the dead-eyed desk jockeys if poked. He'd read old DFAT reports on Timor in preparation for his posting there. Aunty had recommended he acquaint himself with the kind of people he might be dealing with. Handwritten notes in the margins of heartbreaking reports of atrocities against defenceless civilians: rape, torture, murder, massacre. *Boohoo*, chortled one; *Suck it up, princess* chided another. But the evidence of such people was everywhere in plain sight these days.

'Look at your average government leadership spill,' said Driscoll. 'Or look at how vicious the partisan media can be with people who refuse to zip it: survivors of high-school shootings, victims of frat-boy pack-rape, you name it. The hardliners here have had power and influence beyond their wildest dreams for the last decade or two. Now it's on the wane and they don't intend to cede without a fight.'

'But what's the point? Worlds turn. Even if they are on the way out, their time will come round again.'

'Entitlement.' Driscoll stifled a yawn. 'A strutting rooster when everything's going good. A caged feral cat when the end is in sight. They are really bad losers.'

'So what's Graham Winter clawing and hissing at?'

'That, I expect.' Driscoll prodded page three of the profile-cum-backgrounder, halfway down.

Cato leaned in and read a few lines. Yep, he'd certainly seen people killed for less.

***

'Our problem is we have nothing to charge him with, as yet. So what's the point of paying him a visit?'

Pavlou was right. There was no trail, electronic or paper, leading from the murders of Peters and Drummond and the suspicious death of Paul Reinado to this man Winter. Given his background, and the resources supporting him, it hadn't been difficult to firewall him against future prosecution. They didn't even have any whistleblowers prepared to turn against him – José wouldn't testify in any trial where the likely outcome was acquittal or at most a pathetically short sentence. José's hopes rested on Driscoll taking matters into his own hands, and Cato had sold that possibility as a convenient lie. Outside, through the window, there was a soft orange end-of-day quality to the light.

'Simmonds?' Pavlou checked her notes. 'This military attaché, Mark Rintoul. Are they likely to spill?'

'My contacts tell me Simmonds has disappeared and Rintoul has taken long service leave and buggered off to the States.' Driscoll tapped his knuckles restlessly on the arm of Pavlou's guest chair. 'If you really want to apply pressure to Winter, you need Mrs Blasey's help. She'll have the righteous dirt on him.'

Cato grimaced. 'She's just as likely to tip him off.'

Pavlou back to Driscoll. 'You don't agree?' A shake of the head. 'So convince me.'

'No, take my word for it or not. I don't have to explain myself to you. There's nothing stopping me calling her right now. I'm showing you respect by not doing so. Maybe you guys should show some back.'

Pavlou tried staring him down but this was a man with years more practice behind him. Cato stifled a smile at the squaring off. 'Okay then,' he said. 'Let's hear what Aunty's got to say.'

Pavlou arched an eyebrow. 'Aunty?'

Driscoll already had his phone out. 'Pet name for my boss.'

Pavlou caught the expression on Cato's face. 'Don't even think about it.'

***

Jacinta from PR was still smiling all these weeks later. She gave Cato a matey elbow nudge and lifted her chin towards Driscoll standing a few metres away talking on his phone. 'Who's your friend?'

'Rory.' Cato checked the clock on the wall. Just after 5.30 p.m. and a steady stream of CLG office workers were homeward bound. Through the floor-to-ceiling windows, the freeway was clogged north and south at the Narrows bridge. It was nearly dark and there were a few spots of rain on the plate glass. 'We've been waiting ten minutes. Enough is enough. This is official police business.'

Aunty had come up with the goods and Pavlou had given the go-ahead for a preliminary interview. 'In his office is fine by me but happy for you to bring him back here too. Your call.'

They'd phoned ahead and lined up an appointment. This brief delay was probably down to gamesmanship or some last-minute advice from a lawyer.

A tinkle on Jacinta's phone and a few monosyllables later, she led them down the corridor to Winter's office. 'You local, Rory?' she said over her shoulder.

'Victoria.'

'Seen any of the sights while you've been in town?'

'On previous trips, yeah.'

'So you come and go a bit then? Great.' She opened a big, wide, impressive-looking heavy wooden door and ushered them through. 'Maybe see you around the traps.'

Winter had dismissed the lawyer, or else they were listening in from another room. By the look he gave Driscoll, he clearly didn't expect this to go by the book. The carpet was thick and the room befitted his big-cheese status even if there was a chill to it. Still he presented them with a smile and invited them to sit.

'Thank you for taking the time to see us, Mr Winter,' said Cato.

'No problem.' He pushed his specs back to the bridge of his nose. 'I don't think I've met your colleague, Detective Kwong.'

'Driscoll,' said Driscoll.

'Right. And you're a detective too?'

'No.'

'On whose authority are you here, then?'

Driscoll nodded at Cato. 'His.'

Winter must see this was going nowhere. Any further challenges to Driscoll's right to be there and Cato would simply swap him for Deb Hassan or Chris Thornton, both sitting downstairs in the foyer. 'We're hoping you can help us with a few matters, Mr Winter.'

'Call me Graham if you like.'

'Cheers, I'm Phil and this is Rory.'

'All mates, eh?' said Driscoll with a grim smile.

'What matters?' Winter fiddled with a flash-looking pen and straightened a notepad, the only items on his desk save for a closed laptop.

'Do you recognise either of these gentlemen?' Cato slid printouts of driving licence photos of Peters and Drummond across the desk.

He studied them. 'No. Should I?'

'Or him?' A photo of Paul Reinado.

'No.'

'You sure?' said Driscoll.

'Absolutely.'

'Maybe you didn't get a good look at him, and it was a long time ago.' Driscoll brought up a photo on his phone and spun it around so Winter could see. 'How about her? That's his mum, Filomena. You must recognise her, you bumped into each other in March at the Darwin markets.'

Winter focused back on Cato. 'What's this all about?'

'Those people, bar Filomena, are all dead. Murdered.'

'I know. I read the paper, watch the news. What's it got to do with me?'

'There's a thread through their lives and deaths, through recent events, and through people connected with their murders. You're it.'

'A thread? Interesting legal concept. You're occupying my precious time with this ... thread?'

'He's right,' said Driscoll to Cato, grabbing his phone and getting wearily to his feet. 'This is bullshit.'

'Is it?' Cato waved him back into his seat. 'A multibillion dollar pipeline deal to take the oil back to the Timorese mainland. None of the other multinationals or Aussie players will touch it because of the logistics and geology. It's less risky, they reckon, to run it all the way back to Darwin rather than the shorter distance over the deep Timor Trench. One big storm, the pipe ruptures. Disaster. But faint hearts never won fair maidens, eh?'

Winter picked up his phone. 'Jacinta, can you get security in here to remove these jokers? Then when you've done that, connect me through to the police commissioner.'

Driscoll took up his cue. 'Picking the winning side, always tricky isn't it? Bit of a gamble. The Indonesians in seventy-five. We got that right. The Indos and the militias in ninety-nine. Oops. Never mind, move on. Next time stack the decks maybe? Load the dice. The inside running on the oil negotiations. Bingo. Quid pro quo from friends in government, and jackpot for you on mandatory detention and the offshore processing business.'

A knock on the door and four beefy blokes in suits. 'Off you go, lads.' Winter looked at Driscoll. 'Pity I can't have you sacked too.' He picked up the phone and found a smile in his voice for the commissioner. 'Lesley! How are you, my sweet?'

As they were led out the door Driscoll had a parting shot. 'The BIN file on you makes sense now. Those Indonesians know how to pick winners too, eh?'

Winter lifted his hand in a dismissive wave, but the smile had dissolved.

***

'Think it worked?'

They were back in the car park behind police HQ. Detectives of all shapes and sizes ending or starting shifts. Driscoll wondered briefly about that world, whether he could hack the protocols, rules of evidence, all that shit. 'If it didn't,' he told Kwong, 'you've got bog-all else to poke him with. Filomena's testimony that she saw him twenty years ago outside a building in Timor where her son had been abused. José, a man facing life in the slammer, claiming a respected captain of industry told him to commit murder but he never actually met him face to face, just thinks he talked to him on the phone. Simmonds? A sad little yes-man who finally got picked to be on the team and show the pretty girls and bullies he was something after all. Only he's probably in a ditch somewhere.'

'The Indonesian intelligence file?' said Kwong, jangling his car keys. 'The missing thumb drive?'

'Can you see the prosecutors running with that?' Driscoll didn't need an answer. 'The best we can do is stuff up his deals, his job, his life. Bring it crashing down. Hopefully provoke him into a tantrum.'

'He seems pretty cool-headed.'

'Nah, mate.' Driscoll grinned. 'He's pissed beyond measure. He'll lash out pretty soon I reckon.'

'Really?'

'I've been needling these private school wankers my whole life. I can spot a revved-up gubba a mile off.' Driscoll wondered if the guy now remembered him from that CIA training course all those years ago.

They could do little now but sit and wait. If nothing happened they could try another poke or two in the morning. Maybe send his BIN file to the Timorese with the question did they realise who they were going into business with? Or The Hague committee still deliberating on those maritime boundaries – the outcome of which also impacted the pipeline deal. Did Mrs Winter know she had married a war criminal? Prod, prod, prod and watch the fur fly.

***

When Cato got back to the hotel, Sharon had two bits of news for him. 'We're cleared to go back in the house tomorrow.'

'Great.' Ella had climbed up into his arms for a goodnight cuddle. Julie had fed and bathed her before the handover back to Sharon. All that needed to happen now was stories and sleep. 'And?'

'I've accepted the job in Investigations.'

'Wow.' Cato tried and failed to hide his surprise. 'Congratulations. When does it start?'

'Early July.'

'No fallout from the Guthrie thing then?'

'If anything, it enhanced my CV. If only I'd known that earlier in my career.' Sharon slopped some shiraz into two glasses and handed him one. 'Happy days.'

'Here's to you,' said Cato.

They ordered room-service dinner for an hour hence and set about the semi-military covert operation of getting a two-year-old to go to sleep. Stories, milk, dimmed lights, quiet voices. Two seafood risottos and a second shiraz later and they were ready to resume the conversation.

'It'll mean time on the road and shitty hours. Pretty much like your job.'

'Yeah,' said Cato. 'It would.'

'And I really want it. I'm ready for it.'

He looked at her. Yes, she absolutely was. 'I can see that.'

'But?'

Cato knew now what this meant. He could see how important this was for Sharon, for both of them. He looked at Ella sleeping in her fold-out cot. All of them. It all made absolute sense in his head. So why did it feel like a gut punch? Could he actually step up and do the right thing? 'But nothing. There'll need to be some big changes in the way we do things.'

'Yep.'

'Sacrifices.'

'Yep.'

'I'll need to let Pavlou know. Give her notice. Work something out.'

'Yep.'

'A year do it? More? Maybe two, get Ella to preschool?'

'Sounds about right.' She reached across him for the bottle, planting a smacker on his lips on the way. 'Top-up?'

'Cheers.'

'And while we're on a roll – the meds?'

'Hmmm?'

'If you need them to stay on top of things, fine. It's been a tough couple of years. But stick to the expert advice on the dosage and the weaning. No more emergency stashes. Fading out on the people around you isn't a good look.'

'Okay.'

'Ella needs full attention.'

'Got it.'

'Great.'

28

Tuesday 15th May

Driscoll's phone lit up on the passenger seat. A text from an unknown sender.

USB in PO Box 8 Cloverdale, JC

A second message had the QR scan code for opening the PO box.

Cloverdale, out near the airport. Had José had a change of heart? Borrowed a phone from inside to give Driscoll the news? Interesting timing. Maybe Winter was behind the move. Or perhaps Winter had already made a move on José, nudging the Brazilian into decisive action. He checked the time on the dashboard. Nearly two in the morning. He'd been driving around aimlessly for the last hour or so, too wired to go and sit quietly in a hotel room waiting for someone else to take the initiative. Realising he'd had no dinner, he'd grabbed a drive-through burger on his travels and the smell of it haunted the rental car. Should he contact Kwong and advise him of this latest development? No, the man needed some normal family time, some sleep. Whereas Driscoll didn't? Or maybe he did. His mind turned to DSC Nikki Earle and the brief fantasy of a walk along the shoreline near Portland, arms encircling each other's waists like Mason and Mira at Blackmans Bay in Tassie. Yep, that ended well too. Bullshit. Long-term hook-ups never worked. His life was a series of lies, half-truths and fables. Who wants to commit to that? Even now he was out of the game, evasion was in his modus operandi. He didn't trust easily and didn't deserve any back. He did zap off a message to Aunty though, so somebody knew where he was headed. She replied with a raised eyebrow *huh?* emoticon. It gave him some comfort to know he was interrupting her sleep.

Cloverdale in the small hours was as bleak and deserted as he would expect. The area as suburban and forgettable as Brian Simmonds. Driscoll wondered if he really was already dead. Snatched in Darwin, there were a million places he could be mouldering in his grave. Interesting that of all the suburban lawyers Deborah Chan might have chosen to guard her racy secrets and memoirs, she chose him, a former embassy colleague. A man who would, despite his claims to the contrary, have known exactly the implications of her coded diary and journal entries and the truth behind the fictionalised scenes. At least for the Timor chapter anyway. Accident or design? Design surely. Simmonds seemed a tad low-rent to be the usual solicitor for someone like Deborah Chan. She would have been a socialite of sorts, the type to add both levity and gravitas to a dinner party or barbecue. She would have known and dealt with higher-powered and more dynamic lawyers than Brian Simmonds. Did he present himself, once the word was out on her literary aspirations, as her very own and very 'umble servant? Maybe she thought his brief and fringe diplomatic career might be an asset to her, his understanding of the need for discretion and loyalty. He had that in spades, just not for her. It would be good to get a read of those diaries and journals – the whole lot. Maybe that Timor chapter wasn't what got her bumped off a winding mountain road in NZ after all. Note for Aunty: when else might Winter's and Chan's paths have crossed?

Driscoll reached into the glove box for his gun, stepped out of the car, felt a few spots of rain and a snatch of wind. The parcel lockers were in a sheltered annexe to the post office, the access door unlocked. Accident or design? Number 8 was a big locker for just a thumb drive. It was big enough for a case of wine or a holdall or a small body. He scrolled through his phone for the QR scan code and held it up to the keypad. A click and a green light on the door. Then a thunderous crack and a flash that lit up the night sky over Cloverdale.

***

Cato took the call just after four and was out there by five. It was still dark although the eastern sky did show signs of life. A steady rain fell and the wet roads reflected the flashing lights of the emergency vehicles. Police cars blocked approach roads and an ambulance had taken Driscoll away.

The bomb had started a blaze in the adjacent building and the firies were damping it down. Until they'd finished, the scene investigators would have to wait. An outer cordon tape marked the limit of Cato's approach and that was fine by him. Cannington detectives covered this patch and they were already knocking on nearby doors and accessing private and public CCTV. The OIC was Amy Trimboli who, after a brief stint in Major Crime where he last encountered her, had seized an opportunity for advancement with the always busy Cannington D's who covered the badlands of the eastern suburbs. She looked as bookish as ever and he noted on her lanyard that she had been promoted to senior constable. Not bad for someone of her tender years.

'Keeping well?' she enquired.

'Fantastic,' he said. 'What's the word?'

'Your … colleague asked us to ring you. Driscoll, right?'

'He's okay?'

'He received a crack on the head when the locker door blew off but that probably also shielded him from greater damage. He's a bit fried and singed by the flash but most of it went over the top. The paramedics reckon he'll have some blisters and peeling skin for a few days but nothing to write home about. What was he up to, do you know?'

'Search me.'

'He was armed and doesn't have a permit. Or even a job as far as we can make out. Mind you, that's not unusual round these parts.'

'I can vouch for him. As will DI Pavlou.'

'Yeah, that's what he said.' She handed Cato a phone. 'His. We confiscated it. Looks like he was responding to that text message.'

USB in PO Box 8 Cloverdale, JC

Trimboli pushed her specs back up her nose. 'JC?'

'A source.'

'We ran a location check on the number. Last time it was switched on it was in Hakea. Would JC be the Bunbury D you hauled in for the old men murders?'

'You're wasted at Cannington.'

'No,' she assured him. 'I'm not.'

Cato lifted his chin towards the charred and twisted ruins of the lockers. 'Lucky escape or crap bomb?'

'Both, according to the prelim from the fire investigators. Either amateurs or ...'

'A rush job.'

'Again, both are possible. Do you have a perpetrator in mind?'

Cato noticed officers rummaging around in Driscoll's hire car parked just down the street. 'I have suspicions but they lack foundation as yet.'

'Care to share?'

'Sorry. Give DI Pavlou a ring, she'll explain everything. Anything recovered from the locker?'

'I'll let you know once the forensics team have been allowed closer.' Trimboli smiled. 'We'll drop Mr Driscoll's car at the hospital car park and leave the keys at reception. He can come and see us if he wants his gun back.'

Birds were beginning to chirp and warble, and some early risers had gathered with their smartphones to take selfies. 'Who was the locker registered to?'

'A certain J. Carrascalao, but it had been under a different name until today. Some blah blah holdings limited. We're looking into it.'

'Keep me posted. Please.'

'Love your manners.'

***

Driscoll was collecting his discharge paperwork from hospital reception when Kwong strolled through the automatic doors.

'Fancy brekky somewhere?' He waggled his car keys. 'Need to move the motor before I get a ticket.'

There was a cafe a block down from RPH back over on Murray Street. Mainly junior lawyers and office workers grabbing takeaway coffees on their way into work. Kwong surveyed Driscoll's injuries, as did a number of their fellow patrons, gauze on the face and hands, steri-strips over the gash on the bridge of his nose. Embarrassing bald patches and pink blistered skin where clumps of hair had burnt off. 'You were lucky.'

'They reckon I'll be presentable again in a day or two. Meantime might need to get myself a beanie or stay indoors.' He surveyed Kwong's still visible injuries. 'We make a fine pair, the sight of us.'

Their coffees and breakfast rolls arrived. Fried food might not have been the best choice right now. 'Mr W. didn't waste any time making his move.'

'Neither did I. I've forwarded the BIN file to my mate Jens from The Hague subcommittee. Also sent it to Paul Reinado's parents who're well connected into the Timorese leadership. That should start a few ripples. Holding back on ruining Mrs Winter's day for a bit longer.'

'Don't pull your punches, do you?'

'Nah. What about you? Commissioner Lesley come gunning?'

'Not so far. She and Pavlou are old mates. I should be firewalled for a while.'

'Winter will be frothing at the mouth today. Meltdown. You watch.'

'Maybe we should be talking to José again. If he played a part in that bomb set-up he's just got himself into more trouble.'

'Whether he did or not we can use it on him anyway.' Kwong checked an incoming message on his phone.

'Anything?' said Driscoll.

'Home stuff.'

'Nice to see that you and Shaz hit it off. Good for each other, I reckon.'

'So far so good.'

Driscoll finished chewing his breakfast roll. 'That Bunbury cop. Earle? Seems a good sort.'

'Yeah, she does, doesn't she? Forgiven her for tasering you, then?'

'Just doing her job.'

'Love is in the air …' crooned Kwong.

'Know anything about her home life?'

'She's got a kid, school age. Otherwise, no. Want me to ask?'

'I can do that myself, cheers.'

'If you hadn't been in a fire recently I'd say you were blushing.'

'Faint hearts and that.' Another message came through on Kwong's phone. 'Busy boy.'

'Cannington D's would like a chat, if you're up for it, and you can pick up your gun while you're there.'

They dodged across the Causeway against the flow of rush-hour traffic and hit Albany Highway. Twenty minutes later they pulled into Cannington cop shop. The woman who'd interrogated Driscoll briefly while his hair was smouldering was there to greet them.

'Nothing serious, then?' she said noting his injuries. She held out a hand. 'Amy Trimboli.'

Driscoll offered up his bandaged hands in apology. 'Rory.'

She and Kwong seemed to already know each other. They were taken into an interview room and Trimboli was joined by a male colleague. They wanted to know what he was doing in Cloverdale in the small hours. 'As I said at the time, I got a message to go and collect a parcel.'

'And this message came from a phone within Hakea prison. Do you know who sent it?'

'The initials on the message said JC.'

Trimboli nodded. 'JC. Are you aware José Carrascalao was attacked overnight?'

'No.' He exchanged a glance with Kwong. News to him too. 'Is he okay?'

'He's in RPH. Haven't got the details.'

'If I'd known, I wouldn't have discharged myself so soon. Could have stayed there and had a chat.'

She shrugged. 'Sorry to inconvenience you. I understand you're assisting Major Crime with a murder investigation?'

That was one way of putting it. 'Yes.'

'But the exact nature of your assistance is classified?'

'Yes.'

'Get well soon, Mr Driscoll.' She slid his gun and a receipt pad across the table.

He signed the form and pocketed the pistol. 'That's it?'

Trimboli glanced at Kwong then back at Driscoll. 'Not sure if my colleague has brought you up to speed but it's looking like Mr Carrascalao wasn't the lessee of that parcel locker and probably didn't send you that message.'

'Really?'

'Call yourself an intelligence officer?'

***

'So do we go and visit José, or press a few more buttons on Mr Winter?'

Cato pulled back into the RPH car park. Driscoll's hire car had been ticketed. 'I think we need to step back a bit from Winter and see whether your needling strategy is having the desired effect.' He studied Driscoll, the bloke looked spent. Cato lifted his chin at the higher floors of the hospital. 'I'll check in on José, or at least enquire after him. You should get some rest, buy a beanie, whatever. We can regroup later in the day.'

Driscoll frowned. 'I'm not good at sitting and waiting.'

'Never too late to learn. I'll be in the office with the mobile on if you need me.' He rested a hand on Driscoll's upper arm. 'Seriously, mate. You need to chill.'

Driscoll nodded glumly, scrunched up the parking ticket and tossed it in a nearby bin. 'Catch you later.' He climbed gingerly into his car and took off.

José Carrascalao would live, but he'd been scalded with boiling water and stomped and kicked a few times while he was down. He was dosed up on something and having a nap. No visitors allowed at this stage. Cato was happy to leave the interrogation for now. José had obviously been given a warning of the likely consequences if he chose the wrong side. He wouldn't be so lucky next time.

Back at Major Crime, there were a whole bunch of post-it notes on Cato's desk and computer monitor, missed message notifications, and an inbox full of emails. Where to start? DI Pavlou popped her head around the door and got in first.

'Since when did Cloverdale become Aleppo?' Bit of a stretch but Cato got the point. 'Amy Trimboli filled me in. Plus the commissioner is taking an interest for all sorts of reasons.' Pavlou dragged up a chair. 'This isn't going to backfire is it? Your mate James Bond isn't about to drag us down with him, is he?'

'Maybe he'll win the day and we'll bask in the reflected glory.'

'Love your optimism. In the meantime, Chris Thornton is working on compiling actual evidence – remember that stuff? – for the Carrascalao brief, and we've got DPP keen to assess whatever's developing with Winter. I suspect we'll get strong word to back off if nothing is forthcoming soon.' She stood. 'And I'll be inclined to accept their advice. How about we take stock at COB today?'

'Today? Isn't that a tad premature?'

'All I'm talking about is dumping your spook pal. If anything solid turns up on Graham Winter at any time, of course we'll be back onto it. But we can't play by Driscoll's anarchic rules indefinitely.'

'Do anarchists have rules?'

'Stop being a pedant and do what you're told.' Pavlou left the room.

Chris Thornton took her place. 'Got a sec?'

'Sure.'

'Forensics have got fibre traces linking Carrascalao to the Peters, Drummond and Ryan Hodgson crime scenes now, along with pings on his phone which support our timeline of his whereabouts.'

'I thought he would have been more careful.'

'Maybe he was too confident of never being in the frame.'

'Anything concrete linking him to Winter?'

'Nada, except for the burner phone with the ABC numbers on it. It won't be enough.'

'Anything else?'

'We've analysed the communication records for Peters and Drummond around that Christmas Island trip in twenty thirteen.' He slid his iPad Cato's way. 'Check this out.'

An email from Bevan Drummond to Doug Peters. *Great to catch up after all these years and really enjoyed the fishing trip. Pity I'm bloody useless at catching the things. Must be the only bloke in the world who could drop a rod off Flying Fish Cove and not get a single sniff all day. The new job sounds full on and can't say I envy you but certainly pulls in a quid – way better than teacher's wages. Hope I didn't put your boss offside with my two cents worth about ET. Sometimes don't know when to shut up.*

ET, East Timor, presumed Cato. And the reply from Peters. *No probs. It was great to see you again. Fond memories. Don't worry about the big cheese, he's got the attention span of a goldfish. Plenty other stuff on his plate without letting an old lefty like you rile him. Obviously been there and knew his stuff, even that village where we did the wells. Each to his own, eh? Stay in touch and keep well.*

'Winter was the visiting big boss?'

'Yep,' said Thornton, swiping some photos on his screen. 'Found these on other people's Facebook feeds at the school. There he is, happy snaps from the quiz night where Bevan won the fishing trip.' Another shot on the fishing trip itself accessed from the charter company's archives. Five blokes holding up their impressive catches. Drummond excepted. Winter among them holding a monster. 'Drummond spoke out of turn. Thought he was just having an honest and frank exchange of views about Timor over a beer on a boat.'

'During which he gives something away, perhaps unknowingly. The village name, for instance. Puts Winter on alert. Not overly so but enough to keep an eye on him.'

Cato nodded. 'And an eye on his employee Peters, who he now knows was also there in Timor.'

'A call to his snoop mates and tick, sorted.' Thornton shrugged helplessly. 'All supposition and useless in court.'

'But in March this year, shortly after he'd been identified by Reinado's mum in Darwin, something drew his attention back to Drummond and Peters.'

'Nothing shows in the emails.'

'The phone records?'

'No, nothing,' said Thornton. 'But around that same time Drummond starts his internet search on Ximenes. Maybe his web searches were being monitored. Raised the alarm.'

'March. Just a few weeks after Ximenes was pictured at the oil and gas industry conference in Perth in the company of various industry bigwigs.'

'You'll never guess.' Thornton swiped again. Yep, there was Ximenes in a group photo in a seminar about the technical challenges posed by the oil pipeline and the pros and cons for taking it to Timor or Darwin. Third from right, Ximenes. Second from left, Winter. 'Drummond is a retired science teacher. He's into stuff like this. The rest of his internet search history shows that: science, climate change, human rights, Timor. They all figure strongly. But this time he spots a familiar face in Winter and a familiar name in Ximenes and gets to thinking.'

'But that still doesn't explain why he suddenly becomes a threat to Winter.'

'That other Rotarian who was there with them on the well-digging project. He'd described their change of demeanour during that trip.'

'Find him. Invite him in. Today. This morning preferably.' Cato recalled the developments he'd seen during his visit to that Timorese village: the wells, the new school building, the mobile towers and solar panels. The latter courtesy of AusAID and Cormann Logistics. A village elder with sad memories of a recent past. 'And see if you can track down a number for me.'

***

Driscoll was unable to relax, never mind sleep. His view from the motel at Canning Bridge showed a brown-grey, wind-whipped river. The window didn't open and perhaps it was just as well, as the dull whine of constant traffic would have become a roar. Clouds scudded up from the south-west and more rain threatened. The skin on his face and head felt tight and hot and stung like crazy. He'd put a few calls through to Aunty but she wasn't picking up. Did her radio silence presage anything sinister? Some enquiries after his health and wellbeing would have been nice. Surely by now she'd have heard about the bomb and his trip to hospital. A coldness jolted through him. He was overtired, his skin burned, he'd nearly been killed and he was sometimes as dumb as a rock. All roads led to RPH. He'd been there and checked himself out unexpectedly early. Mira was still there recuperating from her gunshot wound. And now José was back in after his prison beating. Coincidence? Or unfinished business.

Driscoll snatched up his car keys and raced downstairs. He buzzed Kwong en route, telling him to drop everything and get over to RPH. 'Check the police guard is still in place and double it. Get Carrascalao locked down if it's not too late.'

When he arrived at the hospital twenty minutes hence, it was clear he was already too late. Half-a-dozen police cars, what looked like a tactical vehicle, lots of uniforms – some of them paramilitary and heavily armed. Patients, visitors, and staff huddled outside awaiting instructions. Kwong met him at reception.

'Third floor of that wing has been cleared already,' he said. 'They're assessing how much more needs to be emptied and working through it. But that's where he is, in Mira's room with her and a nurse as hostage and the police guard dead.'

'Fuck. What about the people who were meant to be in charge of him?'

'The prison escort service for medical transfers? Privatised. Securimat – wholly owned subsidiary of CLG.' Kwong gestured towards a couple of hard-faced gorillas in cheap khaki uniforms being leaned over by TRG. 'They were only obeying instructions, they say.'

They headed for the stairs. 'Are we in communication?'

'Yep. Both hostages unharmed. José is awaiting your instructions.'

'Mine?'

'Their lives in your hands, it seems.'

They were blocked on the second floor by a phalanx of TRG ninjas. One of them placed a big gloved hand on Driscoll's chest. 'And you are?'

'Driscoll.'

The man turned to Kwong. 'He with you?'

Kwong looked around theatrically as if there was anybody else Driscoll could have been with. 'Yep.' Then he made the introductions. 'Rory, this is Dave.' No handshakes, just nods recognising existence.

'So you're the one he's asking for,' said Dave. Fact, not question. 'Done hostage stuff before?'

'Yes.' But not here in Australia, thought Driscoll, and the outcome was often less formal.

'We need to mike you up.' Dave summoned a minion. 'Tristram will do the honours.'

He was also given a stab vest in case it was necessary to get closer. 'So no firearms involved?'

'Only ours. He's got something sharp against the nurse's throat.' Dave showed him a live image on a laptop screen. CCTV feed from inside the room. Mira lying still. Unconscious? Dead? It seemed not. Monitor lights flashing regularly, along with the beep. The nurse grim but seemingly calm and composed. José jittery. Eyes darting back and forth between the door and the camera high on the wall. Dave nodded at Driscoll's holster. 'I see you've come prepared. Who did you say you worked for again?'

'I didn't.'

'Tristram will patch you through to him via the tannoy system. Start talking when you're ready but if I lift a hand for you to stop, you stop. Got it?'

'Okay.'

'No sudden words or thoughts. No codes. No threats. All nice and calm.'

'José, you there, mate?'

A glance up at the camera. 'Cato with you?'

'Yeah, we're all here. You wanted to chat?'

'Been thinking.' On screen the hand holding the knife relaxed a little, resting on the woman's shoulder. 'This ...' A shake of the head and a sad smile. 'All gone to shit, hasn't it?'

'Not yet, mate. Still plenty of time to save the day.'

'They won't let me though.'

'They?'

A warning glance from Dave. No interrogations, just reassurance.

'You know.' José adjusted position, brought the knife up again. 'Doesn't matter anymore for me. But my family. They won't leave them alone. Ever.'

'We can protect them, José. New lives, new identities, new country.'

'Wouldn't work. These people know where to look. Best if I just do what I'm told, eh?'

'That wouldn't guarantee their safety. Winter and his crew don't like loose ends. That's why he's got you here today in with Mira. And when you're gone, the only loose end left is your family. He doesn't know how much they know. Can't take the risk.'

'Ease off,' hissed TRG Dave.

'Devil and the deep blue sea, eh?' José looked up at the camera. 'I need convincing, Rory. There's only one way you can do that.'

'Tell me,' said Driscoll, knowing the answer.

A chuckle. 'Winter's head in a basket. Can you do that for me, hotshot?'

***

'Not sure that's allowed, buddy.' TRG Dave took the stab vest back and handed the mike to Tristram. He turned to Cato. 'Maybe you can explain to him?'

'I think he understands the implications.'

Driscoll frowned. 'Do you mind not talking about me as if I'm not here?'

'You shouldn't be making promises you can't keep,' said TRG Dave. 'Heads in baskets. It's not on.'

'He was speaking metaphorically.'

'Didn't sound metaphorical to me.'

'I'll go and see the man. Go through the motions. Buy time. You guys can have a think until then.' Driscoll left Kwong and the TRG bozo. Eschewing the CBD traffic and parking nightmare, he hopped on a CAT bus which dropped him fifty metres from the foyer of Winter's skyscraper on St Georges Terrace. He wondered idly how many assassinations had been carried out from the convenience and comfort of the Central Area Transit system.

Jacinta from PR was waiting for him on the twenty-third floor with a welcoming smile. 'You're back!'

'He in?'

'Yes, he's expecting you. Follow me.'

At the end of the carpeted corridor she opened up the big wooden door and ushered him through. Winter was indeed home and expecting him. He'd left the shelter of his enormous desk and parked himself in one of the comfy chairs surrounding a coffee table. There was a plunger of coffee, milk, cups, saucers and bikkies. And Aunty was playing Mother.

'White and none, Rory love?'

'What the fuck is this?'

'Have a seat,' said Winter. 'Please.'

Aunty slid a cup and saucer his way and offered a plate. 'Tim Tam?' He shook his head. 'We're calling a truce.'

'Meaning?'

'Meaning we all stop this, go home and get on with our lives.'

'You're joking.'

She scrutinised his injuries. Found her empathetic face. 'You okay? Been in the wars, eh?'

Driscoll flicked his fingers towards Winter. 'Ask him.' Drank some coffee. 'Do you realise what's going on down at the hospital right now? This tosser has got Carrascalao holding a knife to a woman's throat.'

'Nothing to do with me,' said Winter. 'The bloke must have lost it.'

'Aided and assisted by your goons from Securimat.'

'A regrettable error. Negligence. They will be facing disciplinary action.'

'See how hard all this is, Rory? It's chewing up a lot of time, energy and resources.' She bowed her head. 'And I've shown poor judgement at times too. "Beat not the bones of the buried", Rory, love. Shakespearean for let it go.'

Driscoll studied them both for a moment. 'The pipeline deal. Too much potential revenue at stake. Is that what's behind all this?'

Winter shrugged. 'The government royalties alone would halve the deficit and pay for a shitload of pork-barrelling election promises. The Timorese don't have anybody else prepared to take the geological risk with the pipeline that we will.'

'Ximenes, The Hague committee, the whistleblowers, Willie Mason stirring things up. The old men. Everybody putting their pieces of the jigsaw together.'

'All of it troublesome and bad timing.' Winter took a sip of coffee. 'João Ximenes was an ingrate. I created him, turned him from village thug to ghastly celebrity. He got greedy. Playing oil magnate with the big boys. In the end the consensus was he was more trouble than he was worth.'

'But, for a while at least, protected by somebody in the Presidential Palace. That's why you wanted him out of the way locked up in Australia. You couldn't just kill him.'

'And even that luck ran out for him eventually. We did try to warn you off but you were all very persistent. Look, Mrs Blasey's star is on the rise and she'll likely be the new head of a reformed cleaned-out agency, free of the ideological turmoil that beset it these last few years. Clean sheet all round.'

'Win-win,' said Driscoll. 'Except for Paul Reinado, Dougie Peters and Bevan Drummond.'

'You have your culprits for them. Guthrie, José.'

'And Mira Soares, Willie Mason? Handy, him suiciding under your watch. He worked out you were the mystery *malae*, right?'

Winter broke a Tim Tam in half. 'Mason was no angel. Don't fret about him. Ms Soares? Her future is in your hands.'

'How so?'

'I can give you the guarantee José wants that would end all this. In writing if you like – coded of course, but he'll get the message. But I need to know you'll let this drop and go back to your fishing.'

'Or?'

'Or things could get ugly down there. José is a desperate man.'

'All this blood spilled to protect you.'

'Not so much me, although yes, I do pay my way. That ideological line in the sand that I represent, us and them, persuaded my friends to circle the wagons for one of their own. Rally to the cause if you will.' Winter smiled fondly towards Aunty. 'Here's to a less binary future.'

'And what if I did say yes? Kwong doesn't give up so easily and play the game.'

'He's on a deadline. If he hasn't made any progress by day's end, his boss is pulling the plug.' Winter checked his watch. 'And this little psychodrama at RPH is eating into his precious time.'

'Commissioner Lesley doing your bidding?'

'Not exactly, but she's a pragmatist. The state government is also rubbing its hands at the prospect of a slice of the jobs and construction boom. The police minister doesn't want zealots or personal vendettas rocking the boat.'

'What do you say, Rory?' Aunty fidgeted with her cigarettes and lighter. 'Call it a day?'

***

Cato tried to phone Driscoll but nothing doing. José was getting agitated, wanting to know what was going on. Issuing threats. The nurse was losing her calm too, bottom lip trembling, tears running down her face. And still no sign of life from Mira. Out cold. The hours and minutes were ticking down, and the prospects for a peaceful and bloodless settlement receding. Driscoll wasn't going to get a result. Winter wouldn't budge and, much as Driscoll might want to, he wouldn't kill him to appease José. Cato was going to have to intervene. He tapped TRG Dave on the shoulder.

'I need to talk to him.'

'He hasn't expressed an interest in talking to you. Some people are like that.'

'Make the offer. He's not going to last until Driscoll returns.'

TRG Dave nodded at Tristram and the tech patched him in. 'José, mate. Dave here. Need a cool drink or any food in there? Been a while.'

'No.'

'Stephanie's looking a bit upset. Can I have a word with her?'

'She's fine.' A nudge with his spare hand. 'That right?'

'Yes,' said Nurse Stephanie. 'I'm fine.'

'Cato here was wondering if you'd fancy a chat?'

'What about?'

'Anything, mate. The Dockers, the government, the weather.' He looked outside at the rain spattering the window and at the news drones and helicopters competing for a picture. 'Anything you like, José. Cato's a chat machine, wind him up and off he goes.'

'What are you offering, Cato?' Head cocked up at the camera. 'Anything new?'

'You know Driscoll can't deliver what you asked for.'

'Yeah, suppose.'

'I find it hard to believe you did those old men and the kid, Hodgson, just for money. You just don't seem that kind of guy. Did Winter have anything on you?'

'Oh, you should have seen me in my heyday. The original *Assassin's Creed*, mate.' A bitter snort. 'Course he did. Carrot and stick, typical security services approach. I had the choice of doing it for lots of money or not doing it and having the gangs from the *favelas* come knocking once he'd tipped them off. And a couple of them would too, they're politicians and captains of industry these days.'

'Nowhere to run but you keep on trying. Ducking and weaving, looking for a result.'

'Never say die.'

'You might have to, mate. You can't guarantee yourself or your family. Why not just do the right thing, whatever the consequences, this one last time?'

'Nudging him towards the precipice wasn't what I had in mind, Cato.' TRG Dave slipped his Darth Vader helmet on, issued some instructions, and they took up new offensive positions.

'What's happening?' José tightened his grip on Stephanie and backed further into the corner of the room.

'They'll be making a move soon.'

José pulled Stephanie's hair back and there was a yell of pain. 'They better not.'

'Shut the fuck up!' TRG Dave glared at Cato and signalled to Tristram to cut the connection.

'One last go,' whispered Cato. A nod between ninjas. 'José? How about I come in there, there'll be no shooting with me in the way. We talk, sort this out, end it. Live to fight another day. Yeah?'

Silence.

'José?'

They all glanced at Tristram's screen. José couldn't say anything because he was being garrotted by Mira with her hospital tubes and wires.

***

The machine was beeping like billy-o when they got to the room and José was turning blue. The knife was on the floor and Stephanie was shouting abuse at José and landing the occasional punch and kick on his flailing body.

'Yeah, die you fucking coward. You're going purple, mate, and it fucking suits you.' Meanwhile Mira showed no signs of letting go.

TRG Dave stepped in. 'You can stop now, love.'

'I'm not your love.'

'Yeah, right on, sis,' said Stephanie, smacking José hard on the cheek.

Tristram ushered Steph out the door while Dave eased Mira's grip on the improvised garrotte. Finally José slumped to the floor, gasping for breath and clutching his throat. He yielded gladly to the TRG officers and paramedics.

Cato crouched down beside the prone José. 'It's over, mate. You're going to be okay.'

José still couldn't speak too easily. He gurgled something and Cato leaned closer. 'Nikki Earle's desk. Top drawer right. Taped underneath.'

'The thumb drive?'

He nodded. 'Fuck Winter. Fuck youse all. Do what you want with it. I'm dead.'

A shadow over both of them. Cato looked over his shoulder. Driscoll. 'Got something for you.' He took a sheet of paper out of his jacket pocket. 'Dear José, you need have no worries about your family. I will ensure they are safe and cared for. Yours faithfully. Signed and witnessed by two others.'

'How'd you get that?' asked Cato.

'Don't ask.'

'Just did. Is it worth anything?'

Driscoll nodded. 'He'll keep to it. He's in Aunty's pocket now.' He surveyed the scene, finishing with an appraisal of Mira, flushed and pleased with herself. 'You seem perky. On the mend, then?'

29

Within the hour Earle sent through the contents of José's thumb drive, the copy of the one he'd taken from Bevan Drummond after killing him. The drive itself would follow by courier. It contained an unredacted incident report from the Christmas Island detention centre from when Doug Peters was supervisor of the punishment block – White 1, along with a signed and dated statement from Peters to be read 'in the event of his death'.

'Very melodramatic,' said Cato. 'Usually when I see or hear something like that I reach for the TV remote and switch channels.' He pressed print and Driscoll collected the copies. 'Except he wasn't wrong.' Driscoll dragged up a chair.

STATEMENT BY DOUGLAS JOHN PETERS 22/03/19

I feel a bit foolish writing this but I don't suppose it can harm. My acquaintance Bevan Drummond recently drew my attention to a possible connection between my former employer – Graham Winter CEO of CLG Group – and an alleged war criminal from the period of Indonesian occupation of East Timor – one Joao Ximenes. Bev had been paranoid about leaving a trail – he told me all about it over a few beers at my local. He was right to be antsy. I wouldn't be writing this except that weird things have been happening lately. Our landlines ringing at all times in the middle of the night, dog and human shit in the letterbox, unsolicited pizza and flower deliveries. Kids possibly. But both Bevan and me, all of a sudden? I used to be a copper and coincidences were a rarity in my experience. What Bevan and I have in common, apart from being gnarly old bastards, is that we both went on a Rotarian trip to East Timor in 2006 to dig wells. Why? He's a do-gooder and I just fancied getting away from the ratbags for a while.

The previous year there'd been this death in custody incident. Not my fault but I still felt cut up about it, responsible in some way. Maybe the trip would clear my head.

Bevan's weird but you can't help like the bloke. Takes himself and life too seriously. He reads all the news about how the world is going to the dogs, be it from climate change, pollution, war, famine, or general nastiness. Maybe it's a Catholic teacher thing. So he knows all about people like Ximenes and about how corrupt and dangerous the oil industry is. He calls himself a student of history. He's been putting two and two together. I'm hoping he's got his sums wrong but I suspect he hasn't because I've been doing some adding up too.

Anyway, back to the point. We were supervising this well project in a village west of Dili in May 2006. Bloody warm and I was choking for a beer. We needed to clear the area and flatten it to lay some concrete slabs but there was one corner of the field had this old fallen down building. Rubble, that's all it was. I'd asked the elder to organise some young blokes to clear it away but he point-blank refused. He was jabbering away in Tetum and there was no point me arguing – no skin off my nose. I could understand a few words. Diabu, diabu, diabu *– devil, fiend, whatever. And* Lafaek, *their name for the crocodile or grandfather or something. One of the interpreters later told us some bad stuff had happened there during the Indonesian occupation. A torture house, sounded like. They had let it go to ruin since but weren't game to touch it. Put a damper on the trip but that's what you get when you take on these things. Put the willies up us and we were glad to get away not long after.*

It was late afternoon and Cato was aware of the clamour for a report on today's incidents, for an update on the case against Winter, a hundred things lining up to be dealt with but this, at last, was the truth of the matter. Or at least one version of it. Driscoll had, in vague terms, outlined his encounter at CLG during their return trip from the hospital to Cato's office. A truce, he'd said, a deal to let drop everything that had gone before in exchange for, among other things, a guarantee to protect José's family. It stank, even if Driscoll and his cronies were pragmatically right and Graham Winter would never face the consequences of his actions. It still stank.

It must have been a good six years or so later when I met up with Bevan again – 2013. I'd left the Job and been offered a post at Christmas Island Detention Centre. More custody sergeant work basically. Most of the poor buggers who used to inhabit the place had either been sent home or to Nauru or Manus. A handful were there for administrative reasons, waiting to be deported, and the rest were bad bastards being cleared out of our jails. Kiwis, Poms, nasty sorts not welcome anywhere. Bevan was on temporary secondment to the island high school – he was something of a guru in science education it seems. There'd been a quiz night to raise money for some school trip and Bevan won a raffle prize of a fishing trip through a charter company owned by CPS. Lovely night and great to catch up. Soured a bit on the fishing trip when Bev had a run-in with the CEO, Winter, who was on one of his grand tours. Bev couldn't catch a cold never mind a fish. Maybe he was bored and drank a bit more than he usually does. He was going on about what bastards the Aussies were in East Timor, turning a blind eye to Indonesia, stealing their oil, blah blah. Winter wasn't having any of it – said Oz saved the Timorese and they should be grateful. The rest of us just wanted to drink and fish and made that pretty clear by keeping out of it. They got the message and eased off.

Cato reflected on how a few ill-chosen words on a boozy fishing jaunt could end up in those visions of hell in the suburbs a few years later. But maybe that wasn't so unusual. In his experience hell can be conjured at the blink of an eye.

Something else funny happened during those few days. History repeating. A man had died in custody at the Centre. Indonesian, early forties. He'd been arrested when his boat was intercepted carrying asylum-seekers a few years before. He'd served his prison sentence for people smuggling and was at the Centre waiting to be deported back to Indonesia. He hadn't been in the punishment block – my block – until a day or two before but had been sent there since the visit by Winter. Apparently he'd started acting up and misbehaving. None of us knew or, to be honest, cared what he was saying, we just wanted him to shut up and behave. I wasn't on duty that night, overnight, when the incident occurred. Bloody Meeka re-run. The man died after a confrontation with ERT: ruptured spleen, fractured skull, internal injuries, you name it. It was my job to supervise the packing up of his few belongings for shipment back to Indonesia with his body. There had been a slip of paper inside a rolled-up shirt with words that meant nothing to me at the time. After that death in custody in Meekatharra, I got my phone and took photos of the original incident report and of the man's possessions including the note. I never expected to have to revisit the matter but since Meeka I'm a born-again arse-coverer and one day somebody is going to have to answer for what we do in those places.

Cato caught a movement by Driscoll in the corner of his eye. He too, Cato recalled, had played his part in Operation Sovereign Borders. Were these words hitting home, irritating, dredging up unwelcome memories? Was it hypocritical of Peters to retrospectively criticise the system that had paid him so handsomely? Was it any less hypocritical, Cato wondered, for any of us to remain silent and inactive if you really despise the things governments do supposedly in your name?

Bevan Drummond contacted me again six years later, March this year, after seeing Graham Winter's photo in the paper with Ximenes, the suspected war criminal. He reminded me of the incident in the field in that village near Dili and the elder using those Tetum words when he talked about the history of the tumbledown house in the corner of the field: lafaek – crocodile or grandfather, diabu – devil or fiend. I dug out the photos I'd kept on my old phone from Christmas Island – the incident report and the photos of the possessions, that note with the Indonesian words: buaya, setan, and musim dingin. I went to good old Google Translate – buaya – crocodile, setan – devil or fiend, musim dingin – winter. He's writing of a season, I know, not a name. Did this Indonesian guy, Adie Dipa, know Winter in a previous life? Would an Aussie be involved in such bad stuff? We were in Vietnam and now we're in Afghanistan, Iraq, etc. Of course it happens. Even then what of it? Bad shit happens in wars. End of story, water under the bridge and all that. Except suddenly Bev and me get all this weird stuff happening. Stuff the cops would laugh at us for if we tried reporting it. I don't know why anybody should get upset about a couple of old duffers like us but it feels like we're being watched, followed, listened to. So, if anything bad does happen, someone might read this and wonder. Meantime we'll just have to try and be a bit more careful when we talk to each other.

A quick call from Driscoll to a contact in the Indonesian intelligence service BIN confirmed that the dead man, Adie Dipa, had been a young soldier in the Indonesian army unit sent to that village in Timor when Paulho Reinado was taken prisoner and abused. Since then he'd returned to his village near Kupang, fallen on hard times and taken to hiring his boat and his skills to the people smugglers. Then the Timor village elder was contacted by Thornton via the newly installed mobile towers and via the woman in the general store, who spoke passable English. Through her the elder confirmed the gist of the torture-house story and recognised the photos of Winter, Drummond and Peters that Thornton had sent to him.

'But it's still not going to be enough, is it?' said Cato.

'Doubt it,' said Driscoll. 'You guys are the experts on evidence thresholds. Still,' he tapped the statement with his index finger, 'at least you know what happened now.'

'Still doesn't explain Mira's part in this. Why Winter would need her dead.'

'She was writing the story supporting Mason's version of events on the bugging of the oil talks. She was on the opposing side.' Driscoll perked up. 'Maybe, like me, she doesn't realise what she doesn't know. Six months in the camp over the border with Ximenes and his militiamen. Maybe she saw or heard something she gave no significance to. She was fifteen, focused on surviving her time in their grubby hands probably.'

'But if Winter was there during that time, he didn't want to run the risk of her remembering that.' Cato checked the time. Half an hour until Pavlou's close of business deadline. He wouldn't reach the evidence threshold she and the DPP and a jury would need – not by then, probably not ever. 'We need to splash this around.'

'You sure?' Driscoll pushed his chair back and stood up. 'It could all end in tears.'

EPILOGUE

Twelve weeks later

Cato strapped Ella into the bike seat. The day was cool but dry, and she was too excited to worry about trivial matters like the weather anyway.

'Which way?' he said, clipping the catch on her helmet.

She lifted her hand and pointed. 'That way.'

Ella loved the ride down to the beach, especially downhill on Lefroy to the junction with Hampton Road. Cato never relished the return uphill but it was getting easier with practice and he was beginning to feel the benefits too. Sharon had started the job the previous month and was already neck-deep in the long haul of a major drug importation investigation. Most days went twelve or fourteen hours, she would leave and return in the dark and saw little of Ella or her husband. She was thriving and guilty in equal measure.

'It'll settle down,' he'd said over a quick coffee that morning. 'Once you get your rhythm.'

'The scrutiny of others,' she'd nodded. 'It's a bugger.'

'Stop pretending you're not enjoying yourself. I didn't sign up to become the poster boy for stay-at-home dads so you could mope and whinge. Get on with it, lock up those baddies, make the world a better place.'

'Pavlou forgiven you yet?'

'She's too busy to worry about me. José's pre-trial starts next week and she's still fending off Winter's defamation claims.'

Cato and Driscoll had cobbled together whatever they had on Winter and, via an internet cafe in Northbridge, Driscoll had sent it out to all the journalists and muckrakers they knew between them. It had taken a while for the story to catch. Sometimes it would flair and die through one of Driscoll's overseas sources. Other times local Australian outlets would prod it to see if it still showed signs of life. But catch it did, and after a while even the mainstream outlets showed interest and began gathering new evidence of their own. None of it enough for a jury but plenty of it enough for shareholders, business partners, rivals and clients to act decisively. The pipeline deal was off. Timorese opposition newspapers had labelled the CLG–Timor partnership 'Blood Money'. In both countries the government faced an electoral reckoning, sooner or later, and the price was just too high. The dark lords in the Presidential Palace and in Canberra got out their barge poles. Meanwhile, domestically, the government was reviewing its offshore detention regime and the related contracts with CPS as public opinion swung away from both. Winter was ruined, professionally and personally. Had he been involved in, actually participated in, the rape torture of the teenage Paulho Reinado? Mira hadn't recalled him being around during her incarceration with Ximenes, but dimly recalled a *malae* being present when she was traded back for imprisoned militiamen. Whether he was there or not, Mira was more than happy to contribute to the aspersions on his character. Both Pavlou and Aunty were predictably hoppy about developments. Cato and Driscoll had put them on speakerphone as they drove out to the airport to drop Driscoll off for his flight back to Melbourne.

'Rory, for fuck's sake, what part do you not understand about the word truce?'

'Sorry, Aunty. Just he's a prick and I don't live in your world anymore.'

Then Pavlou. 'Philip, I can see where you're coming from but while you spend the next two years on sabbatical being a model dad I'm going to be fighting a rearguard action to save my own career and keep the lawyers from taking your house off you. Winter has powerful friends and a vengeful soul. I hope you appreciate my efforts on all our behalfs.'

'I do, boss. You're a diamond.'

The calls closed as they'd pulled into the airport car park. 'She seems like a good sort, that DI. On balance.'

'She is,' admitted Cato. 'And I suspect your Aunty's heart is in the right place too. If you look deep enough.'

'Yeah.' They'd shaken hands. 'No offence but I'd prefer not to see you again for yonks. Look after Shaz, eh?'

'I will. Any word on DSC Earle?'

'Later this month. A long weekend. We'll see how it goes from there.'

'Keep me posted.'

'Nah, mate.' He'd smiled a final farewell. 'I won't.'

Cato crested the hill at Christ the King ready for the descent towards Freo and the beach. How would the two-year 'sabbatical' play out? Who knew? He had the medication back under control and had agreed a weaning timeline with the doctor. After a shaky start he was feeling better for it. As for the rest? He was even getting back to the piano, polishing up those rusty Chopin nocturnes. Life can be good, he decided. Just do what you can to make it so. 'You ready, Ella?' he shouted as they picked up speed into the downhill. 'One, two, three ... Wheeeeeee!'

***

Driscoll told Yakov the story as the old man laid out the chess pieces ... murder, war, atrocity, greed, ambition, ideology in pure evil form, hatred for otherness. It all sounded wearily familiar to a man who had survived a concentration camp. Driscoll tried to explain the vicious ideological internecine struggle between two factions of the security services. Hawks versus doves didn't do it justice. But now, he said, it was hopefully all over. Aunty had taken over the agency and set about reforming and re-professionalising the spooks under her charge.

'The dimwits, the time-servers, the spiteful fascists, all gone or going, Rory, my dear. Fancy your job back?'

No, he didn't, he'd told her. He doubted they really were gone. Probably mutating, biding their time like a virus. The fishing was good at his place near Portland, and he was too busy trying to make his shack seem less blokey and more homely in time for Nikki Earle's visit next weekend. She was taking some overdue leave, would drop her kid with the grandparents, and fly in to Melbourne. He'd pick her up from the airport and drive back along the Great Ocean Road, show her the sights. Just a couple of things to sort out in the meantime. In Melbourne he'd also drop by and see Mira – well and truly on the road to recovery. She was putting together a series of articles and a podcast on the Timor story: *Crocodile Tears*, a tale of murder, spies and dirty tricks. A major newspaper was supporting both: true-crime podcasts were all the rage – money-spinners and audience builders. Brian Simmonds had still not been found and his wife had slipped away in her coma. The Chan diaries and novel manuscript had been released by the authorities, and there was whisper of a lucrative posthumous publishing deal.

Meanwhile, Driscoll was fulfilling a promise to an old man. A soft rain fell on the still waters of Blackmans Bay and the sun disappeared behind the hills.

'So,' he concluded. 'Last time you saw us we thought it was all about the bugging of the oil negotiations. But it wasn't.' He thought a moment. 'And yet in some ways it still was.'

'It's hard to cheat at chess,' said Yakov, after a pause. 'You cannot tamper with the pieces, dive and claim a non-existent foul, manipulate the rules for a cheap advantage to deliver you victory. It's not that kind of game. Sure, wire yourself to a sneaky hidden computer if you're desperate, but really.' He took a sip of whisky. 'Cheating at chess would be like cheating on yourself.'

Driscoll made his opening move. 'I've come across plenty of people prepared to do just that. Winning is the thing. It's un-Australian not to do so.'

'You think so? When I was growing up here, yes, I encountered bullying and ignorance but the main thing that sticks in my memory is of all the instances of ordinary human decency. My parents had seen it extinguished at Ravensbrück and I had never known it until we came to Australia.'

Driscoll gave away a pawn. 'If you arrived today, fresh out of Ravensbrück, you would be sent to Nauru, out of sight, out of mind.'

'And so I would look for the remnants of goodness in the situation. They are always there, even if it rests with a handful of stubborn resisters prepared to speak truth to power.'

'I envy you your generosity of spirit.'

The old man gave him a sharp look as if he'd just been patronised. 'Maybe that is where Australia lets itself down, confusing generosity, compassion and decency for weakness.' He moved his knight. 'Check. This pathological need to win at all costs, it shames and cheapens you, blinds you to the goodness and badness both in yourselves and in those you meet. It drives you to cheat on the playing fields and in the courtrooms, to bully and cajole those weaker and better than you and to pander to those mightier and worse.' He shook his head sadly. 'And it makes you fragile, takes away your resilience. You are resistant to failure and to difference in yourselves and others.'

'You this, you that. Who is "you" in all this? Not me.' Driscoll blocked the check with a pawn and promptly lost it. 'I don't need convincing.'

Click. Clack. Click.

'Check, again. Don't you? You don't feel you belong to this thing I've described? So what was that job you've just been doing the last ten, twenty years or more?' He helped himself to another of Driscoll's pawns. 'Myth-making is not just the prerogative of the Australian ruling classes. We're all capable of doing exactly that in our own lives. You tell yourselves lies about yourselves and you learn to believe them.'

'Australian ruling classes? You sound like an old Commie.'

'That's exactly what I am. It runs in the family and I'm proud of it.'

'Mate, I wasn't expecting to have a strip torn off me.'

'Huh,' said Yakov. 'Glass jaw.'

'Shut up.' Driscoll felt himself smiling.

'Pathetic.'

Click. 'Check.'

Click. Clack. Click.

'Mate.'

ACKNOWLEDGEMENTS

An earlier draft of this novel was submitted as part of my doctorate thesis at Curtin University.

I take this opportunity to extend my thanks to my supervisors. Firstly, to my thesis supervisors Dr David Whish-Wilson, Dr Sean Gorman and Dr Jo Jones who scrutinised every word more than once or twice and without whose guidance the PhD would never have been completed. Particular thanks also to David Whish-Wilson for expert guidance through the initial candidacy and the novel-writing period. I also gratefully acknowledge the support of APA/CUPS scholarship funding support in the production of the thesis and novel, enabling me to do (among other things) a research trip to Timor-Leste in 2018.

During the novel research and writing period I was welcomed to Timor-Leste by Nivea Saldanha, Luke Millwood and David Senior, all of whom were very generous with their time, advice, and anecdotes. Special thanks to Nivea for checking my Tetun phrases. Nods of appreciation too for Paul McGinty and Beth Hutchinson who facilitated those introductions. Thanks also to Walter Saunders from the 'Fighting Gunditjmara' who read the manuscript and offered his wise counsel.

I cannot express my gratitude to them all enough. Any errors or omissions remaining, I claim as my own.

I think it's important also to pay homage to my fellow scribes who push on through thick and thin (and this last year or so has been both) coming up with great stories and striving to share them with the world and with each other. In particular I'd like to acknowledge Kiwi writer Vanda Symon whose novel *Overkill* helped inspire the Sharon/Guthrie scene. Undoubtedly Vanda's was the original and best and if you haven't caught on to her fabulous Sam Shephard series yet, then do yourself a favour. The legend of *Lafaek*, as told by Rosa to Cato, has been drawn from the following sources: etan.org/timor/croc.htm and visiteasttimor.com/legendhistory-timor-leste. Thanks to Wakefield Press for permission to reproduce a line from Charlotte Jay's *Beat Not the Bones* (Crime Classics edition, 2012).

As always muchas gracias to Fremantle Press and to my agent Clive Newman for continuing to support and promote my literary endeavours. In particular, editor Georgia Richter for her ongoing wisdom and feedback on all matters great, small, and even pharmaceutical.

Last, but never least, my beautiful wife Kath – early reader, muse and love of my life.

First published 2021 by
FREMANTLE PRESS

Fremantle Press Inc. trading as Fremantle Press
25 Quarry Street, Fremantle WA 6160
(PO Box 158, North Fremantle WA 6159)
www.fremantlepress.com.au

Cover photographs from istockphoto.com
Cover design: Nada Backovic, nadabackovic.com
Printed by McPherson's Printing, Victoria, Australia.

A catalogue record for this
book is available from the
National Library of Australia

ISBN 9781925816570 (paperback)
ISBN 9781925816587 (ebook)

Fremantle Press is supported by the State Government through the
Department of Local Government, Sport and Cultural Industries.

Publication of this title was assisted by the Commonwealth Government
through the Australia Council, its arts funding and advisory body.

CPSIA information can be obtained
at www.ICGtesting.com
Printed in the USA
BVHW072240040719
552667BV00001B/10/P